Cadence of the Storm

DELIA DUKE

NIMBUS DYNAMIX LLC

Sign up

Sign up for the mailing list to be the first to know about new
book releases!

WEBSITE
INSTAGRAM
FACEBOOK

Also by the Author

Fate Intertwined

Fires of Affinity

Bonds Unbreakable

A Sultry Betrayal

Clause of Attraction

I saw that you were perfect, and so I loved you. Then I saw that you were not perfect and I loved you even more.

— Angelita Lim

One

RISHA

As I picked up a miniature iris from the dessert table, Cece watched a server carve curls of parmesan over someone's truffle risotto. His job might have been mundane, but the added flair garnered laughs, including Cece's. She decided on a cannoli before we circled back to stand at one of the pedestal cocktail tables we had claimed earlier.

The Sicilian summer-themed gala was in full swing. Despite the chilly October night in Manhattan, the ballroom shimmered like a moonlit vineyard, chandeliers cast soft glow on silk-draped tables. The faint sound of the crashing waves in the background overlapped the instrumental music. No expense had been spared to bring this party to life. Tonight, the ambiance fascinated me more than the strangers around me.

Women dressed elegantly. Men, rich and sophisticated, mingling with the same crowd they knew all their lives. Every time someone opened their mouth, all I heard were million-dollar deals, an exorbitant vacation, a hyped-up restaurant where one dinner would cost the average American an entire month's paycheck.

Other than our dozen years of friendship, Cece and my life were worlds apart. This wasn't my usual scene, and I most definitely didn't belong here. I was attending her father's big sixtieth birthday. And because I had successfully avoided every invitation in the last two years, this one had been an ultimatum. *"Show up, or this friendship is over."* Her exact words. However, I caved into her demands for my own selfish reasons—I wanted to soak in my creativity for an evening; my contribution to give Mr. Cristaldi a slice of his world.

Though he was a Bronx native, his connection to his heritage was as deeply rooted as my parents'. Both immigrants, despite their diverse backgrounds, they wore love for their homeland proudly.

I found immigration to be both fascinating and overwhelming. People would uproot themselves in pursuit of a better life, only to spend the rest of it clinging to the traditions and lifestyle they left behind—fascinating. It came with expectations the next generation didn't agree to—overwhelming. I wasn't standing on a bridge connecting two worlds, but on a wire, stretched tight over someone else's struggle. Meanwhile, I balanced the weight of my own becoming, wrestling between the dreams I didn't choose and guilt for wanting something different.

"How many times do I need to remind you, Risha? Push back." Cece swirled the wineglass between two manicured fingers before tipping her head back to finish the contents. This was her second glass while I tended to my first.

My best friend since freshman year knew me better than anyone else in the entire world. However, she didn't realize her words always sank deeper than she intended, slicing through my bleeding wound. And although I didn't disagree with her observation, people misinterpreted the circumstances surrounding someone leading a double life—living in two separate worlds and belonging to neither.

Self-preservation pushed me to the edge; the need to maintain peace always pulled me back. This ongoing internal battle was half self-sabotaging and half life-affirming resilience.

"What's the worst they're going to do? Ground you?" Cece's

words pulled me out of my head. "That kind of shit doesn't fly in this country."

"You know, you make me sound spineless and weak," I responded, feeling the unrest this conversation always stirred.

"Gosh! No." She dramatically put the glass on the high-table we were sharing then put her hand over mine. "You're too complacent, Risha. You need to fight for your freedom."

"Well ... my dearest friend, sometimes freedom and peace are mutually exclusive. And sometimes, wanting peace means sacrificing freedom," I exclaimed.

"That sounds noble until you realize freedom without peace is just a prettier kind of prison."

"Maybe. But have you ever tried sleeping through a war of your own making?"

Cece raised a skeptical brow to our metaphorical discussion. This argument, I could win, and I needed a win to feel better.

"You're the one who lit the match, and now you cry fire?" she said.

"Some fires are easier to start than stop." *When consequences are not fully thought through.*

"Regret doesn't put out flames, Risha; it just makes you choke on the smoke," Cece retorted.

"Spare me the poetry, please. I'm not ignorant." Exhaustion seeped into me from this conversation. Had I presumed to win the argument?

"You are, and it's quickly becoming part of your personality."

"No, it isn't." I swatted her arm, which broke the unwarranted tension.

Her dyed dark hair bobbed as she let it go. A blonde who had fallen in love with my raven head and had decided to imitate me. Color was easier to change; with length, she struggled. Managing my waist-length hair was another tale tangled in exasperation.

Leaning sideways, I adjust the hem of the tangerine-colored velvet dress that had caught on my pointy stilettos rather too many times. A simple boat neck showing off my neck and shoulders was Cece's pick for the night. I liked the comfort part of it without compromising on elegance. The dress hugged my curves and flared waist down, allowing me to walk with ease.

When I looked up, someone caught my attention behind Cece, and every circuit in my brain rewired itself, syncing to a wavelength that belonged only to him. He was attractive. Scratch that—he was devastatingly gorgeous, with a face that would make even a sculptor weep. The lines of his jaw created an unmistakably sharp chin. His hair was the color of sunlit wheat, tousled with a carelessness that only came from confidence, making my fingers restless to rake through it. Not too neat, not too messy, just perfectly undone. But it was his eyes that made my heart blip. A striking electric blue that flickered with mischief one second and something unreadable the next. Like a storm waiting for permission to break.

Instinctively drawn to him, my wild thoughts started plaguing my mind. My heart raced for some unknown reason while our gazes remained locked. He stood with two equally beautiful men, but none pulled the strings the way he did.

Cece noticed the sudden loss of my attention and followed my gaze to where the three men stood. Turning back to me, she asked, "How's it going with Patrick?" slicing right into the heart of my grief.

I refocused on her. At this point, I wasn't sure who was the worst—Mom, Dad, Patrick, or Cece.

"As good as it can ever be." Sighing, I fidgeted with my fork over the mini pastry because I'd lost my appetite at the mention of his name. Well, I had lost my appetite after she'd thrown one issue after another. My carefully constructed façade would hold until the cracks spread too wide, letting one truth bleed into the other.

Life, in my case. A pathetic one, to add a colorful adjective.

"Remind me exactly why you two broke up?" Cece mused, poking at her cannoli and debating if it was worth the calories.

I groaned internally. Patrick. His name still clanged like a warning bell inside my head. I'd never given people the full story.

Just enough of a vague excuse to earn a week's worth of sympathy before everyone moved on and forgot he existed. I had shoved the mess of that relationship under the rug, hoping time would smother the stench.

Until he came back as my boss in the firm I had bled into and carved a space for myself.

"It doesn't matter. That was a long time ago." I stressed on the word *long*, because five years should count for something, right?

"Don't let him bully you," Cece warned.

"I won't," I said quickly. "This job is the only bright spot I have right now. I'm not letting him dim it."

Cece studied me with reservation, and I was certain a piece of advice was coming. "Take charge. Don't let people shove you around," she added, like she hadn't said the exact same thing ten minutes ago. Then she shook her head. "God, I can't believe I actually liked that guy."

I sighed and decided not to respond.

"I don't understand what happens on the other side of Hudson, Risha. But you should know that none of it was your fault."

Don't go there ... please.

I let go of the fork, rejecting the remaining bite altogether. Unsolicited advice from people who didn't understand my situation didn't exactly work.

"What about starting your own startup? You have been wanting it for so long."

I pushed away from the table with a dismissive headshake. Was this a night of counting my defects? "That was until I started thinking about logistics. Time is my biggest enemy. If I have to put everything on hold and head over to Jersey every weekend to play *happy family*, I can't imagine starting a business. Not to forget, a consultancy firm won't satisfy Verma family needs."

"Like I told you before—push back." Cece rolled her eyes.

She lacked the wisdom of how to live with South Asian

parents. I was neither naïve nor reckless. Not anymore. Not to mention, I was still fixing errors from my past. Caution was my middle name.

Mr. GQ behind Cece once again caught my attention, and my thoughts were tossed into a whirlwind of intrigue and reckless curiosity. Once again, smoothly and successfully, he drew me back into his riveting intensity. His eyes crinkled with mischief when our gazes locked again. My body's reaction to him defied all reasoning.

There weren't many men who could pull off a dusted bronze suit so effortlessly. His tie enhanced the color of his eyes. His smile went beyond his lips; spreading across his face. There was something utterly casual and severely distracting about him that I couldn't pinpoint.

I tried severing the imaginative tie, but he wouldn't let me. His gaze wasn't intense, but seductive and curious. I breathed out when he was called into their ongoing discussion, letting his gaze waver from mine. But even when his concentration moved, the remnant of the smile remained intact.

It almost felt like we had an unspoken trade, something unseen lingering in the space between us. A game neither of us had agreed to play.

Even Cece's next question about Patrick couldn't fully deflect me. I responded, for sure, but I was distracted. When I looked at him again, Mr. GQ was already heading our way. A smile lingered at the corner of his lips with a silent greeting. It should be criminal to be so handsome and so utterly at ease.

Two

RISHA

Picking up a glass of champagne from the passing server, Mr. GQ joined us.

Unexpected but unmistakable heat bloomed inside me. My fluttering chest ran wild, wondering about possibilities. At thirty, one-night stands were behind me, and I ran from romance like the plague. Correction: I ran from all kinds of relationships—period.

His gaze shifted from me to Cece. "Good seeing you, stranger." He leaned over to kiss Cece's cheeks, which she gladly accepted.

"Sorry, I got sidetracked ... How are you?" Cece responded with her casualness, but her hand lingered over his arm, and unwarranted jealousy sparked in my gut. He was a stranger, and I wasn't open to *anything*, yet reasoning was tossed to the wind.

"Never better. Thank you for inviting me tonight." His voice dripped with seduction and honey. "I was wondering who kept you busy through the entire evening?"

"Gosh... my manners." Assuming her hostess persona, Cece angled herself to face me. "Risha, this is Ryan, Taber's best friend and now his business partner. Ryan, Risha, my roommate and best friend."

I watched from close proximity this time to find a physical

flaw I might have missed from afar. A beard covered his face with a golden halo of mischief. My eyes lingered on the curve of his lips —sculpted and infuriatingly kissable. The kind of mouth made for sin and poetry both.

Nope, he was perfect! And he was as blatantly checking me out as I was him.

"Risha..." My name had never sounded so sensual before. "I'm Ryan," he reintroduced himself. Not sure if I mentioned this before, but this man's eyes were hypnotic. And his voice ... it was narcotic, like a drug you'd instantly want on repeat.

Cece cleared her throat. "I guess I didn't introduce you two properly. Risha, meet Ryan McAlister, a real estate mogul and hotelier. And just so you both know, there's nothing common between you two."

She was right. We had nothing in common, and yet I couldn't look away.

Amusement flickered across his perfectly chiseled face. "That sure, hmm?"

"Come on, Ryan." She pinned him with her gaze. "I've known you for over a decade. You've quadrupled your family fortune but alienated yourself from the rest of the world. And Risha is orbiting this universe for one evening."

Mrs. Cristaldi appeared next to me and hugged me before saying, "Thank you for helping Cece with this phenomenal décor. Tony is in heaven finding a little piece of home."

"It was a pleasure. I loved it, actually," I responded with a smile.

"If you don't mind, I need to steal my daughter for a bit." She looked from me to Ryan who offered a polite nod.

"I'm sorry, I shouldn't be demanding all her time, anyway," I answered quickly.

As soon as they left, I realized it had been a terrible move—I felt the full effect of Ryan's presence. He was pulling me into his axis without even asking for my permission, and I was losing control. Like nicotine entering my pores from secondhand smoke.

I cleared my throat to gain semblance. The best way to break the spell was simply to engage in a friendly conversation. It'd kill two birds with one stone—show him he didn't affect me in the slightest and convince myself this chemistry wasn't real.

"So, Ryan McAlister... you're one of these hotshots here."

"And you're Risha...?" His smile was disarming.

"Cece is right; we have nothing in common," I said dismissively, trying hard not to sound disappointed.

"I disagree. We hardly know each other. In fact, the only thing I know is your first name and that you're the most beautiful woman in this party."

Wow! The cheesiest line in the history of pickup lines, and yet it lit a spark inside me.

I leaned closer, taking in his broad shoulders and lean frame. He smelled of musk and worn leather, and something so distinctly familiar, yet I couldn't pinpoint. He was attractive and intoxicating, and I found myself drawn to him with no brakes to hit.

He was also taller than I realized. At five-five, I wasn't short, but even with my heels I came right around his shoulders. From his hand-tailored tux to the Berluti shoes, the man was polished and subtle. Effortless and non-dazzling. Not hiding who he was, but not flaunting either.

"I'm a nobody," I conspired near his ear. Totally unnecessary, but I was falling fast under the spell he was weaving.

Ryan took a step closer, invading my personal space. The boundary that I'd hovered over first, he crossed it next.

"I don't believe you," he said playfully, pulling me further into his thrall.

The sexual tension was a reminder of what I'd been missing for a while. Not that I didn't bring men home from time to time, but things had been... complicated recently. This physical attraction was just a wake-up call that some parts of my body needed servicing.

"Believe me; I am not a millionaire, billionaire, hotelier, not even a sommelier, for that matter. I'm an absolute nobody."

Ryan raised a brow. "Debonair, then?"

I laughed, shaking my head.

"Financier?"

"Engineer," I answered before he went into puppeteer or mountaineer. "Just an engineer."

He flinched, exactly as I had expected him to. I didn't belong among the who's who of the top point-one-percent of Manhattan. I was plain and unremarkable, comfortably stuck in the middle. The hardworking middle class, who spent the first twenty-six years grinding through education to finally get to taste its rewards. Not the struggling class, hustling just to survive. Not thrill-seekers, chasing adrenaline because money was meaningless. And definitely not the academic prodigies whose names graced scientific journals. I was the quiet center—the unnoticed backbone no one saw or cared about, because we had nothing flashy to offer, no sob stories to tell, nothing anyone needed to take from us.

"How can you be nobody, then? Either you fix what's broken, or create something no one even knows they need until they realize it's impossible to live without." His words actually *shocked* me.

Something warm flushed inside, and I forced myself not to let that go to my head. "Very smooth, Mr. McAlister—"

"Nuh-uh, call me Ryan," he corrected immediately. There was a strong magnetic pull I couldn't shake off. I was certain it was all in my head. My libido had hijacked my judgment, drowning out any sense of reality. "Tell me what was the last thing you created," he asked.

I laughed. "You make it sound very fancy, Mr. ... Ryan. I'm just a consultant. My clients tell me what they want, and my team puts it together."

He watched me intently, as if trying to figure me out. I wasn't playing the hard-to-get, mysterious woman, but after everything I had been going through, I couldn't deny this was a refreshing change.

"It seems you're selling yourself short. Ideas are easy to form; bringing them to life is an art—science, in your case."

I swallowed a lump that definitely felt like pain. He was a complete stranger who stirred a *highly* sensitive nerve.

"Is that what you think of me? An artist?" I asked, curiosity taking over my rationality.

Resting his elbow on the pedestal table, he crossed his feet and took a more relaxed stance. His eyes grazed over my every facial feature, giving more thought to the question than required. They lingered a beat longer over my lips, but it was my eyes his gaze shifted again.

"As soon as you walked into the party, you first fixed the flowers on the front, then you smoothed out the drapes, and fixed the smallest of creases on the checkered tablecloths. And all that even before you removed your coat, you ran up to the DJ and gave him the music that has been playing since."

His observations left me stunned. So ... he had been watching me since my arrival, which was more than two hours ago.

"I was pretty sure you were the party planner, or organizer, or something like that." He flared his hand, gesturing at the elaborate theme. "But then you shocked me with your profession. You might be an engineer and an artist, but you're definitely a mystery to me, and I am intrigued."

I was still reeling when he took another sip of his champagne then put the glass down on the table. Guests were slowly moving toward the bar or the makeshift stage where Cece and her mother had retreated to.

"Artist. Engineer. Mystery. That all makes it sound more interesting than it really is." I tried to be nonchalant.

"A fighter," he added. His unwavering eyes held me still. I didn't agree or deny, so he went on. "You love defying reasoning ... you fight because it's your right. Now tell me I'm completely off."

Every cell of my brain screamed to run, but a part of me

couldn't resist the fun. Physically, this man was irresistible, a breath of fresh air, but the best and worst part was he saw right through me.

"A fighter, huh? Maybe you're right. Maybe I like to swim against the current because that's where the real fight is."

"And when the current gets too strong?" he asked, moving closer like we were sharing a secret. Or maybe he was just as attracted as I was.

"I'll still be swimming. Even if I drown, at least I'll know I was fighting." I wasn't sure when we started talking metaphorically or if we were talking about the same thing, but I was as fascinated by him as he was by me. "What would you do, Ryan?"

He leaned in, his breath a ghost over my neck. I forgot how to breathe, terrified of melting into him.

"I'm the storm that stirred the still."

I retracted back to create space, but the hem of my dress snagged beneath my heel, tilting me off balance. Ryan caught my arm on reflex, steadying me from tripping.

Forgetting the accident we just avoided, my knees buckled from the sheer jolt of his touch. Electricity seared straight through me, a wild rush igniting my skin.

Trying to regain some semblance of control, I straightened my spine and pulled myself together. His fingers lingered—one ... two ... three seconds—before slipping from my elbow. I looked everywhere but at him while my heartbeat scribbled a frantic story beneath my ribs. The strength in his hands, the imprint of his palm, I felt his heat trailing all the way down to the middle of my thigh, but I couldn't decide if it was his words or the physical attraction making me dizzy.

He stepped closer, his voice dipping an octave. My body and brain were no longer aligned. Without meaning to, I mirrored his movement. The fine hairs on my arm stood up, pulled by some invisible current crackling between us. His jacket brushed the fabric of my dress and, suddenly, every nerve in me was awake, raw and aware of just how close we were.

The surrounding noise started to fade. The crowd blurred. I inhaled sharply, filling my lungs with his scent. His mouth hovered inches from mine. I parted my lips on instinct.

"Ladies and gentlemen, can we have your attention, please?" Cece's voice broke through the speaker, and the spell cracked.

Burning with desire and fighting for restraint, I stepped back and focused on the makeshift stage, where the entire Cristaldi family stood together. The people around them were cheering with raised glasses of champagne.

What the hell was I doing?

I picked up my forgotten clutch and the coat check ticket from the table. "I have to leave," I said without meeting his eyes.

His hand immediately moved to my back, halting all my thoughts. "You're fleeing even before dipping your feet in the water?"

I had no comeback. I was burning from his touch, his heated gaze. "I have a train to catch."

"That sounds like an excuse."

He inched closer, and any rational thoughts started evaporating quickly. I knew all the reasons to run, but my feet weren't exactly cooperating.

"I don't date," I said, only to prove I was in control.

He didn't respond. He locked eyes.

"I don't do one-night stands, either," I clarified.

"Good to know." He didn't let go.

"It was nice knowing you," I said, making no effort to leave just yet. The pull between us was too strong, almost hypnotic.

"If you leave, it'd end our story before it even began."

"We've nothing in common."

"Are you sure about that?" He slid his hand down to my lower back, and I sucked in a breath. He was baiting me. "You know how easy it is for me to find you, right?"

Cece. Of course, we have a mutual friend.

"Now you're disappointing me, Ryan."

His lips curled into a devilish smirk when he removed his

hand from my back. The heat lingered like a brand under my dress.

"It'll be a lunch when I find you."

"If you find me without Cece's help."

"When I find you..." he corrected me.

"I really hope you don't waste your time," I said, disappointment and desire waging a battle inside me.

I stepped back toward the exit, our eyes still locked in a dare. Waiting for a silent standoff to see who'd look away first. Logically, it should be me. I was the one retreating, after all. But I couldn't tear myself away from him just yet. Couldn't sever whatever this was we shared. Instead, I shook my head, a quiet answer he'd feel more than hear.

"Just a drink then?" he asked, this time louder.

I took two more steps back, almost ready to turn on my heels when I heard him say, "Give me something to look forward to."

I glanced from under my eyelashes for the last time. "I won't let your storm take me down."

Three

RYAN

"Where've you been?" Alan Benson, my chief financial officer, gave a cursory glance from the pile of paper he was buried under. He waved his pen over a line marked with a *"sign here"* sticker and continued skimming down and signing one page after another.

Tall, lean—let me reiterate ... leaning toward frail—with sagging skin, he was in his late-seventies and had mentioned retirement at least thrice in the past year. I ignored that comment on every count. I'd known him since I was a child visiting this office with my father. When I had taken over the McAlister Group, Alan had shown me the ropes. The only person in this office who believed in me when everyone else had written me off as an inexperienced rookie.

"It's only eight in the morning." I settled into the chair opposite his and took in the ceaseless jungle of skyscrapers outside the window. Another crisp morning in the city that didn't look much different from yesterday or the day before. No blizzard or snow, but undeniably cold. From the size of this room to the view from his window, this office was identical to mine. The only difference was, here I got a minute to look around since my eyes weren't glued to the screen or ears to the phone.

Though I was here, my brain was still sifting through endless data to track down one person in a city of eight million. I had given myself an entire month to forget her. Buried myself in new proposals and all the fires I had to contain. I had even gone out with friends for drinks and browsed through all the glamorous women with their never-ending legs. No one held my attention for over a minute. I was tired of plastic and superficial, or women bending backward for McAlister name. Sure, if I took them to the nearest hotel, the sex would be a great distraction, maybe even satisfy the physical need. But that was it—physical satisfaction. Beyond that, there wasn't anything to exchange.

Risha was different from all those other women. She hadn't reached out, even though our attraction was certainly mutual.

At the party she'd caught my attention the moment she'd entered the room, and I hadn't been able to look away the entire night. The dress she'd been wearing had accentuated her perfect curves, sending my imagination on a reckless spin. The way she'd watched and dismissed every individual, while inspecting every detail of the decor had captivated me.

It'd made sense that she was the orchestrator of the entire theme and decor after Cece'd introduced us, but her profession threw me off. An engineer, not an interior designer or party planner, I never would have guessed it. But then again nothing that I'd learned about her fit in a box. She remained an enigma and a mystery, cladded in a gorgeous body, she intrigued me. And I was still getting over the burn that those slight touches had left on my now deflated ego.

She fascinated the hell out of me. For the first time, something other than work occupied my brain. And even after a month, I couldn't get her out of my mind. My desire to see her again had grown to the point of downright distraction.

"Only?" Alan's loud chuckle pulled my attention back to him. "Since when has eight o'clock become *only* eight in the morning for you?"

"Let's get to the reason behind this ad hoc meeting, shall we?"

My workaholic tendency wasn't something I wanted my employees to mock.

"Fine." After a long and exaggerated exhale, he closed his ballpoint pen and dropped it onto the contract he had been signing.

I straightened my tie and leaned back in my chair.

"Let's discuss these upgrades in your pet project, MoxTo. You completely bypassed my decision not to add a revolving bar and restaurant to your five-star hotel. Didn't we discuss that this would be a serious financial burden if the project staggers any further?"

"First," I started, "this is a joint partnership project. I can't make decisions singlehandedly when my other two partners want something else."

"One is a ten percent partner and the other can buy you over ten times," Alan pointed out, bringing in Taber's smaller partnership into this multi-million-dollar project and Nick's net worth. Friends since undergrad, we had turned our friendship into a partnership. A successful partnership, if I must add.

"Second," I continued, like Alan hadn't interrupted me, "adding a revolving bar and restaurant overlooking midtown will make it enticing."

"Another million-dollar expense we can't afford," Alan countered.

"This was always part of the project; we were buried under the bullshit license issues."

"Two years back, when it was *part of the plan*, we didn't have Maine, Rhode Island, Boston, Florida, and Vegas projects running simultaneously."

His frustration was counterproductive. I understood where he was coming from and that we were burning a million a day. But I knew how to run my business, when to pause, and when to push forward. This wasn't the time to put on the brakes. We were stretched thin, but not buried under debt.

"Our performance is solid. This is the time to expand, not hold back," I explained.

"And the crisis with Miami's mayor we had last month? Vegas construction on complete standstill due to heavy fucking rain in that goddamn desert? We are bleeding money, Ryan."

"Part of doing business. We always account for these contingencies."

"Slow down." Alan heaved in frustration. "You don't have to rush. Time is not your enemy here."

"Time is the most valuable resource we have that everyone takes for granted. Everything can be rebuilt and replaced, except for time. Once it's gone, it's gone."

"Ryan—"

"Alan!" I stopped him. "We don't have debts or a board to answer. Trust me; I know what I am doing."

He sagged back into his chair, unconvinced but conceding. "I wouldn't be here if I didn't trust you, but I'm not the only one concerned. Your reckless gambles might start giving people heart attacks soon. And even though we don't have a board, you don't want your executives to lose faith in you, because that would make you question your credibility."

"Reckless gamble ..." I laughed. I wasn't reckless, nor a gambler. I simply took risks my dad never did. Unlike him, I had a lot to prove, and my employees' trust to earn. I knew exactly what I wanted. McAlister Group to be a global brand. It was Dad's dream that he'd never fully pursued, and now it was my ultimate driving force.

"We're in the best shape we have been, so don't get a heart attack before your anniversary or Anne will kill me."

He shrugged, letting it go for the time being.

This wasn't the first time we had argued about the expansion or he had brought other executives' concerns to my attention. Alan and my perspectives were different, and so were our roles in this company.

"Anne will also breathe down your neck for showing up alone

at the party," he reminded me. "Believe me; I understand your singlehood and focus, but not Anne. If it was up to her, you'd be married by now."

And that was the reason finding Risha was imperative. I needed a date for this party. Not a wife or a girlfriend, only a date. With a woman who didn't date. A woman who had vetted me thoroughly after we had made eye contact, but discarded me nonetheless. And the woman I couldn't stop thinking about.

"Are we done?" I asked impatiently. I wanted to go back to the task that had kept me busy all morning.

"Not yet." Alan bobbled his head, suddenly remembering the real reason for this meeting. "David was scheduled to work on the architecture for Maine's phase two, but he's been pulled back into MoxTo again, and Vikki was supposed to start MoxTo's interior this week, but now she has nothing to work on."

"Postpone Maine extension for now. That resort is doing great as is. And for Vikki, she can start with the southwest side of the building." Not the ideal solution, but that would keep her team busy, even if it went at a snail's pace.

A message pinged on my phone. And the text dictated my next move.

'Risha *Verma, Sylosis Engineering. She works at one of our buildings.*'

$$Four$$

RISHA

"You're late," Patrick stated matter-of-factly, not looking up from his laptop screen.

My work had been demanding, but never unbearable or unreasonable... until him. The stress he piled on me had less to do with the job and everything to do with his hatred of me. As the vice president and my direct manager for the last six months, I maintained deference and focused on the fact he often ignored.

"I'm always the first one in and the last one out of this office."

He pushed horn-rimmed glasses up his nose and leaned back in his chair. Tall, with an athletic build, Patrick was a man-next-door kind of handsome. Clean-shaven and always wearing a two-piece suit, I'd seen him in every shade between black and gray. His brown tie accentuated the inner circle of his iris, and the glasses had been a permanent fixture for as long as I have known him.

Patrick and my chapter hadn't just ended sadly; it had ended brutally. How it ended had rewritten my life henceforth. The damage he had caused lived in plain sight, dressed as affection, cloaked in concern. He had lit the match, and the smoke hadn't cleared ever since.

"And yet, the Blackrock project got derailed by a week." He paused for effect. "How did that happen?"

I took the seat opposite him. "Our written specs and customer's understanding didn't align. The specification clearly said copper wiring, which was read, reviewed, and signed by the customer. Last night, we discovered their old machine used aluminum coils," I explained my late evening call with the California-based customer.

"That's a big fuckup. But now they're pushing the blame on us." He interjected.

"I'll handle it," I said without even batting an eyelash. "I have a paper trail to prove that we weren't informed of the material discrepancy to begin with."

"Of course you do. Unlike relationship management, your customer management skills are precision sharp and thoroughly competent." He smirked and continued, "Miss Risha Verma, the perfectionist, known for her due diligence and efficiency. No one has risen the corporate ladder faster than you."

I tried to decipher his insinuation—a compliment or a taunt. I didn't want either coming from him. We were both scorched by the same fire. The only difference was I kept walking while he stayed in the ashes.

"Any particular reason for this jab?"

He feigned surprise. "*Jab*? If I didn't know you better, I'd think otherwise, but you deserve where you are. The youngest director of engineering, heading a fifteen-member team."

I couldn't tell if I smelled bullshit or indignation, but I was certain he hadn't called me to this meeting for my career achievements.

I steered our conversation to relevance. "I'll keep you posted on Blackrock. Anything else you wanted to discuss?"

"As a matter of fact, I do. Nixus reached out for a six-month contract. They want *you* and *your team* for their project."

I ignored the finger pointing in my direction.

Nixus was a multi-billion-dollar security firm that I worked with during my graduate year. They also held a massive in-house engineering team, so the need to outsource it to Sylosis made no sense.

Before I could ask, Patrick went on. "They want to enhance the x-ray machine you helped them build, which translated to needing us. As always, you've made quite an impact there, too. Wherever you go, you leave quite a remarkable impression on people." His words seethed with sarcasm and bitterness.

"I hope this project doesn't start for the next six months." Ignoring his taunt, I reminded him of my team's overcrowded calendar.

Patrick chuckled. "You're joking, right? They are ready to pay a small fortune, but they want this to start immediately."

I shook my head, not ready to take on more than I could chew. "I can't ... *we* can't. My team is swamped."

Patrick folded his arms across his chest. "It seems Nixus forgot to check your calendar before planning this project." Resentment flickered in his eyes, a blaze he refused to fan. He drew in a slow breath, exhaling the weight of whatever war raged beneath the surface. When he spoke again, his voice was even and measured, but edged with steel. "They're ready to pay out bonuses at every milestone. But, I repeat, they want this to be our first priority."

"And what about the other five projects we're currently working on?"

"Reassign them to Sarah's or Ari's team. Borrow a few heads to fill in the gap. I don't know, Risha. You are the director—figure the fuck out."

"So, let me get this right. Instead of hiring more, you want me to ask Sarah and Ari to lend me engineers out of their five-people teams?" My patience was running thin. Our billing hours were triple—not because we were unicorns, but how long we stayed at our desks.

"We're on a hiring freeze until spring." He got up from his chair to his full five-ten height. "They don't have a choice."

"I haven't agreed to this yet. Let me talk to my team first."

"This is not a negotiation. We need Nixus's name on our

client portfolio and also the premium they are ready to pay." He closed his laptop screen, signaling the meeting was adjourned. A power move to show who was in charge now.

Powerless to resolve my team's work-life balance, I grabbed my laptop and left before him. Letting the door bang behind me in frustration.

In my office, I dropped the laptop onto my desk with a *thud*. My love for this job was directly proportional to my hate for Patrick. He was here to make my life a living hell. But this job was all I had. It kept me occupied, kept me sane, and was the only thing remaining that I looked forward to. However, as much as those project deliveries were my responsibility, so was my team's wellbeing. And I was failing them.

A sudden knock filled me with contempt. Every time we entered a showdown, Patrick made sure to come back and flaunt his position just to goad me.

I turned to face the door and was taken by surprise. Shock and excitement swirled within me like a tornado. Butterflies barreled up my stomach, ready to break through my diaphragm and burst out of my chest.

Jesus, fuck. The reaction this man got out of me was unnerving and unfamiliar. Thirty-five days and not a single thing had changed.

My feet faltered as I took a step forward. My brain was still processing the pull instead of forming words. I barely managed, "Ryan? What are you doing here?"

His smile knocked me sideways, and my body stirred with a whole new level of eagerness, singing a tune I'd never heard. Everything that wasn't supposed to happen to me, I felt at every micro-fiber of my being. My senses heightened in response to his worn, leathery cologne. In a gray three-piece suit, he looked every bit as devastating as I remembered him from the party. His smile, the twinkle in his eyes, disarmed me. Either I hadn't been drunk that night, or perhaps, I was under his spell even now. The beard hugged his jawline like it hadn't meant to be devastating, but was anyway. That scruff was equal parts rugged and refined, softening the stoicism in his face, while the mustache gave his smirk a roguish edge.

"We meet again." He stood by the doorway casually. Behind him, I saw Patrick walking down the hallway toward my office.

My fucking life. And my fucking boss.

Grabbing Ryan's arm, I pulled him down the hallway, in the opposite direction from Patrick. "Let's go for lunch."

I didn't need to grab his hand, but it happened on impulse. Part of me wanted to explore what this was. Part of me wanted to run in the opposite direction. This man left me in sorts, making me question if I had ever felt this alive before.

If Ryan was confused by my impulse, at least he didn't show it.

I hastened us toward the exit, and he let me lead.

"Isn't it too early for lunch?" he asked when we exited the fogged glass door of Sylosis' fifteenth floor office and into the elevator vestibule. One elevator was already on our floor. We walked onto it, and I pressed *'lobby.'*

"Is it?" I needed some respite from Patrick. "Brunch then. I am starving."

Five

RYAN

"Stop grinning." Risha jabbed the lobby button five times to rush out of here.

Not complaining—whatever had her spooked had led her directly to me.

"How did you find me?" she asked without a glance.

She smoothed her hands over her skirt then over the coat she had grabbed seconds before leaving her office. Nothing was out of place, of course; she was gorgeous and so fucking flawless. Today, her nude silk shirt and black pencil skirt screamed business. But those knee-high boots were pure seduction. I couldn't take my eyes off her.

Now that she was in front of me, I knew why I had been so fucking miserable all this while. I missed the zing in the air when she wasn't there. I wanted to explore this further, which meant I had this lunch, or brunch, or whatever the fuck she wanted to call this to convince her to spend another day with me.

"I thought it'd take some persuasion to take you out on a date."

I provoked her, and my words had the desired effect. She turned sharply with an expression hovering between annoyance and perplexity.

I feign nonchalance. "Your desperation is so obvious."

"Excuse me?" She turned on me now ready to bite my head off. "You found me, remember."

"By chance." I shrugged, holding any further explanation until she asked.

She didn't. Instead, she looked straight at the blank elevator door and said, "This is not a date."

The floor shifted slightly, and then the door opened. Tugging on her coat, she braced for the cold. In actuality—hiding the effect I knew I had on her.

Electricity had crackled from the moment we'd met, like someone had flipped the switch on a live wire. The signs were all there—her blushed cheeks, the rapid rise and fall of her chest, the way her lips parted and her eyes dazzled when she saw me in her office. The physical tension between us was unmistakable.

I followed her through the lobby. "So, brunch doesn't count as a date then? Good to know. I'm a bit rusty in this department."

She looked over her shoulder as she continued walking. Her eyes squinted as she did so. "This is two hungry people going to a restaurant. It's not considered a date."

Stifling my chuckle, I raised a hand in surrender.

Risha picked up the pace.

I followed closely, matching her strides. I took the opportunity to admire her once more, slender, beautiful, sophisticated—she was a vision. Unlike last time, her long hair was pulled into a ponytail with a few tendrils over her eyes and ears. There was nothing delicate about her, no pretense. Confidence radiated off of her like armor, a quality that put other women to shame.

We exited the office building, stepping out into the crisp morning wind and walked into the first restaurant in sight—Russo's. Judging by the faint smell of fresh coffee and the absence of any other diners, the place had stopped taking breakfast orders, and it was too early for lunch.

"Table for two hungry people who are absolutely,

unequivocally not on a date." I told the hostess as she approached to seat us.

Risha groaned, but trailed after the hostess as she led us to a table halfway across the room. I followed close behind her and we took the chairs on opposite sides of the table. She shrugged out of her coat before sitting down, draping it over the back of her chair.

"Just making sure no one mistakes this for a date," I exclaimed, which earned me a huge eye-roll.

I was enjoying vexing her all too much. No matter how much she attempted to distract herself from the tension between us, the rising pink blush in her cheeks was a clear giveaway of how my presence affected her.

Ignoring me, Risha scanned the restaurant with a critical eye, taking in every detail as she had done at the party. Appreciation flared in her eyes as she took in the intricacies of the upside-down candelabras hanging over the corner booths, but then quickly turned to displeasure when her gaze wandered over to a replica of *Venus Italica* in the center of the floor.

When her almond-eyes finally landed on me, I gave her my best smile.

"What now?" she asked, folding her arms under her breasts.

"Spill it. What's wrong with the sculpture?"

She hesitated, but only for a second. She seemed eager and stated, "They used warm olive tone wallpapers, then green and orange furniture. Those go in perfect harmony."

I followed her evaluation with my eyes as she pointed to the various pieces of décor and balanced colors. The dark wooden floor and large windows made the place cozily intimate rather than airy. It wasn't bad—a blend of old and contemporary.

"So far, I'm with you." I said, urging her to continue.

"The light fixtures have a modern rustic touch to them. That's in harmony, too, adding something refreshing and new," Then turning back to the statue on the pedestal in the middle of the room, she said, "A statue from the nineteenth century is completely unnecessary and serves absolutely no purpose to accentuate the rest of the look."

I had been to this place several times but never paid attention to any of this. Now that Risha had pointed it out, I saw everything through her artistic lens. Her observation made complete sense.

"What will you change?" I asked.

She paused, sweeping her gaze around the room as she considered my question. But then she stopped and locked eyes with me. "Do you own this place?"

I laughed aloud. "Do you want me to?"

With a big eyeroll, she turned to the statue again. "Lemon vines can add warmth and something entirely new, pulling it all together in a cohesive manner."

Her eyes turned dreamy, as if she could see the changes in her head, her creative mind taking over. I could watch her like this all day.

"You know," I pulled her attention back to me. "I would have easily mistaken you for a designer if I didn't know you were an engineer."

"Right." Straightening her back, she turned to face me fully. Placing her hands on the table she narrowed her eyes at me. "Now tell me how and why you found me?"

"How is easy. I gave your name to my security engineer. It only took him a little over three hours to track down the company you work for."

"You wasted three productive hours of that poor engineer just to find me?" She shook her head in disbelief.

I refrained from mentioning the two hours of my own before he'd taken over the search. If given a choice, I would do it all over again. Hell, if I could turn back time, I wouldn't have waited a month.

"And you did nothing to contact me," I responded instead. "You knew who I was."

Her cheeks flushed as she scanned my face. That look was adorable, the red tint rose along her high cheekbones all the way to her perfectly sculpted nose. I was drawn in once again by the flawlessness of her skin. She wasn't just beautiful; she was magnetic.

Then the heater hissed in the otherwise quiet restaurant, breaking the moment.

"What did I save you from?" I asked.

Snapping her spine straight once more, something like panic crossed her face then vanished just as quickly. "I have no idea what you're talking about."

"Come on, Risha. What made you so eager to flee your office?"

"Stop hallucinating. I was hungry—that's all there was to it." She rolled her eyes as if my question was the most absurd thing she had ever heard.

"Yet, you haven't even looked at the menu," I challenged, calling her bluff.

She shifted uncomfortably, sifting through the menu for the first time. We placed our order, but even after the server left, she wouldn't meet my gaze.

Our food arrived within minutes of ordering. Perks of being the only customer. I drank my coffee, while Risha played with her fork, tossing scrambled eggs from one side to another. Whatever was bothering her was keeping her withdrawn from me right now.

"You aren't hungry," I pointed out the obvious.

She dropped the fork and pushed the plate away. "Not even the tiniest bit. I'm sorry; I just needed to get out for a little bit."

"We all have our days. I'm glad I was there."

"You haven't answered the why part yet," she reminded me.

Isn't that obvious? You enamor me.

"I need a big favor. Huge, actually." She didn't interrupt, so I went on. "Next Sunday, I've been invited to an anniversary dinner. Join me as my plus one."

"That's—more than a week away." She sipped water from her glass. "What's the rush to meet today?"

I could be direct, if that was what she wanted.

"What're you doing this weekend?"

She put the glass down without meeting my eyes. "I'll be at my parents' place, in Jersey."

Was there a crack in her voice, or was it just a flicker of my imagination? Before I could read her, though, she tucked that emotion away.

"Something you do often?" I asked.

"More than I would like to, yes." It was just a whisper, but I caught it. "I told you already, I don't do dates."

"You'll be my plus one at the dinner," I clarified, not accepting that answer.

She clearly didn't want to date, and I wasn't looking for complications. Yet, here I was, because I couldn't get her out of my head.

"Come on now; be a sport." I nudged further, coaxing her to give in. "Look, I saved you today; it's only fair you reciprocate the favor."

Risha quirked her brow. "You don't believe in keeping your debts, Mr. McAlister?"

I picked up my coffee cup, taking a sip. "We live in a world of instant gratification, Miss Verma."

I pushed my plate away since I wasn't hungry, either. But I was intent on getting my way. The tension between us was becoming something far more comfortable than I cared to admit.

Her face flushed. "And if we do this, we are even?"

"If you agree, I'll owe you one."

"Hmm, it's that important?"

"Something like that." I couldn't disappoint Anne, and I needed another date with Risha. I needed another reason to spend time together. Her presence was intoxicating and I wanted more. This time I wasn't taking no for an answer. I was determined to convince her to see me again.

"Fine." She conceded with a sigh, pinning me with a pointed finger as she stipulated. "It's not a date, though."

I raised my hands up in mock surrender, a grin chasing the lines of my mouth in response. "I wouldn't assume in a million years."

Satisfied, Risha called for the check. I dropped cash onto the table. She thanked me and got up to leave. I stepped toward the exit, our shoulders brushing as we fell into step. The heat that skated up my arm told a distinct story. I caught her stealing a glance in my direction, lips parting and closing. Damn, she was distracting.

When I opened the door, a gust of wind pushed a strand of her unrestrained hair over her face. Without thinking, I reached out to tuck it behind her ear. My fingers grazed her cheek, and a single stupid brush of touch short-circuited my thoughts. She stilled, and for a second, neither of us moved.

Was this fucking seriously happening to me? I wasn't immune to women. I went celibate since I met her only because I couldn't concentrate on mundane chatter and mindless sex to take the edge off. I wanted whatever this was.

We walked slowly toward her office as if we were trying to stretch the seconds we had together. Her hand brushed mine. The first time felt like an accident. The second made me pause almost imperceptibly. I didn't move away. She didn't either. Our hands didn't quite hold, but they hovered close enough to feel the physical attraction. Like my body found its magnetic pole and couldn't fucking move.

She bumped into me slightly when someone passed too close on the sidewalk. My hand went instinctively to her back, steadying her. All the layers of clothes couldn't cover the heat underneath my palm.

We paused at the street corner, and she turned toward me, sunlight caught in spilled ink.

I leaned into her personal space. "Give me your number," I said casually.

She arched her brow. Amused. Intrigued. "You found where I work, but not my number?"

I removed my phone from the inside of my jacket pocket and held it out for her. "I can, but I thought you'd appreciate it if I ask you instead ... privacy and what not."

She gave a throaty laugh as she took the phone. Her fingers brushing mine again, the touch lingered, burning into a bruise while she typed in her number.

More, the word echoed.

"There." She pressed the phone into my chest. "It's to coordinate next weekend."

As if.

I took the phone but couldn't end it there. Catching her hand, I raised it to my mouth and brushed my lips over her fingers. Her eyes fluttered closed.

Was it my imagination or did she hate how right it felt. The chemistry between us was undeniable.

"I'm not open to anything," she breathed out, the fight in her eyes telling another story.

I paused, alarm bells ringing. "Are you seeing someone?"

"It's ... complicated."

Fuck. "It's a yes or no question, Risha. Are you with someone or not?"

Agitated, she pulled her hand out of my grip. "Technically, no. But that doesn't mean I am looking for something."

I stepped closer and kissed her cheek. She leaned in, contradicting her own statement. The silence that followed colored my raging heartbeats. Maybe she didn't know what she wanted. Or maybe she just couldn't reach it. *Technically*, she wasn't taken. *Emotionally*, she was a mess of contradictions.

Walking away would have been the smartest move. But it also felt like the coward's way out.

"Me neither," I told her.

Six

RISHA

The screech of steel-on-steel grated through my skull as the train pulled into the station. I loathed trains like engineers despised a last-minute design change, or an artist dreaded a cookie-cutter. A perpetual, inescapable plague and a maddening, soul-sucking inevitability which drained my essence and filled me with resentment that refused to dissipate.

The hour-long commute to be with my family was my slow descent into misery, and the return trip only deepened the gloom. Worthlessness and self-contempt haunted me no matter which side of the Hudson River I lived.

And then seeing Ryan sent me back into a spin, like a match struck too close to gasoline, flickering with want and resisting the inevitable spark. His every word echoed in my brain, and his every touch seared like a brand on my skin. Live and pulsating, an electric current. Wanting to say no, but leaning into him for more.

I wanted to get over those hypnotic blue eyes. An unparalleled, desperate need left me incomplete, craving something I shouldn't be wanting. My rebellious streak urged me to live a little, though aware I was flirting with danger. He was making me forget my pathetic past, drowning present, and hopeless future.

Living in two worlds had its own challenges.

When I exited the train station, Sia was already waiting inside her hand-me-down sedan. With the laptop bag hung over one shoulder and overnight bag on the other, I shifted from an advancing corporate woman to an inadequate daughter.

"Hi sweets. Missed me?" I asked with a genuine smile.

A firecracker to the core, Sia, was the youngest of us three sisters, and everything I wasn't.

"Tried and failed." She giggled, bubbling with excitement. "Tell me about your week. I'm living vicariously through you."

If only living far from home meant living on an edge.

"Nothing has changed since last week, or the week before really. One client was trying to be a dick, pushing their negligence onto us, so I had to put him in his place. He called my manager, threatening to take the project away."

"Fuck, seriously?"

I chuckled then glossed over the drama that had ensued, knowing my life would be easier if fewer people knew who my manager was.

"Nothing, I called their bluff. Four hours wasted, but they apologized and promised to pay every penny they owed us."

"You rock, but seriously, you need to live a little outside your work."

"Yeah, it's high up on my to-do list, actually." I said keeping my voice even.

"I can't wait to join you in the city. This wait for college acceptance is killing me."

I turned to face her. "No news?"

"None. I don't know what they're waiting for. I have a perfect score." Her face turned into a cute cocktail of disappointment and animated gestures.

Sia's dream of attending Columbia University was partly influenced by her choice of major in artificial intelligence, but primarily by its proximity to me.

"Don't overthink," I offered.

She smiled. "You know I'm not good at it, anyway."

"Any changes to our weekend plans?" I asked as she turned onto our street.

"None. Tonight's party will be all about tomorrow's wedding. And the wedding tomorrow is just that—a wedding," she exclaimed.

Presence was mandatory for both. The wedding was of my neighbor, Asha, to her high school sweetheart. Now they were bigshot engineers running their own innovation in California. Perfect match, made in heaven. That was all I'd hear all weekend long.

Sia pulled into the driveway and hit the garage door opener.

I'd lived my entire life here before moving to Manhattan six years ago. My mother's expectation that I should refer to India as my country was illogical. But then, I didn't think of myself as an American, either. I never got the opportunity to embrace the country and the culture of my birth.

So, here I was, always questioning the authenticity of my identity—an American concealed behind a façade or a South Asian wrapped in a shroud of tradition?

The moment Sia killed the car's engine, I walked through the garage and foyer and dashed upstairs into my bedroom ... until it was lunchtime at the Verma family.

"You know, Avar," Mom addressed Dad in her traditional endearment. Her short and timid frame remained still, but her head bobbled with excitement. "Raj is visiting his parents this weekend. After finishing post doc, he started his own company; some ... green energy solutions ... I always knew he was the brightest kid."

"Interesting. I should find out about his funding. Everyone is after green energy nowadays," Dad responded with a twinkle in his eye, his scientific mind always drawn to people like him. Quiet and composed, he carried his six-foot frame with ease, and I often wished he'd speak up more.

Mom continued, completely disregarding the food she had spent hours preparing. "We haven't met him in fifteen years, but I remember he was such a handsome kid. Not sure if his profile is already on a matchmaking site. I'll ask at the party tonight—"

"You will not do any such thing unless you are planning to remarry." I lost my calm, and Sia giggled next to me. Tired of Mom's constant nagging, it took little to lose my patience these days.

"How dare ...?" She stopped herself to inhale a sharp breath, and then an exhale with tears ready to jump out. "You're getting old now. When do you think you're going to get married and have a family of your own?"

Queen of Manipulation was her middle name, and I'd learned nothing from her.

"Maybe never. Just leave me alone, Mom," I said, hating myself, because peace took priority over standing up for myself.

"I don't want you to repeat mistakes," Mom continued, always reminding everyone of my error in judgment. "I'm thinking what's best for you. And it's not that you are doing anything important, anyway."

Here came the famous last words. I decided to point out the facts since she had a short memory.

"I'm one of the directors in our company. My team respects me, and I'm earning very well for myself."

"There are thousands like you in every city of every country and in every goddamn company. I don't see anything extraordinary that you do." She pushed the dagger right where it hurt. A town creating an army of high achievers, where the Verma family was let down by their oldest daughter.

"My team develops cutting-edge, innovative products daily."

"Taking someone else's idea and executing them isn't innovation, Risha; that is ... providing service." She repeated the exact words she had heard once from Dad. He'd said it to prove his point, but that'd become my mother's Bible. He hadn't always been this way, but lately, his disappointments had eclipsed his love for me.

I turned to Dad, who sat there like a mute. I had abandoned his plans; in return he had abandoned me. But he wasn't the only one feeling disappointed here. I was, too. I knew I'd have to fight for myself even if it meant risking failure.

"Fine. I'm happy with what I do; does that count?"

"Of course, it does. When have we ever stopped you from anything? We even paid for your useless MBA program, didn't we?" Mom always brought that up in our argument. Not that I asked for their money, but God forbid if someone found out the Verma daughters' education wasn't paid for.

"And it still doesn't change the fact that you're thirty. You need to be married before summer." She couldn't let it go. Wouldn't let it go. Now that Sia was going to college and Ria was already there, Mom had found a new pet project to focus on. Her life's goal was to screw mine.

"Who has given this deadline?"

Why am I here? And why am I sucked into this torture every weekend?

"I know you don't trust Sarika Ammayi, but any OBGYN in the world would tell you that having children after thirty is risky."

Ammayi was my mother's sister, far more progressive than Mom could ever be. But now and then, Mom used her name to quote her own beliefs. Like quoting someone well-versed gave authenticity to her statement.

"I'm confused. Are we talking about marriage or pregnancy? Because I don't need to be married to have children."

The concept of matchmaking was bile constantly sloshing inside my bloodstream; neither could I run away nor swallow the poison once and for all. Mom complained about my age, my choices, but my gripe was she never tried to understand what I wanted.

Not wanting anything was a want in itself, wasn't it?

Why did I have to want anything at all? Always that next step —study, work, marry, procreate. Why couldn't it be enough to simply exist, to breathe without chasing something more? Was it so wrong to live without a finish line in sight? Since when did contentment become a sin?

"Is this why we came to this country, Avar? So these kids can forget our culture, family values, and how to respect their elders?" Mom's temper flared.

"Stop playing the cultural card, Mom. When you don't have an answer, you start with family values." I was at the end of my patience, already regretting my decision to come back home. Not that I had a choice. But it was a choice I wanted to have. Independence and self-preservation fought a battle for control when I stood on my feet, needing space and to rein in my composure.

"Don't forget that she is your mother and all the sacrifices she has made to give you this perfect life. Whether you agree with her or not, the least we expect is your respect." Dad's statement silenced the entire room. "She isn't the enemy here, so stop fighting everyone to prove your independence."

The quiet was so intense it resonated in my bones. He wasn't a man of many words, and in recent years, we've hardly spoken to each other. The disappointment on his face lingered every time I walked into this house now, and we both avoided each other at all costs.

Mom's sobs broke the standoff between Dad and I. The values she'd been raised on demanded obedience, while I was yearning to steer my own life, even if only in fragments. She cried to gain control, displaying her vulnerability and how my pursuit of independence challenged her traditions and beliefs. I refused to show how vulnerable I felt inside. Lonely in a crowd, fighting a war wedging day and night, year after year.

The worst part was this wasn't a war; she wasn't even an enemy—this was my mother. Wars were simple when we knew what we were fighting for, standing up for something we believed in. No, the worst was the endless tunnel with no light in sight. Because, to me, that light was a missing unknown. The sky had been so dark for so long that I'd forgotten what a clear sky looked like.

As Verma daughters, we were all driven by someone else's dreams. There was no space for what I wanted since others' sacrifices became propellers of our destiny. And, as the oldest daughter, I always found myself buried under the heavy burden of expectation. I wanted more, or less, however you wanted to look at it.

"Avar, I'm letting you know, either she marries someone soon, or we contact that Indian matchmaker to help her out," Mom continued, as if my input wasn't necessary. Like it wasn't my life, my future, she was discussing. "She has clients in the US and India, and I heard now she has a matchmaking show, as well."

The monologue continued through lunch; my name tossed around like it didn't belong to me. Like I wasn't even in the room at all.

Neither Dad nor I spoke for the rest of the weekend.

Seven

RYAN

"Hey, boss, you got a minute?" Vikki knocked on my door, halting Alan's latest rant.

His complaints were nothing short of nails on a chalkboard these days. He said, and I quote, I was "bleeding the company dry." The fucking company, founded by my great-grandfather and significantly grown by me, was hemorrhaging cash on overly long and complex projects. Even at thirty-two, if people couldn't trust me, when would they?

I signaled Vikki to come inside, an open-door policy I instated since taking over the company and one which my employees took full advantage of. I didn't buy into the whole boss-subordinate bullshit. I wanted people to speak their minds, pointing out my errors and offering solutions. My policy was made with good intent, but every decision came with its pros and cons, and its share of consequences.

I'd handpicked Vikki right out of her design school. Her two most recent projects had been featured in major magazines. I saw the potential—her unorthodox ideas, boldness that reflected in her every statement piece. I made her an offer against everyone's advice—too fresh, too green, no real experience ...

I wouldn't be where I was if only experience decided one's worth.

Sometimes, people needed a chance to prove themselves, and who would understand it better than the man churned through the grinder? I'd worked four times harder to show my worth. Or maybe I wasn't even given a choice.

She took the unoccupied seat next to Alan. The veil tattoo on her tanned arm exposed below her kimono sleeve showcased her creative talent.

"I was planning to meet you; good you came by." I adjusted my back in the chair. "How was Miami?"

She smiled. "Living and working in a luxury resort on South Beach had its own charm. I must admit, I was getting used to the weather."

Our Mediterranean revival luxury resort in Miami was her latest project. The terracotta roofs, dramatic archways, and lush courtyards with pools and two ten-story wings overlooking South Beach had already been featured in *Aesthetic Style's* October issue. The grand opening was scheduled for next month, adding yet another success for McAlister Group.

"Don't get too used to it. You're far too important to get stuck in one place. Have you visited MoxTo yet?"

She groaned and fell back in the cushioned chair. "That's what I wanted to talk about. It's a mess. I know you want my team to start, but with the construction crew dragging heavy machinery through every open space, it's impossible for us to do anything right now."

"How about the third-floor suite and up?" Alan chimed in. "Since the construction is limited to hundred-and-twentieth and above."

"Or"—her smile turned lopsided—"Ryan's penthouse has been sitting empty for years, I heard."

Where is she going with this?

When I remained silent, she added, "Ryan, I need something

new to work on. In the last six years, I have done all sorts of hotels, resorts, and offices for McAlister Group."

"So, you're complaining? Already?"

"No." Vikki sat up straight. "I love my job."

"Good God. I'd hate to lose a talented designer who just got featured in one of the biggest international magazines." I flared my hand. "Congratulations! You were exceptional once again."

"Yeah, thanks ..." She sighed in boredom. "I need something different this time."

"MoxTo will be different," I reminded her. The highest level of a luxury hotel with every amenity available under one roof. Taber, Nick, and I were going for a shockwave in Manhattan.

"I'm sure it will. You don't believe in cookie cutter projects, and you don't do anything half-ass. But we aren't there yet. It's overcrowded by construction crew, architects, those jokers from the city licensing department. I can't concentrate on anything there."

Her statement made Alan flinch. The last two words he wanted to hear were "delay" and "stalling." Taber had taken a massive interest in the hotel. Beyond his ten percent stake, he was bringing Cristaldi's signature bars and nightclubs into the fold, transforming it into the destination people flew to Greece or Monaco for. Once MoxTo was complete, it wouldn't just dominate Manhattan; it would own the world. Any and all imaginable luxuries under one roof.

But Alan wanted to see the revenue. And believe me; I felt his sentiments—we had been bleeding money into this project for the last two years. To make things worse, our cash flow wasn't exactly the best at the moment. I refused to take a loan. Neither was I ready to discuss these issues with anyone. Because needing help showed vulnerability, and vulnerable, I wasn't. Failing or showing weakness wasn't part of my plan. I hadn't turned my father's multimillions to billions by depending on others. When I'd gotten into the Miami, Vegas, and Manhattan projects simultaneously, I had understood what the challenges were. The stakes were high, but the payoff made the risk worthwhile. I knew it. Alan just needed some convincing.

"What are you suggesting?" I asked Vikki.

"I want to work on your penthouse," she said bluntly. "That place has been sitting empty for years, and it's my dream to work on something personal—not where people spend time, but where they live. Where you can liv—"

"No." It came out harsh. I couldn't cover the void that came with the mention of that place. It was empty because going back meant admitting I had survived without them.

"You don't even live there, boss. Hear me out ... I need a new challenge. I have always—"

"This is not up for discussion, Vikki." I turned my attention to the laptop, mainly to rein in my unease. It wasn't just some penthouse, and definitely not something I was ready to change. The building itself wasn't our biggest property, but the McAlister residence held many memories and a load of nightmares that I wasn't ready to get past.

"Boss—"

"Let it go, Vikki," Alan stopped her this time. He'd been with me through the worst of times and knew a lot more than anyone else in this office.

"Start with Serata on the southwest side on the main floor. Close off the exit points and start right away." I changed the direction of our discussion. Being a luxury hotel meant having multiple in-house restaurants. Serata would be our epicurean heaven right out of Italy.

She exhaled, disappointment plastered on her face. "Sure." Gripping the chair's handles, she began to rise.

"Add lemon vines into the aesthetics," I added. "I want to see Amalfi in there."

"Are you serious?" Her expression morphed into one of amusement even before she fell back into her seat. "You completely overrode my idea when I first pitched it, going into length about the temperature control and natural light and whatnot … What made you change your mind so suddenly?"

Fucking hell. An open-door policy also meant every authority challenged, and every decision debated.

"Tangerine trees were a terrible idea," I retorted with an exasperated snort, remembering our discussion from months ago. I'd killed her idea on the spot.

"Citrus tree," she clarified. "I mentioned tangerine once … And that's not the point. Why this sudden change of heart, if I may ask?"

"You may not." I smirked, trying to be the *boss* here. But then I gave an explanation, anyway. "I played with the idea. It's refreshingly new, something New Yorkers can enjoy in this concrete jungle. The fresh scent of the tree will bring authenticity to Serata Ristorante."

A part of me succumbed to guilt.

But a grin spread over Vikki's face. "I'll start right away," She got up from her chair to leave, not completely thrilled, but satisfied to get one of her wishes granted.

"Make this first priority and keep me posted," I told her before she left the room.

"Vikki wasn't completely wrong, you know?" Alan spoke up as soon as we were alone. "At some point, you have to stop living in this office building and move back to your home."

"I live here because it's convenient," I retorted, not ready to give air to this conversation.

"It's not just about a bed to sleep on, Ryan," Alan said. "It should feel like home, not a hiding spot. It saddens me to see you alone."

It wasn't the first time he'd commented on the matter, and he wasn't the only one reminding me of my bachelor lifestyle. Since Ivy had left, I had no reason to go back to the penthouse. Without someone to share a home, the grandest of spaces could feel like a coffin. And this one was a whopping eight-thousand-square-foot morgue.

I also had no excuse not to move into something new. After all, McAlister Group owned a sizable chunk of Manhattan's real estate. Unfortunately, nothing in this fucking city felt like home. In a city of eight million, I was still lonely.

Not alone, but lonely.

Alone, I was fine with. My work kept me busy, and I knew what I needed in life and how to get there. Being alone kept me focused.

Loneliness was a different matter. I'd felt it when my parents died, when Ivy had left for Boston. The difference between alone and lonely was I could be sitting on the highest pile of gold with no one to share it with. Loneliness was when no one was waiting, no one to go home to.

Alone was momentary. Loneliness stretched for a lifetime, with no end in sight. Alone, I had no problem with. Loneliness was crippling.

An orphan, no matter how old, there was no life outside my work. And that was loneliness.

"A real estate mogul living in a makeshift studio in his office building, and you call this convenient?" Alan shook his head, pulling me out of the abyss. "This isn't normal."

Choosing to ignore Alan, I went back to the list of pending emails I had to respond to. There was nothing to say that would convince him. I had to make peace with my past one day, but that day wasn't today.

"Any news from Ivy? I heard Boston is getting hit by a blizzard."

"So I heard." Now this, I could discuss. Even though Ivy was half-owner of McAlister Group, she had given me complete autonomy on all decisions. I wanted her back. To have her beside me. What Dad had left was for both of us, but hell, this woman was more stubborn than anyone I had ever known.

"Spoke to her last night. She's staying in her apartment until the storm runs its course," I answered as I forced myself to get distracted with work.

"I heard people could lose electricity for a while."

"She is living in a McAlister building with generators and twenty-four-seven security." She was my responsibility, which I took seriously. "I'll be seeing her soon," I divulged further.

A customary visit I maintained since she found every goddamn reason not to come home. The demons of our past had affected us differently. Her solution was to run away and mine to fight back. I was still fighting mine while Ivy wasn't ready to make peace with hers. Hiding wasn't the solution, but when had she ever listened to me?

"Now *that* building was an excellent investment. A few freebies you've given here and there, but overall, that building has always been profitable."

"I'm glad you approve." I smirked. "The only freebie is an apartment to our state senator's granddaughter. Who knows when and where we'll need his help."

He got up with a sigh. Not approving, but agreeing with yet another decision of mine. "Don't forget about our dinner tonight."

"Yes, boss." I gave him a mock salute. A customary dinner with our top executives.

People talked openly when they weren't bound to an office. I wanted every person to enjoy working at McAlister Group and to speak without hesitation. I wanted to earn their trust and respect, and I wanted them to work for me because they enjoyed working here. I wanted to be available to them and approachable, as well. That was why I found living anywhere else a complete waste of my time.

Eight

It was dark by the time I exited the office building, debating whether to brave the subway or hunt for a cab. My stomach growled with a vengeance, reminding me that my last meal had been a cereal bar early this morning. The day had slipped by, and so had the evening. But after a full day of meetings, I was at least leaving the office content. Nixus's project wouldn't begin until December, which gave us enough time to end a couple of other projects.

Deciding to catch a cab, I turned toward the road. The first cab whizzed by without slowing down. I raised my hand for the second one, which got me the same result. When the third cab didn't stop, I conceded and turned toward the subway station. Then, a black sedan pulled up beside me. I looked inside the car through the passenger-side window, and my stomach flipped.

"Ryan?" My voice carried an edge of surprise, the exhaustion of the day bypassing my normal stonewall.

"Get in," he said, unlocking the door from his console.

I wanted to believe it was the hunger pangs sending me off-kilter, but who was I kidding? He'd been invading my every waking hour since we'd last met. A sane part of me wanted to excuse myself; the other part—the insane and wild one, the one that couldn't get him out of my mind—wanted to take him up on his offer.

"I don't want to bother you. I'm heading for the subway." I said instead. My hand vaguely gestured down the block.

"I saw you trying to grab a cab," he said with a small shake of his head. "Come on, just get in, it's really no trouble."

Opening the passenger door, I sank into the warm, plush leather seat. Was it fate that kept crossing our stars, the universe conspiring to test my resolve, or had he sought me out once again? The heavy *cha-chunk* noise, though, signaled my heart's triumph in this round.

"Thanks," I said, feeling the heat rising up my cheeks.

Without meeting his eyes, I busied myself with the seat belt and other inconsequential movements, like where to keep the bags I'd been carrying. It had been almost a week since I'd given him my number, but he had never reached out. Not that I was waiting for his call, or text, or whatever. Okay, fine, I was hoping he would text.

Why on earth does he affect me so much? I couldn't help the deep sigh that accompanied the thought.

He said nothing, not even hello, but his presence caused a dizzying effect, intoxicating and overpowering. With every second that passed, my pulse quickened with his mere proximity. Every time I tried to breathe in, I inhaled his scent. My every exhale called his name. *Ryan! Ryan! Ryan!*

My pathetic life be damned. I cared less about all the baggage I carried. When I was with him, he overtook my senses. The tug I felt for him was stronger than gravity.

He looked, as usual, devastatingly handsome in a three-piece striped suit. His broad shoulders tapered under the jacket. But his smile was missing, and his eyes seemed ... distant.

"Do you always work this late?" he asked as he joined the traffic.

"Off this late is becoming my new routine." I tucked the

laptop bag and purse near my feet and kept it casual. "I wasn't expecting to see you."

"Don't tell me you're disappointed," he tried to joke, but something in his tone was missing.

His words and voice didn't align, but that didn't quiet the rampant butterflies swarming in my belly.

Not in the slightest, I wanted to say.

"Where were you heading before you found me?"

"I'm returning from a business dinner," he explained.

"You can drop me off at the subway station."

He gave me the once-over. "I know where Cece lives; it's not a problem."

"Do you now?" I turned at my waist to face him. Hoping to get a smartass comment, I said, "And here I thought someone preferred asking instead of finding out."

"I own that building," he said dryly.

"Oh!" Of course he did. What else did billionaires do? Buy and sell properties, I guess.

When he stopped at the light, he faced me and said dryly, "I own your office building, too. Not showing off my assets, but I thought you should know."

He wasn't his usual self, that much I was sure of.

"Want to talk about your day?" I asked carefully. Something was obviously bothering him.

Turning his attention back to the road, he pushed the accelerator. His hands flexed over the steering wheel, knuckles blanching with the force behind them. The car moved with the rest of the traffic. I saw people who carried their baggage, and sometimes all they needed was an ear to confess, a shoulder to lean on.

"Do you ever feel like the mountain in front of you is so high you can never reach the top or get to the other side?" he broke his silence.

A million things ran through my head at once. A quiet

unhappiness, I never managed to outgrow. A sad version of myself, I couldn't shed. A woman who couldn't stand up for herself. A daughter who couldn't sort out her differences. The pressure of being a leader who couldn't give a simple work-life balance to her team.

"Go on," I encouraged, because this wasn't about me.

He didn't speak. The street light accentuated his chiseled jawline, and I couldn't help but admire every inch of his perfection. Guiding his sedan effortlessly block after block, he stayed with the light traffic. Locals by now had tucked into their apartments; commuters had long since taken the train home.

Ryan parked outside my apartment building and turned off the engine. Turning to face me, he took my hands in his. With his thumb, he brushed over my knuckles in a soothing circular motion. The shockwave that traveled through me at the contact made it hard to breath. With effort I concentrated on his face and waited for what he had to say.

"Every time I feel like I'm doing something right, ten people line up to tell me how it could all go wrong. When will I be enough for them to trust my decisions? To take my words without second-guessing them? It's exhausting you know? Constantly trying to prove myself. To be taken seriously. If I stop now, I'll go stagnant. There'll be nothing to look forward to, nothing worth getting out of bed for tomorrow. But if I follow my instinct, I risk losing the very people who shaped me into who I am. This fucking conundrum is tearing me apart." A floodgate opened, and there was no stopping him. Every frustration inside him poured out like a freefall.

At first, I didn't notice how tightly he was gripping my hand —I was too focused on his clenched teeth and rigid jaw, each telling its own story of a desperate need for validation. But the sting grew sharp enough to jolt my reflexes before my mind caught up. I pulled back, and he released me instantly.

"I'm sorry, I didn't realize—"

I locked my fingers with his and pulled his hand over to my

lap. "When we climb mountains, our focus is fixed on the summit," I said.

His deep electric irises locked with mine. Even in the darkness, they glowed like bright gems.

"Look down, Ryan. See how far you've come. It's about perspective. It's not always about how much further you have to go, but how far you've led them."

His gaze didn't waver. The air between us buzzed like a live wire.

I went on, "Sometimes, people need reminders of how much they've achieved. Because your goal might be beyond that peak, but their vision didn't even see the flank. They're scared. And that's exactly why you're the leader."

He framed my face with both hands, his grip firm enough to scatter my ongoing thoughts. The urgency of his mouth suddenly upon mine stunned me, igniting a need that tore through me. When his tongue flicked against my lips, coaxing them open, I didn't hesitate, instinct overriding reason.

I burned for him. Every inch of my skin buzzed like it had been set alight. His touch was an aphrodisiac; his presence, magnetic. Hot and dangerous, the kind of kiss that made rules meaningless.

He slid his hands down, tracing the curve of my neck like he was memorizing the shape of his want. With each brush of his fingers, he left a trail of fire, and when he pressed his chest flush against mine, I knew exactly where we were heading.

Forbidden.

His kiss turned desperate, filled with need. Everything about this moment felt so perfect, but my fucked-up life couldn't take any more complications. I had to stop, end this here, before my brain and heart synced into thinking this was a possibility.

I was attracted to him so much that it seemed unreal. But my circumstances, my life ... nothing belonged here. I was on borrowed time, and he was just a passerby who was never meant to be anything.

I conjured every ounce of my will to stop myself. Putting my hand on his drumming heartbeat, I pushed him away. It wasn't just a kiss; it was my weakest moment that threatened to unravel inside me. Every wall, every boundary, every lie I fed myself about what I didn't need was being challenged.

Before I melted into his confused expression or gave in to my desire, I unlocked the door of the car.

"Thanks for the ride, Ryan. Drive home safe," I said before rushing out in a flash.

———

I walked up three flights of stairs, hoping the climb would steady my raging heart. Taking deep drawn out exhales, hoping they would help to calm me down. But nothing could quiet the storm Ryan had stirred inside me. He was everything I should stay away from—too real, too capable of making me feel things I'd spent years learning to suppress.

Every time I looked at him, it felt like standing outside a store window. I could admire him, maybe even dream a little, but deep down, I knew it wasn't meant for me. A life I could look at, maybe even brush against, but never belong to.

We might have been breathing the same air, walking the same streets, but our worlds were parallel. Always running beside each other, close enough to feel, but not enough to touch.

"I'm home," I announced as I unlocked the door and entered the two-bedroom apartment I shared with Cece. It had an eclectic bohemian charm that I'd been given full control to curate.

Every room had large windows overlooking our quiet neighborhood. I'd painted the main wall of the living room scarlet red with dusts of gold and jungle green windowsills. The rest was white to add in the contract. Bright green and gold furniture, with fixtures and paintings adding depth, giving the room a character. Every piece was put together to mean something, to serve a purpose. Nothing in excess because we could afford it or wanted to possess it.

My bedroom was cadmium yellow with one large window, and Cece's was an electric blue that matched her personality.

After changing into my pajamas, when I returned to the living room, Cece was flipping through the television channels. Wearing warm pajamas, her hair still wet from the shower.

"What took you so long? I thought you'd be home sooner," she asked, flopping on one side of the couch. "Let's eat. I'm starving."

"With so many projects on my plate it's easy to lose track of time." I sat beside her. "It was a successful day though, so I can't complain."

She raised a brow, encouraging me to go on while she removed her sandwich from the brown paper bag sitting between us. Picking up my own sandwich I continued.

"After a daylong meeting, we have finally struck a deal with Nixus. The project runs through July. Now we get eight months instead of six, which helps with all the other projects."

"That's a relief. Will you guys still need to work long hours, and weekends?" She unwrapped the Italian sandwich and took a big bite.

"Yeah. There's no way around it yet."

As Ryan's daze started wearing off, my stomach grumbled from hunger.

"Well, good luck with delivering that news to your mother." As she bit into the sandwich again, sauce dripped from one corner of her mouth. I handed her a napkin to clean the mess.

The thought of that discussion with my mother left a bitter taste in my mouth. Unreasonable as she was, I could only hope Dad would understand. Hope was all I had with my mother's expectations and father's continued silence.

I uncurled the wrapper and took a few quick bites of my pastrami sandwich. I was so hungry that my stomach was vaporizing the food faster than my mouth could bite into it.

"I guess I have a few weeks to sit on that unpleasant exchange."

Cece skimmed through a reality show set on an island, and as the camera moved to the Caribbean blue water, it drew my mind back to the man I'd kissed less than half an hour ago. The push and pull of the air between us only heightened my desire. And then the kiss ... it'd been electric. Powerful. The wild in me wanted to lose myself, while my sane brain screamed to flee. The fight within was my quiet collapse.

"I met with Ryan again today. He dropped me off," I announced, ignoring the part how our kiss still clung to my lips. Or how I ran, even though everything felt so right. "I couldn't find a cab when I left work. Coincidentally, he was there."

"Did you now? Twice in two weeks, not sure if I can categorize this into a coincidence anymore." She wiggled her eyebrows with a lopsided grin.

"This one definitely was." I reassured her, *Wasn't it?*

She waved a hand. "Yeah, I believe you."

"He seemed"—I tried to find the right word—"melancholic."

"He lost both his parents when he was twenty-three."

My heart stopped at Cece's words. It was one thing to argue and hold grudges, but I couldn't think of my life without my parents in it.

She kept talking while fiddling with the remote again. "But then, after a year, his sister couldn't take the pain anymore and left Manhattan."

"Oh God ... That must be too much for someone to handle." I didn't even know what I'd been doing at that age, let alone figure it all out. With no support or guidance? I shuddered at the thought of it.

Cece faced me. "From what I know, Ryan puts his heart and soul into fulfilling his responsibilities, whether it's managing a relationship with his sister or taking McAlister Group forward. Taber once told me he doesn't do anything half-assed."

Was he, too, chasing that ever-elusive light, or had he already found his path and chosen it with certainty? Was he a broken soul trying to find his place in this world or a man who'd so much to prove to himself.

I respected people who knew what they wanted and how to get it. A part of me didn't want to think more about him, but I also couldn't help but wonder what other colors made up his personality.

I wanted to know Ryan McAlister.

My phone dinged with a new text message. I picked it up only to see a message from Ryan. *I'm sorry for offending you. I thought ... I don't know what I was thinking. I'm sorry.*

The thing about wanting was that it rarely followed logic. Rules broken beyond reason, craving what was out of reach. The forbidden, the untouchable, the things we knew we shouldn't chase were often the ones our hearts beat loudest for. Maybe it was the thrill, or the illusion of perfection, or just the unattainable. But deep down, wanting wasn't about need. It was about longing for what we were told we couldn't have. And aching all the more for the impermissible.

I panicked. I'm sorry, I messaged back then went back to my dinner and whatever Cece was playing on the television above the mantle.

His message came minutes later. *Are we still on for Sunday?*

You bet, I responded without another thought.

Nine

❧

RYAN

It turned out to be an intimate gathering at The Crimson Hour, mainly known for its fifty feet underground cellar. I avoided most parties—shmoozing strangers for no particular reason was out of my character—but tonight, the crowd was bearable, mostly because the woman beside me captured my attention. If thoughts of her weren't enough, our kiss the other night was an irrefutable affirmation. I wanted her. I wanted to spend more time with her.

I only had tonight to convince her.

In a sheath velvet dress, she oozed confidence. The dove-white fabric covered her from neck to knee, hugging every inch of her curves in-between, and those long, never-ending arms stretched down like extensions. I was awed by her beautiful face, mesmerizing almond-shaped eyes, the plumpness of her lips, and her apodictic perfection. Loose curls slid over her shoulders, grazing the swells of her breasts, and the warmth radiating from her consumed me.

"Anne, Alan, this is Risha. Risha, Alan is our CFO, and his wife Anne," I introduced everyone.

"Happy Anniversary!" Risha wished them with her signature smile.

Her attentiveness was quite the opposite since I'd picked her up from her apartment. Then, she had seemed restrained; now, she was completely present in the moment. Her resting hand on mine was pouring heat into my bloodstream. Our last kiss still burned on my lips, stealing focus every time I breathed. I was attracted to her before. Now I wanted more.

"Thank you, dear. Please rest my curiosity and tell me how you two met." Anne's eyes sparkled with mischief. She was measuring me, weighing what this woman beside me really meant.

"My roommate's brother is Ryan's friend and business partner. We met at their party."

"Which one? Taber?" Alan asked, knowing everyone in my life.

"That's right.," Risha confirmed.

"We are so happy to have you here. And to see Ryan attending parties and with a woman," Anne added playfully.

I smiled, not sure of what to say.

Risha laughed it off.

"What do you do, my dear?"

"I'm just an engineer." Risha brushed it off, just like on the first night we met.

"She's an engineering director with keen eyes for aesthetics and decoration." I looked at the surroundings before I spoke again. "I bet she can tell you ten things they can improve in this place."

Beside me Risha seemed abashed, her skin flushing a color of pink.

"Do I hear pride in your voice, Ryan?" Anne patted my shoulder.

I felt Risha's gaze shifting to me from under her eyelashes.

She squeezed my arm. "Ryan is being kind. I'm getting by with my work," Risha expressed. "Interior decorating is just a hobby if and when I find time."

She really didn't know how to take compliments, even where they were due.

I pressed on. "She works at Sylosis. They are leasing the fifteenth floor in the building in front of our office."

Alan nodded, knowing which one I was talking about. "Aren't they one of the fastest growing offices in that building?"

He asked more to himself, but I answered, anyway. "They are. That's how I found out Risha is short-selling her skills. I happened to meet the president, and he couldn't stop praising their gold-star director."

Risha's jaw dropped in disbelief.

I clarified. "I needed a reason to be at your office. Discussing the lease seemed prudent. My excuse was wanting to understand their growth, and the man was all gaga about you."

"Ryan ..." She pulled her hand from my arm and playfully swatted my biceps, a smile hinting at her amusement. She looked catastrophically gorgeous when she smiled.

"I've never seen this side of Ryan, I hope to see you more, Risha." I didn't realize Anne was observing my every move until she'd said that.

The crowd closed in to meet Alan and Anne. Risha and I excused ourselves and walked over to the bar. We ordered a glass of the house blend each before we settled at a table by the window. Her eyes studied the people in the room. The unshakable attraction was a constant between us. One kiss—just one fucking kiss—and it burned like a fireball. Every time her gaze met mine, the air between us turned to thunder. She sucked in a breath when my fingers accidentally brushed hers. She was as affected by me as I was by her.

"Can we talk about what happened the other night," I posed my question, not ready to let the evening slide by.

She cocked her head, her elbows resting on the table and her face no more than a foot from mine. "Do we have to?"

"Knowing I can't stop seeing you and that wasn't the last time we kissed ... I need to understand your limits and pace, and everything in-between." A bold move, but required nonetheless.

I mimicked her pose until our lips were inches from each

other's. The radiating heat unraveled us both. I saw it on her parted lips. I felt it in my ticking heartbeat.

With much deliberation, she exhaled and moved away into her own space. "I'm attracted to you."

"That's a good thing, isn't it? I still don't see the problem here."

"Well ... it's a problem." She picked up her wineglass and took a sip. Her eyes drifted to the people walking outside. "It's complicated."

"Nothing in life comes easy. Sometimes you need to choose complications to uncomplicate the rest." I followed her field of vision. "It's clear we both are attracted to each other. Explain the complicated part now."

"Cece told me about your parents; I am sorry for your loss." She suddenly changed the subject, making me flinch.

Our gazes locked. She was trying to gain control. "Taking in so much responsibility at that young age must have been tough."

I swallowed my remaining drink and got up from the chair. Tapping the glass in my hand, I asked, "You want the same one?"

She turned her attention to the street outside the window. "I apologize if I upset you by mentioning them."

I walked over to her side, crossing the small table between us. Holding her chin between my finger and thumb, I raised her face until our eyes locked. "You didn't."

Her lips quivered, but words never formed. Our eyes remained locked, and a range of emotions traveled between those almond eyes—sorrow, pain, grief, understanding—but one thing I didn't find was pity.

"I'll be back with our drinks."

Twenty minutes of social dancing later, I made my way to the bar and placed our drink order. It was packed on all sides, so I had no choice but to wait. Honestly, I needed the pause to process everything Risha had said ... and everything she hadn't.

I couldn't shake the nagging question: Had she shifted the focus onto me because I was getting close to knowing her, or was she genuinely sorry for me? When I'd looked into her eyes, they had reflected my grief, carrying a weight I hadn't even given myself permission to feel.

"Now I know why you've been so lost in lala land the past month," Alan said as he made his way to me.

"What do you mean?" I asked, but my gaze remained on Risha. She was talking to a man who had approached her the moment she'd been left alone. Her face was inquisitive and attentive, and she smiled a few times when the man joked. A pang of jealousy hit me in the gut.

Alan chuckled, pulling my attention to him. "She's way out of your league, if you know what I'm saying."

Alan was wise and full of guidance. I might not implement his every piece of advice, but I listened to everything he had to say.

"No, I don't. Please explain."

"Unlike those other women in your world, you can't impress her with money." Alan patted my forearm. "If you want her, you need to offer her the most important commodity of your world—time. She's a smart woman, Ryan. She can't be persuaded by materialistic things."

I had never thought of persuading her with anything but myself. And I wasn't ready to extinguish the fire she lit inside me. Alan was right, however; dating meant an investment of time. I wasn't certain how much time I was ready to commit.

But, was I open to anything less?

With Risha I wanted so much more.

The man standing with Risha made her laugh so easily. A part of me wanted to punch that smile off his face. Another part wondered if I could ever make her laugh like that.

"Sometimes, it's okay to think from here, Ryan." Alan poked a finger over my chest, pulling my attention back. "I can see the way you look at her. Don't wait too long or ..." He turned his head to Risha.

The bartender placed two glasses in front of me. Finally!

I picked them up, intent on returning to Risha when Alan patted my shoulder again. "Don't be an asshole in front of her either. That guy there she is talking to ... that's my nephew."

"Good to know."

I walked over to Risha and the nephew guy, beaming. "What did I miss?"

"Hey." Risha's smile put me at ease. "Ryan, meet Marcus Benson. He's a senior director at Nixus whose project we're starting next. And Marcus, this is Ryan McAlister, the—"

"Real estate tycoon," Marcus announced. "The man who never stops working and doesn't allow my uncle to retire. Your name precedes you, Ryan. Uncle Alan has only good things to say about you."

"Alan is too young to consider retirement." I shook his hand. "And I'm sure everything he said about me is a lie."

"Which part? That you work every waking hour of the day, or that, in the last eight years, no one has left McAlister Group to work for someone else," he stated.

I was surprised by his knowledge of me.

Risha raised her eyebrows, suddenly seeing me in a different light. "That must be tough."

"Just lucky so far. You said both of you are working on a project together?" I changed the subject, not used to being in the limelight.

Marcus eased his stance. "Since I joined Nixus, all I have heard about was our security system and the advanced x-ray machines. Risha became one of the lead architects even though she was just an intern."

"Oh please, don't make it sound bigger than it was. That project was the entire team's effort," Risha exclaimed. Her cheeks started blushing a shade of pink that was quickly becoming my favorite color in the universe.

"I wasn't there back then, but it was your name that came up in every discussion. We never outsource our projects but, for you, we seem to be making an exception. And that's saying something, right?"

She blushed as Marcus went on. I didn't understand every technicality they touched on, but a sense of pride filled my chest. Not just beautiful and creative; she was brilliant, too.

Soon after, dinner was served, and we were immediately swamped with people. I couldn't wait to say my goodbyes the first chance I got. So, that was what I did.

We were the first to leave and enter the parking garage across the street. Grabbing her by the elbow, I pulled Risha close. She inhaled a sharp breath but didn't retreat. Not back, not forward. Just there, between my arms. Her breath feathered over my neck. That pause—half a second, maybe less—held a thousand possibilities. I was desperate to end the distance. This agonizing evening of push and pull seemed like torture.

Caging her between me and the brick wall, I brushed my knuckles against her jawline. Smooth. Soft. Porcelain. With a hint of pink crawling up her neck, she was fucking gorgeous, and that scent of rose laced with sandalwood was fucking with my brain. My chest rose with every breath, heavy with the anticipation of her mouth against mine, tasting her again.

I threaded my fingers through her hair until they rested at the nape. Then I dipped my face over hers. Her lips parted the second we touched, like she'd been waiting for this moment all along. Her fingers curled over my biceps, her chest rising and falling between us. The quiet surrender in her closed eyes and parted mouth was all the consent I needed.

I brushed my lips over hers. She tasted delicious, like roses and wild berries. Sweeping my tongue along her lips before coaxing them open wider, she obliged without hesitation, and I devoured her. Bit by bit, I drank in the way she breathed, the way she moved, the quiet hum of her moans curling through me like smoke.

"I don't want to drive you away. Help me understand you, Risha." My voice was firm, but inside, I was pleading. "Tell me what's off limits."

"I'm scared." She slid her hands from my arms to the opening of my jacket then flattened them over my chest. Her kisses didn't stop, like her mind and body were on two different planets.

"I won't hurt you," I said.

"I know ... It's just... our lives are so different," she spoke into my mouth.

"Maybe ... but life is also short and can be measured in minutes or seconds. Heartbeats. This life is all we have."

"Oh, Ryan, you're confusing me." She deepened the kiss, taking over and not letting me ask what she meant.

My heart stuttered, every cell in my body responding to her. The press of my mouth against hers, the glide of our tongues, pushing and pulling, giving and taking. She tasted even better than I remembered, impossibly more perfect.

Our kiss turned hungrier with every passing second. Her hand remained on my chest, and I thought my heart might beat out of my ribcage. She nibbled on my lips, bringing my complete attention back to where it started. Our mouths clung to each other, savoring every second of our heated encounter.

A car sped past. The bright light, slicing through our moment and breaking the spell. We drifted apart, inch by inch, until I could finally see her. Her light olive skin was flushed a deep crimson. The kind of color that didn't lie.

"You want me, too. Why are you lying to yourself?" I asked.

"We don't belong in the same world." Her voice was so soft I almost missed it.

"Okay. Show me your world then."

"There is no place for you in my world." Risha tried to break away but lacked conviction. She undoubtedly wanted me, but then what could possibly hold her back?

"Then let's make some space," I answered, nibbling on her

bottom lip. Her heat, her taste ... I was committing every moment with her to memory.

"You don't understand. We're different." She looked down to hide her face, her feelings, her wants, her needs, her desires ... me. I was in her mind, and her body wanted me. But I was fighting a force much stronger than both of us combined. The one I couldn't even see or understand.

I cupped her face in my hands, waiting for our eyes to meet. "Talk to me."

She pinched her eyes shut, hiding the whirlwind underneath. "Let's take it slow ..."

"Okay." I kissed her forehead before backing away. "I can do slow."

Ten

RISHA

The sensory lights went on as I walked down the empty halls of the office. Everything sat dark and quiet except for the lights on the engineering floor. The moment I reached the desk, my phone chimed with a new text.

Ryan: If you are working late, I can give you a ride home.

The way my body reacted to the message wasn't exactly reassuring. We had decided to take it slow, but the spark between us didn't just burn—it roared into flames every time we got close. Even the stark reality of my life couldn't dampen the igniting flames.

I knew what I could and couldn't have, and Ryan McAlister could never be part of my fate. My family would never approve. My future had been set in stone the day I was born. And yet, the rebel in me wanted to fight for the unexpected.

Me: Are you free?

Ryan: What do you have in mind? His response was immediate.

Me: Come over to my office. Let me show you what I really do for a living.

Ryan: In that case, I'm bringing dinner.

I was still going through my emails when a knock on the door broke my concentration. And the sight of the man left me mindless.

When I was just getting used to seeing him in three-piece suits, he walked in a navy-blue cashmere over denim. No jacket or coat, as if it weren't another frigid day in November.

He walked into my office with his casual stride and set a large paper bag on my desk. "Am I early or late?" he asked in his casual tone.

"Right on time." I left my chair and walked over to him. "Ready?"

"Always." His smile was genuine, with a hint of mischief. If he thought I was just another puzzle to solve, he'd be surprised. This wasn't about figuring me out; it was about seeing the real me. Because he was right about one thing—I was hopelessly drawn to him. And no matter how hard I tried to forget, I had no control when it came to Ryan.

We crossed the long corridor and entered an open-floor with six large tables—we called them stations. The low hum of machinery and diagrams covering the whiteboards were the background to my life in this room. My entire day could be summed up with these workstations.

Even though we were approaching eight in the evening, the room wasn't entirely empty. Ryan and I walked over to the first station where Zoe was completely engrossed.

When she saw us approaching, she dropped the wires she was working with and eyed Ryan with a mixture of praise and apprehension. She wasn't the only one. I noticed how women looked at him. Alan's party, Cece's ... women everywhere were attracted to him. He was a fine specimen. Let's also add rich, famous, and single.

"Zoe, this is my friend Ryan. I wanted to show him the projects we are working on." I stayed back, letting the two shake hands. Even though she was an introvert, I wanted her to talk comfortably about her pet project.

As a manager, I wanted her to succeed in every aspect of her job. As a mentor, I was getting her ready for the upcoming meeting with Blackrock. Zoe had been handling this project for months now. But it was one thing to know your work and another to present to a client.

"Nice meeting you, Zoe. Want to tell me what this machine is for?" Ryan asked, glancing at the parts scattered neatly across the table. I called it organized chaos.

"We are working on the device to condense the water vapor and then pass through multiple filtrations to make it portable. Drinkable for humans, in this case," Zoe explained in one breath.

Ryan's eyes popped when he swirled his head from her to me. I couldn't help but smile. First, she was nervous, and having Ryan as an audience didn't help her case.

"Do you want to break it down in smaller pieces?" I nudged her gently.

She blushed and took a swig from her water bottle. "I am sorry."

"Don't be," Ryan chimed in. "Think of me as an investor for a product I know nothing about. Now, tell me what it can do and who it can help." He took a step back, giving Zoe more space. I didn't know how he did that, but his gentle voice and stepping back helped Zoe find her composure.

"Imagine living in a desert state where fresh water is a scarcity." Zoe put her bottle back on the table and looked between me and Ryan. I nodded, urging her on. "Despite the climate, there are water droplets in the air, especially during nights and early mornings."

"So far, I'm with you," Ryan encouraged. He didn't even know Zoe, yet he somehow understood what I was doing. I saw this man in different lights every day.

"This generator can capture those droplets from a fifty-foot radius. Condense it to dew-point then drop it into the container where it goes through the filtration and sterilization process to remove all impurities and dust. In a place where fresh water is a priceless commodity, think of finding another source to get clean, drinkable water, pulled straight out of the air."

"Wow. I mean just ... wow. That's mind blowing." Ryan looked between me and Zoe, completely awestruck. "You guys made this?"

I chuckled. "No. It's relatively old technology now. We are enhancing the sterilization process to get 99.99% impurities out, and also increasing the radius so it can pull more droplets from the air."

"And this is what you do as an engineer?"

I shrugged. "My team does it. I only manage customer expectations. I'm just a bridge between what the customers want and what the engineers can deliver."

"She is being modest," Zoe decided to join the conversation. "Not a single thing here would get done without Risha."

"That's quite an exaggeration, Zoe. I'm just lucky to have a great team." I averted their eyes and saw Marty still working at station three.

"Clients want things, but they don't know what exactly and how to get it. We engineers require a clear understanding of those needs, Risha is the brain and knowledge. Bridging the gap between every project here."

"I would've never guessed," Ryan said to no one specifically, still taking in the half-assembled machine in front of him.

"Our projects keep increasing because every client wants Risha," Zoe continued.

"Okay, time to go home now. It's too late already."

"Soon, I have to be ready for this meeting," she muttered and went back to her work.

If it were up to me, this meeting shouldn't be planned for another week, but of course Patrick went over me and had told Blackrock we were ready.

Next, I introduced Ryan to Marty, and then I took him from

one station to another, explaining all the projects we were working on.

Right before leaving, he stopped at station six, sitting completely empty with just a handful of drawings. "This one is done?"

"No, this is a monster of a project that will start next month. Nixus. I'm working on the sketches right now."

"So, what do you think?" I asked Ryan as we sat across from each other in my office. His chopsticks were deep inside the paper container, picking between broccoli and chicken. He sat at ease, one ankle resting on the other knee. My office wasn't big, but I had never thought it was small either, until now. Today, the room felt small, the building small ... even the city itself not big enough to contain him.

He hadn't been sure what I would want, so he had bought extra food. Like, five extra dishes. I'd handed some off to my colleagues. Still a couple of unopened boxes laid on the table.

"I think I know now what Alan meant by you being way out of my league."

"What?" I was flabbergasted by his confession, pausing as I dug into my honey-glazed chicken. . "What do you mean?"

"At the party yesterday, he said I can't sway you with money or glitz, which never even occurred to me. If all the things Marcus and Zoe said were true, and all these projects you're working on ... I fucking don't stand a chance. I am in awe of what you do."

"Let's be clear: I didn't invite you over for a compliment." I wasn't the sharp brain people assumed I was. I'd left the path laid out by my dad because it wasn't mine to take.

"Risha." My name on his lips snapped my attention back. "Nothing has changed." The chopsticks and the box remained in his hand like a prop, held but forgotten. "We are different people

—I never denied that—but what lays between us can't be explained either. It can only be felt. I feel it. Do you?"

He pinned me with his stare until I nodded and looked down into my half-eaten container.

"Thanks for showing me this side of you. I can't help but be impressed by everything you do."

I wanted to pull him close. I wanted to feel all the feelings only he could evoke. I was drawn to him and couldn't stop thinking of the possibilities. The what-ifs.

With all the feelings twirling inside, I went for the biggest question I'd been holding in. "Do you still think I should be an artist, or am I better off as an engineer?"

He regarded my question, giving it more thought than I'd expected. Removing a piece of broccoli, he popped it into his mouth and chewed thoroughly. "Why does it have to be one or the other? You're so talented; how many people can honestly do both? The world is yours, Risha—have it all."

I inhaled a sharp breath but it got caught in my throat and I couldn't exhale.

Noticing my predicament, he raised his eyebrows. "What? You don't think you could handle both?"

I shook my head and turned back to my food. My appetite was gone, but I needed something to keep myself busy. "I am struggling with this job as is. Who has time for a hobby?"

"If you love something, I'm sure you can make time. Even in the busiest of schedules."

"So? You think I can have it all?" I asked.

He nodded without a flicker of hesitation. "I think the world's finally catching up to who you've always been."

Eleven

RYAN

"Where the hell have you been?" Taber slid a crystal glass toward me with a scowl. We were at one of his oldest clubs in the Meatpacking District. Below, the dance floor was packed; up here, the members-only lounge was reserved for Manhattan's finest only. The lounge lacked a flashy, expensive feel; instead of money, it exuded class. Tonight, Nick, Jonah, and I dominated the center of the bar, while Taber lingered on the opposite end. With a half-empty bottle of Macallan within easy reach, I was an hour late to the party.

We always held our business meetings at one of Taber's bars in the evening. I wasn't sure how it'd started, but it had become a tradition over the years. We met weekly to unwind and catch up on our business dealings, but something in Taber's scowl confirmed this wasn't a pleasant meeting. I had been driving Risha home when I'd received a text about this impromptu meeting.

Risha and I had fallen into a routine of dinners, daily chats, followed by me dropping her off at her apartment. I looked forward to our stolen moments. The potent attraction between us remained palpable, constantly searing right underneath the surface. We felt it every time our eyes met, when our fingers brushed against each other and lingered. Instead of launching into another kiss, which we both knew would lead to more, I took a more patient approach, biding my time until she made the next move.

My desire for her had been a slow burn at first. Now it was a constant ache. But rushing her meant risking everything, and she was worth the wait.

I clinked my glass with Jonah's before taking a sip. The smooth liquid sailed down my throat, keeping me grounded in the moment. "When did you fly in?" I asked.

Since he lived in Vegas now and partnered in our Vegas casino resort, Jonah oversaw that project across the country.

"This morning. Dad wants to meet all his sons." He rolled his eyes before taking a swig out of his glass.

As the middle son, Jonah always got the short end of the stick. Darell chased their father's approval, and the media was fixated on Trent, leaving Jonah in the shadows. He had borrowed a million dollars from their multi-million dollar media and entertainment corporation and decamped for Vegas. With Nick's backing and his own grit, he now owned one of the nation's top computer security firms. I wouldn't be surprised if his father's call was about stealing some of that spotlight, or maybe pitching a merger.

Uncharacteristically, Taber lashed out at the bartender.

"Why is he so upbeat today?" I asked.

"Let me get you there, as well." Taber sniped over his shoulder, apparently he had heard me. Clenching his teeth, he walked over and filled my glass for another round. "I received a notice that MoxTo's swimming pool license is revoked."

I flinched. "What the fuck? Why?"

"Because the city's building safety permit department doesn't agree with the plan of a rooftop swimming pool over a revolving restaurant. Some bullshit safety hazard," Taber spat out.

This shit couldn't be happening.

"That makes no sense. This isn't a new request. We've gone

over every safety protocol and we submitted our specs long before the project even began."

Fine, if I was being honest the revolving restaurant was a recent addition, and Alan warned me about potential pushback. I had ignored him. We had rerun all the inspections, covering every hazard.

I turned to Nick, who'd been silent since I'd arrived. From the look on his face, he knew something more than I did.

"Every step went through full scrutiny and inspection before we started construction. Why this sudden change of heart?" I asked.

"Correct," Taber answered in response. "I gave a visit to the inspector and guess who I saw coming out of his office with a wide grin? Nick's fucking enemy."

"So, you're telling us *you* don't have enemies?" Nick retorted, losing his composure just enough to show a crack.

It took a lot to get Taber pissed. And it was unlike Nick to lose control. What the fuck was going on here? And what the fuck was I missing?

"Not as many as you, no," Taber answered, not ready to back off.

Nick stood up abruptly, knocking over the bar stool. "My enemies are jealous, so they come after my business. Unlike yours who come for blood."

"Do not fucking go there, Nick. I am warning you." Taber launched at Nick. Thankfully, the counter stood between the two men.

Shoving my glass aside, I stood up. One hand on each of their chests, pushing them apart. "Have you two lost your mind? What are we gonna gain fighting amongst ourselves?"

"Why the fuck did he have to bring that up?" Taber went for Nick's jacket but failed.

The patrons around us ignored the confrontation like this was a common occurrence. It definitely wasn't.

"You started it." Nick took a step back to compose himself. "I responded."

"Guys, this is exactly what they want, isn't it?" I tried again to put some sense into them.

Taber's deep-rooted Italian history and Nick's single-minded ambition to be number one had earned them more than a few enemies.

There were pros and cons to our joint ventures. We were growing exponentially, which meant everybody was noticing us. And they were jealous. I didn't have enemies of my own, but it seemed I was quickly inheriting those of my business partners.

"The fucker is blackmailing us for a lump sum to reinstate the license," Taber added color to this discussion.

That got me pissed, but a pissing contest wasn't the solution.

"For some here, it means nothing, but for the rest of us, it's a burn."

"You want to go that route, Taber? How many times have I saved your ass?" Nick warned, pointing one finger toward his chest.

"As many times as you have burned my hands," Taber answered, not ready to give it a rest.

"Calm the fuck down, guys," I tried again. One fucking headache was to fix a license problem; another to contain the damage between friends. And the last thing we needed was for people to see the crack in our united front. "Tell me what is really going on between you two," I demanded.

Stepping back, Nick picked up his stool and repositioned himself near the counter. He wasn't a man who would get into fights. I pinned him with a look and waited to hear his side. Taber's glare remained fixed on Nick, but at least he resisted the urge to take the matter back in his hands.

"I took control over Chandler's company. He'd been struggling for years and selling me a few shares at a time to stay afloat. The opportunity presented itself, so I bought the majority share from another board member and pushed him out."

"And now we know the rest of the story," Taber condemned. "The license officer is Chandler's brother-in-law. Not to forget Chandler himself is a close friend of this asshole's father."

What a fucking mess.

Jonah, who sat beside me, gave a low whistle as he finished the rest of his drink. "Nick is a shark, and Chandler was bleeding in the middle of Pacific. I can't blame him for what he did."

He certainly couldn't when they were business partners. This fucking guy, who also happened to be my best bud, had put his hand in every pot.

"Let me talk to Senator Waltman," I told everyone as a plan formed. Another setback would send Alan and those fucking executives into a spin. I couldn't afford another set of grilling. "His granddaughters have been living rent-free for years in the same apartment Ivy is in. It's time to get something out of him, as well."

"It's my mess, let me fix it," Nick interrupted.

I nodded, and together we formed a plan, keeping mine as a backup just in case Nick's didn't work. I took it as progress, a successful meeting by its end. The tension had burned itself out, leaving only resolve. Whatever Chandler or his brother-in-law tried next, we'd meet it together. The four of us had always been unbreakable, and that would not change tonight.

We were making too many enemies though. Individually, all of us had money and respect, but together, we were becoming powerful. Almost untouchable. It'd already started rubbing people the wrong way.

Sometimes we were so close to the problems that we lost perspective or became part of the problem itself. Doing business with friends had its perks—our ideologies matched, our goals were the same—but there was another side to it we often neglected. Mixing friendship and business might be the best plan or an absolute disaster. I believed it was the former. I really hoped I was correct.

"It seems you three have rubbed too many people the wrong

way in this town. Ever considered moving to Vegas?" Jonah smirked, unfazed by the drama that had just unfolded.

Enemies be damned ... We owned this city. I believed in solutions. A levelheaded approach. Quitting wasn't in my repertoire.

"Something on your mind?" Nick asked.

"You know the outburst if this project derails any further."

"I'll take care of it," he said.

And I trusted him.

Twelve

RYAN

I stood at the busy intersection, darting my eyes to the incoming traffic. I hadn't been this nervous since my first high school date. After six months of pining over her, I'd asked if she felt the same. She had. We'd dated until we parted ways—her to RIU, me to Columbia—and ended things mutually. Absolutely no drama and a proper goodbye. When the dating ended, we became friends ... which died down eventually, too.

My relationship with Risha was fluid, moving from one day to another without any labels. No strings or promises, just a mutual need for each other's company.

The source of my anxiety had nothing to do with nerves and everything to do with guilt. I'd taken something from Risha without her knowledge or permission. We'd been meeting every evening, and yet I never broached the topic. What the fuck was I thinking?

The fall breeze carried a brittle edge, but the blood racing through my veins was heating up the entire block. A cab cut through the traffic and stopped right beside me. She waved from the back seat.

All sorts of thoughts swirled from my gut to the chest. Elation. Excitement. Dread.

I stepped forward and opened the door. Risha emerged, smiling wide and genuine. Her nude pencil dress clung to her curves, and the dip in the neckline offered a glimpse of her cleavage. A brown coat hung open, letting the dress do all the talking. She was hot and so fucking confident.

She wrapped one arm around my waist and lightly kissed my cheek. Our lips lingered an inch apart. "I'm ready for your surprise," she said.

Did I say it would be a surprise? More like a shocking blow. What possible reason could I give for stealing her idea?

Taking her hand in mine, we faced the towering white-limestone building. "Ready?"

Her face dead panned when she took in the scaffolding covering it. "Do haunted buildings fall under surprise?" she asked innocently, taking in the doors and windows covered in brown paper.

I chuckled and pulled her with me. "It's not haunted. Now, come on; let's get this over with." I hadn't even realized this was a mistake until I'd seen the message this morning.

Vikki: Your idea is ready for scrutiny. Let me know what you want to change.

My idea? No fucking way. I had to text her.

11:45a.m.

Me: Can you meet me for dinner tonight? There is a surprise waiting for you.

Risha: Interesting! Does seven work?

11:46a.m.

Me: Perfect. I'll drop the location pin.

Risha: Great.

12:02p.m.

Me: Scrap the surprise part ... it's just ... something.

Risha: Okay ... Wanna divulge what it is?

12:03p.m.

Me: No, you decide what you think of it.

1:15p.m.

Me: Hypothetical question: Is it considered stealing if someone took something unintentionally without your knowledge?

Risha: I believe they receive a lesser sentence if it was unintentional.

1:17p.m.

Me: Who the fuck are they? I'm asking you.

1:17p.m.

Me: Hypothetically, of course.

Risha: Seriously, Ryan? I have nothing worth stealing. Now go back to work and let me concentrate on mine. Zoe needs my full concentration.

I punched in the code and walked her through a barely constructed lobby. Unpainted walls, wires hanging from all over, every area we crossed lacked character, but beamed with potential. Risha's eyes took it all in. She moved only because I was guiding her with me.

We took a turn and reached a partly closed door. Soft light emitting from the crooks didn't give away much.

I faced her. "If I overstepped my boundary, we can discuss—"

"Goddammit, what is this big surprise?" With her patience running out, she pushed the door open.

And her eyes widened as she sucked in a breath. Abandoning me, she walked right into the dimly lit room, taking in everything first with a quick scan and then a slow, detailed appraisal.

She touched the vines of the lemon trees. "These are real ..."

I nodded, even though it wasn't a question.

She traced patterns on the table, eyes wandering, taking in the rest of the décor.

To bring the outdoors in, Vikki had used long teak wood tables, giving Serata a rustic feel. Overhead, lights crisscrossed the length of the ceiling, and strategically placed fixtures and temperature controls were supposed to keep the trees inside thriving year-round.

Her inspection ended when we reached the bar. The shelves

were empty except for a bottle of wine, two glasses, and two heated domes that were keeping our dinner warm.

She turned so suddenly I thought she was on the run.

I held her hand and said, "Clearly, this was a mistake. It's just ... we were starting this project, and I thought of your plan for Russo—"

My apologies halted when she rose on her toes and pressed her lips hard over mine. She then pushed my mouth open with her tongue, taking full ownership, and wrapped her arms around my neck. Every inch of her was pushed into me, waist to waist, chest to chest, shoulder to shoulder, nose to nose. Confusion swirled inside me. Did I interpret it all wrong?

I moved back an inch to read her face.

Her lips parted as if she were going to speak, but nothing came. A flicker of something crossed her face—fear? Awe? I couldn't tell. Then she kissed me. Hard. Again. And with a new urgency.

Her voice was hardly above a whisper when she said, "No one has ever done something like this for me. You gave life to my idea."

"So ... you're not mad then?"

She laughed hoarsely and shook her head. "I can't explain what this means to me, Ryan. You breathed life into something I thought in a fleeting moment."

"But it wasn't a fleeting moment," I said, rubbing her cheek with my thumb. "You were passionate about it. You were mentally visualizing the whole place with these vines."

Heat and passion poured in waves when her tongue devoured me, and she spoke into my mouth. "No one has ever cared what I want."

Something inside me snapped at those words. How could anyone not hear her when her every step was so clear and precise? What she wanted, where she drew the line.

I pushed her coat off of her shoulder, letting it fall back. She glided her hands over my chest then wrapped them around my waist. I slid my fingers into her hair and kissed her hard. With every thrust of my tongue, I poured my affection into her. Intensity and need consumed me. I wanted her, needed her ... I wanted to—my dick strained painfully under the zipper—consume her.

"I'm done waiting," she said in a low voice, but it might as well have been a scream in my bloodstream. She had made the decision, and I was just catching up. The scent of her—rose and sandalwood mixed with the citrus—clung to my skin like air.

My pulse hammered under my ribcage as I snaked my arms around her waist, pulling her into me, right where she belonged. Right where I wanted her.

"You sure?" My graveled voice was filled with heat. Want and hunger. But I wanted her to be sure where we were heading. "Once we go this route, there is no holding back. Decide now, Risha. Because this won't be a one-night stand."

"I don't want to stop," she moaned, already closing the remaining space between us. Her hands were on my chest, sliding down like she was memorizing the feel of me. Her breasts pushed into me, her hips thrust into mine with need. She was burning for me like I was burning for her.

I kissed her fast, hard, like I had something to prove. My hand was on her jaw, then her waist and lower, tugging her into me by her hips. She was heat and hunger, responding to my every demand. I hooked her legs around my waist, pressing us closer, rubbing my hardness into her pussy as I half-lifted her onto the edge of the bar.

"Ryan." My name was a gasp from her mouth, and I kissed it off her lips.

With one hand gripping her thigh, the other threaded through her hair. Sliding her over the bar, I opened her legs to make space for myself. Her dress rode up to her waist, showing her white lace panties. *Fuck!* Sometimes the simplest of things were the sexiest.

Pushing her panties to one side, I put my tongue over her clit and started stroking slowly. She tasted like honey, smooth and warm; her skin was butter, melting into my mouth with every slide of my tongue.

She arched her back, pushing her pussy further into my mouth. Her moans were loud, and with every breath she called my name.

"You're beautiful," I said huskily. "Sweet fucking hell. Magnificent."

She thrust her fingers through my hair, trying to center herself. My one hand put pressure on her navel to keep her steady while the other hand roamed over her inner thigh. With my tongue, I pushed the folds of her entrance, and she cried out and thrust herself into my mouth.

I looked up into her sedated brown eyes and said, "Don't move. Let me savor you."

"Stop bossing me ... please. Please." Her voice quickly turned into a plea, a soft prayer in her eyes asking for release. "Please."

But I was nowhere near done. "I'll give you what you want ... just not yet."

I stroked my tongue up and down and around her swollen nub. She whimpered some incoherent words that I couldn't understand. I slid one finger inside her, stroking and sucking while she moaned my name between her every plea. Moving my hand up and all around her, I pinched one nipple through her dress, and a guttural moan left her throat.

"You like that?" I asked over her sex, inhaling her sweet scent.

"Love this ... Don't stop. Do it again ... please."

Removing my finger from her dripping pussy, I pushed her dress further up over her sleek body until it rested over her chest. Then I pushed the elastic of the bra until her bare torso and those fucking gorgeous breasts were on display. Raking my hand all over her abdomen, I grabbed a handful of breasts in both hands. She arched her back and whined with pleasure. I pinched her nipple, and she moaned again.

"Yes ... like that ..."

"Anything you want, precious," I said and went back to consuming her, sucking that sweet little cunt of hers.

She was so fucking wet that I couldn't stop or take my eyes off of her. I continued to pinch and stroke her nipples while my tongue entered her warm, inviting pussy. She thrashed her head from side to side, pulling at the roots of my hair. But this time, she wasn't guiding me; she needed me to support her.

Her moans got louder, setting the whole restaurant on fire. I grazed my teeth over her nub, and she said, "I am dead ..."

"Are you now?" I chuckled.

"Yes. Please don't stop now. Please don't stop ... oh God!"

This time, I slid deeper. Her muscles clenched, and she started milking me like her life depended on this climax.

"I am going to come, Ryan," she screamed emphatically.

I pulled out and pushed my tongue in again and again until she crashed all around me.

I loved her screams. Her thrashing. Spasming into my mouth.

She went over the edge, throwing back her head and swiveling her hips into my face. Her pussy clenched as she trembled against my mouth. I continued sliding in and out so she could ride out her orgasm. I kept moving until the spasms left her body and she slumped against the bar top.

Seeing her undone like that, I could die a lucky man. Lying here in front of me, Risha felt too fucking perfect.

I stood at my full height and pulled her by the hand. She sat up and threw her jelly arms around my shoulders. Forehead to forehead, breathing each other, her skin glistened with sweat, her scent filling my lungs.

"You're too perfect, you know ... I'm having a hard time finding faults in you," she said in a breathy voice.

"I didn't know you were looking for one," I mentioned with a chuckle. Wrapping my arms around her back, I kept her close.

"A girl must try."

"Hmm. In that case, you must spend the night with me. See what else you can discover."

Thirteen

⨳

RISHA

Unlike my office building, Ryan's was at least six floors taller and had cameras and two security guards on duty. It also turned out we were almost neighbors.

The two security men got up from their chairs and spoke with him like the time of day didn't matter—night, in this case, given we had already indulged for over two hours, enjoying the finest wine and steak.

I followed him through the lobby and into the elevator while he stayed exceptionally quiet. I knew I wasn't the cause of his silence, because his fingers laced with mine and he kissed my cheek every now and then. Whatever was troubling him built an invisible wall between us.

We got off on the top floor, crossed a plush carpeted reception, private offices, and conference rooms on both sides of the hallway before reaching another reception area to the mahogany double doors. The building was eerily silent, making me wonder why he had brought me here.

Ryan opened the doors wide and waited for me to enter first. He remained by the threshold, taking in my movements as I walked right into his private office.

When Cece had told me he had taken over his family business,

I imagined it would be more baroque corner office. Definitely not a floor covered in plush blue carpet with everything modern and functional. A glass table took up one end of the room, with two visitor chairs. His chair on the other side looked exactly alike. He wasn't aiming for superiority, but wanted to blend in. His desk was starkly empty with just one laptop and a monitor. I assumed he hated mess.

The floor-to-ceiling glass walls framed a stunning view of the city's sprawl of glittering lights. "You're so lucky. I envy your landscape. My office seems like a dump in comparison."

When I didn't hear any response, I rested my hip on his table and faced him. While it was certainly his office, it felt more than that.

I pointed at the closed door across from me. "There's more?"

He nodded, but didn't utter a word.

"You live here?" I asked.

That earned me another nod.

"How long has it been like this?"

Ryan let out a deep exhale and walked over to the corner bar. Pulling out two crystal glasses, he offered me one. I shook my head, too focused on trying to read the man who'd consumed my every thought since we met.

He poured two fingers of amber liquid, downed it in one smooth gulp, then turned toward the glass wall. He scanned the twinkling lights, but his mind remained somewhere far from the glitz of the city or even us.

"I was in my leadership and ethics class when the messenger walked in to deliver the message of my parents' deaths. Before I even had the time to grieve, the responsibility of McAlister Group was on me. Hawks were lurking everywhere; some waited for me to make mistakes, some wanted me to fail, but mostly everybody was there to take advantage of the situation. Our employees didn't trust me, so they started leaving one after the other. Soon, I found out some of the senior managers were embezzling money from under my dad's nose. They saw a rookie and tried to take over. I caught them and fired them on the spot."

I was unable to even blink as his words kept pouring out.

"Every day, I had to make tough decisions, and my age and zero experience wasn't helping the cause. I had to work harder to prove myself.

"Ivy was going through a difficult time, but I couldn't be there as much as she needed me to be. She moved to Boston to start over, and I fucking couldn't stop her. She needed my time, and the ever-elusive time was my enemy."

Ryan faced me. I didn't know when I had moved away from the desk and walked toward him until I was only feet away.

"I am not lucky, Risha. I was forced into this life with no choice but to make it into my passion. And work is my life now, so I started living here."

There was no regret in his choices, no hint of sympathy sought, but the pain in his eyes remained raw and unbidden, like a wound he had learned to live with rather than heal with time.

Overwhelmed by the surge of emotions, I tried imagining the pain he had been living with for so long.

I couldn't.

There were no measurements of that kind of grief. He'd had to grow up without a warning and assume the role of his father— not just for the people relying on him, but also for his sister. Large shoes to fill, a forced transformation that rewrote his future before he could understand the weight of his loss.

He was living two lives—the one he let the world see and the one he barely allowed himself to feel. On the surface, we had nothing in common, but deep down, we were exactly alike.

The urge to be near him crowded my senses, making it impossible to stay on this side of the silence. Eating the space between us, I wrapped myself around him—not to fix, not for sympathy, but to stand with him in the ache. My mouth devoured his in desperate need, and with every kiss, I tried to tell him how sorry I was for his loss. Sorry for everything he had been forced to carry alone.

With every flick of my tongue, I tried to tell him he was a winner for converting his pain into power. His relentless and uncelebrated strength was something to be proud of. It was one thing to fight external threats, but demons that lived inside the head were the most dangerous ones. And he'd been battling them alone in silence. This man was self-made, forging his grief into resilience.

He cupped my hips and lifted me like I was made of air. I wrapped my legs around his waist, clinging to him as our mouths collided again. The intensity of our kiss brewed an untamed storm. Electric and dangerous underneath all the calm we had been trying to prove we were.

His tongue pushed deeper, claiming and tasting, taking what he wanted. Every wild, brazen kiss fired through my brain like sparks on dry tinder.

I yanked his tie loose, my fingers trembling as I unbuttoned his shirt, desperate to feel him skin to skin. Frantic and wild. His hair was already mussed from my earlier touch, his shirt slightly wrinkled and a button missing. This perfect man was beautifully undone, just for me.

He set me on my feet just long enough to shove the hem of my dress up to my waist then over my head and out of our way. His cufflink clinked when it fell onto something metal. He shrugged off his suit jacket, tie, and shirt. Capturing my mouth with his teeth, we were again back to our maddening and desperate kissing game. Taking what we needed, surrendering to the other's demand. A few more kisses like this, and he might get an orgasm out of me.

He guided us through the doorway and into a dark room. Without missing a beat, Ryan flicked a switch on the wall, bathing the space in a low amber light, never once breaking our kiss. His hands roamed over my chest and taut back while mine raked through his hair, pulling him nearer, needing him closer.

Every inch of distance between us felt wrong and unbearable. I wanted to breathe his air, to lose myself in the pleasure of our bodies. Desperation burned in my veins. I needed this man more than my next breath.

"Tinted glass—no one can see inside," Ryan spoke into my mouth about something I didn't even notice.

"I don't care," I said, because it didn't matter.

I heard his faint chuckle, and the discussion died right there.

Heat flared over me when his chest brushed against mine. We fell onto a soft bed, and he rolled over me. Boxing me between his elbows, his mouth took a dip, exploring down my neck and shoulder and further to my breast. His teeth grazed over my puckered nipples, still tucked under the bra. He sucked, and licked, and nibbled from one side to the other, shooting sweet pain into my bloodstream. I moaned, my body moving under him. He was driving me insane by keeping me between pleasure and pain.

He helped me get out of my bra, panties, and shoes before unbuttoning his pants. His erection pressed through his boxers, waiting for its release. I wrapped my legs around his waist and circled my hips to find some friction. I wanted him inside me.

He held my waist. "Slow down. I want to know every inch of you first."

"That sounds more like torture at this point," I complained.

He chuckled, but stayed on his course. "You've tortured me far too long. I have wanted you since the day we met."

"You don't think I wanted the same thing?" I grumbled.

He looked up from my breasts. His eyes turned electric even in the dimmest of light. "What was stopping you until now?"

I looked away. "I wasn't sure what I wanted."

"And now?"

Our eyes locked as fast as I had broken it a second ago. "You. I want you."

Tonight, I forged ahead without hesitation or second thoughts. I desired Ryan more than anyone else I'd ever known.

From the moment we'd met, I knew exactly where our path would lead. I delayed only the inevitable, battling a war I was bound to lose.

Coming closer, he took my mouth in a frenzy, as if those were the words he had been wanting to hear. The overwhelming nearness of his hard body was already sending shockwaves through my system. My thighs flexed. My nub strained with a throbbing ache. I rubbed up and down his erection to tell him what I wanted, my brain short-circuiting with a damn craving.

Leaving my mouth, he garbled something incoherent and grabbed my waist, trying to control my movements. The torture was too much, and I was hungry for his cock, panting between crave and lust. My core starved to be filled with him. I desperately wanted him to jump to the next phase. But with my freaking luck, this man was *savoring* me.

I rolled us over onto his back and took charge. I explored him with my hands and mouth, kissing every inch of his taut build. I rolled my tongue over every ridge and every sinew of his pectoral. He entwined our fingers and raised our joined hands over our heads. I straightened out on top of him, spreading to feel every inch of his skin. My eyes locked on his bluer than blue eyes. God, he was gorgeous. I rubbed my slick heat over the hardness under his briefs.

I wanted all of him and to surrender myself, all in one moment.

He released my hands, his fingers now on the elastic of my thong. I did the same to his brief. As I pushed the elastic down his waist, he quickly pulled out a condom from his pant pocket.

We rolled again. He got on top. "Patience isn't serving me anymore."

I giggled.

Getting rid of his briefs, he put on the condom. His hard cock stood tall between us before he moved and the tip of his erection nudged my sex, hot, throbbing, and ready to push its way in. I widened my thighs until he settled between and pushed inside. My drenched sex tightened its grip.

Burning desire filled his eyes when he was balls deep. I inhaled, and all I consumed was his masculine scent. He tried to be gentle, but I raised my hips, increasing the thrusts, unable to wait. He slid in and pushed all the way to the hilt.

"I'm fighting my desires to be gentle with you, but you're making it pretty damn hard."

He pushed into me then started to pull out. I whimpered in complaint. He pushed again. Once. Twice. Finding our rhythm.

Pleasure coursed through my veins, taking me back to the high I had hours ago. I felt him in every pore of my being. I felt him coursing through my bloodstream. I felt him inside my brain. And I felt him ticking underneath my chest.

"We fit so perfectly," he garbled into my neck. Our feelings were in sync. "Everything about this feels so perfect. It feels ... so damn good to be inside you."

His words tipped me over, and I bucked into his next thrust. My pulse quickened at an unnatural speed.

His entire body hardened as he slammed into me repeatedly. The restraint he had shown until now was gone.

The pressure inside me intensified tenfold, and a massive orgasm ripped through my core. I called his name and milked his cock, taking him with me to oblivion and beyond.

Fourteen

RYAN

I woke up in a heap of tangled arms and legs, with her one hand around my chest, the other cradling my head. My arms were wrapped around her waist, our bodies pressed, our mouths a breath apart, but that wasn't why I woke up. My damn erection was throbbing inside her, matching the rhythm of her heart pulsating over my chest. I was behaving like a fucking teenage all over again. This was what I got for obsessing over her. Even three mind-numbing orgasms weren't enough.

I craned my neck to see the gigantic clock in the dead center of the wall, its inner golden cogs slowly rotating like a beast always on the hunt. For years, I'd drift off with my eyes locked on that face, waking up only to count how much time I'd lost. I was always lagging, chasing the uncatchable, falling into this bed unsatisfied, and waking up determined to seize more than my wildest aspirations. I was always missing the mark. Time was the most precious commodity in the world. One moment it was there, and then gone forever.

This room used to be Dad's personal conference room, where he held all his meetings. I changed this room into my studio apartment and held all my meetings in the conference rooms scattered around the building. That was my first step in assimilating with the people who made up McAlister Group.

But with every step I took, I felt further and further from my end goal. There was still so much to learn, to achieve, and to give. Earning my employees' acceptance had quietly become the mission of my life. Somewhere along the way, this room had turned into nothing more than a rest stop. At thirty-two, I didn't have the luxury of slowing down, not when the clock kept ticking.

Today, though, the feelings were completely flipped. The ticking clock didn't bother me. I was awake, but leaving the bed, or her, didn't even occur to me. In her arms, I found peace and passion; contentment I never realized was absent.

I never thought I could trust anyone with the parts of me I kept hidden for years. My pain, my solitude, they fueled me, drove me ahead. But with Risha in my personal space, something shifted.

Talking, confessing, pouring it all out like I had been waiting for someone to listen and it wasn't forced. It was instinct. Like every part of me had known she would understand me even before I did.

My cock throbbed inside her, reminding me of the reason for tonight's sleepless night. It had only been an hour since we'd fallen asleep, so waking her up seemed too selfish. But the way her hip moved every few seconds to increase the friction, she needed a release as much as I did. I wanted to give her what she wanted, and I wanted my fill.

I never considered myself a selfish man. I'd built a life on control and discipline. But with Risha, something unhinged in me. I wanted to be selfish. I wanted to claim her as mine, to take what I craved when I craved it. No patience. No restraint. Just this unbearable, pulsing need that didn't care for boundaries.

What the hell was happening to me? This wasn't supposed to be complicated. I enjoyed her company, and I looked forward to spending time with her. I was obsessed with her body, no doubt, but now I wanted so much more than that. Every second with her made me reckless. And the last thing I wanted was to be the reason she ran.

"Good morning," I whispered over her lips, my shaft moving inside her, following the rhythm of her hips.

A faint smile tugged at the corner of her mouth. "Good morning to you, too."

"I'd like to take you home someday," I gave words to my thoughts that had been crashing through me all night.

"This place is nice, too," she murmured, half-sleep, fully aroused, and inhaling deeply. "Everything here smells like you."

Risha wasn't a ball of fire, or a damsel; she was a confident woman. She was independent and talented. And intoxicatingly sexy and so fucking beautiful.

Holding her round ass, I thrust deep inside her. She let out a soft moan, but her eyes remained closed. I invaded her mouth through her parted lips and soon was diving deep inside her mouth, as well. Fucking her on both sides. With every orgasm, I wanted to quench my thirst. Every time we climaxed, I wanted us to be together.

She fisted my hair and moved her other hand up and down my back, scraping with her nails, marking her possession. Leaving a trail of fire and soothing the soul within.

The feel of her fingers, the touch of her skin, the deep penetration, and the way every inch of us fit right was a revelation of sorts.

"Found enough faults to scare you away?" I asked as I leisurely moved inside her, feeling her warmth and slickness around me.

"Mmm, not yet."

"But a girl must try?" I repeated her words.

"Or die trying," she mumbled with a grin. Her skin flushed pink, and it had nothing to do with my words and everything to do with my cock hitting her deep. She squeezed with my every thrust.

"In that case, what are your plans for today?"

"I might have to work late with my team," she answered huskily.

"I'm heading to Boston tonight to spend the weekend with Ivy. Can we meet for lunch?"

"Ahh." She nodded, letting out a soft moan. Her back bucked with the brewing orgasm. Her taut nipples pushed further into my chest, her heartbeat was a heavy rise and fall.

"Umm ... Close ..."

Her moans were the end of me. I moved faster to ride the wave with her.

"Oh, Ryan ... I am ... so close—" Even before she completed her sentence, an orgasm tore through her. Her pussy clenched around me, wringing me in.

I gave it one last thrust before I joined her in the whirlwind and toppled over.

Fifteen

RISHA

I jumped to my feet when a woman spoke behind me. Yanking the duvet, I haphazardly wrapped it around myself for modesty. Noticing Ryan's naked body spread over the bed, I yelped and stood in shock. Should I cover him or save myself?

I looked around but couldn't find the elusive woman anywhere. Instead, the soft morning sun filtered through the glass wall, covering every surface of the room.

Ryan crawled out of the bed, eyes hooded with sleep, not caring about the time of day, or that he wasn't alone, or that someone was still talking.

"... they're asking if you're running late for your eight o'clock meeting."

My eyes took a quick inventory of my surroundings—a king-sized bed dominated the center with a couch in one corner. Instead of portraits or paintings, there was an uninterrupted view of city towers outside, and on the opposite wall was a clock the size of Notre Dame's glass. The time on the clock made me refocus. Eight in the freaking morning?

Beside me, Ryan pressed a button on the nightstand. An intercom, I assumed, and said, "Postpone it by an hour." He stood up to his full height, pulled me by the duvet, and kissed my startled face. "Good morning again."

"I've never slept this late." Although self-directed, my thoughts sounded more like a grievance.

"There's a first time for everything." He winked while pecking at my lips. "Don't freak out on me today. Shower is on your right. You can be in your office soon."

"In the same clothes?" My eyes popped in horror.

He sat down in front of me. "I need to calm you down first." And he opened my legs to make space.

An hour later, I hurried into my office with a sigh of relief. Two orgasms, a shower, and a run to my apartment to change left me no room to catch up on my breath. I opened my laptop and started with emails since my first meeting wasn't until two in the afternoon, and I didn't see any fires burning anywhere.

But no matter how hard I tried, my mind kept drifting back to yesterday's event and the man I parted with an hour ago. I was totally blown away by Ryan. Breathing life into a flicker of my imagination was the nicest thing anyone had ever done. I had melted right there, letting my feelings for him possess my will. The tug of desires we had been meandering had snapped in that instant. I'd let my inhibitions take a backseat and closed the distance I'd been responsible for.

We wanted each other, no doubt. Not a day had gone by when I hadn't thought of giving in. Something about him felt too real, and it forced me—no, stopped me ... told me he was trouble that I didn't need at this point in my life.

That reasoning just hadn't been enough to stop me from jumping into his arms last night.

His every doing was my undoing. Every touch burned into my skin like a scar. Every revelation stripped me down, made me want him even more. And I did.

I let go of the world that kept me on a short leash and lost myself to him. Shutting down my mind's warning, I let my heart and body lead me, where only two of us resided for one entire night. His kisses overwhelmed my senses, making it impossible to think clearly. They drove me crazy, deep and relentless, hungry and passionate.

A hard knock on the door snapped me out of my daydream.

"Risha Verma?" a man in khakis and a T-shirt asked.

"I am, yes. And you are?"

"Delivery." He turned to the other side of the wall and came back within seconds with an enormous arrangement of bright pink roses in a crystal vase. He placed the arrangement in the center of my desk before removing the touchscreen for signature.

I signed off and opened the personally signed note out of the bouquet.

Can't stop thinking of you - Ryan
P.S. Picking you up at noon for lunch.

I smiled profusely as I picked up my phone and texted him: *Nice gesture, but totally unnecessary.*

The last guy I had dated had told me flowers were overrated, too short-lived to justify the cost. That was the thing with finance guys—everything had to add up. Even feelings needed a reason.

Ryan's response came right away. *Just ensuring you find those faults that make you run the other way.*

Me: I see you're trying very hard.

My phone buzzed with an incoming call.

With an unexplainable grin, I swiped my screen and greeted, "Hi, Mom. What's up?"

"Risha, can you take the earlier train and come before six?" she asked, skipping to check how I was. The keys jingled as she searched for the right key in the bunch. On Friday mornings, Mom typically went grocery shopping for the weekend.

"I'll be there tomorrow morning. Zoe, Marcus, and I are trying to finish one project before the customer shows up next—"

"Don't start this," she tsked, cutting me off. "We discussed last week that Neel is flying here for his parents' thirty-fifth anniversary."

Marcus walked into my office, grinning, his eyes focused on the flowers on my desk. But he skidded, noticing the phone attached to my ear. He paddled back, wiggling his eyebrows. People who knew me well also knew this wasn't my usual. Rather, outside of work, I didn't have a life, so these flowers would definitely make some heads turn.

"Please congratulate them for such an outstanding achievement," I answered on the phone.

"You need to stop mocking people, Risha. It's indeed an achievement to live a happy, blissful life with the person you love." She sighed as the door on her end unlocked.

Her definition of love was so screwed up that I never tried to correct her. I admitted, however, that a thirty-five-year partnership was a significant achievement. Love or not. Happy or not. Together was all that mattered.

The molds were prearranged. Higher education was presumed. Marriage in the twenties was expected. Children followed immediately. Love only your family. Be the perfect daughter. Be a perfect mother. Live for your family because living for yourself was considered self-centered. Deviate, and your whole family risked being ostracized.

Thirty years of my existence, and I was drowning in these nineteenth-century mindsets. There were years when surrendering seemed easier. There was no happiness, but at least it came with peace. But then, living with those regrets left me gutted. So, I started standing up for myself. Only to fall on my face.

"Anyway, I didn't call to discuss everlasting relationships

again. I want you to meet Neel tonight. He is a brilliant scientist—"

"Mom," I interrupted her to thwart those plans. "You need to take a break from this matchmaking. How many times do I have to tell you I'm not interested?"

"And how many times do I have to tell you it's not an option. You're thirty. It's high time you settle down."

"I will when I'm ready," I retorted in frustration.

"Now, Risha. Right now. Next year. Before summer." She wasn't ready to end this discussion, pushing me down the rabbit hole again. "Neel is the guy."

"Give me a break, Mom."

"How many times are you planning to disappoint your father, Risha? He can't take another blow from you," she changed her gears, hitting me exactly where it hurt the most. She knew my weakness too well. In another lifetime, I was his weakness, too. Now, we weren't even on talking terms, and Mom took full advantage of that situation.

"You know only you can bring a smile back on his face. And you also know what he wants ... he wants to see you happy, Risha. I want it, too."

Out of everything he wanted from me, settling down just to tick a box was not one of them. But with all things that went wrong in my life, Mom saw a chance of pushing her own idea of a fix, like getting married would magically solve everything between Dad and me.

With my parents, it was never about what I wanted. Even at thirty, I had no right over my own choices. When would it end? What would it take for things to change? Would it ever end? As always, none of it mattered. It was always about them, leaving me no choice but to abide by *their* definition of *my* happiness.

"We're not your enemy, Risha. We only want what's best for you ..." She kept talking, but it was all a muddled blur.

Time with Ryan was a beautiful illusion. A fleeting moment that was now over. Perfect for a night where dreams resided. This call with my mother was an awakening. An unwelcome tug back into the world I could avoid but never escape.

The flowers on my desk now looked pale, like props from a life I'd never get to live. And somewhere inside me, something warm turned cold. My heart sulked quietly ... until there was nothing left.

Patrick knocked on my door before walking in. His eyes first took in the flowers in shock, and then his gaze shifted to my face. I was still on the phone, and my mother was still talking. I didn't know what he saw on my face, but the disdain in his eyes filled the silence. If the call wasn't enough of a reminder of my shortcomings, the look on Patrick's face was. I knew what I had to do.

"I'll be there by six," I said before hanging up.

With my gaze locked with Patrick's, I asked, "Need something?"

It seemed he had a lot to add. Instead, he shook his head and turned on his heel, saying, "You're needed in the conference room."

I was about to follow Patrick when a text from Ryan interrupted me. *Is it noon yet?*

I typed: *I have to cancel lunch.*

With no further explanation, I threw the phone over my desk and left my office.

Sixteen

RISHA

I sulked my way between the food counter and wine bar, offering barely any hellos and definitely no smiles. Not one person in this crowd got more than a glance from me.

Mom intercepted me with hissing reminders to fix my attitude.

She clearly missed the memo: *I don't want to be here.*

Words echoed like a chant, pounded over my tongue, ready to roll out. To keep them in my personal vault, I stuffed myself with food.

"Someone seems really hungry."

I turned toward the soft chuckle, and shock overlapped all the other feelings. Sri Banerjee pulled out the chair beside me and settled in. Her smile was exactly how I remembered it from my childhood. Time had carved sagging lines around her eyes and beneath her chin, but none of it dulled the grace she carried. Elegant and sophisticated, she was still the same poised, self-assured woman I had once looked up to.

Of all the regrets that summed up my life, what I did to her daughter still haunted me the most.

"Banerjee Auntie! I didn't expect to see you tonight." My voice came out more surprised than I had intended.

I caught a glimpse of my mother's scowling face, and it oddly satisfied something inside me. I knew all the lectures I would have to endure when we got back home, but not talking to the woman whom I once looked up to seemed too immature. And somehow, these tiny acts of rebellion against my mother made me feel alive when I was drowning in self-loathing.

"I haven't seen you in years," I said to Sri.

She nodded, and a soft, familiar smile tugged at her lips. "After Virona left for college, I moved to New Orleans. Just returned a month ago."

It made sense now. I hadn't seen her since I'd left high school. Virona had been my best friend since elementary, her house a second home to me, and Sri the person I sought advice from.

From studies to hobbies, Virona and I had similar interests. To say we had been inseparable was to put things mildly. We had dreamed together, planned our futures together. But everything had changed the day her parents had filed for divorce. That single event caught up like a storm in our lives, changing everything we thought was permanent.

Sri moved on. Virona had definitely moved on. I doubted she even remembered me anymore. And I stayed frozen—stuck in the same place I had always been, living with my regrets and chewing on remorse.

I still couldn't understand where I belonged.

"I'm happy to see you, Risha." Sri took my hand, pulling me out of my internal musing.

"Same. I thought I lost you guys forever." Tears prickled at the back of my eyes. I wasn't even sure if I was sad for the people I lost all those years ago or miserable for my inability to stand up for myself then and now.

She caressed my hand and said, "Relationships don't end so easily. Sometimes these breaks do more good than harm."

A sob made its way up, and I picked up a napkin to clear my glassy eyes. The past, when left unresolved, had a way of staying just that—unresolved.

"I don't think Virona will ever forgive me."

She gave my hand another squeeze, but her silence told me what she didn't. Her daughter, my childhood best friend, whom I betrayed in the worst possible way, would never forgive me.

My whole body shuddered when Sri pulled me into a hug. There had been a time when her embrace had the power to take away all my worries in the world. Even today, after all these years, she felt like home. Like how I always imagined a mother's warmth should feel.

"Time heals every wound, my child. What doesn't break you makes you resilient. Listen to your heart—it'll tell you what matters. Then take one step at a time."

Her soothing voice and every word echoed in my brain as I desperately tried to make sense of things.

"It's not easy." A sob ripped through me. There was no holding back today. I was fourteen all over again. "I don't see the light, Auntie."

"Then keep walking until you find that light."

And that was the problem right there ... I didn't even know what my light was. Stuck on a raft, I could look for land. A wanderer looked for an oasis in the never-ending desert. In a storm without a compass, even a flicker became a sign. How would I know where I wanted to reach when I didn't know what I was looking for, where I meant to be?

I was clear on what I didn't want in life, but I never thought about what I did want. Not for a long time. Not since I was in my teens. I'd been leading my life with no goals. How was I supposed to find my destination when I didn't even know what I was searching for?

"Is everything all right here?" My mother's voice broke the melancholy in my heart.

Not willing to fuel her fake curiosity or concern, I blotted my eyes with the napkin again.

"We met after many years. Risha got emotional," Sri spoke to

Mom, giving me time to get my composure back. "It's good to see you after all this while, Rekha."

"We are so happy to have you back, too. This place didn't feel the same without you." Though my mother's voice was sweet, her insincerity could be felt from a mile away. She blamed Sri for leaving her husband, resenting her because she chose herself over a farce marriage.

To my mother, a divorced family could never be happy or perfect, or raise a perfect daughter. I didn't hate her, because she wasn't a bad person. My grief was watching the world move forward while she stayed rooted in her past. She clutched those traditions as if my independence threatened everything she stood for. To her, every choice I made outside her doctrine was defiance.

My expectations and her delivery were always off base.

Sri left after some pleasantries. I started to get up when Mom snatched the napkin out of my hand and gently but deliberately shoved me back into the chair. "For God's sake, Risha ... you want Neel to see you with these raccoon eyes? Why do you always make things hard for me?"

Wrapping one corner of the napkin over her forefinger, she started rubbing it under my eyes, scrubbing my smudged eyeliner, trying to restore a perfect look. But she never asked why I was crying. Either she didn't care, or her obsession with a perfect life drove her away from me. Either way, our relationship was dying every day. I could feel it in my bones, but she couldn't see it yet.

Neel and I exchanged a polite nod when we met at the bar. I busied myself with a glass of wine while he played with his beer bottle. Neither of us wanted to be here but had to fulfill our obligations. This wasn't the first time, and he wasn't the first guy my mother had set me up with. I was used to these awkward evenings now.

My mother's one-size-fits-all solution was to find me a

husband from her meticulously curated circle of friends. Neel was just her latest attempt to "restore balance" in our picture-perfect, traditional family with academic excellence. And I wasn't the only one caught in her matchmaking vortex. Every guy she'd set me up with seemed just as trapped, dutifully playing along as if we were all too clueless to figure out what we actually wanted for ourselves.

My phone buzzed inside my clutch, a reminder that I couldn't avoid the inevitable talk forever. Ryan's messages had progressed throughout the day, shifting from understanding to annoyance, then settling into full-blown frustration. He'd offered to bring lunch to my office, suggested pushing back meetings, even considered delaying his Boston trip. By the time I'd stepped off the train in Jersey, he must have figured out my deliberate avoidance.

He deserved an explanation.

What I felt for him wasn't just passion, but an all-consuming storm that left me both wrecked and whole. The physical intimacy between us was wild, but it was the connection underneath that shook me to my core. Even with all the money and power, he was fighting a battle of his own. And I ... I was too broken to offer him anything in return.

Shattering expectations was my tendency. I'd done it over and over again. Ryan deserved better—someone solid, someone whole. Someone who didn't flinch. I couldn't stand for myself; how could I weather his storm?

He'd resent my disappearance, but I was saving him from getting hurt. He was better off without someone like me. I had no choice but to let him go, even if something broke underneath my chest and hollowed me out. Ryan had done things no one ever had, and he'd done them without fully knowing me. I missed him in ways I couldn't explain, even while convincing myself that walking away was the right thing.

I couldn't even fathom how Ryan had his whole life figured out while I was still struggling to find my identity. We were practically the same age, yet he moved with certainty while I was still lost in myself.

"You've been awfully quiet, so I'll go first," Neel spoke beside me, breaking into my contemplation. "I'm in love with someone else."

It was close to midnight when we walked in through the garage door. Exhaustion clung to me like a thick blanket as I trailed behind Mira and Sia. Sia darted up the stairs, two steps at a time. I wondered where she'd found this renewed energy when, five minutes ago, she could barely keep her eyes open.

"You and Neel looked so good together." Mom's words stopped me on the landing step.

"He loves someone at work," I replied flatly and continued the ascent.

"She's not right for him. That marriage won't last," she shot back.

I turned to face her. "And you know that how?"

"She wouldn't understand our culture, our traditions ..." Mom kept going, but after a while, it stopped sounding like she was talking about Neel. Her every word was aimed at me. "I want you to marry someone who understands our values, who respects elders, who knows the meaning of family. Only someone from our background can give you that."

"No, Mom. You want all of that for yourself."

She moved farther into the foyer, closer to the stairs. "I'm your mother. I know what will make you happy."

"But you don't even know *me*." I wasn't sure where I found the courage, but I'd said it.

"I raised you."

A beat passed while I debated my next words, and then I delivered them. "If food and shelter count as raising, foster homes do that, too."

"That's enough." Dad's voice cut through the tension as he stepped into the foyer. His words resonated with the same disappointment he consistently harbored for me. A constant reminder of everything I'd failed to be. Maybe he wanted to say more, but he held back and turned to Mom instead. "Don't force her into something she doesn't want."

I couldn't tell what that meant. Was it disappointment again, or was he finally defending me? I needed it to be the latter, but I was too scared to ask.

Because he wasn't the only one disappointed here. I had a fair share of complaints, too.

"But I—"

Mom stopped when he gave her a look that said enough.

"Ever," he said, the word clipped and final.

"My work's getting busier," I said into the silence. "I won't be home every weekend anymore." I wasn't speaking to anyone in particular. I just didn't feel like holding back anymore.

Seventeen

RYAN

"More wine?" I asked Ivy when the server approached us with our meal.

"I'll pass. Have to work on the Blue Chip project tonight," she said, pulling her high ponytail over one shoulder.

She got her brown hair from our mother, but the rest of it, including our stubborn chin, we shared with Dad. Her smile used to light up a room once; now it seemed more practiced and forced.

It was getting crystal clear that she had absolutely no interest in McAlister Group. Since Ivy started undergrad, she had been interning with local startups. When I asked why not join our Boston office, she fed me some excuse about smaller projects being easy to manage. I was a decade older and could smell bullshit from a mile away.

Like everything else, she was distancing herself from the last tie that held us together. I was giving her space, but that didn't mean I would let her go. She was all I had.

"Twenty-two made you old." I shot her a displeased look as I filled my glass with Margaux.

"Then I should call you vintage, big brother." She quirked a brow, ready for banter. "Why does it feel like you're running on fumes? Is everything all right?"

I shrugged. I'd been off because the woman I felt a connection with ghosted me after one night. I had assumed things were perfect. I had assumed she was into me. I had assumed it was a start, not an end. *Fuck!* I had assumed too much.

"Ryan, I'm talking to you," Ivy pulled me out of my reverie. "This is the third time you've dodged my question. You need to stop thinking about work and relax a bit."

"Fine. Get involved in the business."

She rolled her eyes, holding back her words. But she had given me the opening, and I pushed further.

"I'm serious, Ivy. This was Dad's dream to expand the McAlister name. He wanted us to build it with him. I took it on to honor that, but I still don't know which direction you're heading."

"They are gone, Ryan. You don't have to live their dreams." She choked on her words.

Avoiding tough conversations didn't just make them disappear. They accumulated until one day you stood in the mess you pretended you didn't see coming. That was what Ivy and I had been doing for years—procrastinating the inevitable discussion.

"Yes, they are gone, but you and I are still here. I found my purpose in his dream. But what about you, what is your goal, Ivy? What do you want? Mom and Dad wanted us to work side by side. Don't you feel you should at least give it a try?"

"No." She held back her tears, but her voice cracked all the same. "They aren't coming back. I want to restart."

"Restart how? By forgetting who you are?"

She shook her head vehemently, but the tears still ran. I didn't intend to make her cry. But everything I was working for would be worthless if I couldn't bring my sister back home.

"It still hurts, Ryan."

"And it doesn't hurt me?" I said, laying my hand over hers on the table. The restaurant buzzed around us—not crowded, just enough to keep our words floating safely between us. "We both lost our parents, Ivy, but why does it feel like I lost you, too?"

I understood her pain because it resided inside me as well. But running wasn't the answer. Almost eight years since she'd left home and not a day went by when I didn't curse myself. She was only fourteen, and I was her guardian; why did I let that happen? How long would it take before I could correct my mistake?

"I have no one left other than you."

"Then prove it."

She nodded, and we went back to eating in silence. One car crash—that was all it had taken to tear our family apart. One wrong turn, and four people were gone: my parents, our driver, and the truck driver, who had turned too fast. The dead were gone, but the survivors suffered every day.

My phone rang inside my jacket pocket. I removed it with fading hope and whatever was left of it vanished when I saw the face on the screen. I cleared my voice and said, "Nick."

"There's a fire in our Miami resort," he said. "They're assessing the severity, but it seems the opening has to be postponed until it goes through full inspection. Cops are at the scene investigating the source of the fire."

"Fucking hell. We're not postponing anything." With two weeks until the grand opening, the invitations were already out. No way I was letting anything get in the way, especially bad press.

"I've called the chopper downtown. How soon can you make it here?" Nick asked. The helipad was over his office in downtown Manhattan for convenience.

"I'm in Boston with Ivy."

Her vacant stare reflected her struggle to comprehend the one-sided phone conversation.

"I'll hire a charter to be in Miami as soon as I can."

"Can you be at the Hanscom Airfield in an hour?" he asked. A small airfield in the Greater Boston area. He had to fly north with this detour, but going with Nick would definitely be quicker than trying to reserve a private charter at this hour.

"Give me two hours."

I disconnected the phone and turned to Ivy. She beat me to it.

"Let me finish school."

"I'll hold you to your word." Standing up, I dropped cash on the table to make things fast. My mind was already somewhere else ... Florida and what awaited there.

"The dishwasher responsible hasn't been seen since the fire," Nick updated me as he slid into the chair across from me. The now calm ocean stretched behind him after a weekend of nonstop thunderstorms, and the sky gave way to the bright sun, bringing everyone out of hiding. Swimsuits, neon trunks, and tourist chatter filled the restaurant. This was the only spot open to the public on the resort grounds—no walls, just a roof held up by a few columns.

For the past three mornings, we'd met at this exact spot. Each day brought a new concern, and the progress toward re-opening crawled on. The fire had hit our main kitchen just before closing. The resort manager had caught the smoke during his final walkthrough and pulled the alarm. He'd saved us from a major catastrophe, but all the equipment and part of the kitchen had been damaged.

"Pretty suspicious, don't you think?" I asked, picking up my coffee.

Two attacks within a month, both targeted at our major projects. Even if I didn't want to point fingers, the pattern was hard to ignore. I'd seven projects running simultaneously, and the three largest tied to Nick, Taber, and Jonah. MoxTo's rooftop pool license revoked. Fire at the Miami resort. Something told me Vegas was next in line. My gut also told me I was paying for someone else's enmity.

"They've assessed the damage." Nick decided to keep it clinical. "Our crew can start as soon as the fire inspection clears. Five days, max." He paused. "I took the inspectors out for drinks last night. They assured me this will be their priority."

"And what do they want in return?" The cynical side of me knew there was always a price.

Nick lifted his fork and took a bite of his scrambled eggs. The sun-drenched November afternoon made our brunch meeting feel almost at odds with Manhattan's typical bite in the air. "They haven't named a price yet."

Which only meant it would be high. And with our opening on the line, we were in a tight spot.

"I also bumped into Senator Waltman," he added casually, mentioning one of the most powerful men in the country.

"And?"

"And he said a rooftop pool over a restaurant shouldn't be a problem. He'll make some calls, clear the red tape from MoxTo."

Of course he would. Waltman lived on favors and didn't call them bribes. But the ask always came. Maybe not now, maybe not in words, but it came. A condo for a granddaughter. An Ivy League slot for a niece. A job offer where one wasn't needed. There was always a price.

"As long as no one asks for our kidneys," I muttered, turning to the sausage and eggs on my plate. I needed the Miami opening locked, needed MoxTo to go smoothly.

What I didn't need was the silence from Risha.

Three days and not a word, not even a one-line text. Whatever we had, it seemed to be over. She didn't owe me anything, and maybe that was what stung the most. The ease with which she'd walked away, like none of it had meant anything. Not the late nights. Not the dinners. Not the way she had looked at me. Not the way she had kissed me like she wanted to burn with me. Her every touch seared inside me.

I had stopped messaging her when I'd left Boston. Maybe it was pride, or it could be self-preservation. Maybe both. But every damn hour that passed, it gnawed. She had slipped under my skin without even trying. And now I couldn't scrub her out.

My phone chimed, and Alan's name lit up the screen. I showed it to Nick.

"What took him so long?" He chuckled.

"Coffee, probably." I swiped and opened my texts with him.

Alan: How's everything going there?

I replied. *The arsonist got away, but we're working on getting everything back on track before the opening.*

Alan: Sounds like progress, keep me posted. Btw, Risha stopped by.

My fingers flew across the screen. *When? What did she say?*

No reply. The kind of pause that made my pulse spike.

Finally, the three never-ending dots popped up.

Alan: Nothing. I told her you'd be in Miami for a while.

I looked up at Nick. "Can you handle things here?"

He stared at me as if I'd grown two heads. I wasn't the guy who bailed during complications, especially two weeks from opening. But right now, I wasn't myself.

I needed some real fucking answers.

He nodded slowly, going back to his orange juice. "No problem. Need anything else?"

"Actually"—I pushed back my chair—"mind if I borrow your plane?"

Eighteen

RISHA

Every hour, I learned new tricks to keep the roses thriving—magnesium for color, prune petals for energy, change water, grow light on a timer. For someone without a green thumb, I took it as a personal win. When my alarm went off at three, I dimmed the grow light to fifty percent using the knob and began tidying up. Two shriveled petals circled the base of the crystal vase. I cursed myself for leaving them at the office over the weekend.

The man who'd sent these flowers had left, but the storm he'd stirred inside me still hadn't settled. The new awakening refused to fade away. He lived like a pulse in my veins, in my muscles, and in my memory. I couldn't shake him. Another chapter closed with pages left blank. Another goodbye that turned into silence.

Maybe this was easier. Cleaner. Because when he was near, reason abandoned me. My body betrayed me, wanting something it had no right to want. The worst was not knowing whether he resented me or had simply forgotten me. Or if he saw me as the woman who'd wrecked what could have been.

"How long are you going to fuss over those damn flowers?" Patrick's voice startled the heck out of me, causing me to jump, knocking the crystal vase with my hand but thankfully not tipping it over.

I faced him and chose to remain unaffected. "You need something?" I asked.

"Yes. Your attention. To the job you're paid to do." He stepped inside my office with his usual grump. "Nixus meeting is due tomorrow. Where's the planner?"

I had come back from Jersey on Saturday and worked straight through the weekend. My entire team was here at least half that time. Something that I had to change. We all loved what we were doing, so we gave more, but that didn't mean a work-life balance wasn't necessary. This Nixus account was a heavy load, but the client was more reasonable than Patrick. The man who should be on our team was playing an opponent.

"I emailed it over an hour ago," I told him and went back to what I'd been doing before. I knew these flowers were bothering him, and then the sudden break when I went to Ryan's office had only made things worse. He hadn't known where I was, but he definitely let his imagination run wild. Because since then he had been snappy.

"These flowers are not therapy. Focus on the deliverables instead." He scowled.

I straightened my back and met his gaze. "Is this coming from my boss now?"

"Who else can it be beside your *boss*?" Patrick emphasized the word *boss*.

"I've been given unrealistic deadlines and still delivered. You have nothing to complain about."

He took a step closer. The only thing separating us now was the edge of my desk. "And if that complain came from your ex-lover?"

I shook my head and walked over to the trash can to add some distance between us. "Then it's none of your business."

"My business—"

"Let it go, Patrick. It's been five years."

His eyes blazed with menace as he closed the distance again. I didn't want to go down a slippery slope with him.

"I want you to feel every bit of this pain, Risha. I want you to burn for someone you could never have."

Disgruntled and delusional, this man was still holding on to the past.

"You're crossing the professional boundary here. It's best if you leave my office," I told him without backing away further.

His eyes moved between my face and the flowers, rage blurring his eyes. "I want these flowers gone or you can leave."

I paused momentarily trying to see through his bluff.

"You can't fire me." I laughed, though uncertainty gnawed.

"You're right, I can't." Anger pulsed between his eyes when he opened his mouth next. "But that doesn't mean I can't make your life miserable enough that you'll quit yourself."

That remark left me stunned. He'd thrown his share of sharp comments over the last six months we'd been working together, but this was a line he hadn't crossed before—threatening the one thing he knew meant everything to me. I didn't know what triggered the escalation or how to pull it back, but one thing was clear: I wasn't backing down, no matter how vulnerable I felt.

"What do you want, Patrick?"

"I want those flowers gone." His face was dead serious and completely unyielding.

And so was I.

"Okay." I yanked the power cord off my laptop and snapped it shut. Walking behind my desk, I packed my purse and laptop. Then I grabbed the crystal vase and the grow-light between my arms and walked out of my office. "I'll see you tomorrow."

I unlocked my apartment door, juggling an armful of chaos. The subway ride with a vase full of water was an impractical disaster, an ill-conceived plan when I'd stormed out of the office. My anger had started to cool, mostly thanks to the water sloshing all over my georgette, semi-sheer white shirt. Worse, in my fury, I'd forgotten my coat. The only upside? I had the train mostly to myself during off-peak hours.

"Holy hell," I muttered, placing the vase on my nightstand and finally assessing my situation in the full-length mirror. My shirt clung to my front, soaked and completely transparent, the fabric now plastered to my camisole, leaving absolutely nothing to the imagination. Even the lace of my bra was soaked in water, and my nipples were erect from cold and consciousness. The skirt was wet, too, but at least it was bright red wool. No transparency there.

While I debated between getting out of the wet clothes or setting up the vase, my doorbell rang. I doubted it was Cece since she had her own keys. Though she could have forgotten them. Assuming it was one of her many delivery boxes arriving, I decided to check just in case. Unlocking the door, I opened it wide. My jaw slacked at the sight awaiting on the other side.

"Ryan?" My axis tilted one-hundred-eighty degrees. The physical need to be in his arms suddenly overtook all reasoning. "Alan told me you were in Miami."

He opened his mouth to say something, but stopped. His gaze shifted from a man seeking answers to seduction and lust. They raked over the wet clothes clinging to my every curve, lingered over my breasts before going farther down.

The tautness of my nipples under his gaze sent a shiver down my skin, and it had nothing to do with the wet clothes. The apartment heater was blasting at full speed.

I took in his frame that filled the threshold. Without a word, he stepped inside, closing the distance between us. Heat pooled inside me, a fire flickering with need. *Shit*! This man was my downfall.

He looked ... gorgeously hot. A stark reminder of why I felt something was missing. His presence was like the winter sun. His scent filled me to the brim—worn leather and musk.

"When did you return?" I asked in a low whisper.

My feet were grounded firmly, unable to move when he

walked closer. The door shut behind him. He took another step closer until we were inches apart. I sucked in a sharp breath. My heart raced with desires I hoped to contain. Without a word, he wrapped one arm around my waist and pulled me into him.

"You stopped by my office." It wasn't exactly a question.

"Yes ... I didn't know ... I thought you were back from Boston."

"You never responded to my calls or texts." Now I heard the hurt. Not accusations, but the wound of betrayal.

"I owed you a proper explanation," I said breathlessly when his hands tightened around my back and his eyes remained fixed on mine.

"That's right, you do." His lips almost caressed mine. Almost, but not quite.

My knees buckled under his touch, but his firm hand held me upright. I found my solid ground in him, and my world shifted once again. Leaving reality behind, I was slipping into this other world ... even if it wasn't real. I didn't understand the pull, but I ached for him like roots ache for rain in a long, cruel drought.

"I visited your office," he said.

That explained how he knew where to find me. It was unusual for me to leave in the middle of the day. Zoe had looked at me questioningly. I'd told her I wasn't feeling my best.

Ryan moved his other hand to my shoulder and up my bare neck to the locks of my hair. Was he reliving what he had missed?

My skin was ablaze. The charge between us came alive the way it always did. A taut live wire pulling the strings.

He brushed his lips over mine. I inhaled, breathing my oxygen through him. God, he made me incapable of thinking beyond reason. When he was this close, there was only one thing I wanted.

Him.

I might not know what I needed in life, but in this moment, in this instant, I only needed him. Ryan McAlister.

"You should know something about me," I said before I lost all sense of reality.

"I'm listening." His voice remained firm and controlled, despite the electricity that crackled between us.

I opened my mouth to talk, or maybe to taste his lips again. Both eluded me. I wanted to authenticate that he wasn't a flicker of my imagination who'd been haunting me.

He pulled back, calling the shots. "Explanation?"

"Right." I had so much to say, starting with an apology for my actions. I wanted to be open and honest; I needed it for myself. I wasn't hiding anymore. "I'm sorry for avoiding your calls and texts."

"That's an apology, not an explanation, Risha. To understand you, I need to understand your reasons first."

"You're right. An apology is meaningless until I can back it up with a reason."

He didn't stop me from continuing, but he didn't let me go either.

Safe. I felt safe between his arms ... or at least that was what my delusional mind told me until I spilled the truth about myself.

"Our worlds are different, Ryan, so I don't expect you to understand any of this, but ..." I sighed heavily. *Here it was.* "I am under pressure to get married and settle down. I am on a borrowed time and the clock is always tick—"

"What do you want?" he asked, stopping me mid-confession.

"*What do I want*? No one cares what I want. I have expectations to fulfill, someone else's dreams to live on."

"I'm asking *you*, Risha. If there are no barriers, what is it you want?"

His words halted my every thought. *An unrestricted life without expectations tying me down. No one questioning my choices, whether right or wrong. No judgment passed. No guilt. No shame. A dream ... that I am allowed to live until I wake up.*

If Ryan wanted to know my dreams, then I'd tell him. My answer came unabashed. "You ... I want you."

He pulled me closer until our mouths crushed. Biting my lower lip, his tongue glided its way inside. All restraint was gone, and suddenly, everything felt too intense. He was filling me with his scent, and all thoughts of reality and dreams merged into one.

I didn't realize I was moving with him until my back was pushed against the couch. He caged me between his chest and the backrest of the couch, and instead of his kiss tapering down, it started padding my brain. I whimpered like an addict needing her next fix.

"Is that what you really want?" he spoke inside my mouth. Sliding one hand into my hair he fisted it roughly, jerking my head back to better accommodate his mouth.

I moaned and wrapped my arms tighter around his waist. My hands moved frantically up and down his back. I needed more. I needed him.

"Don't hold back, precious. I want to know you."

"I want to live. And feel. I want to experience everything you stir in me ... and I want to savor it a little longer," I confessed. "I don't care about anything else. My world, your world, who we are. Never in my life have I felt this unrelenting pull. But I understand if it's too much to ask."

"I want the same things," he growled, losing all self-control. He ran his hands down my sides and gripped the hem of my skirt. Yanking it up and over my waist, then he crouched between my legs.

I looked down only to see that perfect golden-brown hair and bobbing head. And I threw back my head as a sharp moan escaped my lips.

He rubbed against my nub, his tongue invading my wet pussy.

"You're so fucking wet," he groaned, leaving hot breaths. Pulling by my hips toward him, his tongue penetrated deeper. I gave an involuntary moan as his thumb turned between pinches and circular rubs over my throbbing nub.

My first orgasm came in a fury. Ryan didn't stop, nor did he slow down. His tongue moved furiously, pushing me toward my next orgasm. The roughness of his beard grazed my supersensitive skin. I gripped him by his hair and held his shoulder with the other hand for support.

"Oh, please ... yes ... I'm close," I whimpered.

My senses paralyzed. My core was on the brink of climax. His tongue pushed further inside my folds, pushing deep into a bundle of nerves. I cried out, my fingers fisting to pull him for a deeper thrust. Soon, another orgasm tore through my core. I screamed his name and pushed into his mouth. He rode me for a full minute until the ripples subsided and I could see through the haze again.

When I opened my eyes, his deep blues were staring back at my face, with his arms holding me for support and a grin overtaking his face. I smiled, exhaustion and ecstasy battling inside, but my heart felt so much at ease. So relaxed.

I didn't know what I wanted in life, out of this life. But at this moment and time, I wanted only Ryan.

Nineteen

RYAN

Running my hands down her never-ending legs, I removed her panties, boots, and then her skirt. Shirt, camisole, and bra followed before I stripped out of my clothes.

Risha rested her hands on my shoulders, and her knees wobbled under my every touch. She wanted me, and now I understood her resistance. I finally saw why she had kept her distance.

We moved over to the couch, and I settled between her legs. My hard cock stood between us, begging for a release. But there was something more that needed clarity. She wanted me, and I wanted her, but the mountain between us was far more treacherous than I'd imagined.

"I'm sorry for ignoring you," she said without meeting my eyes. "I also want to apologize for leading you on. No matter how much I want you, this is all going to end very badly. I'm not good for you, Ryan. All this will lead to disappointment ... I can't do this to you ... to me."

Disappointment, wants, future—they all seemed familiar, taken directly out of my own playbook. Her future wasn't hers to decide, and mine was already dedicated to McAlister Group. But

Risha ... this moment ... felt too close, too real. A contentment that I could feel in my bones.

"I've spent years chasing the future. A constant battle to prove myself ... It's so fucking exhausting. But then I met you, and for the first time, I don't care about before or after, my past or my future. I just want to be here. With you. Right now."

She shook her head. "But this moment won't last forever. What if you want more? I want more? I can't do this, Ryan. It's too—"

"What if you can't stand my guts in a month? What if your career takes you to the moon? What if our priorities never align? What if ...?" Getting on top of her, I brushed her lips with mine, inhaling her beautiful scent of sandalwood and rose. "There is no end to these what-ifs."

"You're not taking me seriously, Ryan."

"What if you are wrong? What if I am right? What if today is all we have? Are you ready to live without knowing what our time together could be?" I stopped to let her process, and when she didn't say anything, I led her on. "Can you live for today, Risha?"

Silence stretched between us. She wanted me no doubt, but I could feel her fear of commitment. Not even a day? What expectations was she living under?

"Can you live in this moment? In this instant? No future. No pressure. No ask or want ... just be here in the present and see how it feels? Can you do that?"

Her nod was so small I could have easily missed it.

Holding her chin, I raised her face. Her almond eyes were glassy, but a sliver of smile tugged at her lips. And finally she nodded again, processing my words.

Cupping her ass, I adjusted her, guiding her soaked opening to my throbbing cock. That fucker didn't understand the seriousness of the matter. Since meeting her, he had grown a mind of his own. Leaving all reasoning behind, he wanted only her warm, moist, inviting pussy, and the unfathomable chemistry we shared. The rush of wildfires and our maddening chemistry.

With one smooth thrust, I filled her with my cock. She wrapped her legs tightly around my waist. Our connection was so intense that I closed my eyes to fully experience her embrace.

"Which one is your room?" I asked hoarsely.

Without severing the connection and thrusting vigorously, I lifted her and carried her toward the door she showed.

I woke up parched, a little hungry, but more rested than I'd felt in days. I hadn't realized how drained I had been from the chaos in Miami until I'd collapsed into bed with Risha. Or it could be her, curled against my chest, who gave me the calm I craved.

Nick had called to tell me the inspection would be delayed right before I'd arrived at Risha's. We had a team ready and fully equipped to replace the damaged equipment, but we couldn't proceed without the license. Maybe I should feel guilty dumping everything on Nick, but that guilt never surfaced.

The conversation with Risha had taken priority over everything else.

Everything made sense now—her hesitation, the need to slow things down. This was never about me. It was her family that kept her guarded. And what she wanted ... was me. She was choosing the present, choosing *us*, even if it was just for now.

So, I'd make damn sure there was no tomorrow. From this point on, we'd live right here, in the now.

I pressed a kiss on her forehead and slipped out of the bed. Tugging on my trousers, I reached for my shirt. A flickering light underneath the door signaled we were no longer alone.

Crossing the hallway, I spotted Cece on the couch, lazily flipping through TV channels.

"Late night for you, isn't it?" I asked, more acknowledgment than question.

"Hard to sleep with the concert you two were putting on," she muttered loud enough for me to hear.

I walked around the island into the open kitchen, filled a glass from a pitcher, then turned to face her. "Sorry ... I guess. You should be used to these noises if you've been living with a roommate."

Cece smirked, full tilt. "Nice move, Ryan. If that's your way of digging for her sex life, you're out of luck."

"No harm trying." I winked and took another sip. "What happened before me doesn't matter."

"You hurt her, and I'll forget you're Taber's friend." Her eyes narrowed with conviction.

"Ouch! Territorial."

"Concerned," she responded.

Surprised by her tone, I leaned forward, setting my elbows on the island. "Go on."

She clicked off the TV and tossed the remote aside. "Didn't you say you hated drama? Wasn't that your reason for walking away from Kat?"

I stiffened. *That* had come out of nowhere. My ex Katherine had run in the same social circles as Cece, but I didn't know she had been holding a grudge.

"You have to be clearer than that."

She stood up from the couch. "If you can't handle messy, Ryan, keep Risha at arm's length."

"Risha is nothing like Katherine." I pronounced every word. "Kat was entitled, aimless, and exhausting. She wanted a yes-man who'd jump every time she snapped her fingers."

"And yet, here you are," she challenged, crossing her arms over her chest. "Taber told me you left Miami in a rush this morning. And now you're here, in my apartment, screwing my roommate."

Un-fucking-believable. "Didn't know you were so invested in business updates. Last I checked, you were the engineer who swore off anything Cristaldi-related."

"By choice," she shot back. "And I still don't care. But I care about *you*. And her. Which is why I know it's a disaster waiting to happen." She exhaled, trying to find the right words but falling short.

I turned my back and refilled my glass. "You're overthinking."

"She is different, Ryan. Her Dad and she had stopped talking after she left the doctoral program. Her chaos, mess, drama—whatever you want to call it—is different. And you're a straightforward kind of a guy."

She wasn't wrong. I liked the order. Control. Lines drawn in bold black and white with no room for gray. But there was another side of me Cece didn't understand ... I was attracted to Risha to the point where I couldn't think straight.

"I'm not trying to play mother," Cece added, her voice hovering between softer and sharper. "But I'll kill you if you hurt her."

Twenty

RISHA

I opened my eyes to find Ryan's magnetic blue eyes intently watching my face. Our arms were wrapped around each other, and my hair covered his chest. His megawatt smile dazzled me. The smile I should have gotten used to by now, yet it flipped my stomach every time.

"Did I miss something during my sleep?" I asked.

"Except my hard cock, nothing."

"Dang it." I chuckled, and his smile widened. "Did you get a good sleep?"

"Best sleep in days. Thanks." He brightened my room more than the vibrant colors surrounding us. "Is it a good time for some Q&A?"

Speaking like a true boss.

I nodded so he could dive right in.

"First of all, I love your room ... I'm guessing it's your doing?"

"Good guess ... Tell me what you like about it?" I fished for compliments.

My guilty pleasure for as long as I could remember, there was a time in life when I thought designing homes would be my career.

Ryan studied the room, taking in the rustic dresser, wicker

full-length mirror, and the cozy reading corner by the window that overlooked the street and had been one of the most used parts of my room.

"Tell me about this picture on the wall.". His chin directed me to a grainy image of a houseboat constructed from dark jackwood.

A woman posed in front, wrapped in a bright red sari. There was something about her enigmatic smile—a mystery I still hadn't been able to crack. Her body spoke of sensuality, her smile told another story, but her eyes ... they held something else entirely. Emptiness. Guarded. As if she were hiding a truth no one had earned the right to know.

More than the picture, it was the moment I was clinging to. Our last family vacation. The last time Dad and I had been close. He also had the exact photo, minus the woman as his screensaver. When Sia had asked him once why that old picture, he had said, "Because I miss my home." I liked to believe it was a lie. I was on the other side of the lens he looked through.

"I took it a while back," I answered. I could still taste the mugginess in the air, with endless backwater surrounding me.

When I turned to Ryan, he was watching me intently.

"What?"

"How fucking talented are you? You make me feel ... inconsequential." Wrapping his arms around my neck, he pulled me into him.

I laughed. "Oh please. That is a terrible picture, not enough light and most of it is blurred. I'm just trying to read this woman's story. Until then, it stays."

"Hmm." He gave it another thirty seconds, but came up empty. I didn't blame him; she was a beautiful mystery. Then I watched his eyes drift to the nightstand. "I see you're still holding on to those flowers. Did you like them as much as I thought you would?"

Wrapping my arms around him, I pecked at his lips. "Loved them."

"They reminded me of the flush on your cheeks whenever we're near." He deepened our kiss, leaving me breathless. "I want to take you somewhere this evening. Pack an overnight bag."

"Did we decide on sleepovers now?" I quirked a brow, feigning ignorance.

He straddled me, peppering kisses all over my face and neck. "We have some serious catching up to do."

"I'm with you," I agreed, rubbing my hips over his erection and taking charge.

"Good morning." I looked straight at Marty, my second-in-command. Sleepless nights with his six-month-old had carved dark hollows under his eyes, and the stifled yawns said the rest of the story. Then he'd stepped straight into the chaos of Nixus and our mercilessly deadline-driven projects.

"Thanks. I'm having a hard time deciding which one's worse: sleep deprivation and a screaming baby or the fires we're putting out here," he said with a dry laugh.

"I hear you." I faced the rest of the team. They were inching toward burnout. My responsibility was split between protecting them and meeting our customers' demands. It was gnawing at me that I hadn't been fair to these people. "Let's cut down on the late nights. I'll handle the customers' expectations."

"And what about Patrick's expectations?" Marty smirked, voicing what everyone else was thinking. "He wants us to go full throttle on Nixus without missing a beat on everything else."

"I'll deal with Nixus. And Patrick isn't managing these accounts, I am. Now let's walk through all the workload to see where we stand." I pulled up the project management spreadsheet, and we started reviewing.

We went over deliverables, blockers, and what could move faster if we reshuffled resources. Everyone knew their role and understood what it would take to hit the deadlines.

When our meeting concluded, I fired off a quick message to Marcus. After meeting him at Alan's anniversary dinner, our working relationship had evolved into a friendly professionalism. Both of our teams were syncing weekly via conference calls. For next week, I requested an in-person meeting.

His reply came in the middle of my next meeting with Patrick and Zoe. I was sharing my screen when the message notification popped up for all to see.

"Any particular reason for this in-person meeting, Risha?" Patrick asked, raising an eyebrow.

Keeping my tone casual, I said, "Our offices are nearby, it makes sense to meet face-to-face once in a while."

"I see. Add me to the invite." Patrick adjusted his glasses and turned back to Zoe, picking up the project status and timeline on Blackrock.

He acted as if yesterday's confrontation had never happened. He definitely picked that up from me, because the last time things blew up between us, it ended with a brief argument, followed by a long silence. Until he came back as my boss and lit my life on fire.

"This is unacceptable." Patrick's voice cracked like a whip as he pinned Zoe with a stare. "The client wants his machine early next week, not in thirty days like you're proposing."

Across the table, Zoe squirmed, her fingers tightening around her pen. She had a hard time expressing herself, and Patrick for sure didn't make it easy on her. How had I missed this side of him when we'd dated? Oh, right—we'd never actually worked together then, and he turned out to be an ass anyway.

"This project's already a month behind," he barked. "If we don't deliver, they're threatening to take it to another firm."

"We're trying," Zoe managed in a small voice.

Patrick's palm landed flat on the table. "Not hard enough."

"That's funny you said that." I intercepted, keeping my voice even. "You surely didn't think it through before taking on the Nixus project."

His head snapped toward me. His eyes flashed with the same

fury I'd witnessed repeatedly now. This wasn't the first time he'd been reminded that signing contracts behind my back had consequences.

"This revenue is budgeted into this quarter's goal," Patrick said.

"You should've adjusted your budget then," I added, refusing to let him bully a junior or undermine my authority.

His lip curled into something so repulsive I couldn't comprehend what I saw in this man all those years ago. "Who approved Zoe's three-week vacation in the middle of a deadline?"

Zoe shrank further into her chair.

"I did," I said. "Six months ago. She earned it, and it was already factored into the project timeline. We're approaching holidays, people will take time off."

For the next couple of minutes, every time he opened his mouth, I had a comeback locked and loaded. I'd been waiting to prove I'd predicted this outcome.

When he finally realized he wasn't winning, he turned back to Zoe like a vulture. "Cancel your vacation."

"Not happening," I snapped, matching his contempt. "Start dealing with the fallout of your making."

I stood and motioned for Zoe to follow.

"And next time you've something to say to one of my team members," I held his gaze, "take it up with me. Otherwise, I'll be happy to go over your head and have this same conversation with the president of the company."

Then I walked out, pulse hammering but satisfaction coursing through me. No idea where my courage came from, but hell, it felt amazing. First Mom, now Patrick. I wasn't backing down or looking for easy.

Twenty-One

RYAN

I opened the door for the first time in nearly a decade and let Risha step inside. My heart pounded relentlessly, the visceral pulse of memory drumming under my chest. Every fragment gutted and wrecked, my past stirred like echoes trapped in old walls, tugging at chords I thought had long since frayed.

The only thing keeping me grounded was her hand resting on my arm. Then the other hand slid over to my chest, an innocent, unconscious gesture that drew me forward when everything in me wanted to run.

"When was the last time someone was here?" she asked in a tentative voice, staring intently, seeming to count the beats of my heart.

I cleared my throat. "Ms. Johanson is in charge of looking after the place. I asked her to stock up the house for us."

Risha's gaze drifted from me to the foyer. But she made zero attempt to head further within. Instead, she circled her arms around my waist and leaned in closer. "We don't have to go in if you're not ready," she murmured.

"I don't think I'll ever be ready, but I can't move forward until I face my past," I admitted. "Are you ready?"

"I'm ready whenever you are."

Pressing a kiss on her forehead, I led her into the foyer.

Cool air embraced us. Risha paid attention to every detail in the house. I wondered what was going through her head because, to me, it was a ruinous mansion of what used to be. I couldn't see past the horror of death. All the good times we had once shared, lost and forgotten.

Everyone told me to move on to something new, away from my past. A part of me wanted to believe that one day I could. Yet another part told me this was my home. My mother's smile, Dad's laughter, and Ivy's glees and giggles when she bossed everyone around lived in this place. Running wasn't an option, and accepting would make me a man.

"What do you think?" I asked Risha, who clung to me like my suit. I wrapped my arms around her waist, soaking in her warmth and masking the darkness with a desire only this woman could raise from my core.

My mother always named her style modern meeting gilded. Her unique signature was on everything she did. I never paid attention to designs until our hotels started showcasing in magazines, and then of course I met this woman.

"Too traditional?" I asked.

"Take me to your room, Ryan," she said abruptly, halting all my thoughts.

Bypassing the living area, I led her down the hallway and opened the door on the right. I flicked on the light and noticed drawn curtains over the floor-to-ceiling windows. On one wall stood my old study table where I'd once spent countless hours. Against the far wall, a queen bed anchored the room. Across from it, spruced shelves displayed my soccer trophies, spanning high school to undergrad, with a few swim and baseball medals from earlier years mixed in. Mom had called it her pride space—quietly proud, never flashy—so the trophies stayed tucked inside my room. A large TV hung on the wall across from a low couch where I used to crash for long gaming nights.

"Not exactly the kind of room I imagined losing my virginity when I was a kid, but this is pretty close."

"What did you just say? *You* imagined a room where you'd lose your virginity?" I burst out laughing and joined her at my trophy wall.

She faced me with confusion. Like my question was more bizarre than her revelation. "It matters. I'll always remember where and to whom. Unfortunately, neither of it was pretty."

"Pretty? You wanted a pretty boy with a"—I looked around to find a word for this room—"subtle-masculine room? And what did you get instead, if I may ask?"

"Well ... what I got was a friend's basement closet with a pimpled guy who had no idea what he was doing. He used to put on a fake deep voice that he thought was a complete turn on ... but absolutely wasn't." She made an icky face that got another chuckle out of me. "Trust me; it's worse than I'm able to describe."

"I love your imaginative descriptions." I laughed again with abundance. "Why did you do it then?"

She made another face and turned back to the medals, giving complete attention to each one of them. "My mother volunteered through the high school, and I went to a college where my dad was a professor. A nineteen-year-old virgin, I took the matter seriously."

Jealousy stung me out of nowhere. I had no right over her past, but the fact that someone saw her the way I do, touched her intimately, boiled my blood.

Grabbing her elbow, I wrapped my arms around her waist. "Let's pretend to be in college again."

"A role play?" Inquisitiveness turned wicked. "Be careful, Mr. McAlister; I've quite an imagination."

"Ryan," I corrected. "It'll be an interesting study session. Do you want to work on the assignment or should we rather get sweaty first?"

"Crass. Oh my God, icky." She wrinkled her nose.

"What?" I chuckled. "We're teenagers, remember? Boys can't think beyond sex. At least I don't have pimples, and this is better than a basement closet."

Her eyes turned sultry, taking me in from head to toe. She pushed the jacket down my arms and then she undid my vest and tie knot. Pulling the hem of the shirt out, her hands moved inside and over my abdomen. She raked me with her fingers, sending simultaneous jolts to my brain and groin. My skin blazed with fire under her caress. Taking a step closer, she inhaled a sharp breath. Her body shivered. Closing her eyes, she savored every sensation.

The effect I had on her made my mind go wild. Grabbing her ass, I pulled her against my hardened cock.

My hands roamed over the curve of her hips. A low yelp left her throat.

"I've wanted to grab your sexy ass since I saw you playing basketball." I low-hummed into her ear.

"Swimming," she corrected me, playing along.

"On the pool deck." I changed my storyline. "I want those never-ending legs wrapped around me while I push you against the wall. Into the shower stall—"

"Umm, Ryan, your door is open." She broke my train of thoughts. "Someone might come in." Squirming between my arms, she played her part.

We were the only two people in this massive penthouse, and this was the first time I had brought a girl home. Even Stacy, my girlfriend in high school, had never visited because I didn't want my decade-younger sister to catch me making out with someone. The protective brother inside me always took the cautious high ground. The day Ivy had been born, Mom had told me I always had to protect her. Mom was gone, but those words were written in stone even now.

Leaving Risha, I went back and locked the door. But the moment I faced her, all my previous crippling thoughts about being here in this house vanished. Her shirt, skirt, and shoes were haphazardly strewn on the floor next to her, while she gingerly sat on the edge of the bed in bright electric blue lacy panties and a matching camisole, her puckered nipples ready to breach their bounds.

"Fuck!" Unbuttoning my cufflinks, I let them fall, followed by my shirt and belt as I continued to walk toward her. "You're so fucking gorgeous. I can't see anyone else since I saw you. It's like there is everyone else and then there is you."

That part was real. The zing between was impossible to ignore. A constant hum lived right where she was.

"You're not bad yourself. I don't know if you ever noticed, but I haven't missed a single soccer match this year."

So she paid attention to all my trophies.

Her teeth unconsciously played with her bottom lip while her fingers moved over the elastic of her panties. There was a fucking hole in the center right below the elastic, and a tiny gold chime dangled there. My cock screamed inside my pants, asking for a shove, a release that only she could provide.

"I noticed that," I went along. I held her chin between my thumb and forefingers and tilted her head until our eyes connected. Her nipples scraped my thighs, and even through all the layers between us, I was wound up so tight that I might snap.

Her eyes were my anchor. Her smile was my undoing.

Get into the fucking game, Ryan.

Right!

Pushing her back until her back touched the mattress, I moved between her legs. I placed my palm between her breasts, slowly moving down her abdomen to the edge of her panties. Every muscle in her abdomen clenched with my every movement. I tried to control my breathing.

Fingering the metal dangling in the center, I said, "That's my lucky charm." I flicked it with my tongue and gently kissed it. She shivered.

Pushing her fingers into my hair, she pulled my face to hers. I slid my tongue into her mouth. Our teeth clattered, our lips stretched, our kisses grew long and deep, gaining urgency with every second. Her fingers started exploring me inch by inch, from my chest to ribs to abdomen and down to my navel.

I moved one hand inside her hair and held her mouth still while moving the other hand down to her panties. I groaned in her mouth, "I'm keeping these fucking panties."

"I had no idea panties are your fetish." She giggled inside my mouth.

I nibbled on her lip and pressed my chin to hers. "Even I didn't know until tonight. And there's more that I like."

She moved under my weight, sending a jolt of shock. "Do tell. I want to know."

I realized I'd never praised her before, never admired her beauty and perfection. Kicking myself for not doing something so basic, I started reciting her every attribute I was in awe of. "I love the curve of your smile. And those eyes ... storm one second, soft the next. But, either way, they knock the breath right out of me. Your hair is velvet shadows I want to get lost in, and your long neck, arms, and legs are my absolute weakness. You're a temptress in those tight boots and business clothes, screaming not to mess with you, while I die to do exactly that. But underneath all these layers, you're just a girl who wants every inch of my attention. You're a storm I crave, Risha, and a calm I can't resist."

She shivered and raised herself until she was pushing against my chest. Her nails dug into my back, sending shivers through my bloodstream. I was lost in her every touch and in the ragged sound of our breathing, the heat of her moist kisses, and her hips dry humping into my hard cock.

"I want you to fuck me today," she asked or demanded.

The former teenager in me wanted to fuck the hell out of her; the man I was today wanted to savor her every delicious curve, take in her every soundless moan, give her a perfect first sex that she would remember forever. I wanted to consume her and create a new memory to replace the old one.

I hurriedly undid my pants and, with her help, got them down my legs. I ripped open the condom, and she rolled it on my erection. The tip of my cock grazed her entrance, and I closed my eyes, gently sliding inside her.

"God!" she moaned.

Lifting her hips, I began to pump through her inviting pussy, each movement feeling more intense. The pain of her fingernails digging into my shoulders fueled my lust. Her eyes closed, but her moans were loud against my neck. Moving my lips over her brassiere, I pulled one side down and took one hardened nipple between my teeth. I gripped her hair tightly in my fist, eliciting a whimper out of her. She soon started breathing hard against my skin.

"Bite me," I demanded, wanting her marks on me.

She complied—hard—making me pull harder on her hair, thrusting faster with a ferocious need. Our bodies were so in tune, reacting to every touch and sound.

A shiver that ran through my body continued down hers. Stretching her thighs wider, pushing her knees upward, she made more space for me to push my cock deeper.

"Oh God, I love this," she breathed out.

"Yeah?" I took her wrists and pushed them over her head. It leveraged me to deepen the thrusts, causing her to gasp. "You like it when I'm deep inside you?"

"No. Yes. I mean ... go faster." She lifted her hips off the bed to meet my next thrust.

"Fuck," I groaned, feeling myself balls deep inside her.

She turned her face, meeting my neck, leaving a trail of kisses down to my collarbone. I crushed my lips over her forehead, my body moving faster in and out of her. The air conditioner was useless by now; we were covered in a sheen of sweat. Her moans and my groans filled the room. The glow of the light played on and emphasized her every curve. She was a masterpiece lying beneath me in complete surrender.

I watched her body straining, her hair mussed and sticking to her damp forehead, the tendons in her neck and shoulder stretching agonizingly tight. I outstretched my arms over her head, planting another kiss on her forehead.

"Oh, Ryan. I am ... close," she whimpered into my neck. She arched up her back, her hips meeting me, needing to find a way to pull me deeper into her.

I'd never wanted to consume someone as much as I did when I was inside her. And even this didn't seem close enough. I wanted to feel all of her. I wanted to possess her. Body. Mind. Soul.

I pushed down her legs and shifted my weight. It undid her, culminating in an overwhelming orgasm building inside us. A ragged breath was her only reaction. A guttural grown left my chest.

I was close, at the brink of my climax, when she said, "Please, please, please," again and again.

My cock turned rough and steady. Her hips circled, as savage underneath as I was above.

"I'm there. So close ... please."

"Anything you want, precious," I growled, biting into her shoulder.

She screamed as she came, her nails digging into my wrist, the taste of her sweet sweat on my lips. My voice turned hoarse and deep, something even I couldn't recognize, and with one last deep thrust, a powerful orgasm tore through me.

Twenty-Two

RYAN

"I always wanted to be a designer." Her words were nothing more than a whisper against my neck. I didn't realize when I'd dozed off after that mind-numbing sex until her words stirred me up.

"It started with designing my sisters' rooms. When their friends saw it, they asked me to help with theirs. Soon, I was helping every other kid on the block. I just finished elementary school, and soon, it became my summer vocation. My best friend, Virona, joined in just to hang out, but within a year, she started loving it, too. By next summer, we had our whole lives mapped out."

I lifted my hand, and she slowly sank into my chest. A soft smile graced her lips, though a shadow lingered behind it, like the memory held something ominous. I stayed quiet so she could continue.

"We were so proud of what we were doing that I told my parents one day," she said, her voice turning quieter now. "Mom laughed it off. Said it was a cute hobby. But this wasn't a hobby for us anymore. We'd poured two years into it. People loved what we created. We weren't charging money, but it felt … so real. Tangible.

Ours. By the end of middle school, we had everything planned—Harvard design school, internships maybe, moving to Manhattan when school was over. Virona and I together at a design school. It was our vision, our mission in life … until it wasn't."

"Wait—why? What happened?"

"Mom put her foot down. She told me it was time to come back to reality," she said with a hollow chuckle, her smile turning into something bitter. She was lying next to me, but she wasn't here. I was holding her in my arms, but her mind had drifted off somewhere.

"Why couldn't design school be a reality?"

She looked at me with a mocking smile. "Because it wasn't science. There's no future without science, apparently. Art could be a hobby, sure, but not a career. Not the perfect life they imagined for me."

"And you accepted that? Just like that?"

A dry laugh escaped her lips. "That's precisely what Virona said. She was so mad at me for giving up on my dreams without a fight." There were no tears, no trace of remorse, only a hollow edge to her voice suggesting a part of her had died that day and never found its way back.

My chest tightened with sudden, irrational anger. I didn't know where to aim it—at the girl who'd stayed silent, or the mother who hadn't listened, or at a world that decided dreams were only valid if they fit into neat boxes. What else had she gone through? And it struck me again how little I knew about her, despite her dominating my every waking thought.

I had taken over my father's empire, but I'd known since birth what I was going to do. No one had pushed me into it. No one had swayed my decision. I always knew what I wanted. There were no expectations weighing on my shoulders, no pressure to meet some legacy I didn't choose. I just knew. And I did what I wanted. Maybe the timing wasn't ideal, and everything had happened too fast, but I never had any doubt about what I wanted when I grew up. I doubted my parents would've stopped me if I had wanted to be something else.

Ivy had been raised with the same freedom, encouraged to do everything she wanted, from Harvard to dance schools. Nothing was off-limits. *Without dreams, there's no purpose in life*—those were my mother's exact words. We were taught to dream, to stretch beyond our reach, to chase something bigger than comfort or convenience.

It never occurred to me how lucky and privileged I was until now.

Support wasn't just spoken in our house; it was given freely. No hesitation. No conditions. Whatever we wanted, whatever made our hearts race, Mom and Dad made sure we had a shot.

"You hate me for not standing up for myself?" Risha asked without meeting my eyes. Embarrassment and self-loathing weighed her down. I saw a tear running down into her hair.

All the while, she had been hiding her vulnerability under that hard shell. Disappointments she had gone through and accepted what life threw at her. I'd seen her work and how good she was. Cristaldi party, her bedroom, Russo's, me stealing her idea and making Serata. So much more she could have been, if given the opportunity.

"No one can take your talent away from you." I peppered kisses all over her face until she came back to me and snaked her arms around my neck. Her hands moved down my back, and she rolled her hips over my cock until it started throbbing between us again.

This time, her kisses were wild. She pushed one hand into my hair and fisted roughly. She was taking what she wanted—a need for control over her life. Was that the only thing she lost, or was there more to it? *Leaving the doctorate program, pressure to get married* ... Every word echoed inside me. She was struggling.

I wanted to say she was beautiful, smart, talented, and so much more, but she knew that already. A confident woman who didn't need praise to know her worth. She needed control, and my body, to dull the pain inside.

I lay down on my back and let her take the lead. She straddled my hips, adjusting herself and fisting my semi-hard cock. Her eyes blazed with fire, and her body shuddered with lust.

"Take whatever you want, precious. I'm yours."

My hands held her waist. Goosebumps scattered all over her as my hands trailed from her hips and up.

"I want you," she said, closing her eyes and feeling my every touch. "You make me forget reality."

I want to be your reality.

I didn't say that out loud. How I felt about her was scaring the shit out of me, but saying aloud would definitely send us both running in the opposite directions. I wanted her happy. I wanted to see her smile. I wanted her to have the entire world and anything that her heart desired.

I wanted her to want me.

Twenty-Three

RISHA

I woke up in an empty bed, body sore, heart tranquil, and strangely clearheaded. Not a single thought clouded me, and for once, I was content. I just *was*. Present. Unburdened. And maybe that was the secret of living in the now. It came with its own quiet perks. No pressure. No expectations. No pretense. Just … me. The real me for once.

It had been a lifetime since I'd delved into that painful chapter of my life. Only Sri and Virona knew how crushed I had been when Mom had shut the door on my dream. Talking about it last night had dredged up every shadow I thought I'd buried. The sting of it, that helplessness, Mom never cared about what made me happy, never asked what I wanted. Sri always sensed my pain and told me to be strong. And Virona had stood by me as best as she could until when *she* had needed me—

Don't go there, Risha. Don't ruin this one morning you feel at peace.

Forcing myself to stay in the present, I glanced around at Ryan's room, half-masculine, half-teenage-boy's den. This wasn't him anymore, but somehow, it still felt like his home. Like the last remnant of a simpler time. He'd outgrown the room, maybe the entire house, but this space remained suspended in time.

I had seen the darkness reverberating behind his eyes when he'd opened the door. The waves of the past crashing into his present. He wasn't okay by a long shot, but yesterday, he had taken the first step in coming back home.

Unlike me, Ryan was strong.

And all the dark clouds had vanished when we'd started our little game. I wanted to believe I wasn't the only one content in our little bubble.

I turned to the clunky old clock perched on the nightstand, a far cry from the one he had in his studio, and saw the time. Six a.m.

Once again, I wouldn't be the first one at the office today. Strangely, it didn't bother me even the slightest. I was truly appeased.

Pushing the comforter aside, I walked into the attached bathroom. It was empty, just like the room, but contained that distinct scent of Ryan—worn leather and musk. The lingering fog on the mirror suggested he had already showered.

I picked up my duffel bag, which Ryan must have retrieved from the foyer where I'd left it.

I used the toilet, brushed my teeth, and took a quick shower without getting my hair wet. Then I changed into a moss-green turtleneck sweater dress with the hem stopping mid-thigh. I pulled my black knee-high boots up my legs and then ventured out to find the man I wanted to see.

I felt him even before I saw him. Stopping at the end of the long corridor, I took in his beautiful contour. Black slacks, a white undershirt, and fully concentrating on whatever he was preparing on the stove. The muscles of his biceps flexed every time he flipped something on the pan. I should know it by the smell, but my nostrils were still filled with his scent. He was whistling, and I wondered if he did that often. I didn't recognize the song, but his expression mirrored my own emotions.

Was I overthinking the whole thing going on between us?

Maybe.

I still didn't care. I was living in the moment.

As if sensing my presence, he looked up, and our eyes held each other for a beat before his face lit up into a full-fledged smile.

"Good morning, precious." He pulled a bar stool from the island and gestured for me to join him.

Pushing away from the wall, I walked up to him. "That's my nickname now?"

"You feel like one. If you don't like it, I have a couple of others ready." He flipped an omelet; now I noticed and walked over to the coffee machine. "Angel. Dollface. Sunshine—"

"Precious will do," I put a stop to his pet names, already liking the one he had given me. A simple term of endearment no one had thought of before.

He faced me, and a wicked smile touched his lips. "Minx. Vixen. Peach. Lovebug. Honeybee," he continued, his voice turning more playful with every name.

"Are you done?"

"Not quite."

"Go on then."

He straddled me with one arm and kissed my cheek. "Precious suits you."

I picked up the knife from the stand and started cutting the washed strawberries while I thought of a smart comeback. Nothing came to mind. A word of endearment, perhaps? Even that felt like an exercise my brain wasn't ready for just yet.

Instead, I said, "So, you can cook?"

"Don't keep high hopes; I haven't done it in ages." He slid a coffee pod into the machine and closed it. Removing the omelet onto a plate, he tossed some cut mushrooms into the same pan and drizzled it with oil spray and salt. I loved the way he concentrated on every part of the process, like his entire focus shifted into that one particular task.

And for the next few minutes, we concentrated on preparing our breakfast.

After switching off the stove, he went back to the coffee

machine and poured the coffee into two cups. I followed him to the other side of the island and pulled out a chair beside him. Lifting a forkful of omelet, he took a bite and praised his own handiwork. I did the same. It was good. Not too salty or spicy, with the right amount of paprika.

"What are you doing this afternoon?" Ryan asked.

"Meeting Cece for lunch," I said. I had seen her message when I'd come out of the shower. Mostly, we caught up during dinners, but it had been two days since we'd done that.

Ryan's eyes grew momentarily distant at my mention of Cece's name.

"We both have a past, Risha," he said earnestly, meeting my gaze with a steady intensity.

I nodded, letting him know I was right there with him.

"I don't give a damn," he continued, "but if you want to go over and dissect every relationship I've ever had, we can spend the whole day doing just that."

"That sounds completely unnecessary. And a massive waste of time," I replied, confused by the sudden detour.

He nodded in agreement. "That's what I thought."

"Do you ... want to go through my list of men?" I asked, uncertain where this conversation was even heading. Did I give him any indication that I wanted more than what we had? I wasn't looking for more, and Ryan seemed like a straightforward man.

"Unless there's a threat I should know about or some old flame you're still holding on to, I don't give a damn."

I released a breath, not realizing I'd been holding. "Nope and nope. Other than what I told you already, there's nothing."

"Good," he exclaimed. "Then let's not waste our present dragging the past into it."

"I couldn't agree more."

He shifted without missing a beat. "So ... full honesty—what do you think of this place?"

The sudden change of direction made my head spin.

Seriously, was I still caught in a haze of our night together, or was he moving at lightning speed?

I looked around. Every piece of furniture had so much character. I was sure every corner held a story of its own, but a nagging feeling gnawed at me. "Honestly, Ryan, home is made with people. This must have been a beautiful home once, but today, it lacks warmth. I blame you and Ivy for turning this into a museum."

Hurting his feelings hadn't been my intention, but he wanted my honesty, so that was what he got.

He exhaled, letting the fork drop to his plate. "I don't disagree. How do you feel about redoing this place? I want to move back here, but I don't want to live in the past."

"You're kidding, right?" Shock didn't even begin to cover what I felt at his bombshell declaration.

Asking for my thoughts at a restaurant was one thing, but changing the house he'd grown up in? The one his parents had built, piece by piece, memory by memory—no fucking way. That was far more intimate, way too personal. I wasn't equipped for that kind of transformation.

In fact, I wasn't equipped for any of it. This wasn't just about picking colors or rearranging furniture. This was the home where he had once shared laughter and loss, where every corner probably echoed with the lives of people he loved and memories he cherished. The idea that he trusted me with something so personal, so sacred—it didn't just scare me; it paralyzed me.

"This is my home, Risha. My house that I want to turn into a home again. I can't see myself anywhere else but here. But I can't live here with all those memories haunting me. Those beautiful memories I created growing up are now tainted by how everything also ended right here. I want you to help me turn those terrible memories into something new."

"Ryan ... I can't." I didn't even realize I was shaking until he pulled me into his arms. "This is an enormous responsibility on anyone's shoulders."

"That's why I think you're the right person. I trust you to do justice to this place and to me," he said softly into my hair.

But I wasn't nearly convinced. He thought too much of me when I was nothing. No one. Nobody.

"Even if I wanted to—and I'm not saying I will—I'm not equipped for this kind of change, Ryan. Having a vision for these designs is one thing, but doing the real work needs lot of experience, expertise, and technique, schooling ... No, I'm not equipped for this."

He kissed my forehead, my jaw, my cheek. I was convinced he had lost his mind, and he was determined to convince me otherwise. I also had a feeling he was already swaying my decision, because panic was one part of it, and saying no to an opportunity like this was another. My mouth and brain were in sync, but my heart was already jumping giddy.

"I'm not setting you up for failure," he said. "I see your talent and trust you more than you trust yourself. Vikki and you have similar taste. I want this to be your vision while she makes it into a reality."

"Who the hell is Vikki?"

"You'll find out when you come to my office."

I was hyperventilating because my heart and brain were fighting for supremacy, and I wanted it to stop. I wanted Ryan to stop before I changed my mind. Before I uttered the word that I would ultimately regret. "Even if I want to, I don't have the bandwidth to take on such a huge project."

He removed his arms from around my shoulders, and I immediately felt bereft. Handing me my coffee mug, he said, "First, you need to calm down and consider your options before rejecting it outright."

"Oh, fuck, Ryan. I hate you. You're dangling the sweetest carrot at the worst of time. I work seven days a week."

He chuckled and put one arm over my shoulders again, pulling me closer to him. He knew he'd almost convinced me when I heard my voice crack with a *but* or a *yet* after every sentence.

"I'm sure you'll figure it out."

"What if I screw things up?" I asked.

"Then you start over," he answered with complete ease.

"What if you don't like it? What if Ivy hates it?" My voice wavered.

He looked at me, calm in a way I envied. "I trust you. As for Ivy ... leave her room the way it is. Let her decide what she wants to do."

He wasn't helping my cause.

I squirmed and closed my eyes. He kissed me nonstop. My heart was convinced; my brain had already lost the battle. And Ryan's confidence seeped into me as if what he was suggesting was the most ideal, the most obvious ...

"This is my dream," I gushed out.

Twenty-Four

RISHA

I was riding a high so fierce that nothing could drag me down, not calls with furious customers, not Patrick's accusatory eyes, not even Cece's cautious reminders to tread carefully around Ryan. She'd told me he was driven, chasing success like oxygen, and his single-minded determination was his sole motivation. I told her that kind of purpose deserved admiration. Ryan wasn't following expectations; he was fueling his own fire.

She reminded me of the other side of the Hudson. My mother's persistence and my father's disappointments. She wasn't wrong. But she wasn't entirely right either. That chapter was shelved, even if temporarily. The only call I'd answer was from the one man who hadn't called me in five years.

To ease Cece's mind, I told her Ryan and I weren't exactly a thing. No labels, no promises. Just this moment, and whatever it meant while it lasted. Working on his penthouse was the icing I couldn't walk away from.

The rest of my day went by so quickly that, one minute, I was in the elevator to go out with Cece, and the next, I was heading out to meet Ryan and his designer, Vikki. I sent a quick text as I entered Ryan's building.

Me: Taking the elevator up.

Ryan: Come to my office. Vikki is running late.

When I reached outside his office, Bobby, his receptionist said, "His last call is running over, but he wants you to go right in."

Okay then. I guess I was the only one on time.

I found him at his desk when I walked into his office. I closed the door behind me while I heard at least three voices other than Ryan's short, "This is unacceptable," and "give me solutions."

When I faced him, a familiar twitch just above his collar gave away his tension. The urge to ease him took over as I crossed the space with a single mission. He looked up, and our gazes met. And just like that, a sense of relief washed over him.

"This is disturbing news, Peter. Why hasn't this come to our attention until today?" Alan's distinct voice filtered through the speakerphone.

"We were given false promises. As soon as Mr. McAlister and Mr. Branson left, those guys went back on their words," a heavy-voiced man said.

I dropped my purse and laptop bag onto the chair opposite his and walked over. His eyes raked me from top to bottom, devouring me. When I was a foot away, he pulled me into his lap and kissed me madly. His rough, unrelenting mouth and the press of his hands on my breasts sent goosebumps tearing through me.

I gave in to the heated rush, in him. My fingers pushed into his hair, forcing my tongue inside and taking some ownership of the situation. Our kisses grew deeper; our touches turned wilder. Consuming each other like this moment was all we had.

He grabbed my ass and straddled me around him. His hardness pressed between us, eliciting desires. It didn't matter that we were breaking all professional boundaries, that his entire office was buzzing with people, that his assistant was sitting right outside, or that he was on a conference call, accessing something that I couldn't comprehend but sounded serious ... I didn't give a damn. And he was losing himself in me.

We just *didn't care.*

I rubbed my pelvis against his hardness. His hands frantically roamed up and down my back. Pushing my dress up and over my head, he dropped it on the floor. Sliding the bra over my chest, his mouth moved immediately to my breasts. I sucked in a breath, trying to hold back a moan. He … didn't care.

He wasn't wearing a jacket or vest, but that wasn't enough. I yanked his shirt, buttons flying all over. I didn't care what the cleaners would assume. Maybe draw a conclusion of their own.

"Mr. McAlister, what do you think?" the heavy-voiced man spoke again. It stopped Ryan momentarily, but certainly not me. I rolled my tongue over his cheek and started sucking his earlobe.

"Contact the councilman and remind him about our arrangement," Ryan said. I was certain the man had already gone over the councilmen, officers, and arrangements, but he started over anyway.

Leaving my breasts, he tried to concentrate on the call this time. I rubbed my hips back and forth, needing the friction. A short moan slipped my lips when his hardness pushed into my soaked panties. He put one finger over my lips and whispered, "Ten minutes."

I couldn't give a damn.

I wanted to distract him. He did the same to me, pushing his way into my every thought since he had dropped me outside my office building.

Sliding off his lap, I sank to my knees on the carpeted floor. Boldly cupping his cock in my hand, I fondled him through his dress pants. When I looked up through my lashes, he seemed half-shocked and oh so fully aroused.

I unbuttoned his belt and zipper, and cooed in a whisper, "I'm bored, but you carry on."

I freed his hard cock and sucked in a breath. His crown dripped with pre-cum. I pulled his pants and briefs down his hips and thighs, and he cooperated without breaking our eye contact. The scorching heat in his gaze could melt an iceberg. I was at the front and center of his thoughts at this particular moment.

"Risha," he breathed out in a hushed whisper, his eyes hot

and tender. He cupped my neck, his thumb brushing over my jaw. "What're you doing to me?"

"Excuse me, Mr. McAlister, can you repeat your question, please?" the man from the other end of the call spoke again.

I stifled a laugh, covering my mouth before anyone heard me. Ryan cleared his throat and said, "Sorry, let's push this call to tomorrow. Bobby will reach out to reschedule." Without waiting for a response, he disconnected the call.

Heat seared his eyes as he leaned over and claimed my mouth. "You're going to pay for this."

"With pleasure," I answered nonchalantly. Wrapping my hands around his hardness, I licked him from root to tip.

***

Ryan opened his office door and crossed to Bobby. She gave him the name of a conference room, where I assumed Vikki was already waiting. He placed his hand on the small of my back and guided me forward. His touch was both possessive and intimate, sending a zing through every nerve ending. It was a jolt of awareness and a sharp reminder of how effortlessly perfect life could feel when we took the reins into our own hands. When we stopped thinking and just lived.

When I looked back at who I had been mere weeks ago, the change was staggeringly obvious. I barely recognized that version of myself. We were taking things one day at a time, and sure, this relationship might be temporary ... but right now, in this moment, everything felt exactly as it should.

Ryan was right about one thing: nothing in life came with guarantees. I wouldn't have known how right it could feel to be with him unless I had taken that leap of faith. And I was glad I had. Every minute spent with him felt like a moment dipped in bliss. No regrets. No fear of what came next. Just me, him, and the rare peace of finally living for myself, even if it was temporary.

We turned the corner. My smile matched his.

"Ready?" he asked.

I was.

That was until Ryan opened the conference room door.

All my feelings came crashing down to a shocking halt as I came face-to-face with a ghost from my past.

Twenty-Five

RISHA

I paused mid-step, making Ryan stumble beside me. The room felt instantly void, a shock that no warning could have lessened. My confusion ricocheted off the seemingly never-ending space as the walls started closing in on me from all sides.

"You all right?" Ryan asked, then followed my gaze to see what I was looking at. Rather, who I was looking at. "You two know each other?"

"Vir—"

"Vikki Banerjee, hi." Virona recovered quicker than I did. Walking up to us, she extended her hand while speaking to Ryan. "We went to school together but ran in different circles."

The blow hit me straight in the chest. Every buried memory rose like a cloud of smoke. All the days we'd spent together whispering secrets in the dark, building dreams and scraping them until new dreams emerged, were now just another thing lost to time. Another weight I carried inside.

Cece was my friend now. She knew this version of me—polished, composed, guarded. But Virona had known the *real* me. The raw, unfiltered, unformed girl before the world had asked her to be someone else. Virona hadn't just heard about my heartbreaks; she'd *seen* them. Virona hadn't just listened to my guilt; she'd *witnessed* it and observed the subsequent transformation. She'd seen me turn my pain into armor, as innocence faded into silence. She'd always been there for me. She'd known me at my worst and also my truest self.

But when the tables turned and my best friend needed me …

Of all the regrets I carried along, betraying Virona sat at the top. A regret I couldn't get over, an outcome I couldn't change. Not a single day had gone by when I hadn't thought of her. I had rehearsed countless scenarios of our reunion, but nothing could have prepared me for what was actually happening.

She deliberately chose not to know me, incinerating the tie I'd already severed.

Ryan's grip tightened around my back, but I couldn't tell if Virona's words had convinced him or left him with a follow-up question. Because the woman who had walked in with him minutes ago had vanished, and the one standing beside him now was staring at a ghost.

"I remembered you by a different name," I said, taking the hand she had extended toward me.

She pulled it away as soon as I held it.

Tucking all the jumbled feelings inside, I tried to pull myself out of the sinkhole.

"People change; it's only apt to change names, as well." Leaving us behind, she walked over to the other side of the table and pulled out a chair for herself. The signs were small, almost imperceptible, but it was starkly clear. She was distancing herself. Not even a *"how've you been"* or a *"hey, I didn't know you live here."* Instead, a total brush-off.

Though after everything I'd done, did I expect anything different? Did I deserve anything different?

Probably not.

Hope was a cruel thing, though. It kept you going even when there was nothing left to hold onto. It stayed long after reason had left the room. It let you swallow your guilt and make you imagine a different tomorrow.

"Thanks for meeting us at such short notice. Now that you two know each other, we can get the introduction out of the way." Ryan's voice broke into my rumination as I forced myself to join him. "How is MoxTo coming along?"

"It's crawling," she answered with a sigh. The dramatic roll of her eyes was my first glimpse of the girl I once knew. Time had passed, her name had changed, but so much of her still remained the same. The way she wiggled her nose before launching into an explanation of the pushbacks—it was so her. Tucking that stubborn strand of hair behind her ear, the one that always annoyed her, but never enough to grow it out—familiar. Her fingers drummed that old rhythmic *tap, tap-tap, tap,* on the table, like she was trying to drown out her own discomfort without giving it all away.

Her gaze stayed locked on Ryan, but I noticed the flicker. She was watching me. Just like I was watching her.

Her hair was shorter now, a straight razor cut that hit just above her shoulders. Sharper. Bolder. And the tattoo peeking from under her sleeve was new. It clashed and belonged at the same time. Her rebellious streak took her to places I could never be. There had to be a story behind that tattoo, and God, I wanted to know it.

She was also leaner now, physically harder somehow. But the distinct confidence she carried was impeccable. In ripped jeans and a T-shirt, it almost seemed she didn't owe anyone an explanation. Typical.

I wanted to ask her everything. About the years I missed. The pain she bore. The people who stayed, and those she lost. I wanted to peel back the layers and find my friend again.

"Risha?" Ryan touched my elbow to get my attention. "I was saying the lemon vines at Serata was your idea, which Vikki brought to life. You two have a lot in common when it comes to design."

Because we grew up reading the same books and magazines for three fucking years.

"It was a vague concept." I couldn't take my eyes off her. "I love what you've done with the place! You're extremely talented."

"Thanks. It was my original idea until Ryan shot me down," she responded, averting my gaze.

"I agree. Vikki did suggest orange trees, but I shut it down," Ryan mentioned.

"Citrus trees. I said citrus trees," Vikki corrected with a tsk, and I couldn't tell if it was my presence—or the fact Ryan only agreed after I'd suggested it—that had her so flustered.

Ryan chuckled. "Fine, fine. I'm not trying to take away your thunder. You've more than proved yourself on every project."

"I'm not a kid, Ryan. I'm not looking for praise. I know what I can do," she answered, dismissing his light-hearted comment.

Completely unaware of the simmering tension between the woman beside him and the one across, Ryan kept switching between Virona's praise and banter. I loved seeing this casual, relaxed side of him, as well. No inflated ego, no god complex, no invisible line separating him from the people who *technically* worked for him. Just a man with solid character and a knack for making everyone feel like they mattered.

Ryan cleared his throat, pulling my attention back to him. "Since MoxTo is *crawling*, and you're looking for a challenge, I have another project that you wanted, anyway."

Virona's eyes flickered, but she remained guarded.

"I want you and Risha to design my penthouse. Her vision, your execution. Consider it a joint project."

It didn't take too long for her to respond—in annoyance, of course. "I'll lend you my junior designers for the job."

"That's not what I asked, Vikki." Ryan's voice tightened slightly. Just a hint, but it was there.

"That's what you'll get, Ryan," she snapped, making it abundantly clear where she stood.

"It's not an ask," Ryan clarified. The playfulness in his voice had dissipated.

"But it's a refusal from me, anyway." Virona got up, ready to end the meeting. Beside me, Ryan did the same. I wasn't sure whether I should follow suit or let them hash it out. "Your penthouse was *also* my idea, and now you want to give it to *her*? What is she, your girlfriend or something?"

"That's none of your business." Ryan's jaw flexed as I looked from one to the other.

"Ryan," I lightly touched his arm to pull his attention, "My work leaves no time for anything else. Let Vikki have the project, I'm sure she'll do more justice to the house than I ever could."

"Who the hell do you think you are to give me anything?" She pushed her chair so far back that it crashed into the wall and returned. "I've spent years studying this. I went to a freaking school and came out top of my class. And suddenly, you want to claim designing it was your idea to begin with? Why are you even here? Is this even your world to be in?"

Shock hit me. My face burned hot, chest tightening with a sting. She resented me. And she didn't even try to cover her feelings.

I had no claim over what she had spent years training herself to do. This was a hobby I had chosen *not* to pursue. I'd already made my bed with my fate, so why was I still restless, wanting something I had given up so easily?

I shouldn't have agreed to Ryan's outlandish proposal. I should have made an excuse as soon as I saw who was on the other side of the room. Virona would never forgive me. Not in this lifetime. Not in the next.

"Can someone tell me what's going on here? I'm clearly missing a link you two are privy to." Ryan looked from Virona to me.

Before I could excuse myself from this project, Virona moved toward the door. "You should ask your *girlfriend*."

Ryan turned to me. Although his face remained inscrutable, the pulsing veins in his neck left little to the imagination. "Do you want to tell me what the fuck that was about?"

I slumped back in the chair with a heavy sigh, deciding to

come out clean. "*Vikki* is Virona. We were best friends until I betrayed her in the worst possible way."

"What the fuck!" He pinched the bridge of his nose, clearly exasperated by the drama that ensued. "What are the fucking odds?"

One in eight million, I thought. The entire population of this island. And seriously, what were the odds?

"She was right, though; I lack talent. She should be the one taking on this project, not me."

"That is neither of your decision to make. And I don't remember asking for anyone's adv—"

The door opened with a heavy force before Ryan could complete his thought.

Alan barged into the room. If I thought Virona and Ryan were furious, I was thoroughly mistaken. The fury was turning the old man's face bright crimson, like he was getting the worst kind of stroke.

"You left in the middle of a bloody call? Didn't I explain how important this was?" he spoke to Ryan, completely ignoring my presence. "Fucking commissioner was on the phone with us. Do you know how long it took me to arrange that meeting?"

"He was on the call, but not onboard with us," Ryan answered.

"So, you convince him, charm him, or pay him off—do whatever the hell it takes to get that damn inspection and license on time," Alan snapped. "First, you leave Miami in the middle of a shitstorm, and now you bail on an important meeting? You just flipped off your top execs when two of them are already tired of your antics."

Clearly, I was stranded on a minefield with no way out. Ryan dropping that call was solely my fault. I wanted to distract him because he seemed tense, not realizing how important that meeting was. And the Virona shit was squarely my fuckup.

"I can't do business in fear, Alan. Let them leave," Ryan said with finality.

"Are you sure about that? Because if this turns into a regret, you'd have no one to blame but yourself." Alan turned to leave the room.

"I've seriously started to wonder who the fuck owns this company," Ryan rapped out. "Every employee thinks they can talk back and walk out on me."

Alan turned on his heel, not calm, but trying. "I've set the meeting back with all the players in Miami. You're not leaving this office until the matter is settled."

The door shut behind Alan, and a heavy silence fell.

Before I could apologize for interrupting his meeting and setting off this chain of clusterfuck, Ryan told me, "Fix things with Vikki."

"Ryan, I think Vikki should—"

"I need *you* to do the penthouse. Now, do what you have to do to fix things."

And he stormed out.

I was the cause, and I was the consequence. The whole damn fallout.

Twenty-Six

RISHA

I managed to reach my apartment without breaking down. Without looking for Cece, I went straight for the shower in my attached bathroom. To wash away the past. To muffle the sound of my cries under the liquid curtain. To make sure no one saw just how broken I was.

Seeing Virona again, after all this time, was almost as painful as when our friendship had died. We'd both grown up, and yet we were still sixteen.

I knew she would never forgive me after what I'd done. And yet, there was a foolish part in me that hoped we could forget, forgive ... move on. I thought time could erase damage, that memory would blur the sharp edges. Of course, I had been horribly wrong.

Wrung out and empty, I finally dragged myself out of the bathroom and crawled under my comforter. And just like that, my body shut down.

I felt him in my dream.

Ryan's lips brushed my forehead. His arms cocooned me. His

warmth pulled me back from the dark. Even in sleep, he was rescuing me from my painfully ugly scars. He was taunting me with those soul-deep kisses, his hands moving over me like I was something sacred. Every inch of me leaned into him, wanting more, needing him like my dying breath.

My name on his lips was a whisper of need and reverence combined. And when his tongue slid into my mouth, when our kiss deepened and stretched into forever, I felt him in every cell of my being. I felt him everywhere. His weight. His heat. The scrub of his beard. The uneven breath against my skin.

It wasn't a dream. He was here in flesh and blood, every inch of him. And I held onto him like he was the only thing keeping me from drowning.

"Ryan, it's you," I whispered onto his lips, scared I'd wake up and the dream would shatter.

"Better be me, precious. I don't want you kissing anyone else like this." His humor lacked mischief, but his return relieved my uncertainty.

"I thought you wouldn't come."

"There's no place I'd rather be," he mumbled. His kiss intensified, and his hands reached my breasts through the tank top. "I came back as soon as I was done with the meetings."

Pushing the top down my shoulder, he took my breast in his mouth. His desperation contradicted his calm tone. How the day had turned from perfection to disastrous, I couldn't even fathom, but an apology was irrefutable.

"I'm sorry to disturb you in the middle of your call. It was unprofessional—"

"Don't apologize for being you." Ryan propped up his torso so he could look into my eyes. The nightlight created a dim halo. "You have every right to my time and body, just the way I have on yours."

"Virona was right; I shouldn't be here. My life is a mess, Ryan, I shouldn't be pulling you into this mire."

He hovered over me. His elbows took his weight, and his

erection rubbed against my boy-shorts. He lowered his mouth and traced the seam of my lips, taunting me and proving to me what this chemistry meant.

"Can you stay away from me?" he asked.

"I want you. So fucking desperately." I cried out. The thought of not seeing him, not talking to him, not feeling him around me —inside me—left a hollow ache so deep it echoed endlessly.

Virona had been right, too. I had started weaving a dream I knew would unravel before it could ever be real. Another dream crumbling. Another need unmet. Another road never to reach the finish line.

"Stop thinking, precious. I don't care what she said." He read my thoughts. "You remember our promise? Now. Today. This moment. Don't let anyone else take that away from us."

"But she's right."

"She is not. I can bring someone else who's more than willing to work with you."

I shook my head as much as his face would allow. "I can't do that to her, Ryan. I left her once. I can't take away what she wants. I pretend to be a designer while she is a real artist."

"Don't think less of yourself. And to me you're everything. This time with you is the most precious thing I have. And I refuse to waste another moment talking about someone else." His face lowered, cutting the light.

His kisses turned wild, sucking all disturbing thoughts away. The more I opened my mouth, the deeper he went. His body pressed until all I felt was his muscles and our labored heartbeats. He wanted me with a maddening intensity, and he didn't stop until I was in that moment with him. Only remembering him. Only wanting him.

Giving in to this moment, surrendering myself to him ... I was starting to forget everything that lay outside this room. Goosebumps traveled like wildfire, short-circuiting my every nerve ending.

"You crave me."

"I do." There was no denying when he could see right through me.

"You feel empty without me." He was mocking me now because he knew the control he had over me. Ryan consumed every part of my brain. If it were just physical, maybe I could try to ignore the need, but my heart, soul, and body ... they were all attuned to him.

"Yes." I breathed him in. Gripping his hips, I arched upward to feel his hardness.

He pushed my legs apart and settled in between. His erection was hard and hot, pushing through my entrance. My panties soaked with his, and I rubbed myself against him to find some friction.

He pushed the elastic to the side. His two fingers lightly caressed the length of my entrance.

I couldn't stop touching him—down his back, over the curve of his hips, back up again along the sides of his chest. My nails dug into his muscles, holding him tight in the anticipation of taking him completely, filling me with him.

He pushed gently against me, spreading me open as he slipped just the tip inside and held it there. His fingers dug into my inner thighs as if he was resisting going wild. His lips moved, his tongue running between my breasts, along the exposed skin of my chest. His torturous mouth shifted between nibbles and lashes, moving over one puckered nipple to the other. Left to right. Right to left.

The room echoed with my moans. Ryan called my name, as if it were a plea and a prayer to him.

I touched him frantically, gripping him whatever way I could get him. I rocked my hips, trying to get more of his cock inside my soaking heat, hoping that with just a push, he could slide inside me.

The tables were turned, and tonight, he was in control. And I didn't know what he was thinking because his whole concentration was only on my breasts.

"Ryan, please, I want you ... inside me," I cried out.

A rumbling chuckle broke through him when our gaze locked.

My eyes pleaded, my voice filled with frustration as I raised my hips to take in his girth. His tip grazed the entrance, but he wasn't open to give in. He was only prolonging the torture to prove how much I wanted him.

Dammit. I knew I wanted him. Right now. Right at this moment. I. Wanted. Him.

My heels rocked up and down his calves, finally locking at his waist. "Please, Ryan, I am dying here."

I meant it. Literally.

He grabbed my wrists and pushed them over my head. Then he lowered his head so our foreheads touched and finally pushed deep inside me. He mumbled something I couldn't comprehend.

I was breathless as he moved in and out of me. With every thrust, his speed was turning faster than the last.

"I can't get enough of you, Risha, and it's obvious you want me too."

"I want you every day," I whispered against his neck, unable to hide the depth of my feelings for this man. It was never just physical between us. Physical, I could handle. But with Ryan, since the day we'd met at Cece's party, there was more to us than just this fiery chemistry.

We moved in perfect synchronization. Our sweaty skin sliding against skin. I raised my hips to meet his every thrust. My locked legs against his waist pulled him deeper. I was getting close, my cries becoming louder.

"Give it to me," he voiced with a ragged desperation, commanding and pleading all at once.

I closed my eyes and called his name. No oxygen was left in my brain. I was filled with him to the brim. Pleasure swamped me, and the telltale sign of an orgasm built tight in my belly.

"I want to feel you to the core, precious. Milk me and take me to the hilt."

"Oh God, Ryan." I squeezed him inside me, and I felt him

growing harder than a rock. He deepened his strokes, lifting me off the bed with every thrust. My orgasm crested deep inside, waiting for him to join.

I clenched him wildly, unable to hold back. Nothing in the world felt as good as this.

I let the rush build inside us, overpower us, consume us, crush over us ... and together, we let it go.

Twenty-Seven

RISHA

I woke up to hypnotic blue eyes looking down at me, undeniable proof that last night hadn't been a dream. Every sore muscle in my body agreed, humming with the memory, his every touch ensued and pleasure imprinted on my mind to last forever. Either he was inside me or I was on top. We used our bodies to convey what we couldn't articulate.

We had hardly slept, and yet I was more refreshed than ever.

The glaringly obvious problem though, remained unaddressed between us. And right next in line was my un-fucking-professionalism. I had no idea what had gotten into me yesterday. Regardless of what Ryan had said last night, Alan was furious. He didn't bring up the cause, but it was starkly obvious I was *the* distraction.

"Before we dive into your questions, I owe you an apology for my behavior at your office. It was—"

"Fucking awesome. Mind blowing hot. I don't think I can ever work at my desk without thinking of you on my lap ... on your knees."

His words sent me into a spin. I had loved every second of it, too, but we weren't in our twenties doing irrational things. Like getting caught with his dick in my mouth. His door had been unlocked. Bobby, Virona, Alan—anyone could have come in.

With his wicked smile intact, he carried on, "I appreciate you getting me off that call."

"You were stressed." I knew what I had seen on his face, in the desperation of his kiss.

"You're the only one who noticed." He wrapped his arms around my waist, drawing me closer as I leaned back against the headrest.

"It didn't help if you had to get back on the call right after." When he didn't respond, I got the drift. "Do you want to talk about it?"

Taking my hand, he rubbed his thumb over my knuckles, thinking. The effect of that touch knocked me out, and butterflies floated up my belly. This touch wasn't sexual. It was intimate.

"There was an arson at our Miami resort that's scheduled to open by the end of next week. The cops lost the guy who started the fire, but that's not even our biggest problem. We need a clean inspection certificate from the health and safety department before reconstruction can begin."

"And I'm guessing you flew back for me without resolving that?" I asked, another crisis unknowingly weighing on my conscience.

He nodded, still tracing lazy strokes over my knuckles. "Nick was handling it, so I left. We were told everything would be sorted right away. But, of course, nothing ever goes that smoothly. As soon as Nick stepped away, they changed their mind."

"Should you go back and handle it yourself?"

He lifted my hand to his lips, brushing kisses along my fingers. "Yeah. I can't give anyone a reason to doubt my commitment any longer."

"You shouldn't." I nestled closer. "I'll miss you while you're gone."

"Me, too. I was trying to avoid going back, but it will only drag things out. No one wants to push back the opening. It'll hurt our reputation." He drew me against his chest, his mouth warm against my hair and neck, but his mind was at the Miami crisis.

I nodded against him. "How long will you be gone?"

"Not sure at this point. I'll keep you posted. Now, tell me what happened between you and Vikki."

As soon as he mentioned her name, the energy inside me shifted to a hesitation that had always lingered when it came to her. A regret I'd carried quietly for years.

"I thought you two were best friends. When did it change?" Ryan pulled me out of my internal thoughts.

"High school," I whispered. "She was Virona Banerjee when I knew her."

"She still is," Ryan interjected. "Vikki is her preferred name. I didn't make the connection when you mentioned her."

I nodded slowly. "Growing up, we were inseparable. Her house was like a second home to me, and I was closer to her mother than my own. I know it sounds strange, but—"

"It doesn't. We connect with people in ways that defy logic or even bloodlines. It's all about the wavelength, our emotional frequency. Some people just get us without needing a label or explanation."

I nodded again, agreeing with Ryan and letting his words settle over me like a balm.

"Her parents were unhappy, but they stayed together for years, probably for Virona's sake ... I don't know. And eventually, they divorced. Amicably, I think. I don't know what triggered it, but it crushed her."

I could still see her face from that time—eyes swollen from crying or sleep deprivation, voice tight with anger and confusion. Everything used to make her upset. Everyone had let her down.

"She didn't care if her parents were unhappy. She just wanted them together. She wanted that normal family life."

"Kids can be selfish," Ryan murmured, trying to piece together a version of Vikki he might have never seen before. "But she was in high school by then; did it really matter that much to her?"

"It mattered more because she was surrounded by traditional conservatives where divorce meant failure. She became an outcast overnight. And I"—my voice cracked—"I betrayed her. Because my mother told me to."

Ryan's expression mirrored the shame I'd been carrying. He'd always seen me as composed, strong, successful. Now he saw the real me and what I'd buried beneath that façade. Tears streamed down my face.

"I wasn't allowed to see her anymore," I admitted. My voice turned thick, and my throat closed up with pain. "My mother volunteered in my school to make sure I stayed away from her. I watched Virona fracture every single day, and I did nothing. I let her be completely alone."

"Your parents ..." Ryan began then stopped, unsure of what to say.

"Pre-historic monsters?" I offered with a bitter laugh.

He huffed. "I don't think the concept of families was even invented in those times. I was thinking of traditionalists."

I exhaled. "My mom's whole world revolves around outdated traditions. The world has moved on to the twenty-first century, but she's still clinging to those old values—academic excellence, family honor, the perfect picture of a happy household—even if it's rotting inside. Her idea of perfection is so rigid, so specific, and I was always expected to fit in it, without questions. She knows exactly how to twist things, turn the house into a pressure cooker. Either way, we all end up doing what she wants just to breathe."

"And your father?" he asked gently.

"Silent. Growing up, I idolized him. Our relationship was made of this unshakable bond, at least until controversy tainted it. He would rather watch me drown than stand up and support me." A tear slid down my cheek. "And so, I wasn't there for Virona when she needed me the most."

A raw and jagged sob broke free from my chest. I covered my face with my hands and let it all out—for the spineless girl I'd been, for the friend I'd abandoned, for the time I could never get back. I didn't even realize when Ryan pulled me tighter into his arms until I found myself sitting on his lap, clinging to him like a lifeline.

"It's not too late, precious." He stroked my arms, trying to quiet my sobs, tracing slow, soothing circles as my chest rose and fell.

I was a storm of emotions, torn between the past I'd been handed and the future I longed for. Wrestling with the identity forced on me and the one I desperately wanted to claim.

And Ryan just held me, letting me untangle my emotions without a word. Sometimes, that was all we needed—someone to hold us and be there.

He moved sideways, holding me between his arms, and then I heard a soft rustle in front of my face. When I opened my eyes, I saw him holding a piece of paper between two fingers. Without a word, I took it from his hand and unfolded it. A ten-digit number on one line, followed by a six-digit code on the next.

"What is this?" I asked.

"Vikki's cell phone. She's working at MoxTo's thirteenth floor. The code is to get inside MoxTo." He smiled.

"Can't you see she hates me?" That ship had sailed decades ago. What part of yesterday didn't he understand?

"And she'll continue to hate you until you make things right."

I started to protest, but he silenced me with a single finger over my lips, continuing his speech.

"You were wrong then, but now you have no excuse not to fix what's broken."

"Ryan, no, I can't. I can't face her."

"Didn't you say that was your biggest regret?"

"Yes, but—"

"How will you ever move forward unless you fix your past?"

"You don't understand. She'll never forgive me." I was

shaking as panic gripped me. I avoided confrontations. Rather, I succumbed even at the thought of it.

"And what if she does? What if she is waiting for you to apologize so she can move forward too? What if she is waiting for her old friend back? Don't you want to find out? Don't you want to work with her on the penthouse to relive old memories?"

"No. No. No." Each no was louder than the last. Panic seized my chest. "You're asking too much of me. I'm not good at this."

"This is your shot to right the wrong. Let yourself free of regret," he insisted.

A sob left me. "You have too much faith in me, Ryan. I'm weak inside."

"I disagree. You're looking for an escape, but deep down, you don't want to be a coward. Sweetheart, you're standing in your own way of who you are and who you want to be. You know you messed up. Now it's time to face the consequences. That's the first step to easing your conscience."

My voice was slightly above a whisper, and my eyes felt heavy and wet. "I thought of her every day, but I never came up with what I'd say to her."

Once again, he tightened his grip around my waist and pulled even closer to his chest. He rubbed his lips across my forehead and said, "You have the entire day to figure that out. She'll be at MoxTo until six."

"What? *Today*?"

His deep chuckle rumbled between us as he cradled me in his arms and carried me to the bathroom. I heard a yes between our kisses.

After gently setting me down on my feet, he turned on the shower, letting the water warm. I caught sight of my reflection in the mirror and winced—puffy eyes, dark circles, a shadow of the mess I felt inside. I didn't understand what kept Ryan here, especially after seeing who I really was.

He joined me at the vanity. That was when something else caught my attention. His toothbrush sat next to mine; razor, bottle of cologne next to my makeup. Personal things that made this space his, too. I remembered the duffle bag I had glimpsed earlier; the suits hanging neatly on the rack. At the time, I hadn't thought much of it since we were too wrapped up in talking.

Yesterday, I had left my stuff at his penthouse. Today, he'd brought his things into my apartment. In that unspoken exchange, I realized we weren't just living in the moment; we were barreling from the present into the unknown—together.

Twenty-Eight

RISHA

The constant calls and endless meetings weren't enough to quiet the churn in my chest today. Even the controlled chaos of the engineering floor couldn't shake the unease sitting heavily in my gut. I held that scrap of paper like hope wrapped in fear.

Ryan had told me to fix things, but he hadn't told me how. And, *pfft*! If I knew how to fix relationships, my dad and I wouldn't have wasted years in silence. Dad had never learned how to express, and I had never learned to reach out.

For the engineer in me, fixing a broken device was easy. If it didn't work, I could strip it apart, rewire, start over. Relationships didn't come with schematics. Unlike machines, we humans were made of heart and emotions. Our hearts broke, our emotions shattered. Disappointment taught us lessons, and self-preservation guided us forward.

I had broken Virona's trust in the worst possible way. If I hadn't been able to forgive myself, how would she?

At least a hundred times, I dialed her number, thumb hovering, heart pounding, only to press cancel instead of connect. At least fifty times, I considered driving to my parents', burying myself in that suffocating quiet where Ryan couldn't find me. Silence had taught me how to disappear in plain sight

But I wasn't fifteen anymore. And the worst had already happened. She hated me. Period. From here, we could either stay in this state or move forward. And for once, I didn't want the easy way out. Ryan believed in me, and I didn't want to prove him wrong.

When the office clock neared noon, I walked out. The determination that had flickered all morning dimmed as I entered the six-digit code in the MoxTo building's keypad. I unlocked the door and took in the changes since my last visit.

The space was packed with bubble-wrapped furniture and chandeliers waiting to be unveiled. Every taped corner and edge screamed opulence and luxury.

I stepped into the functional elevator and hit thirteen. A week ago, I'd stood in this exact spot, not knowing what the hell was happening between me and Ryan. A part of me wanted to detour and relive that night. The desire in his eyes. The silence that burned. And then that explosive orgasm. But that was just my fear trying to avoid confrontation.

I forgot all the rehearsed apologies when the elevator opened on the designated floor. She was sitting on the floor, legs crossed, completely absorbed in a massive square of paper rolled on the edges across the carpet.

In a single year, she'd turned my dream into hers. In three more, she'd made her decision to be a designer. She'd achieved what I had only talked about. And God, she looked stunning in her element. Loose black slacks cropped mid-calf, an oversized top slipping off one shoulder, bearing a flash of red tank and half a tattoo that covered one arm.

Virona sensed me and looked up. "What are you doing here?" she asked flatly.

"How have you been?" I pretended this was a normal exchange.

She barked out a dry laugh. "Fucking great. Can't you tell?" She gestured around, and I took in her creation.

Crimson carpets. Crystal chandeliers. Black wallpaper with velvet roses rising off the surface, a rectangular mirror, a tall vase waiting for something bold. Everything around us demanded every bit of attention. It was a pure reflection of its creator.

"It's breathtaking," I said before I could stop myself.

Her lips curled. "Huh. You'd know."

"Not as well as you do," I replied, skimming the little details now. "But I'd say the room directory would look better on a gold plate instead of black."

"I've already ordered the correction," she said without missing a beat. "They messed it up."

"You still run your projects like a bullet train?"

She exhaled slowly, not amused. "Don't pretend you know me."

"And what if I want to know you again?"

A pause, and then, "Go home, Risha."

I walked deeper into the lobby, feigning interest in a crystal vase, mostly just trying to steady my heartbeat. "I met Sri last weekend."

Virona clicked her tongue. "She's a fool for going back to that suburbia. She doesn't belong there."

"True," I agreed one-hundred percent. "She's too progressive for anyone there to understand her."

"And you're different from them?" Her voice sharpened, and her eyes closed to a slit.

The jab landed close to my gut, curling me inward. I winced. "You really think I'm the same as them?"

"You made your choice, showed your true colors."

"I was trying to keep the peace." I shook my head, denying her accusations.

"Call it whatever you want, Risha. It was still a cop-out." Her eyes cut through me. "You're just a polished version of your mother. At least she isn't living a double life and pretending to be someone she's not. But you ... here, you're the smart, independent woman and back home, you're one nod away from marrying whoever they pick next."

I sucked in a breath. Even after all this time, she saw right through me.

"You didn't just say that."

"Oh, I haven't even started."

"Take that back." I outwardly raged while inwardly crumbled. Self-doubt unexpectedly swallowed me whole, making me question who I really was. "You don't know me anymore."

"And I'm not interested in knowing you, either. Say what you're here to say and get out. I don't want to see you again."

There was no easy out, so I gave her the only thing I had—the truth.

"Fine. I'm here to say I'm sorry. For everything. For not being there when you needed me most. For when I saw you in pain and didn't reach out. I was weak. Maybe I still am. But I'm not my mother. You're right about my double life, but this is who I am now. The girl on the other side is pretending. And I'll do whatever it takes to prove that." Exhaustion hit me on every front. I wasn't lying, right? To her, or to myself?

"I'm proud of you, Virona. You did what I never had the guts to do." I turned toward the elevator and hit the button, jamming it repeatedly, ready to be done with this.

"You only had to stand up for yourself, Risha." Her voice broke through just as the doors cracked open. "No one should force you to be someone else."

"I wasn't as strong as you."

"My only strength was having my best friend beside me." Her voice trembled behind me. "Do you know what it was like those years alone? Carrying all that shit inside, with no one to tell?"

"And you think it was easy for me? Watching you disappear piece by piece and hating myself for not doing anything?"

"Don't make this about you!" she snapped.

I swiped at the pooling tears and faced her. "You're right; it wasn't about me. I failed you, but don't think I forgot you. I thought about you every single day. I just ... couldn't face you."

My voice dissolved into silence. The kind that swelled behind your ribs like a held breath that was never let go.

I turned to leave again because, really, there was nothing left to say. Whatever Ryan had hoped for, he was wrong. This relationship had drifted too far from shore, and no tide was strong enough to carry it back.

"You can try to make it right."

I froze at her words, knowing exactly what she wanted. It wasn't mine to offer, but I'd bend heaven and hell to make Ryan hand her the penthouse.

Virona stepped closer, trying to read my expression.

"I'll talk to Ryan about the penthouse. I don't want any part in it," I said with absolute determination.

"You have to work to earn my trust."

"I will, however long it takes," I said, a little confused.

"We'll do the penthouse together."

"You're serious?" Now, I was stunned.

"You heard me. We do this together, and you apologize every day until I believe you."

"Done." There was no second-guessing, no other thought in my mind except that I needed her forgiveness.

"My schedule's tight. When I say I need you there, you show up before I do. No excuses."

I should've asked what kind of commitment she was demanding. I wanted to tell her, her schedule couldn't be worse than mine. Instead, all I felt was the rush of getting her back.

"I'm in."

Rushing into my office, I headed directly to the conference room, already five minutes behind schedule.

"Excuse my tardiness," I said to Marcus and Patrick, seated on opposite sides of the table. I slid into the chair between them. "Lunch hour traffic is the worst."

Marcus agreed with a nod. "You didn't miss anything. I was updating Patrick on the madhouse I've been caught in."

"Aren't we all in some sort of madhouse?" Patrick responded as I fired up my laptop.

"The difference is you guys are thriving in your madhouse, and I'm struggling in mine," Marcus said, shifting his focus to the projector screen linked to my laptop. "Let's get this started."

And for the next hour, I did just that. I walked him through what we had done so far and where we were heading. With the majority of my team focused on this project, we were working on all cylinders. I fielded Marcus's questions, and his growing admiration for our work became unmistakably clear with each passing moment.

With his last question answered, he leaned back in his chair, fingers laced behind his head. "This is serious progress, Risha. We weren't expecting you to hit these deadlines. Honestly, we thought they were a stretch to begin with."

Patrick jumped in before I could respond, flashing his typical PR smile. "We always deliver full-proof efficiency, every time."

Ignoring Patrick, I said to Marcus, "Which is exactly why we need to slow down. The late nights are bleeding into weekends. My team's stretched thin, and it's starting to show."

Marcus opened his mouth, but Patrick cut in again.

"We've always delivered, Risha. That's what we do."

"And it's unrealistic," I responded in a clipped tone. "I'm responsible for my team's well-being, not just the projects and clients' expectations."

A heavy silence settled as Patrick's icy stare clashed with my defiance. If he thought he could dictate my team's efficiency and hours indefinitely, he didn't know me at all. Marty needed time to bond with his son. Zoe wanted to see the world. Holidays were around the corner. I'd promised them balance, and I intended to deliver.

I also wasn't about to back out of what I'd promised Virona. A lot was on the line—a friendship to mend, a promise to keep, and a dream I wasn't ready to shelve. Ryan gave wings to my dreams, and I wanted to fly.

Marcus cleared his throat and reached for the two envelopes beside him. "That's actually why I came in today." He slid them across the table toward me, each marked with a handwritten name. *Sylosis. Risha Verma.*

"What's this?" I asked.

"Your bonus, as promised," Marcus answered. "I wanted to deliver it in person and thank your team directly. And also to tell you our engineering timeline has shifted by three months."

I blinked, unable to find the right words. "You're sure?"

"I was sure an hour ago, unless you want me to call and confirm?" Marcus said.

Patrick cleared his throat, letting us know he was still there. "What does that mean for Sylosis? Will this change the rate? The bonus structure? Because I've accounted for every contingency in my budget and, frankly, Risha springing this on us—"

"If you ever doubt whether she's good enough for Sylosis, know that our doors are always open to her." Marcus didn't let him finish. He turned to me and continued, "I've no doubt you'd be an excellent fit in any department of your choosing."

Warmth spread through my chest at knowing at least someone in this room had my back. "Thanks, Marcus, but I'm not bailing on my team. They're why I show up every morning."

"We could build a department around you," Marcus said. "We'd give you the autonomy you deserve."

Patrick's smile thinned into a line. "Let's not get ahead of ourselves. Risha's not going anywhere."

"Then treat her like the asset she is." Marcus spoke without hesitation, but his eyes held a critical stare. "Word is, she's the star of this firm."

Patrick's jaw flexed. "Believe me; we know. That's why she gets away with stunts like this, or showing up late to client meetings."

Marcus chuckled, waving him off.

I reached for the second envelope. "What's this one?"

"Ah, right," he said, as if remembering. "That's a personal thank you."

I peeled it open. Two tickets to the New York City Ballet's Spring Gala stared back at me. "This is ... this is too much."

At my side, Patrick bristled. "Personal gifts aren't appropriate."

"Everything is appropriate where Nixus is concerned," Marcus said without blinking. "And if we can sign big bonus checks, we can hand out NYCB tickets as well. You can't just go out and buy them, so there is no price tag attached."

Marcus got up from his seat, and Patrick and I followed suit. Honestly, I was still reeling from the gift. Two tickets that couldn't be bought.

He shook my hand, nodded curtly at Patrick, and turned to leave. Then he paused at the door and faced us once more. "Oh, and rumor has it we're not the only company waiting to snatch her up."

The moment he left, the air shifted, with Patrick's gaze turning bitter. "What the fuck was that?" he asked, as if I had answers.

"I have no intention of leaving Sylosis, if that's what you're asking," I clarified. The last thing I wanted was a rumor or a replacement.

"You didn't think of talking to me first about your team's mental health?" Skipping my earlier comment, he dove right where his ego was bruised. "You made me look like an asshole in front of our biggest client."

I closed my laptop with a frustrated sigh. "I've mentioned it six times so far. You have a habit of ignoring what you don't want to hear."

"Yet, you never took such a bold step until now. The roses, long lunch breaks, going over me and directly approaching the client? Care to explain what's going on?" He walked to the door, right on my toes. "Don't bother answering, your distraction's here," he sneered, brushing past me.

Ryan stepped closer and raised his brows. Whatever had transpired between me and Patrick wasn't private anymore.

"Did I walk into a firestorm?"

"Don't worry about him," I said, clutching my laptop. "My boss just got reminded that I'm a hot commodity and is perturbed that I told Marcus we're dialing back the crazy hours."

Ryan grinned. "Ouch. I could feel the steam from the hallway."

I rolled my eyes and led him down the corridor. "That man can't stand me."

"There's always a reason," Ryan hinted. "Did you ever try to find it?"

I pushed open my office door and dropped my laptop onto the desk with a sigh. "I think I've hit my limit with human feelings for today. I met Virona this afternoon."

His grin deepened, spreading all the way to his magnetic blue eyes. "She called me. I'm proud of you."

Something inside me tangled. I couldn't remember the last time anyone had ever said that to me.

I cleared my throat. "Is that why you're here?"

Ryan hesitated. "Yes. No. Mostly, I just wanted to see you. Though there is another reason."

"Well, don't keep me in suspense, Mr. McAlister."

He leaned casually against the doorframe with a lopsided smile. His gaze pinned me, and I stopped breathing. God! The effect this man had was impossible to understand.

"Can I take you out? On an official date?"

I tried not to smile but failed. "Someone's in a good mood. Don't you have to be in Miami?"

He straightened his back, moving one hand into his side pocket. This man knew how to pose, like I always thought of him —GQ Sauve. "I sent Nick instead. I wasn't ready to leave just yet."

I crossed my arms, amused. "Then it's a date. I've got something to share with you, as well."

Twenty-Nine

RYAN

My hand stayed on her back as we wound our way through the narrow alleys of ancient Kyoto—a Ninja's Den tucked into Tribeca, styled as though we'd stepped through a portal into the old-world. Barrels were swapped for barstools, paper walls sliced clean down the middle by samurai, and the uneven cobblestone paths guided a thin stream of water through shallow gutters along the edges. It was dimly lit, eerie with theatrics, and I cursed under my breath for choosing the least romantic spot in the entire fucking city. What the hell had I been thinking when I'd made this reservation? The woman beside me deserved candlelight and champagne, not shoji doors and artificial smoke.

Her dress clung to every curve as if it had been sewn onto her like a second skin. Black, sleek, and utterly sensual, with a bold sweep of white slashing across her chest. The satin sculpted her form, folding over her arms and cascading into a short train behind her. She was not only beautiful; she was the epitome of sexuality. Everything about her was elevated by elegance. I'd seen a thousand women in a thousand dresses, but no one even came close to Risha. A unique woman and, for now, utterly mine.

I hadn't been on a date in years, but I knew how to make an impression. With Risha, I was off balance, out of my depth in the best and worst ways. I couldn't think of anything extravagant enough to impress her, so I had brought her somewhere that mattered to me. I used to come here with friends when I wanted to forget the world and just be.

With Risha, I didn't want to conjure perfection but remain true to myself. Someone worth knowing without being proven.

The hostess stopped beside a white-brick alcove and gestured us toward a table tucked between two wooden benches. I turned to Risha, who was analyzing the place with the same intense, reverent attention she gave to every structure she came across.

Her sharp inhale as my fingers touched her skin was all the invitation I needed. The electricity between us came to life, crackling, waiting to ignite. Holding her arm, I pulled her into me, our lips just inches apart, suspended on the edge of surrender. She caught my hand in hers, lacing our fingers together, grounding me in her.

Our first official date.

Her body melted into mine. She slipped her free hand into my hair. Her lips—warm, soft, devastatingly perfect.

I tangled my hand in the mane of her curly waves, pulling her closer. I cupped her back, tracing fire along her spine, and pressed her tighter into my chest. She teased her tongue over mine, and I deepened the kiss, chasing every breath she gave me. She opened for me willingly, beautifully, and I took all of her—the sighs, the gasps, the taste of Risha.

Her back bare beneath my palm, I couldn't stop touching her, couldn't stop kissing her. Time disappeared until reality nudged back in. A polite throat clearing snapped us out of the moment.

I opened my eyes just in time to see the server bowing slightly, her gaze respectfully lowered. "We'll begin with the sake and first course shortly."

With one final deep and reluctant kiss, I eased away. I helped

Risha into her seat then pulled down the heavy curtain that looked like a rag but felt weighted. A farce. "I know this probably isn't the most conventional first-date spot—"

"Are you kidding me?" Her eyes gleamed. "This is fucking brilliant. A masterpiece tucked in the middle of the biggest concrete jungle. Every part of it is crafted with ancient history. Do you know how rare that is in commercial design? And did you notice the smoke trickling out of the gutter? Or those rats in the corner?"

I couldn't stop grinning. "You know those aren't real, right?"

She laughed and leaned across the table conspiratorially. I instinctively leaned in. "When I bent down to fix my shoe strap," she whispered, "I touched one. They've wrapped rat skins over brass molds."

I jerked back as if electrocuted. "You touched a gutter rat?"

"Technically ... yes."

"Great. We're going to be patient zero for the return of the Black Plague."

She rolled her eyes at me, the corners of her mouth twitching.

I smiled at her hint of irritation when she couldn't find a comeback.

"So, it seems things went well with Vikki," I said, changing the subject.

Her lips turned into a wide smile. "It's a long way home. I don't know what I've done to deserve another chance from her, but I'll take it."

"Everyone deserves a second chance, precious. You just need to ask."

Risha nodded at my words and wrapped her hands over mine. "Thank you for everything ... The old me would've retreated back. Today, I feel relieved."

"I'm glad you feel that way." I felt joyously overwhelmed that I could fix something in her life. She was beautiful and smart, and now I knew she wasn't perfect. It only made her human.

I removed a small box from my inside jacket pocket and set it in front of her.

"What's this?"

"Open it," I said.

Her brows knit together in confusion when she did so.

"Vikki wants to meet you at the penthouse first thing tomorrow." My explanation didn't help her get the gist. I inclined my chin toward the key in her hand. "Figured it'd be easier if you stayed there. One thing you should know about Vikki: she doesn't know when to call it a night."

Risha chuckled, tucking the key within her palm. "She really hasn't changed much then. But this is ..."

I pulled her free hand and kissed her knuckles. "No second thoughts, no regrets. Remember?"

She nodded hesitantly, wanting the same thing, but something always made her cautious. If only I could solve that mystery.

I heard a distinct throat clearing before the curtain was pulled back. A server in his black ninja uniform and a samurai holder strapped around his chest bowed to both of us. We shifted back, making space for him to serve our warm sake and deconstructed Sakizuke, the chef's special that had put him on the world map.

Risha busied herself with her chopsticks.

"I didn't check if you like Japanese before bringing you here." I admitted.

Risha's smile was genuine. "You did good, Mr. McAlister. It's one of my favorite cuisines. Now, tell me the reason for our date tonight."

"God, you're presumptive. Why can't I bring you on a date for no reason at all?" I threw on a fake pout.

Her eyebrows arched as her hand, holding the empty chopstick, froze. "Instead of a text, you showed up at my office. You already gave me the key to the penthouse, but the veins on your neck are still ticking ... Spill it out, Ryan, because I know you still have something up your sleeve."

Since Mom, she was the only person who noticed that faint pulse. What was she doing to me? Stirring something I didn't know how to name. It wasn't just easy between us; it was seamless, effortless, magnetic. We didn't need to try.

Beneath all that flow of familiarity, something unsettled curled in the pit of my stomach. Because for all we were, we still weren't anything defined. And suddenly, that absence—of label, of certainty—haunted me more than I wanted to admit.

Keeping those wild thoughts aside, I pushed through our conversation.

"Fine, you got me there. Something important is coming up in Spring, April-end to be precise. I want you to be my date."

She raised an eyebrow and started processing the timeline. I knew my asking was outside the terms of our *relationship*. We had decided to live in today, and everything I was throwing at her—from designing the penthouse to being my date in five months—was out of that spectrum. I was stacking the pieces for her to understand this wasn't casual and we weren't ending anytime soon.

"Another anniversary?" she asked. I shook my head, and she said, "Shit, it's your birthday."

I chuckled, deciding to stop her from imagining further. "It's a black-tie gala event, Promise Beyond Loss. Usually, I skip it, but I'm the keynote speaker. I don't want to go alone, so ... will you ...?" I hesitated.

"Of course, I will, Ryan. If it's important to you, I'll be there."

I spent the whole day figuring out how to persuade her to something so far off. And here she was, agreeing instantly without giving another thought.

Nonchalantly, she went for the fish in the bowl. Why did everything seem so easy with Risha? Even the silence between us didn't need a filler.

"Ryan, I want you to join me for something, too," Risha said, clearing her throat.

"Anything, precious," I said without hesitation.

Her next smile filled the entire space between us. "I received a gift from Nixus, two box-seat tickets to NYCB."

A dark pit opened up in my gut to swallow me whole. Risha didn't see the shift, and continued on.

"It's been my dream to go there since I saw their performance on TV as a kid. Dad and I spoke for days about it, but there were no tickets available, or at least the ones we could afford. Will you join me?"

Her eyes filled with expectant hope.

My mouth reacted before my brain could come up with a tactful answer. "I can't."

"But you just said *anything* I want." The sting of my refusal quickly became her disappointment. This was the first and only thing she had asked. One fucking thing. And I couldn't give it to her.

"I can't, Risha—"

She raised her hand to stop me. "You don't need to explain."

I couldn't stand her disappointed look, but the fear was crippling me from the inside, not letting me breathe, let alone explain. A decade since the incident, and I was still buried in the past.

"I am sorry."

"Don't worry about it. It was a stupid request anyway." She gulped down the entire sake. Her inscrutable expression heightened my sense of regret. She could read me so easily, while I couldn't.

"Will you not come to the gala with me then?"

She glared at me, barely concealing her frustration. No tears, no anger, but pure frustration. "This is not tit-for-tat, Ryan. I don't know your reasons, but I respect you enough not to question them. And, it's not reason enough to fight or argue, or tell you I won't go with you somewhere that is important to you."

I took her face in my hands and kissed her with everything I had. Before she could understand, I filled her with ardor. Love couldn't even come close to how I felt about her. And no fear of uncertainty or newness of this relationship scared me from holding back these feelings.

I was madly and irrevocably in love with her.

Thirty

RISHA

The next two months vanished in a blur. I woke to Virona ringing the doorbell and was the last to bed after locking up. It felt like working two jobs—and the damn adrenaline rush left no space for sleep. I partly blamed Ryan. Not that I was complaining.

He made me feel wanted, like I belonged on a pedestal, and then proceeded to worship every inch of me.

I was riding a high that refused to crash. Limitless and without a boundary. If happiness had a shape, this would be mine. Like standing barefoot on a rooftop during sunrise, heart racing, arms open, daring the sky to swallow me whole. Because, when it spat me out, I would still be part of this world. My perfect world.

We spent the holidays together, working during the day and wandering through dazzling holiday markets at night, sharing steaming cups of cider while standing in lines for Stroopwafel. Work was part of our lives, so we powered through a few hours before letting the city pull us outside. The streets glittered with lights, shop windows glowed like snow globes, and even the chilly air felt warmer with Ryan beside me.

We spent Christmas Eve with his friends, but the rest of the season was ours—late-night dessert runs, stolen kisses under every Christmas tree we walked by, and little traditions that felt like they belonged only to us. By New Year's, it felt less like the city was sparkling and more like we were.

When the holiday season ended, we eased back into our previous routine.

It didn't take long for Virona and me to slip back into our old rhythm. No, she hadn't forgiven me yet. Yes, we bickered over petty things—design mismatches, clashing palettes, stubborn sketches. And yes, she never missed a chance to remind me that she had the degree and I didn't. In the end, we settled it the way we always had: rock, paper, scissors.

Today, my phone rang mid-conversation, cutting short Virona's jabbering about the master bath tiles. I tried to locate the phone amidst the chaos on the kitchen island—swatches of velvet and leather, chipped paint samples, a measuring tape coiled like a snake, and the blueprint of the penthouse half-buried under our crimson sketchbook. The island had unofficially become our command center, cluttered with the beautiful mess of a redesign in progress.

I finally spotted its flashing light underneath it all.

Fishing it out just before voicemail kicked in, I murmured, "Sorry," already stepping away. "I have to take this one."

As I walked toward the vast glass wall framing the skyline, I lifted the phone to my ear and said, "Hey, sweets. How are you?"

"You won't believe what I'm about to tell you." Sia's excitement practically vibrated through the phone.

"You want me to guess, or should I let you have the stage?"

"Yes. No. Don't guess—I want to say it." Her voice climbed higher with each word. "I. Got. In." She screamed the last part so loud I had to yank the phone from my ear.

"Holy shit! You did it!"

"Yes! Yes! Yes, I did!" Her joy exploded through the line. I could almost see her spinning through the living room, arms flailing with giddy disbelief. "I want to come for another campus visit. Can we grab lunch?"

"You bet." I grinned, swept up in her wave of happiness. I couldn't believe that, in six months, she would be a subway ride away from me.

"Okay, I'll send the date I can take off. Now wait, Mom wants to talk to you."

Before I could even respond, she passed the phone over.

I pinched my eyes shut and braced myself. Though we'd spoken a few times in the past months, our conversations had been extremely clipped and base level practical.

"Hey, Mom."

"You heard the news, right?" Her voice brimmed with pride, and I couldn't help but smile. Columbia had been Sia's dream. "Now she wants a huge graduation party and a new bike for college."

I laughed. "She's earned every bit of it."

Sia had worked late nights, early mornings, and participated in sports she barely liked just to make sure her transcript was airtight. At one point, she'd maxed out her honors courses, chasing excellence like it owed her something. I never doubted her, but she'd been trying to prove herself to a world that only expected excellence. So now, if she wanted a party that could be seen from space and a sleek new bike? Hell yeah, she deserved it.

Then Mom's voice cut through my thoughts. "No one's going to show up to her party if you keep skipping theirs. Can you come this weekend for Ari Auntie's event?" Her tone was pointed and precise, and her aim was dead center. Guilt.

I sighed. "I can't, Mom. I've got pending deliverables."

When I turned, I caught Virona watching me out of the corner of her eye. She gave the slightest shake of her head—subtle, almost imperceptible, but I noticed.

"Raj is flying in from California. He wants to see you—"

"Mom! Stop," I cut her off mid-sentence. "I've already made

myself clear on your matchmaking attempts" I hissed, making sure no one else could hear me.

"You're making a mistake," she snapped. "He called me specifically to ask about you."

"I. Am. Not. Interested," I whisper-barked, each word heavy with finality, so there was no room for doubt. "You're forgetting what Daddy said."

"He said it in the heat of the moment and regrets it ever since."

I doubted there was any truth in her statement. My father was not a man of impulsive words. If he said something, it came with deliberation. Telling her that, though, would only ignite another argument. And I wasn't ready to sink into her vortex of manipulation. Not when my life was finally moving forward.

"I'll come home when Daddy asks me to." I hung up before she could respond.

I walked over to the island, currently buried under today's hard work and half-eaten sandwiches, to find Virona wrapping things up. I appreciated her silence on my conversation. If asked, I might've lied to avoid confrontation. My new self would have laid out the truth, making it clear things remained the same on the other side of the Hudson. To avoid lies or confrontation, I offered, "Don't worry about this. I'll clean up once we're done."

She gave me a knowing smile. "Let's call it a night. We've finalized pretty much everything. I'll ask my assistant to place the final order. Tomorrow, we'll start with the kitchen remodeling and work our way in."

A team of people already worked in the daytime as we completed the last of the designs. Staying here during the work might seem chaotic to some, but I found a peace that was hard to explain.

"I can't believe we made it through without murdering each other."

"Don't be so dramatic, Risha." She smirked. "Our ideas never clashed. You just argued for the heck of it."

I smiled and looked down. "You still know me better than anyone."

"It seems that way … unfortunately."

When I glanced up again, her expression had softened—no challenge or argument, just genuine warmth.

"I haven't seen Ryan this happy before," she said gently. "He's an incredible boss. Driven. Grounded. Respectful. Ridiculously focused. But now he smiles in this effortless way, like it's second nature. You're the reason behind that. He wasn't brooding before, but now when he laughs, it's like something lights up from within."

I was caught off guard. Because the feeling was mutual. I was the moon drawing light from a star that never dimmed. Ryan made me feel seen and celebrated. Whether it was a bouquet in a shade that matched my blush or a surprise lunch delivery when I barely had time to breathe, he made sure I knew I was on his mind, even when we were apart.

He was present. Not just in body, but in spirit. Not just when we were together, but when we were apart.

"You've changed, Risha." Virona's voice pulled me back. Then she stepped forward and did something I hadn't expected to happen. She hugged me tight. "It's a good change. Stay like this."

And just like that, without another word, she turned and walked out of the penthouse.

After clearing the mess spread all over the kitchen, I entered Ryan's bedroom. He was still on his laptop, working. Focused and freaking shirtless. In just a pair of black silk pajamas, he looked every bit a supermodel right out of GQ. The slightly mussed hair over his forehead was my doing, a remnant of when he stepped out of the shower this evening and silenced my half-hearted protest in the most reckless, delicious way I couldn't deny. We hadn't been alone, but my protest had been too weak to be heard. He was insatiable in bed or otherwise, like his penis could feel my presence before his eyes even scanned me in a room.

Not complaining, the effect he had on me hadn't dimmed in the slightest. His presence itself made me feel like a goddess. His touch electrified my every living cell. His voice was the melody I wanted to hear, and his kisses were my lifeline. I was getting addicted to him, his body, his—

"Are you going to join me or make me wait?"

"But ..." How did he know I was here?

He pushed the laptop onto the bed and headed straight for me. His hypnotic eyes burned me from the inside. It'd been months, and he still left me breathless, like the day we first met.

"GQ Sauve."

"What did you just say?" He tilted his head, half-amused, half-intrigued. His steps slowed down, but he moved closer, nonetheless.

"When I first saw you ... at Cece's party, I named you GQ Sauve. You were so incredibly handsome ... so mesmerizing."

My breath hitched when he wrapped his arms around my waist and pulled me closer. "And yet, you left with no intention of finding me," he complained, his lips inches from mine, teasing me with his breath.

I held his biceps with one hand to steady myself, and the other moved over his chest. His shallow breathing and deep inhales were just a promise of how this night would end.

"I'm glad you found me. I wouldn't have known otherwise how it feels to be ..."

"Don't hold back, precious." His lips brushed over mine, sending tingles down my spine.

"With you," I finished. "You make me happy."

If happiness had a shape, this would be mine—barefoot on a rooftop during sunrise. Ryan was my sun that never set.

Thirty-One

RYAN

The best part of my day was waking up to her, distracting her from early morning work, hearing her giggle, taking a shower together, and then getting ready as a couple. You got it. I found myself another workaholic. But no one was complaining here. Definitely not me.

We understood each other's demands at work and accommodated each other's schedules however we could fit. These little blissful moments in the morning and using each other's bodies all night long were our only escape. I was greedy for her, wanting more. I started this penthouse project to keep her close, but it was keeping her busier than I had hoped. Happy, but fucking engrossed to the point her nights bled into the mornings, and mornings stretched into nights.

Looking at her reflection in the vanity, I asked, "Are you up for a weekend getaway?"

She dropped the blush case into her makeup bag and searched for something inside the pile. This bathroom had a double vanity with his and her sinks, but it wasn't big enough for all of Risha's beauty products. I also didn't know one person needed so many.

"I can take a weekend off. I'm sure Virona—*Vikki* wouldn't

mind," she responded as she removed a black and gold lipstick case.

I pulled her until her back rested against my chest. Our eyes met in the mirror, and I blurted, "Why haven't you ever asked to move into the master bedroom?"

She turned around and smacked a kiss on my cheek before walking out. "I like this room. Even though you've outgrown it, it still feels like you."

I followed her into the walk-in closet. Even that was a quarter size compared to the master suite. I didn't know what I did to deserve her, but everything about Risha screamed right. *She* felt perfect. *We* felt right.

As I drew closer, I noticed her fingers tracing the NYCB tickets she'd had for weeks before they dipped further inside her purse. One bloody thing she'd asked, and I couldn't even give it to her.

"My parents were returning from that concert when a drunk driver hit their car."

This time, the words didn't choke me. The dull pain was still there from that day's memory, but it wasn't enough to drown me or make me react. Today, it was nothing more than a fact, which didn't have a painful trail of lingering sadness.

"Ryan." Her voice was barely a whisper. She left her purse and came closer. "I'm sorry. I didn't know."

"I loved them so much ... No amount of time can take those memories away from me, but I also want my future to define me, not my past." *And you're helping me*, I wanted to add. "I'm trying to move forward."

"Take as long as you need. There is no set time for grief."

I nodded. It still didn't help that I couldn't give her something she wanted. "You said you wanted to go there with your father. Why don't you go with him?"

She pursed her lips and hesitated for a few seconds. "It's different between us now. We hardly talk to each other."

"It only takes a moment for the world to change right in front of your eyes."

"I know … believe me, I know," she agreed, like she had experienced something similar, but did she really know what I was trying to say?

What if there were more layers to her? What if I was only scratching the surface while assuming I knew her well?

I wasn't sure what came over me when I asked, "Have you ever loved someone, Risha?"

She shrugged as she removed a black dress from the hanger. "Love is a weighted feeling. An unreasonable emotion that's demanding and needy, and I have nothing worth offering."

"It doesn't have to be," I said, taken aback.

She laughed dryly and busied herself getting into the dress. "Then what is it? Blindly agreeing to everything? Or push your expectations even if it makes the other person unhappy? Or is it the demand of time? I don't want to be in love if the expectations are so screwed up, so overbearing, that the fun is taken out of it. I want to be in a relationship where my opinion matters and a conversation takes place before any decisions are made. If love means manipulating your loved ones to get what you want, then it's a stressful game of chess I'm not equipped to play.

"If love is choosing one person over the other, I don't want that either. And why do people have to fall in love? Why can't they rise above with someone they care? Respect, space, and just being there for no other reason than just wanting to be. That's what I want. Not love."

I was reeling and trying to understand the woman in front of me. "Is that why you are with me? Because there is no commitment or expectation?"

She busied herself with her boots without meeting my gaze. "I like that there is no label to whatever we have. No expectation, no future to work toward. Just today. Now. We live in the present, and it's liberating."

Her words hit me like a sledgehammer dropped dead center of my chest. Was that what it was? No future? No expectation? I was so deep I couldn't imagine a future without her. Everything we had right now, right at this moment, was what I wanted permanently for us.

I wanted to take her to the gala, not as my date but as my girlfriend. I was in love with her, so why couldn't I openly express my feelings? Why couldn't I tell her what I wanted? How I felt?

A selfish desire grew in me, wanting her to love me, want me, and be with me more than *now*. But her idea of love threw me completely off. And it again took me back to the same question I'd been trying to suppress: how much did I really know her?

I tried relentlessly to focus on work—that day, the next, and the day after. Every evening, I left the office with a firm resolve to tell her exactly how I felt. But when I met Risha, everything between us moved so seamlessly that words seemed needless. Superfluous.

She was right. Even without a label, what we had was already more. Something rare and absolutely whole. The two magnetic puzzles connected with their pairs, so why topple the balance or invite unnecessary chaos?

And yet, a part of me craved that label.

"I hope you're monitoring the Vegas situation," Alan broke in after finishing the call. After Nick had smoothed out the Miami situation, the gala had gone as planned. I had flown down for the night for appearance's sake and returned as soon as I was no longer needed. So now, Alan had already moved on to the next project. It seemed he couldn't finish a project even before I started one. "Though those contractors aren't our headache, if things escalate, our project will stall. We don't need another bleeding expense."

I didn't have direct employees in Vegas, but that didn't mean I could wash my hands of problems. If they worked for McAlister

Group, they became my responsibility. I wasn't as worried, though.

"I had a call with the union leader already. Everything should be resolved now," I said.

He nodded, moving on to the next thing, and then the next. "You heard about that nasty storm? Boston lost multiple power grids. I hope Ivy is all right."

"That property has backup generators and twenty-four-seven security. I wouldn't let her live in just any building," I said dismissively. She was, and would remain, my priority.

"It's not the building I'm worried about."

I unlocked my phone just as our next call with the Miami resort manager started. Alan took the lead on our end. I went online and ordered everything Ivy might need for the next month. I'd be hearing about going overboard, but there was no such thing as too much when it came to my little sister's well-being.

When I left Alan's office and headed toward mine, my phone buzzed inside my jacket pocket. I pulled it out with reluctance. Three messages from Kat that morning had gone straight into the trash, like all her other messages since last year. Engaging in any conversation meant giving her hope, and that was the last thing I had in mind.

My screen lit up with a photo of Nick from our teen years. That boyish playfulness frozen in the image had long gone. Now he called for work alone. Something had shifted. Something inside him had hardened. He was either aloof or too busy chasing the impossible.

After graduation, we had all sailed off in our separate boats and on different currents, chasing our own dreams and conquering personal fears. My dreams had been changing slowly, shifting and dissolving; my future had taken new shapes. The things I had once believed didn't carry the same weight. My ambition alone no longer felt enough.

A future. A life. A home filled with new memories and happiness. I wanted more than just proving myself to the world.

"Tell me," I said, picking up the call.

"I wanted to run MoxTo's grand opening dates by you." The biggest fucking news of the year, and he said it matter-of-factly.

"What do you have in mind?"

"I just got off the call with marketing. We are looking at the first week of June. It gives us enough time for press and other logistics."

I waited for the relief to settle in, but it didn't. I tried explaining the unease, but no particular reason surfaced. Perhaps the waiting had lost its excitement. Perhaps the obstacles were turning me into a pessimist.

"I expected more excitement." Nick broke into my thoughts like he could read me.

"Sorry, I was just ... thinking. This is great news, though. June sounds good."

"Indeed," he murmured. "I'll set up a meeting to go over the next phase. Taber has to take over bars, restaurants, clubs, and the two spas. I can have marketing contact journalists around the world and make sure our hotel is booked for the entire summer. Can you make sure construction and interiors are done on time?"

"I got it," I replied, the unsettling feeling persisting.

I was about to disconnect when Nick cleared his throat.

"Anything else?"

Pausing briefly, he inquired, "Could Mindi manage MoxTo?"

Melinda Conner—Mindi, as she liked to be called—was Nick's latest fling. She managed one of my hotels on Fifth Avenue. A luxury hotel, though nowhere near the scale of MoxTo. She was smart, capable, and reliable. But I had my doubts about her running something three times the size of the largest hotel she currently oversaw.

I believed in giving chances ... *if* they came to me directly. Mindi didn't. Instead, she had climbed into bed with my friend and business partner. And now her real intentions were starting to show. But then, Nick wasn't the type to ask for favors, so whatever this was, it must have taken some convincing.

"Don't let your personal problems come to work," I told him before disconnecting the call and dialing Vikki. She might need to switch her team around, making sure MoxTo took priority.

She picked up on the third ring, and I updated her. She told me her team was already working on the seventy-eighth floor.

As much as Risha needed to make amends with Vikki, something told me Vikki also wanted her friend back. However, her clipped answers and temperament indicated something wasn't quite right.

"Can you put me through to Risha?" I asked.

"She's gone," Vikki answered tersely.

"What do you mean, she's gone? Where did she go?"

She tsked with palpable irritation. "Why are you asking *me* questions? Isn't she *your* girlfriend?"

She wasn't, but I didn't need to give that clarification to anyone.

"Instead of questioning my relationship, why don't you tell me what you know?"

She muttered something under her breath. "All I know is her father called, and five minutes later, she left without a word."

That explained nothing. "So, you didn't ask where she was going?"

"I'm sorry, Ryan, but I don't usually interfere in other people's lives. Especially not in their dating lives."

My stomach dropped. "I don't appreciate riddles; tell me what you know." I emphasized each word through my gritted teeth.

Her dry laugh only heightened my frustration. I didn't realize I was pacing back and forth in the lobby until Bobby said something. I marched into my office and slammed the door shut.

"You really don't know her, do you?" Vikki asked. Her words hit me like a gut punch, stealing the air right out of my lungs. "She does anything and everything her parents ask her to do."

Why the hell was she talking in circles? "I know she and her father were at crossroads, but I never asked for details."

"I like you, Ryan. Not because you're my boss, but I genuinely like you. But you're either too naïve or willfully blind."

"Come to the fucking point, Vikki."

"The point is the woman you're dating lives two separate lives. One that you see and the one she really is."

"Where is she?" This time, I asked with authority. "And do not give me some bullshit that you didn't pry. So, tell me, where did she go?"

Thirty-Two

RISHA

Sliding out of the cab, I smoothed my hands over my black turtleneck, straight down to the waist of my jeans. Today, I hated my father, my mother, my entire life. But most of all, I hated myself for doing this—showing up to something I didn't want, hiding from someone who didn't deserve to be kept in the dark.

A part of me splintered, but I didn't stop. I walked straight into the black hole, fully aware of what it would cost. A relationship without a name that felt more real than any other relationship I had ever had. But my father's voice steadily echoed that was impossible to ignore. *Don't be so stubborn, Risha, and don't make a big deal out of a dinner. If he can fly all the way from San Francisco, I'm sure you can find an hour to see him.*

His expectations had always shaped me, bent me, broken me. And yet I followed without a fight.

I stepped into Chadz and walked up to the maître d'.

"Risha!"

I turned at the sound of my name and saw Raj. The man who refused to let go of the possibility of us.

Growing up we were acquaintances. He lived in California now, but we'd crossed paths at a party a few months ago, chatted casually, and laughed over small talk. I hadn't thought much of it then. Clearly, I had been wrong.

An inch taller than me, lean and fit, his muscles outlined by a snug, navy-blue V-neck and well-fitted jeans. He hadn't always looked like this. As a kid, he'd been soft around the edges. Now he was logging serious hours at the gym, so he flaunted it.

"I'm so glad you could make it." He came closer for a side hug.

"Dad mentioned you were in the city for work?"

He led me to a table set for two. Formal, a little too intimate. Unlike all the dates I'd been pushed into by my mother, this one felt curated.

"Yeah, I wrapped up a meeting with investors and came straight here. I heard you wouldn't be able to make it to my parents', so I figured we could catch up in the city."

Great. I groaned inwardly. One thing about South Asian families was that they were overly intrusive. Period. No regard for feelings or boundaries, no consideration of where to draw the line.

I wanted to prove Virona wrong. I wanted to show I could stand up for myself, and against my parents'. But I was wrong. I'd been lying to myself all this while. I caved the moment my phone lit up with one word: Dad.

What had I really expected from him? That he'd take my side? Stand up for me instead of his wife? Once again, he had failed me, and I had given in to their unreasonable demands.

"Your mom also said you've been buried in deadlines. Even working weekends?"

Just fucking great. What else had she shared? My goals? My blood type? My next of kin?

"Yeah, I'm under a bit of pressure," I said, keeping it vague.

He nodded, opening the menu. I mirrored him even though I had zero appetite.

"I get it. Happens to me all the time. I can't even remember my last real vacation."

I looked up. "Don't you run a unicorn startup with multi-million-dollar funding? And you're here; isn't that technically a vacation?"

A grin spread across his face. "So, you *do* remember our last conversation?" When I didn't respond, he continued talking. "I came for my parents' anniversary and some investor meetings. And—"

He paused as the server arrived with a bottle of red wine and crab cakes.

"I hope you don't mind," he said. "I ordered ahead. I was starving after that four-hour marathon of a meeting."

So, he *was* genuinely here for work, and I was an afterthought. That somehow made this easier, and some of the inside knots untwisted. We placed our dinner orders, and the server disappeared.

"It's all right. I was with my colleague when Dad called. I'm not really hungry."

"Sorry if I pulled you away from something important." His apology seemed genuine.

"Don't worry about it. It's not your concern." I had lost Virona once again, and so had Ryan ... but I couldn't pin the blame on the man in front of me. If anything, I was to blame for not standing up for myself.

He dove for the food after filling our wineglasses. "So, what're you working on right now?" he asked right before putting a forkful of crabmeat in his mouth.

"Unfortunately, I sign NDAs on all projects. I can't talk about work." That wasn't entirely true. Non-disclosure agreements limited the *details*, not the broad strokes. But I wasn't in the mood to talk. I didn't want to get animated and excited. Basically, I didn't want to give him the wrong idea.

"Okay then, something not covered under *NDA*." He air-quoted and smirked like he knew I was full of shit. "We're growing fast. More funding means more hiring. And with that comes ... people. Emotions. Drama."

If I had to sit through the dinner, I needed something to talk about, and this seemed like a harmless topic. "So you want free advice on your people's problems now?"

He grinned, unashamed, looking younger than his age. "Talk to me about science or finding investors, I'm solid. But once feelings get involved, I'm lost. You did your MBA, built a reputation for delivering on tough projects while managing a large team; how do you manage all those egos at once?"

I thought of Sylosis, my team, all our mess. I wished management, especially Patrick, saw them as real issues worth solving. "You need human resources for that."

"I have a team. Problem is, they go strictly by the book."

We spent the rest of dinner talking about team dynamics and management styles. His challenges mirrored ours—startup growing pains.

"My only advice would be to listen. Most problems come from people feeling ignored and unappreciated."

He pursued that line of questioning, and I responded, imagining Patrick asking the same.

"You're damn impressive." He lifted his glass and clinked with mine. The evening was easier than I had expected. It didn't help the unsettling feeling inside me, but the innocent chat made it easy to go through the hour.

"How about you join me?" he suddenly asked out of nowhere.

This time, I laughed. "So ... this *was* a recruitment dinner?" Internally, I laughed even more. My mother's vision of matchmaking, smashed by startup reality.

A chill swept over me. My hair stood on end. From the corner of my eye, I noticed a couple passing by. The woman's red dress was sleek and expensive. From her teardrop earrings to her matching bracelet and heels, she *oozed* old money. Blonde curls spilled perfectly over her shoulders. The scent of her perfume wafted when she crossed our table.

They reached the table ahead of us and started to settle. I

couldn't see her face, but I noticed the source of my chill. This woman had come with Ryan. Our eyes met for the briefest moment, and he looked away—just looked the fuck away—and focused on his date.

A fucking date.

How had he even known where I was?

And then I remembered.

Virona had overheard my call with Dad. Of course, she had to tell. Other than the fact that she hated me, Ryan was also her boss.

"I want to offer you a partnership," Raj dragged me back into our conversation. He gave a nervous smile, looking more boy than man. "What you bring to the table, the way you think ... it'll be valuable. Together, we could build something that really matters."

He went on and on, but it was too late. I'd already checked out. Emotions surged inside me, too tangled to name. Jealousy. Anger. Betrayal. Like lava rising in my chest, streaming down and melting everything soft in me. Ryan's betrayal gutted me in ways I didn't think were possible.

Why did it feel so wrong when I was doing the exact same thing?

Our only difference was my discretion and his inconsiderateness.

Would I be okay if he snuck around behind my back? No, fucking hell no. He. Was. Mine.

And as soon as that realization hit me, everything felt too complicated.

"So, what do you think?" Raj asked.

My eyes remained on Ryan and the blonde, my chest burning and shrinking simultaneously. I didn't even know how it was happening, but I could feel the burn all the way to my core.

Ryan squeezed her hand, and she shook her head as if she were crying. Every cell in my body was telling me to walk over and confront the drama.

"Did I lose you, Risha?" Raj spoke as he tilted his head behind him to see what had caught my attention.

"No ... sorry, I was processing it," I said, pulling him back into the conversation. "It's a generous offer, and one I don't deserve."

"That's not true," he said. "If there is anyone who can take this company to the next level, it's you."

Ryan moved over to the other side of the table and put his hand on the blonde's shoulder. The fucking bitch kissed his hand, and I noticed the tears rolling down her cheek. The heavy makeup and all the mascara, however, remained intact. I fucking hated her perfect little face.

Fire exploded in my brain, and Raj continued with his perfected pitch.

Ryan said a string of sentences that, naturally, I couldn't hear, but really wanted to know. She put her hand on his and nodded obediently. I wish I could yank those perfect curls back and fucking tell her he wasn't available.

Raj moved forward to say something again, forcing me to look at him. "This is the most unromantic proposal, but I'm sure you don't expect romance from a geek. I know I'm moving too fast, but no one reaches anywhere by going slow. Marry me and be my partner in life."

"Will that be all, Sir, ma'am?" The server approached with a jug of cold water, obstructing my view of Ryan and the blonde. I wanted to snatch the jug out of his hand and throw it over the blonde. Or maybe Ryan. Why not both? What if they were kissing each other while this man and Raj discussed the dessert menu?

"Check, please." I sprang into action, throwing the napkin on the table. I got up from my seat.

Raj looked at me in surprise. But at the other table, that fucking asshole who was supposed to be mine couldn't stop consoling the blonde.

"Thanks for the offer, I'll take a rain check."

Thirty-Three

RISHA

Frustration clung to me as I unlocked my apartment. My heart splintered, and shards ground behind my ribcage. It had been months since my last visit here, and that, too, had been a hurried grab-and-go, collecting essentials before I turned my back on this place. The apartment was dark and silent, confirming I was the only occupant. I flipped on the lights as I crossed from the foyer into the living room and then my bedroom.

My phone lit up with my mother's face. Of course, she'd call. Word spread quickly within her circle.

I swiped and snapped, "What?"

"Tell me you didn't say no to Raj?" Her fury crackled through the line. But mine burned hotter.

"I did. And while we're at it—don't ever set me up with another guy," I said what I should've said years ago.

"What did you just say?"

"You heard me loud and clear, Mom. Your manipulation ends right here."

"Don't you dare—"

"Pass the message to Dad, too. I am done." I hung up and flung the phone across the bed.

Then I grabbed the vase Ryan had sent after our first night

and tossed it in the trash, wanting the spell he had over me to break. It didn't, but I wouldn't stop until I succeeded.

Next, I crossed the room to the picture of the houseboat, the one that always made me think of my father. Unceremoniously, I yanked it from the wall and threw it. The frame broke in two. I didn't need his love if he didn't care about me.

Each person remained true to their character. My mother was overbearing, manipulative, but predictable. My father stayed true to his role—silent, nonconfrontational—always siding with his wife, a reflection of tradition. Ryan remained within the borders of our relationship. And I played my well-versed role of an obedient daughter. Then why did it hurt so much? Why was I so fucking disappointed?

Against all the odds stacked up against me, I wanted Ryan.

I wanted it to be different.

I wanted him to be mine.

I wanted him so desperately that it hurt.

And I couldn't wrap my mind around who was at fault. Ryan or me? The moment I had walked out of the penthouse, the moment I had chosen my father, was the moment I had decided to let go of Ryan, hadn't I? I had chosen.

And, as always, I had chosen my father, who never stood up for me. I had given up on the one man who had given me the world. Happiness. Contentment. A reason to smile. Ryan had valued me and appreciated me for who I was, not rejected me for who I couldn't be. With contempt battling within, I couldn't understand how to move forward from here.

My bedroom door burst open. I turned, startled—

Ryan walked in without a word, heading straight for the chair by the window. His face was unreadable, but the distance between us spoke volumes.

"You seriously didn't expect to leave without an explanation, did you?" His eyes waged a war under his calm persona. I could almost hear the throbbing of his pulse. "What were you thinking when you went on a date with someone else?"

I forced myself to calm my racing heart. "It was just a dinner, not a date."

"You want to argue on semantics now? Let's see." He typed something on his phone then walked over and handed it to me, screen up.

I stared at his Google search: *Is going out with someone for dinner considered a date?*

Yes, inviting someone for dinner is generally considered a date, particularly if it is one-on-one time ... and so it went.

I groaned inwardly and let the phone fall onto the bed.

He picked it up and walked back to the chair. "So, about that date ... why did you go out with another man?"

I was furious with him. And myself. And confused by my raging emotions following the evening. Sitting at different tables with different people, I hated that woman, but mostly, I hated him.

"You have no right to ask when you did the exact same thing."

I walked over to the dresser and busied myself, taking time removing a tank top and pajama shorts—not because they were a hard find, but I wanted to wait for him to say something. I wanted to hear that she was a nobody, that it was all an act to make me jealous. Because, swear to God, I was still burning.

He remained silent for nearly a minute ... the longest minute of my life. His silence made my mind go all sorts of wild. Had he been seeing her all this time while I worked on his penthouse? Was she someone from his past he was rekindling with now that we were over? The anger took a different form, and my eyes prickled.

I didn't notice when Ryan walked up to me.

"Ask." He let the word hang between us.

Suddenly, facing the truth terrified me. Would the mystery be less agonizing than the confirmation that he was no longer mine? The odds were even, meaning heartbreak was unavoidable.

I inhaled sharply before confronting him. "Who is she?"

"We dated in the past," he replied. My stomach lurched into

the sinkhole. "I ended it almost a year ago, but she texts me every few weeks."

A secret. I started to walk past him toward the bathroom, needing time to hide my overcrowding emotions. "You decided to give it another chance ..." I put it out there to see what would stick.

He wrapped his fingers around my elbow and turned me toward him. His gaze remained on my face, searching for something. Hurt maybe? Shock? Surprise?

Jealousy festered within, gnawing at my insides like a parasite refusing to die, poisoning everything it touched. She had Ryan, and I had already lost him.

"I told her I don't make decisions I'm not sure about. She is moving closer to her family in France."

I exhaled and stepped closer, but he pulled away, saying, "Your turn."

I fought to control my confusing and frustrating emotions. These overwhelming feelings and all things he'd taught me to be ... I didn't want to regress. If this was our end, I at least wanted us to leave with honesty and truth.

"I lied about not dating," I said. "I go out with men my mother *forces* me to. And hate myself for doing things I don't want to do."

His grip on my elbow tightened. Pain shot through me, but I didn't dislodge. He wasn't interested in my actions, but in the reason behind them.

"It's like a box I have to check before I can say no to my parents," I said.

He let out a bitter laugh. "So that's what this is? The mystery behind your non-commitment. You fuck me to take the edge off while you parade around with husband options. Tell me: do you fuck them, too, or am I the only detour?"

His every word landing a blow, my anger rose with his every accusation. I turned on instinct, hand lifting, but he caught my wrist mid-air.

"I never lied to you. Never played you." My voice shook.

"Could've fooled me this morning, but I'm not stupid enough to trust you after this."

"Get. Out," I spat. "And don't come back."

"The feeling is mutual. But don't think you can get away without an explanation. I have the right to know." He pulled me by my wrist, making our bodies collapse. Electricity ran through my veins. My stupid body hadn't gotten the memo yet.

It was over. We were done. I should have been livid after his accusations, but all I felt was heartbreak and unrest. Of all the relationships I'd had, none had felt as real or wrecked. I had let myself dream. I had believed. I had let him in. I had lived without fear or rules—and this was the price for letting my guard down.

"Now talk," he seethed through gritted teeth.

My surroundings blurred, and I couldn't tell if it was the urge to protect myself or the pain of losing him that hit harder.

"I never wanted this. You came after me."

"Bullshit," he called me out. "You wanted me as much as I wanted you. Maybe I initiated it first, but you never backed off, never said no. Now keep that bullshit aside and start talking. I want the goddamn truth."

Ryan detested me, and all I saw in his eyes was contempt. My two worlds collided in the worst possible way. Living two separate lives came at a cost, and someday or another, I knew I had to pay the price. With Ryan, the price was my heart and the truth that would set him free, ending the most perfect thing I ever had.

"I do what is expected from me. I used to do it to maintain peace in the house, but then it was to find my way back to my father. Every time I pushed back, he pulled further away—until five silent years stood between us. So, today, when he called and asked me to meet Raj for dinner, I thought ... maybe this was my way back to him." A dry sob tore through me. I didn't even know who I was crying for anymore—the daughter still aching for her father's love, or the woman mourning the loss of a man who had given her everything.

"I don't expect you to understand this, Ryan. We both belong in two very different worlds." I paused as a tremor passed through me. My throat tightened, and more tears rolled down my cheeks. "I told you I'm living on borrowed time, and now you know what that means. I'm sorry for being selfish. I just wanted to live and feel without dwelling over the consequences."

My knees started to grow weak, and I realized the only thing keeping me from collapsing was Ryan's grip. His arms were anchored firmly around my waist as I was pressed between him and the dresser.

"I lived for the moment, not realizing that even the present is fleeting. I'm sorry you had to see the real me." I wished the floor would swallow me whole, erase me, spare me from stacking my confessions, but that was wishful thinking.

"Now you know the real Risha. The scared, obedient daughter who can't stand up for herself ... who desperately wants her father's love and that lost affection more than anything else. I am a lost soul, Ryan, a woman masquerading as someone I wish I were. This is the real me. A fragile mess, pretending to be strong for a world that never bothered to look closer."

My sobs became uncontrollable. I couldn't face him. I couldn't break away. I was a mess who didn't know how to redeem myself. I didn't know what else Ryan wanted to hear, because he still wasn't letting me go. And all I wanted was to crumble and fade until there was nothing left of me.

Thirty-Four

RISHA

I woke up to the morning sun spilling across the room and a massive headache. I tried to move. *Yikes!* Turning from one side to the other felt like a milestone. I was in my bed ... I looked down and realized I was still wearing my jeans and black turtleneck from the day before. And then I remembered Ryan carrying me to the bed while I sobbed uncontrollably.

I tried to get up, but a fresh wave of nausea washed over me. I groaned.

"Easy. Here, have some water." Ryan's voice came from the other side of the bed.

I turned too quickly, sending a rush of pain from head to toe. "Ouch! Ryan? You're here?"

He paused. "I can't tell from your voice if that's a delight or a blow?" He came closer and held out painkillers and a bottle of water. I took them from his hand and washed down the pills in big gulps while he lurked close by.

I placed the empty bottle on my side of the nightstand. "Thanks. I ... I wasn't expecting to see you, that's all."

"Hmm, is that right?" He didn't move away, and I didn't know what to do next. My heart was drumming half with excitement to see him here and half with a dread that he stayed to say his final goodbye. Ryan never did anything half-assed.

I didn't want him to leave, but I had nothing that would make him stay either. And then I remembered one more thing we never covered yesterday. "I told Raj no. The guy I met yesterday ... before I left—"

"I never asked you, precious. That's how much faith I have in you," he exclaimed, cutting me off.

I faced him, cursing under my breath as a sharp throb pulsed from the sudden motion. "How? Why?" I asked. I didn't deserve his faith or trust. What I had done was unacceptable, and he had thrown the same thing back in my face. It hurt like crazy. I burned.

He tucked a loose curl behind my ear, his touch too gentle for the storm we'd weathered. His eyes were calm now, with no trace of last night's contempt. This softness, it pulled at me, but I didn't trust it. Didn't trust *us*. Not when wanting him felt so close to hurting myself.

"Your eyes never left me. I don't understand this pull, but it's not something either of us can walk away from. It's stubborn and constant, like we're wired into each other," he explained.

I nodded because I felt the same irresistible tug. He lived under my skin, etched into every breath I took. I felt him in my bones whether he was near or we were miles apart. And that was the problem—the pull between us wasn't one-sided, but this version of me wasn't entirely me. My eyes prickled with a fresh wave of tears.

"Now you know not to trust me."

"And yet, I do. I didn't understand your reasons until now," he said. With the back of his fingers, he slowly trailed my jawline, sending a wave of warmth down my neck and up into my cheeks. I held my breath, afraid that even the slight rise and fall of my chest might break this moment.

Ryan paused just beneath my chin, tilting up a fraction to

lock our gazes. His eyes held a tug-of-war between staying distant and closing that last bit of space.

"Vikki was so upset when I left. I'm sure she will never think I'm good enough." My voice cracked.

Ryan moved closer, his lips inches from mine. I closed my eyes, inhaling his scent, this closeness I craved from within my gut. I was too scared to touch him, say anything that could topple this precarious balance we had just started.

"It doesn't matter what people think," he said in a breathless voice. Flicking his tongue over my lips, teasing and urging in a way that I could barely stand.

"I've not been with anyone else since we met," I clarified another one of his accusations from last night.

"I was upset, precious." He moved his hand from my chin to my hair to pull me in and close the gap. "Trust was never in question, do you agree?"

I nodded slightly, our lips caressing, and then I shook my head. "I was so jealous when I saw you with that woman. You held her hand. You washed away her tears."

The pain of that moment hit me with a vengeance, cutting right through my gut. I moved and fell on my back and closed my eyes to hold back tears. The image of Ryan with another woman was so thoroughly etched in my brain that I couldn't see beyond last evening ... He had seemed so far away, almost unreachable.

And then he pushed me to my breaking point. I wasn't a woman who cried often, yet Ryan had broken through the last of my defenses.

"How long were you two together?" I asked.

"Two years, on and off." With his weight on his elbow, his torso hovered over me. He inched closer.

"That seems long. Why didn't it work out between you two?" The jealousy hadn't died fully. I needed to know she wasn't a threat.

"I don't do messy, Risha. I'm a man of straight lines. My whites are whites and blacks are black; there is no in-between.

Katherine came with a lot of drama and with no substantial goals."

His words should have sent me running. He was choosing wrong all over again, but before I could talk, he said, "She used to lie, manipulate me into doing things I didn't want. I'm done with all those games. So, Risha, is there anyone else? Anything I should be aware of?"

"No." I'd nothing to hide. Though my past had been complex, my present was unblemished. Whatever thread Ryan'd woven around me wouldn't snap. I wanted to be here with him. Because he completed me.

His presence hummed through every nerve, his warmth soaking into my skin, chasing the cold buried deep inside. And yet, the unsettled unease lingered. My eyes burned behind closed lids, a knot climbing my throat, swollen with all the things I wasn't ready to say.

"You laughed with him, at his jokes, Risha. Do you want to know what it did to me?" Ryan's words caught me off guard.

I nodded without opening my eyes, wanting to know everything.

He ran his lips across my lips and jaw, up my cheeks and nose and eyelids. His free hand moved over my breasts and down my abdomen until he pulled the top up and over my chest.

Using his teeth, he pushed the bra, freeing my breasts. His mouth latched onto a nipple, moving from one to the other while he kneaded them in pure desperation. A violent craving burned inside me so potent I'd have done anything he asked me to do.

"I felt possessive and territorial. I didn't know how to sort my feelings because I'd never felt like that before. I wanted to hurt him so badly and drag you out of there until everyone knew who you belonged to. Unreasonable I was, but it killed me that I had no right on you." His wet kisses and warm breath started moving down my abdomen. I arched up, wanting more contact, all of him. "That needs to change right now," he announced.

I nodded vigorously, even though he couldn't see my agreement. "Yes," I let out.

Climbing down, I claimed his mouth. He kissed me deeply, tantalizing me with his tongue, making my knees impossibly weaker. I was glad to be lying down on the bed.

He broke away just enough for our gazes to lock. "You are mine."

"Yes, I am," I breathed, getting drunk on his taste and scent. I kissed him back, wanting every second of the connection we'd missed. "And you're mine."

He growled like a lion nursing its wounds. "Let me show you how we fit so well together," he said.

Quickly, my doubts faded away, and I knew exactly what I wanted in life. All the wrongs I had to right, all the mountains I had to move …

I was ready.

He took off his clothes. I did the same, wanting nothing more than him inside me, making me whole again. If our words were vows, the physical need was the cement solidifying the truth.

His body hovered over me before he hitched my leg over his shoulder, stretching me to the fullest. I gasped as he ground over me, connecting his cock over my opening. He pinned me with his hips, rocking gently with a promise of what was to come.

I slid my hands onto his neck and tugged him to my mouth. I kissed him hard. My pebbled nipples dragged across the light hair of his chest.

He kept his weight on one hand, and the other touched me everywhere—neck, shoulder, breast, waist, and finally my clit. He fingered me gently, gliding between my swollen nub, reaching up to the sensitive spot he knew where to find. I quivered on the edge of release. He slowed and moved south.

"Please, Ryan," I begged. "I want you inside me."

I circled my hand over his hard length, his hot skin between my palm and the pre-cum dripping from the head. I positioned him at my opening and guided him inside. Slow and deep, he rooted himself completely. The sensation was intense. Complete. I fought the emotions that surfaced in my brain, wanting to say the words I had no reason to hold back.

My chest felt heavy, like I was about to burst. Desperate to hold back my words and wanting to say them at the same time, I kissed him frantically, our tongues tied in a game of supremacy. I needed this. Him.

I shifted wildly beneath him, wanting the fiction and his cock moving faster. I wanted to own him and to be owned.

He drove into me hard and deep, again and again. I came quickly with his name on my lips. Tears flowed down my cheeks as waves crashed over me. He saw them and kissed them away, making me feel more than I thought possible.

"Ending us would destroy me, Ryan," I blurted out. "Give me a chance to redeem myself. I don't want you to remember me by the woman you saw at the restaurant. Even though I live in two worlds, this is who I am. This is who I want to be."

He crashed his mouth onto mine in a feverish rush. No words were uttered, no promises made, but everything about this moment felt as real as it could get.

"I want to take you somewhere," he said. "Will you come with me?"

"Wherever you want to take me."

Thirty-Five

RYAN

For February in the Hamptons, the weather turned out to be a borrowed day from spring. We walked downtown, shared ice cream, and stole each other's donut bites. If a word could sum up this day, I would call it a dreamscape. I couldn't remember the last time I had been this relaxed. Finding pleasure in simple things was becoming my new normal.

We roamed around without a care in the world. Our arms entwined, our grip firm. Risha seemed carefree, and I was happy. Genuinely happy. Since we met, our lives have been utterly busy. My work, her work, penthouse, and then ... last night. We needed a break to remind us why we had started seeing each other. To live and enjoy these brief moments. Step toward the future without sacrificing the present.

If last night was any indication, it was a stark reminder of how easy it was to lose everything we had built for ourselves. I needed her. I loved her ... yet there was something that nagged at the back of my mind. She didn't believe in love, and trust was hard-earned. Between us, trust was never a question, and her promise meant more than any hollow confession.

While Risha darted in and out of the boutiques, I slipped into a shop I had last visited with Dad. I didn't know what I was looking for, but I was certain to find something here. *They carry something for every expression*, Dad had told me.

My phone rang, and I picked up as soon as I saw Ivy's face on the screen. "How's everything? I've called you twice."

She exhaled a big sigh, as if I had been worried for nothing. "Everything's fine. I'm fine. The building lost power for half an hour before the generator kicked in. My phone died, and I forgot to charge it."

"How smart." I walked from one showcase to another, scanning everything, but nothing stood out.

"I'm sorry ..." she faltered. Neither was it new, nor would it likely change. She juggled internships and undergrad, yet kept her phone at arm's length as if preserving a refuge from a world that demanded constant connection. "I promise you've got nothing to worry about. I'm staying in and focusing on finals."

Ivy was predictable that way. I had been worried because she hadn't picked up my call, even though I knew she and her roommate were in their apartment. Her building's security guard had updated me already.

"Good. Keep it that way until the city's power grids are restored and everything's back to normal."

"It seems you've memorized Dad's every piece of advice."

"What do you mean?"

"Showing love in ways that matter instead of just saying you love me ..." Ivy reminded me of something Dad had always used to say. "My entire apartment is overstocked, thanks to you."

I let her words sink in. *Show love in ways that matter.* That was what I had to do to reach Risha, to show her that loving someone didn't have to feel difficult. She was right; love should liberate, not burden with demands and expectations. And right on cue, I found exactly what I needed. Amory & Vale hadn't disappointed my father, and they didn't disappoint me, either.

"I have to go, but stay indoors and keep your phone charged. If you need anything, remember I'm just a phone call away."

We reached the Harbor Grill overlooking Block Island Sound. The sunset on the horizon cast a pink and orange glow. Sailboats and returning surfers only added more character to this unusual temperature. As New Yorkers, we seized every opportunity for good weather. The storm wreaking havoc in Boston would reach us within a day—a calm before impact.

"This is a gorgeous view, Ryan." Risha let out a deep sigh. We sat on opposite sides of the table, taking the view through a glass wall. "So serene."

"I remember coming here with my parents ... Not much has changed." I looked around. Our ancestral home was a couple of miles north of the sound; a house where my parents got married and I spent many summers.

"Tell me about your parents." Risha nudged me with genuine curiosity.

I couldn't remember if I'd ever let myself talk about them since their deaths. "They were two bodies with one soul. So completely in tune with each other that sometimes they finished each other's sentences." I smiled, thinking back to all the nights we stayed up laughing, so rooted to the present, as if there were no tomorrows.

"Grief goes through phases. At first, there was the numbness, when I was just trying to process the stark reality. Then disbelief set in, a desperate hope that someone had made a mistake or maybe I was trapped in a nightmare. After that came the anger ... wondering why they had to do everything together—if Mom had stayed home, Ivy and I would at least have had one parent."

Risha placed her hand over mine in silent support.

My mind was already spinning back through the memories I'd locked away. They hadn't gone away, just settled in, making a permanent residence I carry with me every day.

"But when I step back from resentment and think about

them, I'm honestly glad they left together. I can't imagine either of them living without the other."

"You're very lucky to have grown up in a loving family, Ryan." She squeezed my hand and looked at the sailboat moving toward the horizon. "It's heartbreaking that they're not here anymore, but no one can take away those wonderful memories you made with them."

She was right. Every time I thought about them, I had so many wonderful things to say. So many beautiful memories we created together.

I looked into Risha's eyes, and all I saw was melancholy. I couldn't understand how my closed album left me smiling, while hers, wide open, brimmed with sadness.

"Tell me about your relationship with your father," I asked.

She entwined our fingers but didn't look at me. "We've been estranged for years now. I've disappointed him enough ... and I'm not proud of it. We're both stubborn, but the difference is he shuts down instead of opening up, and I walk away instead of staying and trying to fix things. In the end, nothing ever gets resolved."

"Cece told me once he was upset you left the doctorate program. Is he still holding that against you?"

"He definitely wasn't happy when I walked away from it and chose an MBA instead, but he kept his disappointments to himself. Honestly, I didn't ask. At the time, I didn't know exactly what I wanted, but I was certain it wasn't the path he carved for me."

"And now ... do you know what you want?"

Something unreadable tugged at the corner of her eyes, but I couldn't understand what was turning in her mind. She fell silent, letting the weight of it hang between us.

When she finally spoke, it stole my breath.

"I want to be you, Ryan. The kind of person who stands firm in a storm, without letting it break you. Someone who doesn't care what people think or say, or what life throws their way. You set your own goals ... and you live by your own rules. I admire your strength, and you're who I want to be."

A part of me shattered, the last barrier I hadn't realized I'd still been holding. A crack right down the center, followed by a rush of warmth flooding in. She hadn't just touched my soul; she'd unmade and remade me, resurrecting something I'd thought was long dead.

Without a moment's doubt, I crossed over to her side of the table, slid my hand up her arm, cupped the back of her neck, and drew her toward me in a rush. Our mouths met, a collision forged by all the things we hadn't said and all the promises I hadn't yet made. Her lips opened under mine, yielding for me to deepen the kiss, to taste her softness and take away her vulnerability.

I pressed into her, closing the space between us, until I could feel her heartbeat against mine—wild, alive, matching our frenzied kiss. My grip tightened to anchor her and to let her know I was there. I wouldn't let her down. And I fell without reserve, without a safety net, without turning back because whatever storm stirred within her, I was right in its center.

I slid my hand up, my fingertips following the slope of her shoulder, cupping the back of her neck, tugging just a little, tilting her toward me to deepen the connection. Her breath faltered against mine with a shaky rush that made my pulse accelerate. We fell into a passionate, vulnerable exchange. A conversation without words. A confession without promises.

I pressed forward, my grip tightening, slipping upward to feel her skin, her softness. The constant zing spiraled, igniting something raw within. The spark turned volatile, crackling into a storm ready to split the sky. Our mouths moved in unison, letting all the promises I hadn't yet made seep through to her. Promises to stay, to hold, to redeem until there was only us. We would face our future together not as two wounded creatures, but as two people choosing each other, over every obstacle, until there was nothing left but us.

Saying I loved her wasn't enough, so I decided to prove it instead.

We resumed our seats when the server showed up with a bottle of local red wine and a basket of warm bread. As soon as he left, I got up from my seat and resumed my earlier position next to Risha.

"I want to take you to the New York Ballet," I said without any hesitation or doubt.

"You don't have to—"

"I know. I want to." I knew I was all over the place, but right now, my emotions were frayed. "I got something for you."

I removed the emerging monarch chrysalis pendant from my pocket and showed it to her. "May I?"

"It's ... beautiful, Ryan." She pushed her hair aside.

"You're not the only one changing, Risha. I'm changing, too. This pendant represents transformation, letting go of the past and becoming someone new. The next chapter. A new beginning. And us."

Whatever storm she was, I had no desire to be anywhere but at its center.

Thirty-Six

RISHA

The New York City Ballet was exactly how I imagined it to be. Surreal. Spellbinding. Transcendent. Ethereal. Seated in the balcony suite, I couldn't believe how my childhood dreams were unfolding. The man who paid attention to my every want had tucked all his emotions and fear away like a warrior. And he'd done it for me, the man who only knew how to lead by example.

When we exited the ballet and entered the limousine, I couldn't help but notice his tight knuckles and pale skin. I kissed him deeply, rolling my tongue with his in desperation, pouring in the possessive demands, filling him with my ardor. Each time I thought our kiss couldn't get any more intense, he found a way to make it deeper.

"How lucky am I to have found you ...?" I spoke inside his mouth between our ragged breaths.

"I found you," he gave me a factual reminder.

"Semantics."

Foregoing the banter, he slid one hand into my hair, while the other kneaded my breast over the dress. He was trying to forget where he was. The demon wasn't the concert; it was the monster that awaited outside the threshold, ready to swallow him whole.

This drive from the ballet to his penthouse was where he'd lost his parents, and now he was taking the ride with me.

He was still hurting yet unable to shed a single tear.

"I know it's hard. I know." Hot tears pelted my face as I mourned with him. "I'm here with you."

Ryan kissed my tears away in a silent *thank you*, then trailed down my neck, my bare shoulder. He slid his hand from my breast to the small of my back, clutching me like a lifeline. Something solid to anchor him as he stepped across a threshold he couldn't cross alone.

Hiking my dress up, I straddled him. He pressed against me firmly, showing me how to calm him, what he needed from me. Without another thought, I unzipped his pants.

With a sharp exhale, he said, "I want to bury myself inside you if this is the last breath I take."

His words struck deeper than he probably intended. He was saying he'd choose me if this were his last breath. If he were at death's door, I was the one he'd want by his side. More silent tears slipped down my cheeks.

The limo screeched to a sudden stop. Ryan's hand pressed hard, pulling me into him. Panic spread across his face. We looked outside at a band of pedestrians crossing. The moment they cleared, the limo again eased into the traffic.

Holding Ryan's face, I said, "I've just found you, Ryan. There is nothing in the universe that can keep us apart. We are not dying today. Or tomorrow. Or anytime in the near future. Do you understand that?"

Taking his face in my hands, I kissed him with everything. He kissed me back with the same unbridled force. I ran one hand down his chest, through his dress shirt and vest, and down until I held his unforgiving hardness in my palm. And all I could think about was erasing the sadness with our unforgettable moment.

I rocked my hips against him, stroking myself with his cock. He groaned breathlessly, his lips pressing hard against me. I was intoxicated by his scent and aroused by his arousal. I reached for his fly and the belt buckle, freeing the buttons. He scooted up, carrying me with him, so I could lower his slacks and briefs.

When he fell heavily into my palm, I squeezed him gently, my touch tender. He was hard as stone with his head bobbing with glistening pre-cum. I inhaled a sharp breath, my mouth drying to take him. But when I started to slide down his lap, he held my waist and said, "No. I want to be inside you."

I didn't have time to protest as Ryan gripped my thigh, sliding his hands upward until his thumbs pushed the black lace of my thong to one side. His pad sliding through the slickness of my desire.

"You're always ready for me," he whispered, pushing two fingers through the folds, scissoring to open me for him. "Why does everything between us feel so right?"

"Because we are." Setting my hands on his shoulders for balance, I raised myself on my knees to gain the height to take in the crown of his thick cock. His hands moved to my hips either to support me or to anchor himself. His breathing grew shallow, yet his gaze remained locked on mine. The memories of his past, along with where we were, started to fade away.

"I crave you," he groaned. His erection brushed over my folds, making me empty and desperate. And then his sharp breath whizzed past my neck when I slowly took him in, inch by every inch, until he was balls deep inside me and calling my name.

The lust-filled air brimmed with pheromones, warming up the air-conditioned space surrounding us. My skin was flushed and tingled, and my breasts heavy and tender, wanting his coddle.

"Risha ..." His hands flexed restlessly between my waist and my hips. "God, Risha, you feel so good."

I closed my eyes, feeling vulnerable. Everything I'd ever wanted but never expected to find, I'd found in him. This moment felt achingly intimate, wrapping me in his arms, in his world. The rest of the world blurred past, but with him, I felt centered. I'd found myself by losing myself in him.

With a palm on my lower belly, he used his thumb to gently

circle my throbbing clit. My core clenched from the sweet pleasure, and I took him in deeper than I ever had. He garbled my name, his fingers going laxed over my skin. I looked up from under my hooded eyelids and saw this beautiful man sprawled beneath me, calling me like I was his prayer. He left me feeling vulnerable and powerful, all at once.

Sweat misted my skin. I rode him, sliding from the crown of his head to the bottom of his root. He was throbbing inside me, and I was rippling around him. Squeezing him. Trembling on the verge of orgasm.

"Fuck." He removed his finger from my clit, making me whimper into his neck. "You're milking my cock so hard, precious. I don't want to come so fast," he explained.

Ryan knew my body; he knew me better than I knew myself. Gripping my hips with both his hands, he urged me to slow down.

"Ryan ... I can't ..."

"No," he complained. A sheen of sweat covered his face.

Leaning forward, I slid my tongue along his lips. His hips churned from the shockwave coursing between us. I lifted myself up, sliding carefully when he stopped me with his hip and said, "Slow down. You can't come without me. And I want to savor this moment."

I lowered myself, taking him into me again. Our eyes locked as the pleasure spread from the nucleus where we were connected. I pressed my lips to his, kissing him as I rocked my hips, riding the maddening build of orgasm with every movement of his long, hard penis moving inside me. He was melting my core and throbbing so desperately for his release.

He arched back, and the shift in position made me gasp. He pushed a sensitive bundle of nerves, making it impossible to hold back.

His tongue savored me with deliberate strokes, tasting me with unhurried licks of devotion. I reached for his hair, directing his mouth for my pleasure. He growled, stroking my mouth with slow, sensual strokes of his own. I matched him, my skin damp and too sensitive, and my core clenching, sending a wild shiver up and down my body.

"Ryan ..." I was losing my mind as my body started to take charge, ferociously riding his cock until the tension burst and the grinding hunger started to take over the rest.

"Yes ... love ... now ..." he groaned inside my mouth. His hands took charge of my hips, commanding our rhythm. His cock furiously started rubbing over those sensitive nerves, and his girth filled me to the max.

"*Ryan.*"

He pulled me into him as the orgasm exploded through us. The spasms burst out of my core and radiated outward until he filled me up. I wrapped my arms around his neck and witnessed him fall apart. I moaned, my body jerking with every pulse of pleasure. We held each other close for a long time as our bodies rode the rest of the sensation.

"Thank you," I heard him say softly. "I never thought I could cross this bridge on my own. You make everything so seamless and easy."

The sincerity in his voice unraveled me. My feelings for him that I couldn't comprehend until now took the shape of a word and without a second thought, I said, "I love you, Ryan," meaning it.

He looked at me in disbelief. Not upset, no hesitation, but a mix of shock and ... I wasn't sure if I also noticed ... excitement?

"I thought ... You don't ..."

"I was wrong." I knew where he was going. I wasn't capable of falling in love because the concept was foreign. "You proved me that I don't need to *fall* in love. Since I met you, I've only been rising ... as a person, as a woman, as a friend, as a lover. I feel stronger with you. My feelings for you have only been growing, and now it has reached where I can't control it. I have to tell you how I feel. I have to tell you how much I love you."

In a flash, he pulled me close, holding me in a tight, fierce embrace. He wrapped his arms around me as if he never wanted to let go, and I could feel the rapid beat of his heart—an unspoken affirmation of everything I'd just revealed.

Thirty-Seven

RISHA

While Ryan and my relationship was strengthening each day, I couldn't say the same about Virona and me. She didn't bring up my father's last call, but she also didn't forget the incident. Our working relationship continued with minimal communication. With the penthouse project wrapping up, this was our last week—rather, our last evening—to mend things between us. Something miraculous had to happen for that to come true, because Virona wasn't merely upset, she'd checked out on me.

Also today, the atmosphere in the house was different. Cece joined me at the penthouse, and Ryan had been testing working from his new home office. He pulled me into his office thrice in the last hour, pressing grateful kisses against my lips; mostly, he couldn't stand the distance. He missed that one weekend we'd stolen for ourselves almost a month ago. I did, too, and only hoped this lingering work in the penthouse would wrap up in a week or two.

Virona had several people working in the master bedroom suite, the last room that needed an upgrade. The kitchen and living areas had been the first to be remodeled, so Cece, Virona, and I took over a corner of the sectional couch.

"I've heard bits and pieces of you over the years. I'm glad we finally met," Cece told Virona while handing her a glass of red wine she had just poured. "I can't believe you two met in Ryan's office, of all places."

"What are the odds, right?" Virona raised a brow and took the glass. She settled on the pristine white leather couch opposite me and Cece.

"I love what you two have done with this place," Cece said, still taking in the changes. She was our first guest and someone who was also familiar with the old penthouse.

Someone walking in might do a double-take. The once-gilded interior, all polished marble and ornate crystal, had transformed into something freer. White walls now covered soft strokes of earthy ochres, sage greens, and muted corals—sunset tones danced with the shifting light. Virona and I had swapped the crystal chandeliers for soft glass pendants in dusky blues and dusts of gold, casting a mellow glow across low-slung furniture.

Also making sure the past hadn't been erased, simply folded in, on a new walnut shelf sat Ryan's mother's porcelain birds. Her carved wooden mirror, which she had hung by the entryway, had been moved next to the window to add more natural light. It was important to me that Ryan and Ivy's home didn't feel like a clean break. I wanted it to be a tribute to the past and a celebration of the present, a seamless blend of all they'd held onto and all they were becoming, where love that had roots met the life they were growing.

Ryan loved the changes and had spent every moment outside of his work here with me. I only hoped Ivy felt the same way Ryan did.

Her room remained untouched so she could decide which direction she wanted to go. And also, I put all the old furniture into storage in case they ever wanted to go back to their past.

"It was all Risha's vision. I just played along," Virona said evenly, brushing off her effort with a subtle shrug.

"That's not true. We argued a lot over what goes where and which color goes on which wall," I reminded her.

"You argued for the sake of it. Sage and dusty green were practically the same color," Virona tried correcting me.

I raised both eyebrows, feigning absolute shock. "I can't believe you just said that. The master of home aesthetics says sage and dusty green are the same."

She rolled her eyes, not taking the bait. "You know the furniture you chose would go with either of the two colors. Just because I said dusty green, you had to pick sage."

A part of me warmed with contentment that she still understood me, in however small a proportion it might be. I missed growing up with her; a part of me still missed all the lost times, but now that I'd found her, I wasn't ready to lose her again. With so much time wasted in holding onto old resentments, I was ready to move forward. Like a snake shedding skin, I wanted to shed my old self.

"It's fun to see Risha arguing for the sake of it. I always found her too mature for her age." Cece's words brought me back into the conversation. "I figured she was born thirty. A wise woman who couldn't do anything wrong."

Virona snorted with wine in her mouth. She wanted to swallow, which she did, but it went into her windpipe, and she coughed vigorously. Cece rushed to help her.

Through the hallway, my eyes met Ryan's. I didn't know when he had walked in on us, but his smile warmed my heart. I mouthed, "*I love you*." The more I said it, the more I regretted not saying it before because I had fallen for this man the day we'd met.

He leaned casually against the wall, arms folded across his chest, with no intention of leaving. He sought to refresh my memory of his earlier summons. "*Lose your friends. I need you now.*"

"I won't call her wild, but Risha had a strong streak about her. Head strong and unbudgeable, if that is a word." Virona's words pulled me back to us girls. "She had a fire inside her, and her dad was the catalyst."

"I didn't know she and her dad were that close." Cece tried to put the two together.

"They were inseparable ... like they played a game of their own, and the rest of the family was an add-on. Risha's mother, however, was a different story altogether." Virona rolled her eyes.

"Okay, enough." I wanted this conversation to end. This was our second bottle of wine and definitely the last, I hoped. "Leave my parents out of tonight's discussion."

"I don't get it, though. If Risha was so close to her dad, then why did he stop talking when she left the doctoral program?" Cece intervened, trying to put the puzzle together.

"That couldn't be the reason for the fall-out. Mr. Verma had high expectations from Risha, but I can't imagine he'd stop talking to her for any reason whatsoever," Virona said.

My chest pounded, but the reason remained a mystery. Maybe it was just that my past and present were colliding, and my future was standing right within earshot.

"That's strange," Cece tried again. "Only two things happened around the same time. Her change from doctoral to MBA and her relationship with Patrick."

"Who's Patrick?" Virona shot back.

"Her ex-boyfriend and current boss. An ass now, if you know what I mean." Cece waved her free hand dismissively. "But Patrick can't be the reason. They had a wild and crazy relationship, but they both were head over heels. Her mother was totally—like, absolutely—against their relationship, but her father ..." She turned to me with a questioning look. "Was he against Patrick, too?"

Virona interrupted before I could speak. "If she was seeing someone outside their community and her parents discovered it, I can totally see her mom losing her shit. No way the Vermas would ever be okay with that. And this"—she gestured around the room —"is anything but a farce. One day very soon, she'll run home, play the perfect daughter, and do whatever they say—like she always does."

Her words stung. I couldn't believe the perception she had of me.

Cece shot back, "I disagree. You think she's weak, but she isn't. She stood up for herself and joined MBA, didn't she?"

My ears and eyes burned. These two women, my two supposed friends, were dissecting my life like I wasn't even there.

"What do you think happened with Patrick?" Virona asked Cece, completely bypassing me.

"I ... don't remember." Cece turned curious eyes to me.

"Huh. I can bet my life that her family disapproved," Virona continued. "Trust me when I tell you, she'll retreat—it's just a matter of time. Changing programs is one thing, but she didn't change her career. Her mother would never approve of Ryan ... Wait until she finds out. I bet Risha will not even get a chance to say goodbye."

"Enough." My hands shook with the anger surging within. "You think you've figured me out, don't you? You're wrong."

The main door opened and closed. I didn't have to look up to find out that Ryan had left. Gone.

"Then prove it, Risha," Virona said. There was no anger, or challenge, nor an ounce of smirk. I wasn't even sure what point she was trying to make, but right now, she pissed me off to the point that I didn't want to see her face again.

"Get out of my house!" I screamed, my face flushed, tears welling in my eyes.

She put the wineglass on the side table and stood. "Gladly. Except, this is not your house."

I didn't know how to react. I wasn't the kind of person who lost it like this, but all I wanted was for her to get the hell out.

She beat me to it, though, throwing one last dagger over her shoulder. "I don't know who Patrick is, but your thing with Ryan will crash and burn just like it did with him."

"Get. The. Fuck. Out!" I screamed in disbelief.

Her words planted a seed of doubt I couldn't shake. Everything I'd worked so hard to build in myself suddenly felt like it was collapsing in on me. Was she right? Was I about to lose again? Were Ryan and Patrick really the same kind of man?

"If you really like Ryan, then do him a favor. Leave him alone. Because that man has fallen for you. Leaving a string of heartbreak *is* your pattern, Risha, but it fucking hurts. The trail of destruction you leave behind might be a joke to you, but it alters other people's lives."

Thirty-Eight

RISHA

The thing about collisions was they could turn into either fission or fusion. Fission split things apart—like nuclear power or atomic bombs—while fusion forced them together, creating suns and stars. Both were powerful enough to destroy life or create something new, depending on the conditions.

In a controlled environment, and in optimal doses, I knew the steps to follow, how to hone their power, and what the outcome would be. Theoretically, I knew. In an unpredictable setting, I didn't know what to expect. What was going to come next? The outcome was unknown.

All my texts to Ryan went unanswered, and his side of the bed stayed empty as the night bled from pitch dark to soft pink and finally to full daylight. I wrestled with myself about whether to give him space to process or go find him and explain.

The thing about space was, it didn't come with a finite deadline. Leave it unattained for too long, and it festered. I'd learned that the hard way.

With Dad, space had stretched into years of silence until that was all we shared. With Patrick, it hardened into bitterness. And with Virona ... well, that silence had gone so deep there was no salvaging it now.

Of all the relationships that had ended bitterly, the deepest cut was from the one I'd expected the most—my father's. I'd waited for him to reach out, to argue, to fight for me. Instead, he let it rot in silence. I refused to repeat that mistake with Ryan. I loved him. I wanted to fight for us, to reach him if he couldn't reach me. I wanted to explain, to answer every question, to give him every truth he deserved. More than anything, I wanted him to fight for me, too.

In the office, I was a walking, talking robot who knew what needed to be done, but neither my mind nor heart was at work. When I didn't hear back from Ryan by four, I called his office.

"Hey, Bobby. I've been trying to reach Ryan."

"Risha, how are you doing?" she asked chirpily, getting my hopes high. Even if Ryan was upset, at least he hadn't told his secretary about it.

"I'm good, thanks. Can you transfer me to Ryan."

"He's been holed up in Alan's office all day. It seems there is a huge problem going on with our Vegas site," Bobby filled the gap, giving me much-needed relief. He wasn't upset, just busy with his work.

"Is there any way you can fit me in his calendar today?" I requested. I had the freedom to enter his office at any time, but I never misused my power.

"Sure. It's hard to tell how his day looks since he has canceled all his meetings, but ... let me try." She spoke while I heard a few clicks, and then my heartbeat sped up when I heard Ryan's muffled voice.

Bobby told him I was on the call.

Heart pounding in my chest, I waited to hear him take the receiver. He had called me before for no reason but to hear my voice, and he'd never let my call go unanswered.

"Ryan is getting onto a conference call. But he can call you at six, if that works for you." Bobby's voice filled me with disappointment and hope.

Hope ... Stay positive, Risha.

"I can come over to the office," I suggested before she could decline.

She penned me down by the time I ended the call.

At ten minutes to six, I was about to leave when Patrick walked into my office and settled on the chair in front of me. "You won't believe who I just got off a call with?"

I shut down my email and other apps, ignoring him.

"Circle just called. They need our—*your*—expertise for their next project. Might I add it's a two-year contract." Patrick lathered up his excitement as he settled his hand on the back of the other empty chair.

Circle was one of the largest corporations in the country. Their products and services ranged from pharmaceutical to gaming and everything in-between, with an in-house talent of fifty-thousand-plus engineers. Why they needed Sylosis' services should have been my next question, but I didn't give a damn. My relationship hung by a thread. Salvaging what I cared for the most —*who* I cared for the most—was my only priority.

"Please take this to Ari or Sarah. My team is pretty swamped already with the Nixus project," I said as I opened the bottom drawer to get my purse out.

"In case I forgot to mention before ... they need *you* and *your team* for this project." Sarcasm dripped from his every word. Patrick took a more relaxed stance like he didn't see me ending my day.

"In case you don't remember, we are fully booked for the next several months," I responded . Technically, I would be free in a matter of weeks after the penthouse work was complete. But working on that project had whetted my appetite for more. I wanted to dedicate a fair share of my time outside of work to my hobby.

And my team was enjoying these sane work hours after finding their work-life balance. Zoe had travel plans, Sal was planning his wedding, and Marty was going home on time to be with his wife and son. I wouldn't take away their personal time.

I powered off my laptop and unplugged it. "My answer remains the same—we won't work on anything else until the Nixus project starts to taper off."

"That's not how we work at Sylosis." Patrick stood up, visibly exasperated. "We work. We manage our client's as well as family's expectations. This is not new. I want your head back in the game, Risha. Your new romance needs to take a backseat, maybe you need to manage your *new boyfriend's* expectations."

More than his words, how he said them rubbed me the wrong way. By air-quoting new "boyfriend's expectations," he was pissing me off intentionally. Worse—I took the bait.

I jerked up from my chair. Next, I shoved the laptop into my bag. "I don't know what *your* expectations are, but I'm not changing my team's expectations. I won't ask them for overtime, and we won't take on any new projects until the end of summer. Unless you're ready to hire more engineers."

Without waiting for a response, I left my office. If he had to say something, it could wait until tomorrow. My skull ached from all the life choices that I'd had to defend.

Ryan was still on the call, but Bobby told me to go in.

I closed the door behind me, and when I turned, I noticed the heat in his eyes that I felt inside me. Memories of my first visit here burned like hot flames, and hope bubbled inside me. Everything between us had always been salvageable. I wasn't ready to accept that we couldn't cross this barrier as well.

I walked toward him with a determined step.

As I approached his desk, he motioned to the seat across from him. I swallowed hard, took the seat, and waited.

And for the next ten minutes, I watched his frustration rolling with every rapt question to at least five people on the call. Not once did his eyes turn toward me. Crew on strike, a broken water pipe, an inhumane work environment, blames thrown in every direction—that was the gist of what I learned.

"Continue with the call. I'll join back as soon as I can." Ryan killed the connection and turned his gaze to mine, but something inside him had already shifted. The warmth was missing. "Sorry, I didn't expect it to run so long."

Cold. Distant.

"Everything all right?" I asked. My concern was genuine.

"Vegas construction has paused. Things had been escalating since last night."

"Oh." The reason for his absence gave me a spark of hope. "I know it's lame to ask, but anything I can help you with?"

He turned his gaze to the computer screen.

Everything between us is salvageable ... I repeated in my head like a chant.

Leaving my seat, I walked over. He neither stopped me nor asked me to retreat. I took it as an invitation. Taking a stand opposite him, I pushed my hip onto his table. Heat burned between us, but he made no attempt to pull me onto his lap.

When the silence started to turn awkward, I said, "I'm sorry you had to find out about Patrick that way. He and I met in business communication class. We found out he was working at a company where I was interning. We dated for six months during my MBA."

He still didn't ask anything, but I didn't want to stop. I had nothing to hide. And I refused to repeat my old mistakes.

"We dated without any branding or name tags. Just went with the flow."

"That's you written all over it," he said. The vein on his neck ticked, a telltale sign of his distress.

I decided not to take offense. "He was nice, and it was my first real relationship. I went along for the ride until reality hit me. Our worlds were very different. *We* were different. Not like the way Virona expressed, but ... it was ... never meant to be."

"Was it a realization or because you didn't love him? Or was it because your parents said so?"

"Because I knew so. Because I wasn't in love with him ... and because my parents said so." I was ready to lay it all out. "It's true I keep my both worlds separate, but that doesn't mean I loved him or there is nothing I wouldn't do to be with you. Patrick and you have nothing in common. I love you, Ryan. I don't think I felt this way with anyone else before."

"But you left him because you didn't want to disappoint your parents," he insisted.

"There's ... more to it than summing it in a short sentence. My dad ... I love my dad too much, Ryan. He is my first love, and no one can replace him. I don't see you as a person who would ask me to choose. Will you ... make me ...?"

I couldn't form words, and he didn't wait for me to complete them. Standing up, he kissed me with everything. He cradled my face and stroked every inch of me. My heart rolled out of comatose, but I couldn't make out the meaning of the kiss.

His strokes tugged between desperation and anxiety. His hands moved between my jaw, neck, and into my hair. I wrapped my arms around his waist and pulled him closer, trying to erase the distance of the last twenty-four hours.

But just as quickly as he had pulled me close, he pushed me away, saying, "All this time, I thought I was getting to know you, but you kept me in the dark. I don't know if I know you at all."

"You know me more than anyone ever has."

"You're like an onion—the more I peel, the more layers I discover." He shook his head and moved to the window, distancing himself. "I don't know what to believe anymore."

"Nothing has changed from yesterday to now," I pleaded my case.

"Everything has changed. The way Patrick disliked me, I always knew he was in love with you, and now I know the backstory."

"He. Hates. Me," I spat out.

"Have you wondered why?" His sharp gaze cut through me. "Hate doesn't exist without love. You don't hate someone unless, deep down, you loved them first."

"You're making a mountain out of a mole hill. Patrick was a mistake I'm still paying for. You're jumping to conclusions without knowing all the facts. I don't want to lose you over Patrick, Ryan. I breathe you. I love you. You believe me, right?" I wanted to hear him say he loved me back—not just imply it in a million ways, but say it out loud.

The jarring sound of his phone interrupted us.

He pushed away from the window and cursed under his breath. "It's Alan. He'll want me to get back on the call."

No matter how bad the timing was, I nodded and moved away so he could take the call. Between us, we never blurred the line between work and personal life. We knew when work took priority and personal issues needed to take a backseat.

"Go home. I'll see you when I get out of here," he said. Again, without meeting my eyes.

I wanted to remind him that our issues were unresolved. That I was ready to answer his questions. That he hadn't responded to my messages.

"I'll wait here," I said instead.

He pulled me into his chest and kissed me again. And then he was gone.

Thirty-Nine

RISHA

I woke up in his attached studio, bathed in the morning's golden light. The large clock on the wall told me I was late—it was already eight.

Just like last night, the only occupant in the bed was me.

I checked my phone—no message. I walked into his office and found it empty. The cynical part of my brain wanted me to take the hint. My heart gave all sorts of excuses. Deep down, I knew I was beyond the point of self-preservation. I'd completely and thoroughly fallen in love with Ryan.

After a quick shower, I grabbed one of the three emergency outfits I kept there. Then I used his vanity and got ready with whatever bare minimum I carried in my purse. Outside, Bobby was already at her desk like she had never left, except her clothes were different from yesterday's.

"Good morning, sunshine," Bobby greeted me cheerily. I was used to her exuberant greetings. Everyone in this office knew we were dating.

"Good morning. Do you know where Ryan is?"

She tilted her head in confusion. "What do you mean? He's in Vegas already. He left last night with his business partner, Nicholas. Didn't he tell you when you two met?"

I prayed to God she didn't see the shock on my face because I distinctly remembered no mention of going to Vegas. I had even told him I would wait here, and he still hadn't said a word.

Feigning complacent, I asked, "Did he leave a message with you?"

"Um, no." She looked at me like I had grown two heads. "Did you check your phone?"

"My phone is dead," I quickly lied and rushed out.

On my way to the elevator, I checked my phone again in case I had missed something. No voicemail. No text. No email.

My heart took over before my mind forced me to shut down and send another message. So that was what I did.

Me: I heard you're in Vegas. Call me when you're free.

"Conference room. Ten minutes," Patrick announced, suddenly appearing in my office doorway. "We've signed the contract with Circle. Let's go over logistics."

I froze, still clutching my coffee. *Circle.*

"You signed the contract?" I asked with a mix of disbelief and dry amusement. He'd crossed this line before, but I wasn't the woman who'd let it slide anymore. "Are you making decisions on my behalf now?"

I was certain he had seen this coming, so he immediately turned aggressive. "On Sylosis's behalf. I'm the vice president who refuses to let a multi-million-dollar opportunity die because you're having a personal meltdown. Now, let's go."

The mug hit the desk with a dull *thud*. A wave of heat rose along my neck. My personal issues never affected my work, but his accusations were becoming hard to swallow.

"If you made the decision for someone else, I don't need to be in that room. But if you made the decision on my behalf or my team's, then I don't give a damn if you're VP or the second coming. I. Refuse. To. Take. This. Project."

He blinked in surprise before the mask slid back into place. For a split-second, he fought between which role to assume: my colleague or ex-lover. The man I once liked or the man I now loathed. The man who thought I wouldn't walk away or the one who saw me leaving.

"You understand you can't talk to me like this anymore, right?"

I did. It was unprofessional. But he'd been pushing my buttons for far too long.

"And you understand you can't bulldoze my team and call it leadership, right?" I mimicked his tone

He crossed his arms, taking a defensive stance. "That's not how companies work, Risha. Especially startups. You need to stop playing the billionaire's girlfriend and remember the career you wanted so much."

The sting landed deeper than it should have.

"Don't you dare bring my personal life into this," I snapped. "My dating life is not your business."

"Right, but my work is my business. My business is also growing this company. And my business is calling out women like you who want the corner office but can't handle the fire that comes with it."

"I handled a lot of fire before you even walked in here with your insecurities," I pushed back. I felt the prick of tears behind my eyes, but I fought them back. "If you can't separate your feelings from your work, that's not on me."

His mouth tightened. "You think I care who you date?"

"I think you care more than you're willing to admit. And instead of dealing with it like an adult, you hijack my decisions to make a point."

"I'm doing my job."

"No," I said firmly. "You're lashing out because I left. Because I didn't choose you. And because you've been replaced, which your ego can't handle."

His nose flared as he inhaled and exhaled, trying to find his next words. "At least he got the version of you that I built. While I had to deal with an absolute mess."

That was it.

"Fuck you," I spat out. My voice turned lethal. Final. "I quit."

I didn't wait for his reaction; I shoved past him. The hallway stretched in front of me like a vacuum. I couldn't see forward, but I didn't look back. I wasn't just walking out on him; I was walking out on the last part of my life I had held so close.

I spent the next week at the penthouse, waiting for Ryan, for a message, for anything. I felt the silence in my bones, in the sharp ache of every hour he didn't call. Still, I waited. It felt like déjà vu.

My heart had always known when to let go, when to stop hoping, and when to move on. The thing about love was, it never played by the rules. It defied all reason. Until that fragile thing broke.

The reason I extended my superfluous stay was the continued remodeling of the penthouse. Without Ryan, the space seemed haunted, despite ten people working fourteen-hour shifts. I finally understood why he had abandoned this place, why he had buried himself in his office building instead. A house, whether eight thousand square feet or eight hundred, meant nothing without someone to share it with. Today, in all that space and luxury, I felt more alone than I ever had in my entire life.

This had been the best chapter of my life, but even the best of pages came to an end. It was time to start the next one. Time to let go. Once the decision was made, my mind followed suit—calm, clear, always a realist.

"The work is almost complete, Miss Verma. We just need to fix the last claw-foot bathtub when it gets delivered," the senior decorator told me.

"Do we have an estimated timeframe of delivery?" I asked.

He shrugged. "Two to three weeks when I last checked. That was three days ago."

The following morning, I packed my personal belongings and locked the penthouse. After dropping everything back in my apartment, I went to MoxTo.

The place had transformed into something wild and beautiful. I noticed bits of Virona in every corner. A part of me was proud of who she had become; a part of me felt broken for a friend I'd lost forever.

I asked three people before I finally figured out where she was. When I exited the elevator on the windy rooftop, I was greeted by a swanky glass pool, multiple bars, a dozen men on duty fixing tiles and mirrors, and right in the center was Virona, shooting instructions in every direction.

I walked over to her and said, "You got a minute?"

She turned fast to face me. Confusion ricocheted between her eyes, but all she said was, "Risha ... I wasn't expecting you."

"Other than the tub, the rest is done." I placed the penthouse keys into her hand. They were just keys, but handing them over felt like tearing away from the one place I felt seen.

"I didn't mean for Ryan to hear us."

"It doesn't matter," I said, meaning it. "You can do your final inspection before handing over the keys to Ryan."

"I know you blame me for what's happened between you two, but believe me; I never thought I'd be the reason for your breakup." Her words carried guilt, not repentance.

I was trapped by her prejudices, and there was nothing I could do to escape them.

"There are things I blame you for, Virona; breaking up my relationship with Ryan isn't one of them. We both have moved so far from each other that we can never find our way back again. It doesn't mean I'm not proud of who you've become. I wish you all the good things in life, and I'll follow your career, but this is where our never-meant-to-repair relationship ends." I turned back to the elevator, which was still open. "Goodbye, Virona."

Cece and I ordered Chinese takeout and then curled up on the couch, letting mindless television fill the silence. She didn't press, didn't ask, and didn't try to fix anything. Whatever she guessed about my situation, she kept to herself. And like a true best-friend, she gave me exactly what I needed: time, space, and the kind of company that made breathing feel easier. I was grateful for her presence because the suffocating loneliness had started to feel like quicksand. Without her, I might have sunk into it completely.

I'd been hurt before. Emotionally bruised, heart cracked here and there. Back then, I always had a distraction—school deadlines, university chaos, work that never paused. Life had been loud and full, and in that noise, the pain was easy to push aside. Not erased, but buried just deep enough not to interfere. This time, the stillness gave it space to grow. There was nothing rushing me forward, nothing demanding my attention. Just me, the ache, and too much quiet.

I woke up on the couch the next morning. Cece was at the other end, flipping through channels like it was a weekend. My broken heart was twisting inside me, a constant ache not ready to subside. I wanted to say everything I'd been holding in. The things I'd never told anyone. The things I had wanted to share with Ryan before he assumed we'd end the same way things had ended with Patrick, that I was too much of a mess to handle.

So I did. I spilled it all—words, sobs, broken pieces of whatever was left. I talked until there was nothing left to confess. No more shame to tuck away. No more embarrassment to hide behind.

Forty

RYAN

"I need results, Bob, not excuses." I was beyond done. It'd been a month, and I was still cleaning other people's messes. This one had already cost us millions, and I wasn't in the mood for another round of damage control.

"The new crew can start in a week's time, but the city contractor won't let us move forward. It's a sticky situation here," Bob explained meekly, as if that would soften his incompetence.

Sticky, sure. That was what he was calling it now.

"I don't care how *sticky* the situation is," I fumed. "I won't pay that scum a dime more than we already have."

The silence in the room resonated with my soul. Nick shifted in his seat. Alan looked like he wanted to flee but thought better of it. I was hanging by a thread. It wasn't the dry Vegas heat that was getting to me, but the whole damn mess.

And the worst part was, none of this was supposed to be *my* mess. Nick had been pushing to expand. Taber wanted his name on a Vegas tower. Jonah wanted to partner with us so he wouldn't feel excluded. I'd signed off because it had made business sense.

Who the fuck was I kidding? I believed in it, too. Or maybe I just wanted to keep building because it kept me from falling apart.

But now I didn't even know what I was chasing.

Somewhere along the way, I'd let my focus slip, which had led to three hundred workers walking off before I even got here. Three hundred people had lost faith in me. And I hadn't even seen it coming. I thought their demands had been met—end work by six, medical insurance for their families. Nothing outrageous, right? But instead of giving them what they deserved, Bob—the smug ass standing in front of me now—had lined the pockets of a city official and let those hard-working men rot.

I stared at him, rage pulsing behind my eyes. Not because he had screwed up, but because I had. I was supposed to lead. I was supposed to know. But I'd been too busy chasing something—rather, someone—who was nothing but a mess of her own.

I fucking hated mess.

All I wanted was simplicity and straight lines, everything that wasn't complicated. Risha's past and present were so tangled up that it was impossible to extract one from the other. Impossible to move forward.

And now I was losing the one thing I stood for. Belief in me to lead.

"Vegas is not the same as New York, Ryan." Bob pulled me in, or out of the mess I was drowning in—I couldn't tell which one. "You hired me to help you deal with problems like this. The officer realized he could extort more money from you rich guys. He won't budge until he gets another five million."

"I won't pay another dime," I said with finality.

"Then you might as well shut this project down. Walk away from the construction and leave Vegas." Bob shoved himself back into his rickety chair like this wasn't his circus anymore. His makeshift office couldn't be more than ten-by-ten, and today, Nick, Alan, and I had boxed him into the corner.

My anger wasn't directed at Bob, but at the truth in his words. I didn't have power in this city. Not like I did in New York. But I wasn't ready to admit defeat either.

"I won't—"

"Take a break, Ryan," Nick cut in from my right. "This argument isn't getting us anywhere."

"We're on the same side, Ryan," Alan said calmly. "Bob's just the messenger. No point shooting darts at him."

Finding support, Bob quickly jumped in. "That's what I'm saying. I want this resort as much as you do. In five years, you'll have a say in this city. Right now, you're just another big-pocket outsider trying to break in."

Nick stood and shoved open the crooked door, letting the suffocating desert's early April heat rush into the cooled air. "Bob, give us the room. You'll get the money."

"I want the old crew back," I bit out. I was already yielding to his demands, but I wasn't ready to abandon the backbone of this industry. "I'm not bending on that."

Bob nodded and slipped out without another word.

I turned on Nick and Alan. "Stop fucking telling me what to do. I'm the one sweating it out in the middle of a goddamn desert, not you two."

"You could've flown back with me the next day. No one forced you to spend a month in Vegas," Nick shot back.

"Fuck you." My throat burned. "There's been some fucking disaster every day."

"And you're telling us none of this could've been handled from your New York office?" Alan narrowed his eyes like he already knew the answer.

I looked away. Because he was right. Nick was right. I didn't even know what I was doing here anymore.

"You know she's good for you, right?" Alan brought up my miserable, pathetic state without Risha every single day. "You're easier to work with when you're not in tunnel vision mode."

"I'll be in a better mood when people stop quitting on me," I fired back. "I'm tired of people walking away. I'm tired of this bullshit. I'm tired of—"

"Make up your freaking mind! What exactly are you upset

about?" Alan's voice cut through mine. "The crew wasn't even on our payroll."

"They were still working for me. I take that as a personal failure."

"Or maybe you're just pissed at Bob, who's actually trying to do his job," Nick added.

"I disagree." My words clipped out sharply. "Bob's more focused on lining the city officer's pocket. I wouldn't be surprised if he's taking a cut."

Alan shook his head, unable to decide if I was paranoid or spiraling. Nick said nothing. He *knew* I was spiraling when I had argued with a drunk stranger last night. That was way out of character for me.

"At this point," I said, heat rising to my face, "I can't stand Bob's guts—"

"Or maybe," Alan cut in again, "you're just pissed because you're avoiding Risha. The woman you can't fucking live without."

"My personal life is none of your business," I said through gritted teeth.

"It becomes everyone's business when your personal shit starts bleeding into your business decisions," Alan said without missing a beat. "I don't know why you're avoiding her when it's starkly clear you're miserable without her."

I turned my back on both of them, but the walls were too thin, the room too small, the silence too loud. I could feel their eyes on me. Alan's admonition and Nick's silence.

I had come here to fix this construction site. But what the hell was I even fixing? I couldn't tell.

"Here are your keys." Virona walked into my office a week after I got back from Vegas and dropped the penthouse keys on my desk

—*the ones* I'd given Risha. "If anything needs to be changed, let me know."

My focus remained on the half-drafted email to Bob about the permit copies.

I'd moved back into the studio next-door because it was easier to ignore what I'd walked away from. Turning off feelings made it easier to stay focused on the priorities. My work. McAlister Group.

"Thanks, Vikki," I said dismissively. The day I'd gotten back, I had received the pendant I'd given to Risha. She had mailed it back with five painful words: *I don't need this anymore.*

Vikki didn't budge. Instead, she waited until I turned my attention to her.

"I was wrong, you know. I judged her with my sixteen-year-old lens. I let my bias get in the way. I had no right—"

"I understand you two have a history." I went back to typing.

"Yes, that we do. But I also let my prejudice do the talking."

"That's not my place to comment." I tried to shut her down, tried to stay detached. I tried not to listen or hear. *I tried.*

But Vikki didn't move from the edge of my desk. And no matter how indifferent I tried to act, I couldn't stop the part of me that wanted to hear Risha's name. I wanted to know where she was. What she was doing.

My eyes flicked to the corner of the screen. Half past noon. Lunchtime.

She was probably out with her colleagues ... maybe with Patrick. Her boss, the ex. The rising bile wasn't jealousy, but stemmed from how little I really knew. I had trusted her fully and stupidly. Despite that, I was only just beginning to understand the woman I thought I could build a life with.

The thought of her cheating had never crossed my mind, but the omissions were harder to ignore. Four months together, and I still hadn't unraveled her knots, still hadn't seen all her scars. Understanding Risha needed more time than I could give.

My work demanded focus, proof of my worth, even if those

goals felt hollow lately. I needed my head clear, needed to realign, needed her out of my system. But she lingered no matter how far I pushed. A shadow at high noon, impossible to outrun.

I wanted her more than peace, more than success. The summit I'd been climbing no longer existed because she'd become the only thing I craved. A drug I had to wean myself off of before she rewired every part of me, before I forgot who I was without her.

"She was wrong then, and I was wrong now. Please don't let me be the reason for another decade of misunderstandings." Vikki's voice pulled me out of my self-loathing.

I summoned all my strength and met her gaze. "That's between you two to resolve," I said.

"There's nothing left to fix. She gave us another chance, and I blew it. And the worst part is, this time, I can't blame her. But I don't want to be the reason her happiness disappears. You gave her that, Ryan. I saw her really smile with you, laugh like the world wasn't crushing her for once."

"You got a minute?" Alan walked into my office, sparing me from answering. I had nothing to say to her because words weren't forming the right sentences anymore.

"Yes. Vikki was just leaving," I said without pause.

"Now I know how it feels to live with regrets," she said as she walked away.

I tried for the umpteenth time to clear my head, not to let her words play with my decisions. What she'd said or thought didn't matter. Risha was a disruption. A storm that split my neatly drawn lines. I'd made peace with walking away from that. I was better off without her. Now, I just had to learn to live with my decision.

Alan took the chair across from me. "Sylosis is backing out of the lease they signed three months ago. They don't want another floor anymore."

Normally, that wouldn't even be on my radar. I had twenty

high-rises in this city. One tenant walking away wasn't a crisis. But Sylosis mattered ever since I'd found out Risha worked there.

"Why?" I kept my voice even.

"It seems Risha resigned. So did her entire team. The news is the company's about to lose two of their biggest clients."

"Say that again." I tried to keep the surprise out of my voice but failed miserably. It was unlike Risha to make hasty decisions.

"From what I gathered, she resigned over a month ago. Then, last week, her entire engineering team walked. The projects they were handling—"

I didn't hear the rest. Or maybe I did, but nothing landed. My brain was already spinning in one direction—*her*. What the hell had happened? I thought her work was everything. Wasn't it? It used to be.

My hand hovered over my phone. Every message I'd ignored still sat there. Read. And reread. Left unanswered. She hadn't reached out since I'd left for Vegas. She'd left the ball in my court, and I'd chosen to drop it.

A part of me wanted to call her, see her, talk to her. The other part reminded me of what life looked like now. Vegas was back on track. The crew had returned. MoxTo was opening in a month. My speech at the gala was coming up next week. My focus was finally where it needed to be—on things that mattered.

When I left my heart out of the equation, everything worked better.

"You're making a mistake letting her go," Alan said, watching me too closely. "If you find someone who makes you happy, you don't walk away from them."

"You can leave if you're done," I cut him off. "I've got work to finish before the dinner with the execs."

He shook his head in disbelief.

I stared at my phone screen. Ten seconds later, I unlocked and called Bob instead of emailing.

Forty-One

RISHA

I walked the streets of my neighborhood, looking at the various boutiques, stopping to praise the uniqueness of each window. A city with an amalgamation of old and new, funk and eclectic, tradition and contemporary ... a city that breathed life and drew everyone into its heart, transforming them into New Yorkers over time.

I'd been living here for six years but had never stopped to appreciate everything this place offered. From the smallest pretzel cart to the largest museums, a walk in Central Park to a film festival—all the things I missed all these years in this city finally filled me with a sense of belonging. Three steps back and one step forward, I surrendered myself to discover myself.

I still didn't know where I belonged, nor what my future held, but there was freedom in not knowing who I was and what I wanted to be. Sometimes, all we needed was a clean slate to start over. The fog had to lift to recognize what waited beyond it. Only when the vision was clear, did we finally see what was there to be found.

Sylosis' CEO, Cal Jenkins, had reached out the moment he had found out I'd left the building. Marcus had reached out with a job offer when he'd heard the news. Circle recruiters had done the same. And then Raj had offered me a twenty-five percent partnership in his company, minus the offer to marry. He had confessed he was an ass and would start with friendship and partnership instead. He wanted to take on the challenge to learn to be romantic. I'd politely declined every offer.

I needed to find myself before I could commit to the next chapter.

My mother's angry rants jammed my phone until I stopped picking them up. Not answering to anyone or fulfilling expectations had a sense of freedom, as well. Dad had called me only once. The man of few words had finally decided to meet me. Tomorrow after visiting Columbia with Sia, he asked if I was available for lunch. I accepted his invitation. I also had to break the news at some point that I had quit my job. And that I'd joined design school. I wasn't ready to commit to a full degree, but I wanted to learn what I didn't know—slow and steady, at my own pace.

Cece and I had grown closer than I thought possible, like a sisterhood through unresolved entanglements and the quiet times we shared. It was liberating to have that one person I could be completely raw with. Someone who didn't just know who I was, but understood who I used to be and saw who I was trying to become. Walking that uncertain road with her beside me made the emptiest days feel less hollow. And when the nights turned cruel and I cried myself to sleep, her nonjudgmental presence was the only light I held onto.

Rounding the corner of Spring and Greene, I entered Café Rainbleu through one of its two glass doors. I scanned the double-occupancy tables, expecting to find Marty at one of them, but stopped short when I saw him waving from the far end of a long table, pushed together to seat my entire Sylosis engineering team.

"Did I miss a secret team reunion?" I half-laughed, hugging the familiar faces I'd spent four years working alongside. Of all the ties I'd tried to untangle and distance myself from, these people still held a piece of me I hadn't realized was missing until now.

After the usual "how've you been" small talk, I dropped into the empty seat beside Marty. My stomach churned when I noticed another empty chair. "Are we expecting someone else?" I asked carefully, praying it wasn't Patrick or Cal.

"Ignore that for now." Marty waved it off with a smile. "We've got some big news."

"Don't tell me you're having another kid. It's too soon," I teased. "And Zoe's doing stand-up. Reco is off to Texas. Sal's finally locked in a wedding venue ..." I rattled off each of their personal life updates like a reflex, stories we'd shared during our weekly meetings.

"Impressive," Marty mocked. "But zero points. The real news is, we all followed you. We quit our jobs."

I blinked. "You did what?"

"Every one of us," he said, grinning now. "We're out. No more Sylosis."

"Why? When?" I stammered, my jaw halfway to the floor. "Are you all insane?"

Zoe giggled, but it was Marty who answered. "We meant it when we said we worked there because of you. After you left, everything started falling apart. It didn't feel like home anymore. We figured it was time for a fresh start."

I should have been flattered. Instead, I was peeled open. I hadn't earned this level of trust.

"This is so erratic. Do you need reference letters? Interviews? I can help in whatever capacity I can," I offered, turning instinctively to Zoe—the youngest and the one I always looked out for.

"That's not why we're here," she mumbled.

"We're here to work for you, Risha," Marty added with an unwavering smile. "Your team is ready. Start your company, and we'll build it with you."

"You've all lost your minds." It came out uneven, part

whisper, part stunned confusion, disoriented even, like I was still catching up to them. "I don't even know what that means. We don't have a client. No office. I can't pay anyone. We would have to earn before I can even think about salaries."

I must have started hyperventilating, because Marty placed his hand on my arm. I still couldn't catch my breath. What had they done? I carried a sense of responsibility for them, but this was something else entirely. A company. Livelihoods. Families. Futures. This was too much responsibility to take on when I was still figuring myself out.

"You can't be serious," I managed with a shaky voice.

"I doubt any of them are known for their sense of humor," a familiar voice chimed in.

"Marcus?" My confusion shot straight past surprise. "What are you doing here?"

He pulled out the empty chair, wedged himself between Zoe and Sal, and said, "Well, when the camel refuses to go to the oasis, the oasis comes to the camel."

"That metaphor makes no sense."

He shrugged. "You turned down my job offer. But when I found out your entire team had quit, I reached out to them, and they said they'd follow you. So now, I'm following them. If you're ready to start your company, Risha, Nixus will be your first project."

My lungs tightened. The weight of being someone they could trust overwhelmed me. "This is a crazy idea."

"It's not," Marty said calmly. "Like you have said, every obstacle is a beginning. Work from a coffee shop, work from home—we already know how to work together. Nixus is just the start; other firms will follow. Build something that reflects your values and ethics. Real work-life balance. Make it what Sylosis never was."

"You love designing homes," Zoe added boldly. "I want to travel the world. If this is your company, we can do both and still do the work we're great at."

I thought of Ryan and the weight he carried, the expectations he shouldered, yet he held his empire together without breaking. I'd learned so much from him, and I'd so much left to prove—not to anyone but myself. I needed purpose. Maybe this was my sign.

Maybe this was my next chapter. My blank canvas.

For the first time, the fog lifted its hold on me. The blur gave way to clarity, and something unfamiliar stirred: zest. Wild and terrifyingly real. If this were my next chapter, I would call it "Ayati Technology."

"My treat tonight," I announced as Cece and I slid into our usual booth at the local Chinese place. "What do you think of *Ayati Technologies*?"

"Never heard of them." She skimmed the menu, not really reading. Predictably, she folded it shut and looked toward the server waiting to take down our orders. "Chicken Lo Mein. Shrimp with basil."

"Shocking," I deadpanned, handing over my menu without looking. "Egg drop soup, please."

The server didn't even blink. He knew our routine by now and took off with our orders.

"So, what do they do?" Cece went back to our conversation.

"The question you should be asking is: what *will* they do?" I emphasized, feeling the spark in my chest that made my fingers twitch and my leg bounce beneath the table.

She arched one brow. "What's with the face? You look like you're about to launch a spaceship or something."

"That's not happening in this lifetime, but I've got something better." My smile turned into a grin. We'd had this conversation before, but the gap between my want and perceived possibilities seemed insurmountable.

Cece's expression changed as she leaned over the table. "You're not gonna make me guess, are you?"

I shook my head, the grin widening, if that was even possible. "The real question is: do you want to know what Ayati *will* do?"

She narrowed her eyes, sensing the buildup. "What exactly are you not telling me?"

"Who owns the damn company, Cece?"

Her confusion melted into recognition. Then her mouth fell open. "You did *not*."

I nodded. "Paperwork's filed. I submitted it before I left the apartment."

A tiny squeal left her as she reached across the table and grabbed my hands. I laughed profusely and told her everything. From Marty's announcement to Marcus's unexpected arrival. Every twist, every turn, every insane second of it.

We stayed in that booth brainstorming long after dinner plates were cleared. Tomorrow, I was meeting my team to dive into the Nixus project, followed by lunch with Dad and Sia, and then I'd sign the temporary lease for our new coworking office. I wasn't diving in blindly this time. Life had taught me to move forward with hope in one hand and cautious optimism in the other—like wading into uncertain tides not to conquer the waves, but to rise and float with them.

Cece leaned back, sipping her tea. "I need a favor."

"Whatever you want." I was still glowing. If she'd asked for a kidney, I might have offered one.

"Mom sent me two seats to the Promise Beyond Loss Gala this Sunday. I want you to join as my plus-one."

My pulse stumbled. I couldn't believe it was April-end already. Ryan had asked me to the gala back when we'd still been together. I was sure he'd forgotten, but that didn't lessen the pain. I hadn't been avoiding him outright, but I wasn't exactly lining up for a front-row run-in, either.

"He doesn't get to own that space. He was an ass," Cece exclaimed.

"He wasn't," I said quickly before my emotions ran wild. "And I'm not hesitating. I'll join you."

"You can protect him all you want, doesn't mean I will. That man looks at you wrong, and I swear I'll key his precious car or spill a drink on his pristine tux."

I huffed out a laugh, but it didn't quite reach my chest. "Let it go, Cece. I'm not angry at him."

"But you're sad because of him."

I stared down at the blank space on the table. "That's on me. I let my guard down again, let hope fool me into thinking maybe this time love would stand by me."

She didn't say anything after that. It felt good knowing someone fully saw me and still accepted me. I paid the check, and we stepped into the warm spring night, but her words lingered long after.

Love wasn't built for me, and maybe that was okay. Because, this time, I was building something for myself.

Forty-Two

RISHA

Jasmine & Cardamom was nestled between Lexington and Broadway, a small Indian bistro with terracotta planters lining its windowsills and a chalkboard out front that read, *"Spiced Chai & Soul Comforts Inside."* Once upon a time, it used to be my favorite spot in the city. Dad had discovered it during one of his surprise visits after I'd joined Columbia; he'd said he missed seeing me. That was before everything between us fell apart.

I paused outside the door, pressing my hand against my belly. It wasn't nerves but grief that hadn't found its voice yet. So much was left unspoken because he never asked and I never explained. People said time healed everything. I called bullshit. We only swept things under the rug until it couldn't hold and everything spilled into the light, impossible to ignore.

Let it go, Risha. Your next appointment is in an hour. Your life is changing for the better. You don't need people who don't need you. People who don't love you. Talk to Sia, have a minimum conversation with Dad, and get out before things get tense.

I pulled the door open and walked into the soft amber glow. The scent of cumin and saffron floated everywhere, lunchtime chatter buzzing, white walls depicting Indian deserts and camels created a cozy atmosphere. I spotted Sia first, waving with both hands, her excitement brightening the corner they were seated in.

Tucking all emotions in, I plastered a smile and walked over to them. Dad busied himself scanning the menu, like he didn't already know what he'd order. Tandoori chicken and daal fry.

"Hey, sweets." I opened my arms.

Sia got up to hug me, and I clung to her longer than usual, craving the connection. Familiarity. Love.

Dad looked up and gave me a nod. "Risha."

"Hey, Dad." I slid into the seat beside Sia and across from him.

The server arrived promptly. Sia and I decided to split a chicken tikka masala with naan.

"Add tandoori chicken and daal fry, please," Dad added, barely looking up.

I stifled a laugh.

"So"—I turned to Sia—"how was the campus tour? Any second thoughts?"

"Are you kidding?" She beamed. "I've already sent in my acceptance."

"She was here to soak it in. Decision's done a while back," Dad chimed in.

"That's our go-getter." I regarded my little sister with pride. "Next time you come here, just crash with me. No need to make Dad chaperone you."

"He invited himself," she said with an eye roll. "When he heard I was meeting you."

Dad busied himself pouring water into our glasses. He certainly wasn't here out of sentiment. Either Mom had sent him to talk sense into me, or he couldn't bear the idea of Sia traveling into the city alone.

Sia's energy cut through the tension. She animatedly described the buildings she'd visited, the bookstore where she hoped to get a part-time job, and her plans for decorating her dorm. For a while, Dad and I just listened. We laughed and remembered how to be a family. She was a burst of energy.

Then came the turn.

"By the way, you've lost serious weight," Sia observed. "How stressed are you?"

"How many deadlines are you juggling these days?" Dad chimed in right after.

"Actually," I began hesitantly. I thought the hardest part would be telling him I'd left my job. But now, I wasn't sure how he'd react that I'd started something of my own. He'd never had much respect for the service industry, always calling it derivative, not innovation. "I founded my own company."

Dad blinked. "And your job?"

I couldn't tell if the shock was good or bad. "I left Sylosis a month ago."

"Wow!" He looked away, absorbing it. "So many choices made, and we're just finding out. I didn't realize we'd grown so distant."

"If spending every weekend under one roof made us close, then you're lying to yourself." I should have stopped here, but I couldn't hit the brakes this time. "It was all for show. We were playing the happy family because that's what Mom wanted."

My insinuation made him flinch. Sia shifted beside me. Guilt prickled at the edge of my conscience. This was supposed to be her moment of celebration. But when else? When would there ever be a "right" time to say these things? To speak the truth I'd buried for so long? How else would he ever know how deeply his silence had cut me, how often I'd looked for him, only to find he'd already turned away?

"You can't hate your mother, Risha. She isn't a bad person." It stung when he chose to defend her.

"I don't hate her, Daddy. Rather, she is the only one I understand. Don't agree, but understand. She comes from a traditional family where the world is still living in the past. But I wasn't born into that world. I didn't grow up around those values. I'm so confused all the time that I don't even know where I belong. I didn't even choose this country. You did! You chose to build this life. You chose to marry Mom. And that meant it was your responsibility to bridge the space between us."

My voice trembled. "Being a good husband isn't the same as being a good father. You can't keep siding with her and expect me to always be the one who adjusts. It doesn't work that way. You stretched the elastic so far, Daddy—eventually, it snapped. And once something breaks, it doesn't just go back. We're not machines that reboot and restart. We feel. We carry the hurt."

I reached for my water glass, gulping it down to fight the lump rising in my throat. The pain had been building for years, and now it burned to speak it out loud.

His face fell. "It's not like I didn't try," he finally said, sighing heavily. "But your constant defiance left no room for compromise."

"*My* defiance, huh?" I couldn't believe he'd said that. "Choosing my own path is defiance to you?"

"You wanted to be ... ordinary. And I even accepted that," he spat out, reminding me of my transition from the doctoral program to the MBA.

"What's wrong with being ordinary?" My voice cracked. "Why is it so shameful to want happiness over ambition? To step out of a race that only leaves you emptier the further you go?"

"But you were never meant to be ordinary, Risha."

"And what if that's what I want? Why is it not good enough for you? Why do you want a version of me that suits your needs? Why isn't who I am enough for you?" I rasped.

The server returned with our food, but I barely noticed. I wasn't hungry anymore. The lump in my throat choked me with anger and disappointment and those tainted, irreversible memories.

"You know what I remember most about high school?" I started again, not caring that the server was still standing beside us and forgetting this lunch was supposed to be a celebration. He had opened up the can of worms, and I couldn't put the lid back on. "Not my science fair trophies or top grades. I remember sketching designs long after midnight because I wanted to be an interior designer. I remember the agony when Mom told me that wasn't a real career. And I remember you, standing in the doorway, saying nothing."

His face stiffened. "My God, you're holding grudges since that time?"

"Yes. And if I start listing everything else, we'll be here until tomorrow."

He slumped back in his chair. "Your mother and I made sacrifices—"

"For us. Yes, I know. We were reminded of that every day. But don't act like they weren't for yourselves, too. You made your choices. You don't get to use them to control mine."

"And then *that* boy ..." I felt the air leave my lungs. "He destroyed everything we believed in." Dad shook his head as if reliving the nightmare.

"How many times do I need to apologize for that? Have you never made a mistake in your life?" My voice trembled.

"Yes, I did," he said. "When I chose to stay here instead of going back home."

"Right. You made that choice. Right or wrong, it was your decision and your regret. Now let me make my own decisions for once." I stood abruptly, letting the napkin fall from my lap.

"We didn't want you to make wrong choices. We only want to protect you, Risha."

"I'm thirty years old. Let me fail if I must. But let the failure be mine." I turned to leave, stopping only when I saw Sia's face marred with pain and confusion. "I'm sorry for ruining your lunch. I'll see you when you move."

Dad's voice chased me. "So, this is it? You're cutting us off now?"

"No," I answered without turning around. "Those ties

snapped a long time ago. I'm just done pretending they're still intact. You were my hero once, but now I can't even look at you."

His silence followed me out.

The city moved with me as I stepped into the street. Warm wind tangled my loose curls. The sun glittered above me. My eyes stung, but I didn't wipe the tears away. Once again, they spilled in abundance.

Some chapters were best closed before the shadows grew long.

Forty-Three

RYAN

"MoxTo Suites are booking up quickly," Melinda, Nick's plus-one of every event, used the lull in conversation to update us on the numbers. "With a month to go before opening, it appears we're heading for a sold-out summer."

"Good," I said. The update didn't warrant further discussion.

Six months ago, I wanted MoxTo to be complete, done with Miami, Vegas to run smoothly, and people to trust my judgment, but now none of it held weight. My desires had changed, and a constant hollowness consumed my every waking moment.

"What about restaurants? Have we finalized all five?" I asked before Mindy felt the need to fill in the silence again since that was what she had been doing for the last half hour.

"Matsuhina's contract is on my desk," Nick answered. "Everything else is signed. Three6T, Serata, and all the bars are under Taber's umbrella."

"Oh, and this morning, we locked in the two-year contract with Ms. Benedict. She's thrilled to take over MoxTo's spa operations," Melinda added.

Small talk wasn't necessary; not every lull needed buffers, and I didn't need company just because they thought I was sinking. Men didn't talk about feelings—Nick and I were fine, even if he saw me slipping. His solution was simple: take work off my plate. And I appreciated that. His date, though, thought MoxTo updates and gap-filling would impress us.

The venue buzzed with Manhattan's elite. Golden shadows slid across polished marble floors, glasses clinked, servers floated past with silver trays, and a quartet played soft classical music no one paid attention to. If it weren't for the speech, I wouldn't be here tonight. No part of me wanted to put on a tux, walk into this room, and pretend like I wasn't falling apart. But showing up was part of the job—and right now, I had one. Walk the gala. Smile for photos. Sell the illusion.

I wasn't the man to dwell on mistakes or second-guess my decisions. I calculated, took risks, and moved on. Regret was a slow unraveling, though—an unfamiliar territory. It lingered tight in my chest, dulled behind my eyes, catching me off guard in the middle of meetings and appointments. I could keep it together in front of everyone, but I couldn't fake clarity I didn't have.

I wanted her. Needed her. Risha was the air I breathed, and I'd let her go like she'd meant nothing to me. Not even a goodbye. Just ... fucking silence. I had never expected regret to become a permanent state of being. Yet here I was, living with it, day and night. And it ate through everything I built like acid.

"Did you know she'd be here?" Nick asked casually, sipping his drink.

I followed his chin until my breath left in one clean shot. Her grip on my heart pulled tight, like a rope yanking me toward her. My Risha.

She stood across the room in a strapless peach gown that hit my every waking desire, pulling me back to the first time and how everything had changed after. Her sleek bun bared her long neck and the soft slope of her collarbone.

My heart raced. My body betrayed me from admitting how badly I'd fucked this up.

She was in deep conversation with Cece and Anne, like I hadn't wrecked her and walked away. I watched her for a long time. Her eyes never scanned the room, even though she knew I'd be here. Part of me wanted to believe she was here for me; the rest knew she didn't give a damn. Risha had always been the stronger one between us.

"Are you going to talk to her, or just stare?" Nick asked.

And say what? *Sorry I ghosted you and pretended you meant nothing? Sorry I moved into my old studio after all the work you'd put into the penthouse?* She'd given the keys back, and I hadn't called. She'd returned the only gift I'd ever given her because *she didn't need it anymore.*

Fuck the pretense. I couldn't live this half-life any longer. Even now, in my sleep, I reached for her like a habit I couldn't break.

Crossing the room, I walked straight to her.

"Do you have five minutes?" I asked, skipping all unnecessary pleasantries.

"Ryan." She didn't look surprised. "I was just—"

Anne swooped into the spotlight. "There you are!" She beamed. "We were just talking about you."

I bent down to kiss her cheek. But I wasn't here to talk to anyone but Risha, who looked flawless. And beautiful. And totally in control while I was falling apart. Her presence was lightning pulsing through my veins. Our attraction was intangible; a constant thrumming that never dimmed for a day.

Nothing felt the same without her. Our last argument and all the misunderstandings meant nothing compared to what I felt for her.

Cece grabbed Risha's wrist. "Let me introduce you to Preston. He can help you with the office space for Ayati."

What now?

"Don't be silly." Anne waved Cece off. "Ryan will find her space in his building."

"Thanks, but I've already rented a co-working space," Risha cut in. "I'm not ready for a lease yet. It's too much overhead when I'm still figuring out expenses."

I stared at her, partly in shock and party admiration. "You ... started your own company?"

"She did," Cece snapped. "You'd know if you hadn't disappeared."

My jaw locked, but no argument there.

Anne blinked between us. "Wait—are you two not together anymore?"

"No, they're not," Cece said before either of us could respond. "Excuse us, Anne." She took Risha's hand and walked straight over to Preston Landry—my direct competition.

My feet refused to budge as I watched Risha offer him the smile that had once been reserved for me.

"Mind telling me what happened, Ryan?" Anne asked, pulling my attention back. It seemed Alan wasn't sharing my personal life with his wife.

"I made a terrible mistake," I openly admitted for the first time. "I didn't know how to be part of her life without screwing up everything I built for myself. So ... I ran away—literally." My words poured out like vomit.

For someone who'd spent a lifetime mastering control, I felt everything inside me shatter.

Anne gave a sympathizing nod. "Love is hard to find and easy to lose. Keeping it is the real hard work."

I shook my head, fully aware of how badly I'd screwed up. Not a day passed without missing Risha—her voice, her laughter, the way she fit against me like we'd been made for each other. Every time I reached for the phone, pride told me life was fine without her, and ego yanked me back, daring me to fake a strength I didn't have.

"I already lost her."

"Are you sure?" she asked. "Because, from where I'm standing, you're still watching her like she's yours." I couldn't answer, and she kept talking. "You can accept the outcome of your mistakes, or fix it. Fate doesn't write the ending, Ryan—you do."

I let her words sink in. Anne had only met Risha twice and, like Alan, she'd always said we were good for each other. Spectators often had more clarity than the people caught in the scene.

Across the room, Risha stood with Preston, nodding politely while he talked.

I approached with a newfound resolve, not caring what I was interrupting. Stopping in front of her, I asked, "Can we talk?"

Her lips parted slightly, and I didn't know what she'd say. But for the first time in months, I was ready to listen. Taking Risha's hand, I headed for the exit.

We reached the now-empty lobby when she pulled her hand back. "Ryan, stop."

I faced her and took her face in both hands. Her skin warmed beneath my palms.

She searched my eyes, and her lips were so close I could feel the pull of them. She scanned my mouth, and for a second, I thought she'd lean in.

Of course, she didn't. Instead, she rested her hand against my chest. Not pulling me in, nor pushing away. Just ... there.

"How are you?" Stupid question. Anyone could see how much weight she'd lost.

"Good," she said but didn't ask how I was.

I wanted to tell her I was dying without her. I wanted to beg her to take me back.

"Congratulations ... Ayati?" I asked. "What does that mean?"

"Moving forward." Her answer was clinically concise.

"It's beautiful," I said lamely. Then, inhaling a long breath, I let out, "God, I missed you so much."

Our mouths were so close it was hard to breathe without inhaling her scent. Want and restraint collided in the tight space between us. I brushed my thumb along her cheekbone, memorizing the shape of her face I'd touched a thousand times but never with this much uncertainty.

She inhaled sharply when I rested my forehead against hers, grounding us both in the silence that pulsed louder than words.

"I was a fucking coward." My voice came out shaky. "I was scared, and then the Vegas project exploded. Four hundred people left overnight."

"You were needed there." There was no accusation in her voice, no spite.

I wanted to promise her the world, but I was too afraid to even speak. I waited a burning minute of tension, knowing I'd follow her anywhere, even over edge, if she so much as twitched.

"Can you ever forgive me?"

Her body trembled the slightest, but she stayed composed, refusing to show me how deeply I'd shattered her.

"You don't owe me anything, Ryan."

"I should've stayed. I should've responded to your messages. I should've—fuck, I should've shown up. The least I should've done was listen to you when you came to my office."

She shook her head, moving away until I felt her absence. "You did the right thing. Trust me; I'm not upset."

A foreboding churned in the pit of my stomach. "When you love someone, you fight," I said. "You demand, you claim, you burn bridges if you have to. So demand something from me, Risha. Ask for an explanation. Give me something to fight for."

I heard my name echo from the overhead speakers.

She recoiled further. "You should go."

"I made a mistake," I whispered, but she was already looking past me.

My name rang out again from inside the ballroom, this time louder.

"I don't blame you. You like clean lines, and my life is chaotic in every direction."

"Then give me the chaos," I said, stepping closer once again. "Give me *you*."

I couldn't elicit any response from her, like she'd already lost hope in me. I never understood which was worse: not knowing there was hope, or the finality of everything I knew ending.

"I don't regret us, Ryan. But that doesn't mean we were meant to last any longer."

"Just"—I inhaled a sharp breath—"give me a chance to prove to you that I won't leave this time."

She looked away. Her decision was already made. And I realized she wouldn't trust me, no matter what I said.

We both turned again when my name was called.

"You should go," she murmured. "They're waiting."

I took her hand again because letting go wasn't in my bones. We walked back toward the hall. The surrounding noise grew with each step we took, breaking the quiet bubble we'd been in minutes ago.

Just before we reached the threshold, I leaned in and said, "Wait for me. We're not finished."

Forty-Four

RYAN

I stepped onto the stage. Two tables back, I caught Risha slipping into her seat beside Cece. She averted her eyes, but I felt her in every cell of my being.

I removed two notecards from the inside pocket of my jacket, glanced at the prepared words, and then tucked them away. Tonight wasn't about perfected lines; it was about the truth.

"Thank you for being here to support children who've lost everything far too soon," I began, my voice steady despite the tightness in my chest. "I was twenty-three when I lost both my parents in an instant. That night changed everything."

I scanned the crowd, making eye contact with each person. Until a few months ago, I wouldn't have even considered speaking about my grief. I kept my feelings boxed up and buried deep, convinced that showing pain meant losing control. But grief never stayed buried forever. It bled through quietly. You only learned to move around it, or try to at least.

"There's a silence that follows loss and creeps into your soul. You wake up and realize the world is still spinning, and somehow, you're supposed to keep up. But it's cold, and it's lonely, and every memory becomes something you're too afraid to touch, as well as too scared you might forget."

I paused long enough to find Risha again. Her soulful gaze was locked on me, providing all the strength I needed to expose my vulnerability publicly.

"And for the lucky few, someone walks into that silence. Not to fill the space, but to make it bearable. They see the cracks and don't flinch. They don't try to fix you; just quietly stay by your side. And before you realize it, you start breathing again ... you start *living* again."

My voice dipped. My eyes couldn't leave her. "That person doesn't always know the impact they made. They don't ask for credit or praise. They just show up when it matters most and keep showing up. And for someone like me who didn't believe in second chances, they suddenly became the reason I started to find hope again. So, when you find that rare person, hold on to them because that one person is enough to change everything all over again."

The applause came before I had even finished. Some gave a standing ovation. Some dabbed at their eyes. I barely noticed anyone because none of them mattered if Risha hadn't heard what I meant—if she didn't understand what I'd said without saying her name. She was the air I breathe.

Risha had given me my life back. She had taught me how to live again. And now, I just wanted the chance to be the man who could give her the same.

By the time I reached her table, I was met with an abandoned seat.

Grabbing Cece's elbow for attention, I asked, "Where is she?"

"Ryan," Cece exhaled, stepping into my path. "That was a beautiful speech."

"Cece ..." I cut in. "Where's Risha?"

She pursed her lips, debating. "I told you both this was a mistake, but neither of you took me seriously."

"Spare me the lecture and tell me where she is."

"Don't you get it?" Her voice dropped to a whispered hiss,

but the resentment stayed. True to her warning, she hated me for hurting her best friend. "You can't be what she wants."

"I can be everything she wants." The words hissed out before I could stop them.

"You can't, Ryan," Cece fired back. "All Risha wanted was for you to stay by her side, but the second things got complicated you vanished."

"I panicked. So what?" I snapped, running a hand down my face. "She's made mistakes, too. We all do, but then we fix it and move forward. We don't just quit."

"No." Cece shook her head. "You didn't just panic. You shut her out. You *cut her off*. The moment she tried to explain, you slammed the door in her face and walked away. Just like her father."

Her last words hit harder than the rest.

"She left everything, Ryan," Cece continued. "Her job. Her family. You think she's strong—oh, she is—but that doesn't mean she can take every hit and keep standing."

"What the fuck are you talking about?" My head spun. Her words were ten steps ahead of me, and I couldn't keep up. People moved around us, but the world started to blur. I didn't care about anything except getting to her, about understanding what I'd been too stubborn to listen before.

"You really don't know anything, do you?" Cece asked in disappointment.

"Isn't that the problem?"

I had thought I could ignore her past. But when her past was still showing up in her present, standing in her office ... it wasn't something I could pretend didn't affect me. I didn't even remember what made me spiral that day, only that it had ended with me walking out. And regretting it ever since.

"Tell me everything. Please," I begged.

"They dated during her MBA," Cece answered in a steady voice. "Her mom hated him and made it very clear. When Patrick found out, instead of letting Risha handle it like an adult, he stormed into her dad's office and started laying down the law. No humility spared. He disrespected her father in front of his colleagues, questioning his values and calling them outdated."

I clenched my teeth.

"When Risha found out, she was furious, but he refused to apologize. He told Risha to pick between him or them."

"Jesus." I let out a sigh.

"Her dad never forgave her for bringing Patrick into their lives. Her mom used her wrong decision to control Risha. Every decision, every setback, was thrown back at her. You think she's independent? Well, that came at a cost. She's been labeled rebellious, difficult, ungrateful, just for wanting to live on her own terms. Half her life has been spent cleaning up the fallout, trying to keep the peace. And the other half proving she's still worth something even after being told she's not enough."

"Fuck," I muttered.

Cece looked at me. "She's lived her whole life stuck between two worlds, trying to keep everyone happy. She was doing it, barely, but then you came in. And for the first time, she didn't *have* to juggle it alone. She was happy, Ryan. And then, just like that, you left without a word. Imagine her pain. Her dad never stood by her, and you decided to leave because she was a mess."

"I ... didn't know. The whole time we were together, she didn't let me in. She didn't—"

"Who lays out their ghosts on a first date, Ryan? Who unloads mistakes and embarrassments by the second or third, or even the hundredth? Sometimes, it takes a lifetime to really know someone. Why the hell did you expect to know her in four months?"

I didn't argue. I couldn't. I'd walked away from the one thing I never wanted to lose. And now I wasn't sure if I'd ever get her back.

Forty-Five

RISHA

At half-past five I slid my laptop into my bag and glanced around the room. Half the team was still here, eyes glued to screens, fingers dancing across keyboards.

"All right, guys," I said, stretching both hands over my head, "go home."

Marty turned halfway in his chair, arm slung across the back, his smirk already in place. He looked like he hadn't slept in days, but he also had an unshakable permanent grin firmly in place. Fatherhood suited him. "You do realize we're not doing this for a paycheck anymore, right?"

I gave a knowing smile. "I know ... but you have a baby who wants you to hang the moon. You should go home and prove him right."

He chuckled with deep satisfaction. "I worked from home last week without asking permission. Zoe's on the road, and we're still delivering. We're working harder than ever, but on our own terms."

He was right. Ayati was becoming what I had always envisioned. Providing my team the flexibility they deserved. It was another story that we'd a long road ahead. Two potential contracts I wasn't ready to sign, a team I couldn't afford to fail, a space too cramped to breathe, and no cushion if everything fell apart. I was flying without a roadmap.

"Did you sign them?" Marty asked, reading my thoughts.

Word traveled fast in our industry. We'd talked through the contracts, including Circle's two-year project, as soon as the clients had reached out. Everyone was on board for additional work, except me. More work meant more revenue, sure, but it also meant more hiring, more pressure, and more risk.

"Not yet," I admitted.

"You're gonna need more space. Engineering, design, operations—it won't scale in this workspace."

My axis tilted. I felt the shift before my brain processed his voice. Like the room had inhaled all at once, stealing the oxygen from my lungs and replacing it with a tight, electric silence.

"It's a nice setup you have here, but too cramped for the expanding business." Ryan approached my workstation, surveying the floor we occupied.

Butterflies stirred low in my belly, wings beating out a rhythm I hadn't felt since the gala last night. And then our eyes met, and the ground beneath me wasn't there anymore.

"Look who finally remembered we exist." Marty couldn't hide his surprise. He walked over and gave Ryan a firm handshake. "Good to see you, man. Missed your Chinese takeouts, and definitely missed the smile you bring to our boss's face."

At Sylosis, before I could establish a proper work-life balance for my team, Ryan had made a habit of stopping by in the evenings, bringing not only dinner for us but also for everyone else. The team had warmed up to him not because he was a billionaire, like Patrick would snidely remark every time, but because he showed up like any regular guy trying to spend time with the woman he liked. And Ryan had made a sincere effort to get to know everyone.

"I was an ass. And your boss doesn't take crap from anyone. Neither does she believe in second chances," Ryan said.

My stomach knotted, and irritation flowed through my veins.

"Ryan." I pushed to my feet, turning toward him. Electricity rippled through the space, coiling low in my belly, daring me to close the gap. "Why are you here?" I asked, clearing my head.

"I texted you several times." He neared my desk.

Marty turned back to his desk, attempting to fade away. The problem with shared workspaces was the lack of privacy.

"I've been busy."

He stepped closer, entering my personal space. All it took was his smooth, unhurried, familiar voice, and my body suddenly remembered everything again. A month of distance, all the silence … meant nothing.

I looked around to gain my composure back. Everyone seemed either preoccupied or pretentious.

"I told you not to leave." He wasn't upset; he was hurt.

It had all been too much. Seeing him at the gala, telling myself I wouldn't be affected. But I had been, in the worst possible way. And then—

"It was a beautiful speech," I told him.

His posture relaxed. "I meant every word."

I nodded, knowing that feeling would fade because that was how life worked. We were all shaped by the lives we came from. Tastes could evolve, habits could shift, and lifestyles could be molded, but our core values always stayed rooted. Pretense could only carry us so far. Without a solid foundation, it was bound to crumble. And that was exactly what had happened between us.

"We were good together, Risha—you know that."

I nodded again, unable to disagree. What we'd shared had been real, for that moment. A present we'd lived fully. But that moment had passed, and we'd stepped into a future that no longer belonged to us both.

"Being good *together* doesn't mean we're good *for* each other."

"You're comparing me to your past. Give me a chance to prove I'm not Patrick or your father."

I knew everything Cece had spilled to him, which was the reason I hadn't responded to his texts. If Ryan were anything like Patrick, I wouldn't have fallen for this man. But our worlds were so far apart that no bridges were made to join these paths.

"Every decision you make shapes your employees' futures. You don't need distractions, Ryan; you need support. And all I've done is disrupt all your perfectly laid plans."

"You've always been my biggest support. I miss coming home to you. Those months with you were the best I've had in years. I'm a better man when you're beside me."

I remained quiet.

"If you're wondering where I've been all this time, I won't lie to you, Risha, I panicked. I didn't think I could be there for you and still take care of everyone counting on me. So, I pushed you away before you could leave me ... I was so fucking wrong. Every day I stayed silent, I drifted too far to find my way back. But nothing I've built means a thing if I don't have you to share it with."

I shook my head, unsure of what to say. His silence had gutted me raw, and I wasn't sure I could survive another blow.

"I understand you don't trust me," Ryan said. "Let me prove to you I'm here to stay."

"You want this now, but it's a lot of work. It's not a switch you flip and everything falls in order."

"I've never shied away from hard work."

To add distance, I moved backward until my legs hit the desk. "You hate mess and drama, Ryan, and my life is messy. It always has been, and it always will be."

"I want *your* mess," he said earnestly. "Your fire. Your chaos. I want you, Risha."

He stepped closer and took my hand. I swallowed hard, my resolve threatening to crack. Why did he hold so much power over my heart?

With his thumb, he rubbed my knuckles, sending wildfire up my arm. "Give me a chance," he repeated.

I looked away, swallowing the sting behind my eyes. Everything I'd felt for him, everything I'd wanted to say, sat inside me like a weight that refused to lift. His silence was deafening, etching a scar deeper than resentment ever could. I'd been hurt before, but this loneliness was something else.

"Let's start over." He put my hand on his chest and raised my chin until I looked at him. "It's still synced with yours, precious. Nothing has changed."

"You taught me how to love," I said softly. "You made me believe in myself. You showed me love that made me brave, but loving you was my beginning, not the destination. It's time we both find our way forward."

He didn't speak. His chest rose and fell as if his body were processing my words.

"I'll always love you," I whispered. "But we live in entirely different worlds. Not every story is meant to reach a happy ending. Sometimes, the wisest thing is to walk away when it's still beautiful." I turned and walked out the door, past the man I loved and into the life I was building on my own.

Forty-Six

RYAN

I hadn't gotten to where I was in life by letting someone else dictate my path. I'd written my story thus far, and I fully intended to write the next chapter too.

Risha didn't trust me anymore, and maybe she had every reason not to. I'd taken the coward's route once, but I wouldn't let my mistake define me.

I respected her choice, but I wasn't going to give up on proving I could be the man for her. If building a bridge between our worlds was the only way, then I'd lay every damn brick myself. A man who constructed skylines wasn't easily discouraged by hard work.

I waited at a small café across from the university, buzzing with students and their hushed conversations. Whitewashed walls, half-draped in hanging planters and lined with gold-framed bold black-and-white photos, clashed against the earthy calm of the space. I wondered if Risha had ever been here or if she'd pointed out its flaws.

To my right, the door opened, and the man I'd only seen in online lectures and faculty directories stepped inside.

I stood up from my chair. "Mr. Verma. Ryan. Thank you for meeting me on such short notice."

He pulled out the chair across from mine. "Tell me how I can help."

"Would you like a coffee? I've heard the macchiato here is worth trying."

"I don't drink coffee in the afternoons," he said flatly. "But you can order yours."

I'd hoped this would be a straightforward conversation in a neutral space. Clearly, I'd underestimated him.

I walked to the counter and ordered one coffee for myself. I didn't even want the caffeine; I just needed the time to gather my thoughts. To center myself before diving into the conversation I'd come here to have. To listen. To understand.

When I returned to my seat, he met my gaze with steady scrutiny. "So, what brings you all the way to New Jersey, Mr. Ryan?"

There were days I missed my parents, and then there were days when I was painfully aware that I was alone in the world. No one was here to guide me through moments like this, or to remind me how to speak from the heart and not mess it all up. Sitting across from Risha's father, I wished they were still here.

"I'm not sure if Risha has ever mentioned me during your conversations," I began.

"She hasn't," he replied curtly. "And now I'm starting to wonder why. But go on." His posture remained rigid, defensive, like he were reliving his disastrous past encounter with Patrick.

I pushed past the hesitation and began again. "First, let me say, you've raised an extraordinary daughter. She's not just brilliant, but deeply passionate, too. From engineering to interior design, she marvels in everything she touches. I've rarely met someone so talented."

He blinked, clearly surprised. Maybe Risha hadn't told him just how much she'd accomplished, or maybe I was reading too much between the lines.

I pulled my phone from my jeans pocket and opened the photo app. Sliding it between us, I began scrolling through the images. "This is the penthouse she designed, working nights and weekends over the last few months."

He leaned in, studying each picture. Shock flickered across his face. Whether it was pride or disappointment, I couldn't tell.

"And this," I continued, "is my new restaurant. It's already featured in *NYC's Architrave Magazine*. Risha dreamed up the concept. Her childhood friend, Virona—who now works for me—helped bring it to life."

At the mention of a familiar name, something shifted in his expression again. Still unreadable.

"I can't give Risha full credit for this, but without her vision, this one-of-a-kind restaurant in the middle of Manhattan would never have existed."

His gaze hardened. "So this is how she's spending her time now?"

"Actually ... no," I replied, switching off my phone and straightening in my chair. "She's not working on these kinds of projects anymore. She launched her own firm—Ayati Technologies. It's already growing faster than she expected. She dedicates every waking hour to its success. She is already a very successful entrepreneur and a self-made woman."

He frowned. "She's wasting her talent on something so ... miniscule."

"That's where I respectfully disagree, Mr. Verma. Talent isn't wasted when it's used to build something meaningful. The respect she's earned in the industry is no less than the admiration your students hold for you. If academic achievement was the only measure of success, we wouldn't speak of Edison, Watt, Ford, or Musk in the same breath as Einstein, Curie, and Hawking. And yet, we do."

He stiffened again, but I pressed on. "What I'm saying is, just because Risha didn't meet *your* expectations doesn't mean she failed. Right now, she's working on some of the most sophisticated innovations in the world. A cutting-edge x-ray scanner, water extraction from air, carbon-capturing concrete. That's not miniscule—that's revolutionary."

He shook his head. "All someone else's ideas. She's just executing them."

"It takes vision to dream, but it takes brilliance to build, Mr. Verma. To bring ideas to life, Steve Jobs had a vision, but Steve Wozniak made it happen."

"You're throwing out a lot of big names," he said with a dry edge.

"Only to make a point," I replied evenly. "I say this with complete sincerity: I'm proud of her. And I won't stop until you see her for who she is."

He studied me now, more curious than combative. "And what do *you* do, Mr. Ryan?"

"I'm just a real estate guy," I said, brushing it off.

"The owner of McAlister Group can't be *just* some real estate guy." He smirked. "Don't look so shocked. If you had time to research me, I had at least since our phone call to research you."

I grinned. "Touché."

He narrowed his eyes once again, his guards up. "Does she know you're here?"

I hesitated. "No, she doesn't. She broke things off with me. Not because she doesn't love me, but because she's certain you and I can never bridge the gap between our worlds. I am here to prove her wrong, and I won't stop until I do."

He regarded me quietly.

His voice softened a little when he said, "If you two aren't together, then how do you know all these things about her work? Her company doesn't even have a website yet."

This time, my smile was genuine. Maybe he didn't know how to express love, but the bond they shared and the feelings were clearly evident. My answer came easily this time.

"Just because we aren't together doesn't mean she's not part of my life, Mr. Verma. I have to prove my worth and show her I can be the man she can trust, and I won't stop at anything until that happens."

For a long moment, he said nothing. Then, a small smile tugged at his lips. "Huh, it seems you've fallen pretty hard for my daughter."

"No, sir. I *rose* with her. Every moment I spent with her reminded me of what truly matters. I've always believed in working hard to earn respect, but she taught me it's not a one-time transaction. Character is built with consistency. To show up every day and prove ourselves with every decision we make. With Risha, I didn't have to question my feelings for her. I didn't have to chase her. She made me see that love is a choice we make. It's the truth we live with."

His eyes remained locked on mine. I didn't know what he was looking for, but I came here with nothing but honesty, and that's exactly what I wanted him to see.

"You're a lucky man, Mr. Verma. You're Risha's first love, even if she can't always say it out loud. For me, she's everything. But I'm not enough on my own. She needs us both. I'll never ask her to choose, but I'll fight for my place—not above you, not instead of you—but beside her, because that's where I belong."

Forty-Seven

RISHA

After signing two new contracts, hiring four more engineers, and receiving our first official check, Team Ayati finally had something to toast. For the first time, it all felt real, like I'd stepped out of a haze and landed in a life I had once envisioned.

When the team asked where to celebrate, I suggested Russo, where Ryan and I had gone for our first *not-a-date*. Everywhere reminded me of him anyway—no point in avoiding the places we'd been. The memories didn't need permission to follow me around. And the ache in my chest didn't dull because I was busy.

But even surrounded by laughter and mimosas, something inside me stayed numb. Like I'd reached the summit and had left something vital at the base. The success was tangible, but it felt strangely hollow. I'd finally had what I wanted once, yet it didn't look like my future anymore. Not the one I had imagined with Ryan by my side. Not without my father in the picture.

Ryan lived in every inch of me. His memories kept me company. His words anchored me when doubt crept in. I only had to close my eyes, and he was there—guiding me, grounding me, reminding me of who I was. Even in his absence, Ryan was the anchor I leaned on.

Mid-brunch, my phone buzzed with a message that stole my breath.

Dad: Spend the day with us.

I hadn't realized how much I was waiting for him to take the first step. Since our last tense conversation, neither of my parents had reached out. I stayed in touch with my sisters, but home had grown silent.

That was the thing about living between two worlds—to keep one, the other had to be severed. And by refusing to choose, I'd only half-lived in both. When I had chosen, it still didn't feel like peace. Both of my worlds felt like an exile.

I raised one hand to hail a cab when I noticed Patrick approaching from the corner of the busy intersection.

"Risha, wait," he called out.

I didn't owe him anything, yet a small, persistent nag told me there was something to resolve. I let the cab go as he reached me.

"Hi." He rested a hand on his waist, eyes tracking the crowd.

"I have a train to catch, so be quick," I said, not giving him much rope.

"Train, huh ..." He pulled on his tie's knot, visibly exasperated. "Because of your father, I lost you, and now because of you, I'm losing my job."

I laughed dryly. This man had some nerve.

"Because of you, I lost my father's trust, and my job. Point that finger at yourself instead of me or my father."

"I. Loved. You." He blazed fire. "I did everything to make you mine."

"Then you did it all wrong because you never tried to understand me. I wanted a partner to stand beside me, not to wage war on my behalf."

"Maybe ... I was wrong—"

"You were most definitely wrong."

"—maybe I screwed it up. But you never gave me another chance. You were so quick to break up and move on."

And there it was. The closure he never got, because I'd left without an explanation. I had severed all ties without explaining his mistakes.

"I liked you, Patrick, but I never loved you. And how could I ever love a man who disrespected my father and wasn't ready to apologize?"

"I ... I thought—"

"You *didn't* think—that was the problem. My father is irreplaceable. You didn't love me, Patrick; you wanted to claim me. And I refuse to go from one cage to another."

His shoulder sagged from the weight of my confrontation. His next words were barely above a whisper. "I love you, Risha. Even after everything, I still love you."

"I am so sorry that you fell in love with the wrong girl. My heart belongs to two men and you're neither of them."

Excitement coursed through my veins as I boarded the once-dreaded transit. When I arrived at my destination, Sia was waiting, as always. Arms folded, eyes warm, the first bridge back to the life I thought I'd left behind.

"Hey, sweets." I pulled her into a tight hug.

"Thank you, Risha!" she blurted, squeezing me even harder.

I smiled, looking back at her. "Okay ... what did I miss?"

She took a step back, keeping me at arm's length, and I saw the tears she had been trying to hide. "We live off your strength," she exclaimed. "Every time you stand up for yourself, you're standing up for all of us. You take the heat and make it easier for the people following your path."

My throat closed up. I'd been so caught up in my own battles that I hadn't realized I was fighting for more than just myself.

"Mom backs off now when we speak up. And Dad listens more. Talks more. It's like he's really trying."

I listened as she talked the entire drive home. And when we walked through the door, it felt like the last six years had never happened, like the distance, the cold silences, had been a bad dream.

Dad played his old vinyls, the ones that had filled our home growing up. When Sia tried to trade Beatles for Billie Eilish on her Spotify, it turned into a full-blown debate. Mira joined Sia. I sided with Dad. We were loud, interrupting each other mid-sentence. I couldn't care less about who was right. I just wanted to soak in the sweet mayhem of what we'd once been.

Time slipped through our fingers, hours dissolving like sugar, and still, no one, especially Dad, asked about Ayati. Not a word about the company I'd built from scratch, or the contracts I'd signed, or how I was managing an ever-growing team and client load. I told myself it didn't matter; his silence wasn't a verdict. I told myself I was happy. That this—being together again—was enough.

Then Mom joined us, siding with Sia on Billie Eilish.

"Wait." I nearly choked on my water. "You're telling me you prefer *her* over, like, classical sitar and tabla?"

"They're different," she mentioned with a shrug. "Billie's voice is haunting. Adele's is velvety and soulful. Now, don't look so shocked—I listen to more music than all of you combined."

Shock wasn't even close to how I felt. Mom didn't know me as much as I didn't know her. Suddenly I felt an overwhelming urge to know her as well.

Laughter erupted from the other end of the room, and for a second, I felt something close to weightlessness until I saw the time.

"Mom, I have to have an early dinner and head out. I didn't bring my laptop, and there's work piling up."

She glanced at the clock over the mantel. "Any minute now, Risha. Just waiting for our guest."

My stomach dropped. No, no way. This couldn't be their plan. Not after a perfect day. They couldn't possibly try to set me up again.

I didn't have time to react before the doorbell rang. Sia rushed to answer it. And then everything happened in slow motion.

The door opened, and Ryan walked in, his presence shifting the room's energy. He greeted Sia like they'd known each other for years, asking about her school, suggesting familiarity, before moving on to Mom for a quick word. Then his eyes landed on me.

"What ... is going on here?" I asked, stunned, my gaze locking with Ryan's as the air punched out of my lungs. "What are you doing here?"

"Ryan, is our guest." Mom's tone was as casual as her words were shocking. "Since you stopped visiting, he's been keeping us company. We've been getting weekly updates on you and Ayati."

"Did you really think we wouldn't be curious about your progress?" Dad's voice came from behind me.

I broke eye contact with Ryan and turned to Dad. The tears I'd been holding back broke free. "I thought you didn't care. This wasn't what you wanted for me."

He placed his hand gently on my head. "The only thing that matters is what *you* want. I'm sorry, Risha, for not seeing that sooner." Then he glanced toward the foyer, where Ryan stood.

I could feel his eyes on me, but I couldn't face him. I was a bundle of nerves and emotions with just enough control to keep from falling apart.

"You've got a good man there. Losing him would be a terrible mistake."

"Oh, Daddy ..." I wrapped my arms around him, not caring for my tears soaking into his shirt. "I was just ... so scared to disappoint you again."

He wrapped his arms around my shoulders like he'd done when I was a kid. "Making mistakes doesn't mean you've failed. It means you're trying. Patrick was a misstep, and you fixed it. But this man is a keeper."

I was unable to find the words. I didn't want them either. All I needed was right here—my father's acceptance and Ryan's unwavering love. Without even saying it, he had proven it time and again.

Dad pulled back just enough to look me in the eye. "I've made mistakes, too—underestimating you, with my unfair expectations, and also for not standing by you when you needed me most. I'm sorry."

I shook my head hard. I didn't need the apology. Just this moment was enough. Just the realization was enough. And deep down, I knew who had made this possible.

My dark knight.

My way maker.

A transversal man who didn't just walk between two worlds, he bridged them. For me.

I was in my bedroom when the soft knock came. I didn't need to ask who it was—I felt him before I saw him. When the door creaked open, Ryan stepped inside and quietly shut it behind him. I stood motionless at the bedside.

"Growing up, I imagined my girlfriend's room would look something like this," he said, scanning the space. His eyes moved from one wall to another, pausing on each piece of art, every stacked book. "A bed surrounded by bookshelves. Classics tucked between contemporary—*Emma, Persuasion, Little Women* ... and then Jackie Collins? Seriously?"

I ran straight into his arms, my body moving on instinct, wrapping around him. My lips crashed into his, silencing everything I wanted to say and he needed to hear. Everything could wait.

I needed his mouth, his skin, his warmth. I needed him like I needed air, and more. Tears still clung to my lashes, and my mascara had long since surrendered, but none of it mattered. I didn't care.

He kissed me back like I were the only truth he knew. One

hand anchored me by the nape of my neck; the other pressed into my back, keeping me so close that even breath had no room between us.

"You did all this ... for me?" I murmured into his mouth. "You broke your rules and stepped into my chaos?"

"I was a fucking fool." His breath turned ragged. "I thought I wanted easy, but then I met you and knew what *right* felt like. You'd be out of your mind if you think I'd let you walk away."

"So you fought?" I whispered, kissing him harder, needing more of him. "With my dad? My mom?"

"Nah." He smirked against my lips. "They're good parents. I actually filed for adoption."

I choked back a laugh. "Seriously? You know that makes you my brother, right?"

"We'll work around the legalities. There's no way I'm letting you keep them all to yourself."

He slid his hand lower, gripping my hips, pulling me flush against his growing hardness. I moved with him, gasping into his mouth, every nerve lit and hungry. I melted into his light, soaked in his fire. For the first time in what felt like forever, I wasn't just whole—I was *home.*

"I need you," I whispered. My words were barely forming between our kisses.

"Let's wrap up the dinner. There's a McAlister hotel ten minutes from here."

"Skip dinner. Let's leave now."

He groaned, running a hand through his hair like he was bargaining with God. "Tempting, but your mother's finally warming up to me. It only started after I complimented her food."

"You?" My brows shot up. "You've been eating her spicy food?" I couldn't imagine that in a million years. Every time we went to an Indian restaurant, he came out fuming through his nose and ears.

"Long enough that I can handle it without breaking a sweat."

My heart cracked open. I hugged him tighter, kissed him harder, wanting to imprint myself onto his soul. "You know you don't have to do that right?"

"I know. It makes your mother happy." He smiled. "And I've also struck a new deal to see them once a month. Then it won't be too spicy for me."

"Look at you." I rolled my eyes. "Striking deals with my parents behind my back."

"You can't complain now. You were on a spree to severe every tie that touched you. Someone had to keep the relationship going."

Hoisting on my toes, I kissed him gently this time, holding his arms, his warmth seeping into me. "You don't have to do this, you know," I reminded him.

"I know ... I enjoy spending time with them. Your dad and I actually get along well. Losing my parents taught me that happiness doesn't always arrive in grand gestures. It comes quietly and remains for a flicker. And sometimes, when one chapter ends, another begins in the most unexpected way. These tiny slices of heaven are all we really have. And they deserve to be noticed, cherished, never taken for granted."

My eyes prickled again at how we looked at the same things from such different angles. "I love you, Ryan. You're the best thing that has ever happened to me."

He cupped my face, kissing me slow this time. Reverent. Anchoring. "Then don't shut me out again. Even if I mess up, fight *with* me, not against me."

My tears slipped again, but this time from something whole.

I kissed every part of his face—his lips, his rough jaw, the razor-sharp nose that was my absolute favorite.

"I promise," I whispered, and this time, I meant it with everything I had.

Forty-Eight

RISHA

We managed to reach the hotel without tearing each other's clothes off. Instead of heading to the reception, Ryan walked me straight to the elevators.

"Your fuck pad?" I quirked a brow.

"Seriously? You think I'm a thirty-something going around, fucking women?" he pointed out, not appreciating the insinuation. "I've been using it when I come to see your parents. It seems they like to talk, especially your sister, Sia."

I pecked his lips. "You seriously did all this for me? Spent your time in Jersey? For me?"

He pulled me into an embrace. "Not that anyone was waiting for me in Manhattan. At least here, I had people I could talk with about you."

My heart ached, trying to absorb his every word. He had jumped through hoops to reach me, while I had cried my heart out thinking it was over. He had been bridging the gap between our worlds, while I had been breaking ties with everyone.

The moment the elevator opened on the top floor, he took my hand and walked me into his presidential suite—carpeted wall-to-wall with the soft glow of lights, a light curtain flowed from the floor to ceiling glass walls. The room was cool, but heat scalded my skin.

Ryan pushed me into the nearest wall, and his lips claimed mine. "I missed you, madly," he breathed in. "Missed touching you, talking to you ... spending nights with you."

He moved his hands under my sundress. His hardness pressed into my navel. I moaned, pushing my hips forward, rubbing my panties over his knuckles to get some friction.

"I missed you, too. Every second of my day, you were in my thoughts."

He dipped his mouth to my neck and down my chest, pressing warm soft kisses in its wake. I tried in vain to suppress my need, but the sensations his kisses elicited were my undoing.

Sitting in front of me, Ryan bunched up my dress in a fist and pushed it over. He kissed my thighs and moved his way up and inside. He removed my panties with expert ease while I pulled and tossed the dress out of the way. He reached for my wet pussy and licked into the slickness.

"Oh God." A shudder ran through me. I gripped his hair to ward off the sensation.

He parted me with his fingers, and his warm, velvet tongue followed. The pleasure had me clenching uncontrollably. Sliding his fingers into my throbbing vulva, he made circles over my clit with his tongue. My head fell back as pleasure soared through me.

I arched, pressing into his mouth. He added another finger and delivered another blow, knowing exactly where my most sensitive nerves resided. His teeth grazed my clit, taunting me with restraint and just enough pressure to push me over the edge.

Clasping a hand to my mouth, I cried out, "Ryan!"

Maintaining pressure, he continued to pleasure me until I came once. Twice. And again. Then he stood up and wrapped me in himself like a blanket, hunching against my shoulders until I was boneless and out of my mind with a hunger so wild to have his cock inside and pounding.

I whimpered, asking for him, for his cock to be submerged

inside me, his tongue inside my mouth. I wanted to possess him, just the way he had possessed every part of my heart.

My lips parted when I noticed the hard outline of his jeans.

He wrapped me in his embrace and carried me to the bed. I took the hem of his T-shirt and glided it out of the way. He helped me undress him without unlocking our lips. I tasted myself on his tongue, feeling intimate and raw.

His erection pressed into my belly. I went for his belt buckle and zipper. The fierceness of my need for him overwhelmed my every other sense.

He crawled onto the bed, making me fall backward, shifting me until I was comfortably tucked under him. With his legs, he parted my thighs and made space for himself. Taking my breast into his mouth, he took a hard suck before he gave the same attention to the other one. He teased the tip with his teeth, and I arched into him.

I hooked my feet around his hips in a feeble attempt to pull him closer. He didn't budge. Instead, his one elbow plopped next to my shoulder and the other hand caressed my inner thigh, close to the place I wanted him to be.

"I need you, Ryan," I cried out. "Don't make me wait. Please."

I was driving with anticipation.

He started low, kissing the tip of my toe. A jolt of desire rode through my sex. I clenched my pussy before it short-circuited.

He trailed wet kisses up my calves, my knees, my thighs, over my belly, down to the crest of my belly button. I quivered under his touch. Then he languished over my breasts, my collarbone, and into the dip of my neck. The edge of his nose trailed up and down my neck, sending wildfire across my every cell.

He nipped my lips, making me lunge for his. Every part of me stood at attention; my nipples were taut with need. He held his cock and rubbed it over my throbbing vagina, lubricating it with our cum. I clenched the duvet, needing to ground myself and get ready for him.

He entered me in one swift motion. I cried out, fisting my hands to gain control.

"Did I hurt you?" He slowed down. His eyes were gentle, and kind, and worried.

"No ... It's too much. I missed you too much," I mumbled.

His lips were on mine then, kissing me gently then hard. Frantic. "Me, too, precious. Never question my intentions when it comes to you."

I moaned inside his mouth and nodded my head, though he couldn't see my agreement.

He drove into me again and again. Hard and fast. Losing self-control and every restraint. His depth made me spasm around his cock. I could hardly breathe in anticipation of the orgasm building inside me again.

I dug my heels into his thighs, urging him deeper, faster. More. I was desperate for him. For the building climax. I pushed my fingers into his hair and pulled them hard. I needed more. The rest of him.

I met his gaze, filled with desire. "I love you, Ryan. I'm madly in love with you."

After everything we'd been through, I wanted him to know my feelings for him had never changed. They had only grown and taken many forms and shapes. My heart beat for him. My dreams belonged to him.

He paused, pulling back just enough for our eyes to meet. "I never doubted that."

A sob left my chest. "Thanks ... for believing in me." I meant it. "Make love to me."

And he did just that. For the rest of the night, and into the morning when the sun sore high. Our every lovemaking was a reminder that we were made for each other.

When he slept, I got him fired up. Our kisses, every touch, turned into hungry demands, and we took each other again. Each time, no less earth-shattering than the last until we both collapsed in each other's arms and started all over again.

Epilogue

Ryan

The city had been hit with a heatwave, even though summer hadn't officially begun. Every corner radiated heat and humidity like it had swallowed the sun whole and tried to wash it over with all the water in the ocean. Sidewalks shimmered, glass towers trapped the warmth outside, and even the Hudson looked lazier than usual. Thanks to global warming, June felt more like the sticky heat of July.

Summer in Manhattan had a rhythm of its own, and this time, I was ready to move with it. Not faster. Not ahead. Just enjoy the ride with every passing day. At the next light, I blinked up at the skyline, wondering where all the time had gone. It was just yesterday when the fall season had barely reached its peak—the night I first met Risha and my entire world changed.

Excitement thrummed through me as I picked Ivy up from the airport and took her to the penthouse. She was stunned the moment she stepped in—not so subtle, and an imperceptible flicker of surprise. Even though she was disappointed by the changes, my little sister had grown to mask it.

It wasn't the change she resisted; it was the bitter side of the past we both were trying to shed. Continuing our lives, writing the next chapter, while cherishing our best memories. A part of me wanted to tell her everything—how my life had shifted, how I'd changed. But our conversation moved too fast, jumping from one subject to the next before I had the chance to talk about myself.

I left the penthouse promising I'd be back by seven. Tonight, I wanted my sister as my plus-one to MoxTo's inauguration. She'd hidden herself for too long in that cocoon of self-preservation. I wanted the world to see her and to know of her existence.

At four on the dot, Bobby buzzed in through the speaker. "Risha is here, Ryan."

"Send her in." I fired off one last email to Bob in Vegas, reminding him about shaded cooling areas for the men working on our site. A hundred fucking degrees—bodies could practically evaporate in that kind of heat.

That was the last email of the day. Every other thought left my brain when Risha walked in with all her radiance. My breath left at the sight of her. Even after spending every day together, sharing every night, somehow, it still wasn't enough. Instead of dulling the ache, time only sharpened my need.

I wanted more.

"Hi. Is she here?" She quickly scanned the room.

"She is. I mean ... not exactly *here,* here. I dropped Ivy off at home to unwind. She wanted to shop."

Risha had been eager to meet Ivy, but right before leaving for the airport, she'd gotten an emergency call from work. Zoe had run into trouble assembling equipment, and Risha had to jump in.

Closing the distance, I kissed her without warning. She wrapped her arms around me in confusion at first, and then in surrender. I drank her in—her scent, her softness, everything I'd missed in the past few hours.

"There's something I want to show you." Pulling back, I took her hand and gently tugged.

"That's why you made Bobby call my *assistant* to set up a formal meeting?" she teased. "You do realize I'm the CEO, CFO, Receptionist, and also the assistant of my company, right?"

"Duly noted." I led her across the office and through the hallway to where my studio used to be.

She gasped when I opened the newly installed door. "What the hell, Ryan?"

The room mirrored the brightness of my office, but everything in it was tailored to its future occupant—a sleek desk with two wide monitors positioned beside a cozy corner perfect for client meetings. On the opposite end, a six-person conference table for her long project meetings.

"This," I said, "is your new office. And the floor below is fully furnished for Ayati."

Her eyes widened. "Ryan ... I can't afford this."

"You're my girlfriend," I reminded her. "I've never spoiled you with gifts or extravagant vacations. And the only thing I ever gave you, you returned to me."

"I didn't return it out of spite, Ryan," she exclaimed. "It symbolized change. Shedding everything I once believed to become someone new. My note meant I'd broken free of my chrysalis and finally learned to fly ... and it was all because of you."

"Oh ... why didn't I think of that before?" I said earnestly.

"I never stopped loving you. Not even for a second," she added softly. "You're the storm that built me into what I am today. I found myself only after braving through the cadence of your storm."

My heart shuddered from the pedestal she'd put me on. I pulled her close and kissed her with all my passion.

When we broke our kiss, she said, "But ... I need to build this company on my own."

"You don't need to prove anything to me, precious." I kissed her forehead. "I can't explain how proud I am of you. This is not support. I would like to stand beside you."

She let out a sigh, nodding and agreeing. "What happened to your studio?"

"I don't need it anymore." I smiled. We had officially moved into the penthouse the day we had returned from Jersey a couple of weeks ago.

She looked around again, smiling warmly, soaking in the change. "Wait—what happened to your giant clock?"

I grinned and pulled out a large, wrapped frame from behind the desk. "I don't need to measure time anymore. Now I know who I'll be spending it with. So, replace it with this."

Her brow lifted in half-curiosity, half-suspicion, but when she tore off the paper, her mouth dropped open. She stared at the restored canvas that had once hung in her bedroom and the one she had broken in anger.

"You fixed it?" Her words were a bundle of tears and whispers.

"It meant something to you, so I brought it to my office. And after your dad told me the story behind it, I couldn't leave it sitting broken." It was the image of a woman on a houseboat. I hadn't understood its meaning until I spotted a similar image on her father's laptop during one of our chats.

The picture was their memory, their connection, and a piece of their hearts.

Risha and I weren't chasing sparks or getting lucky with timing. What we were building wasn't fleeting. It was deliberate and engineered. A relationship anchored on the strongest foundation and poured with honesty, reinforced with trust.

I knew how structures rose and fell. I'd seen skylines change, the best of luck turned sideways—even steel had limits. What we were creating was made to last. Beneath every storm and every setback, what held us steady was the groundwork we'd laid beneath. The cadence of our storm had passed, but even through that, our foundation was solid. Strong enough to carry us through anything. Together. As one.

"I'm not trying to replace your father," I clarified. "I'm not here to take his place. All I want is a small space that's mine. So now, when you look at it, I hope it's not just your father you see … but me, too."

"You already take up all the space in my heart," she said, her eyes turning glassy. "I don't see clearly without you anymore, Ryan." Her lips met my chest.

Even through all the clothing, my heart zinged.

I brushed my knuckles against her cheek, enjoying the sensation of her smooth, radiant skin. "There's more," I said with a crooked smile. "Two things, actually." I led her through the small connecting hallway between our offices. From the closet, I pulled out two gowns—one orange, one champagne.

"For MoxTo's inauguration gala?" she inquired, draping the dress around herself as she spun in a slow circle to admire the flare.

"They reminded me of you."

She looked up, smiling. "Do you want me to get ready in the apartment tonight?"

Of all the things I loved about her, it was her ability to read my mind that I loved the most.

I nodded.

"You haven't told Ivy about us yet?"

That was part of it, but not the whole reason. "We will do it together."

After Risha left, I sent a quick text to Nick.

Me: Sure you can handle everything?

Nick: I got this. Don't worry about MoxTo. Ivy's safe with me.

Me: Thanks, man. I'll text you later.

Nick: Good luck.

Risha

"A limo, Mr. McAlister?" I teased with giddiness as Ryan opened the door of a sleek, black stretch limousine. It reminded me of our limo ride after the ballet. With heat pooling between my legs, I climbed in and slid toward the middle of the black leather seat. The mini-bar glimmered under recessed lighting, and the bench stretched so long I could have sprawled out for a nap.

While I smiled at the decadence of it all, my eyes landed on Ryan—and the sheen of sweat across his temple. The tension in his jaw was evident, the way he kept shifting like he couldn't get comfortable.

MoxTo had kept him up for nights. From every review to the selection of the team, Ryan had been focused on every aspect of this hotel. And now that it was finally over, I was certain he couldn't wait for the night to go perfectly.

He pushed a button that closed the partition between us and the driver. The nerve on his neck throbbed violently. He wasn't himself. Could it be introducing me to Ivy or her impression of me?

I leaned in and kissed his neck. His chest rose and fell fast beneath my hand when I pressed it against him. "It'll all go smoothly. You have nothing to worry about," I said reassuringly.

He breathed hard, moving his hands around my waist until he was caving me into his chest. I layered my lips with his, cupping his face, and feeling his uneven breath. The heat emanating from him drove me wild.

He ran his hands up my back then unclasped my dress and pulled it down to my waist. His eyes burned at my pebbled nipples. "I need you—right now," he urged in a low growl, his voice wrecked.

"I'm yours, Ryan. You know that already." I brushed his lips, peppering tiny kisses on every inch.

I watched his eyes move with his fingers from my neck to my shoulder and down the length of my chest to the flat of my belly.

Standing up in front of him, I let the dress pool around my feet.

"Jesus, Risha, you're not wearing panties?" he groaned.

I smiled with excitement. "The fabric's too light. Would've ruined the lines." Straddling over his lap, I started rolling my hips against him in tiny circles until he groaned, feeding the burn that pulsed between us.

His head fell back, and he breathed out harshly. "Fuck."

I reached for his belt, fingers deft as I pulled it free then lowered the zipper and rubbed his hardened cock through the boxer briefs, slowly and teasingly. My need grew faster as his cock pulsed under my palm.

His grip tightened on my thighs, sliding upward, nearing the place I wanted him to touch. My pussy throbbed in anticipation. And then, with no warning, he slipped two fingers inside me.

"Ryan." My breath hitched.

"Jesus, woman, you're drenched."

An unnecessary answer slipped from my lips. "For you."

He moved his fingers in a frenzy to give me a release. I remembered where we were and that he couldn't ruin his pants, so I arched up to push his pants and briefs down his legs. He scooched up, helping me, but not giving me a break. I moaned in pleasure, reaching for the climax he always made sure I reached first.

He pumped his fingers, working me until my breath came in broken bursts. I arched, pushing my breasts toward him. I was shaking by the time my climax hit, clinging to his shoulders, my mouth open but soundless. Only when I was undone did he finally slide inside me. And he let go. Let me take control. Let me move.

And I did.

By the time we were dressed, I realized the car had stopped.

"Shit, we're late," I muttered, spinning around so he could clasp my dress.

"That was a quick realization, precious." Laughter rumbled from his chest. The tension he'd carried around seemed to have finally cracked, and I was glad I could ease him, even a little.

I adjusted his slightly crooked bowtie and smoothed my hand down the lapel of his tux. "You're going to kill it tonight."

He gave me that smug little grin I'd grown addicted to, then stepped out and offered his hand. I took it, carefully maneuvering my heels and gown out of the car. The moment I stood next to him and looked ahead, my breath left me.

"Where the hell are we?" I blinked several times at the empty dock stretching before us. No flashing bulbs or velvet ropes. No hotel and absolutely no MoxTo in sight. Just quiet darkness ... and the sound of the water lapping off of the dock.

"A quick stop," he announced. "I want to show you something."

"Seriously? Of all the times, tonight is your time to show me something instead of where you need to be?" My protest went unnoticed as he led me forward. The wooden dock creaked beneath our feet, and the air smelled of river, pine, and summer.

I tried to make sense of it but came up completely blank. New office, restoring the canvas, and now another something? He had been waiting for months for this night, and now he decided to take a detour?

Then I saw the outline of something distinctly familiar rise from the shadows. A houseboat. Not a two-dimensional photograph or a desktop background. A real, full-scale houseboat. The same one that had lived in my memories for years.

My knees locked, unsure if I was hallucinating or high on drugs. After that mind-numbing encounter in the limo, nothing was off the table.

"Ryan?" I whispered, too stunned and too sure it wasn't either of those. "What's going on?"

He didn't answer.

I moved forward, needing to see the boat more closely. The moonlight barely providing light.

Then I felt something brush against my leg and looked down.

"Holy shit." My breath escaped.

He was down on one knee. A ring in his hand. A *ridiculous, breathtaking, heart-stopping, huge, and gorgeous* ring.

"Let me say this," he began in a steady voice. "I thought I had my life mapped out—goals, the future, what was expected of me, where I wanted to be in five, ten, fifteen years. Then you showed up. And I realized I was chasing all the wrong things. I realized none of it mattered without someone to share it with. You showed me happiness isn't just dreams and success; it's having someone who stands beside you through the highs and lows. Before you, I was a robot. You made me human. I want your love, Risha. I need you by my side."

His words and the honesty in his eyes wrapped around my heart like a tightrope, pulling me taut. He looked at me as if I were the only thing that made sense anymore.

"You made me see what actually matters. What would finally make me *happy*."

His words swam in my ears as my vision blurred with tears.

"Fuck it," he muttered suddenly, rising and pulling me into his arms. "I love you with everything I've got, Risha. Marry me. Make me the happiest man alive."

I reached for his collar. I was dizzy, breathless, and ecstatic. "That's how long it took you to say you love me?"

He pulled back, confused. "What do you mean ...? You were waiting for me to say I love you? You should've just asked."

"Who *asks* if someone loves them?" I swatted his shoulder.

"Well, I just thought you knew."

"Well ... I most definitely didn't." I pushed off his chest and turned to the houseboat again, still wrapping my head around it. "How did you even get this here?"

He tugged me gently back into him. "Custom-built. Sourced

the exact specs from the pictures your dad has. It took few weeks, but *ta-da*." Ryan flared his hands and, just on cue, the lights lit up the boat.

A warm, golden glow spilled through the windows, casting soft shadows on the water. Old, glowing memories came back to life. He wasn't just proposing; he was offering me a new home in his world, one that didn't collide with mine but fused into it seamlessly, like two rivers merging into one. A life that combined where I came from while making space for where I belonged, where we were heading together.

"Precious"—he brushed his knuckles along my jaw—"don't make me wait."

I tilted my head, pressing a kiss to his hand. "I fought the world for you, Ryan. And I'd do it all over again." Then I looked up and smiled, my heart overflowing. "Of course it's a yes."

Thank you for reading Cadence of the Storm! I would really be grateful if you leave a review on the Amazon, Goodreads, and or Bookbub. Your reviews are the best gift you can give to an author.

Much love,
Delia

Dedication

My book is dedicated to those wonderful women who carry the weight of other people's expectations every single day while trying to break free; to those unfortunate daughters who trudge under inherited traditions without understanding them or wanting to be part of it; to those rebellious few who stumble, rise, and keep moving forward with grit, determination, and persistence until they forge their own paths.

This is a story no one hears about. We see superficial perfection and mistake it for a wonderful life, unaware of the struggles and choices behind it.

This book started as a romantic story until it tugged at something far deeper. I'd gone down a rabbit hole while writing this story and ended up seeing parts of myself in it. There were nights I couldn't fall asleep, lying in bed and replaying my past, wondering what I could've done differently, what choices might have let me embolden myself. What's shocking is that decades later, I still see women facing the same struggles. So, as you read this book, if you recognize even a small part of yourself, celebrate your victories—and remember, it's never too late to make a change.

I hope our journeys, despite their flaws, lead us to places we can call our own. I hope the weight of expectations never extinguishes the fire within. I hope the times we stayed silent, reminds us to choose differently when the baton passes to us. And I hope we pass our courage and strength to the next generation, so they don't have to go through the same struggles we did.

It wasn't always the worst, but it was more than a scar. And there is no shame in demanding—we deserve more. Choosing happiness is our indelible right.

Fate Intertwined

Haunted by my past, I found solace in running away. That's how I ended up in Boston. Here, I, Ivy McAlister, have everything I need: a caring boyfriend, Mike, who wants me to move in with him; a spot in the Harvard MBA program that I have worked hard to secure; and life away from Manhattan, where I can sleep without being tormented by my nightmares. My needs are met, but my wants are not...

The problem? The man of my dreams and my boyfriend are two different people.

Nick was unattainable then, and he is unavailable now. Nevertheless, he is a force of nature, the very essence of my life, the guiding star of my universe, and the eternal object of my desires. He has the power to make me whole again or break me into pieces. I ran away from him the day I was going to confess my feelings to him. He let me go and never came after me... until now.

Fires of Affinity

I hated Nick with all my might, but I had loved him with the same passion, too. His dominion, his lies, his deception. I needed time to heal with love and hate battling for supremacy...and I could only have one of them in my heart.

Five days is all it took me to change the trajectory of my life and move back home to New York City. With cautious optimism and a hopeful countenance I, Ivy McAlister came here to be with the man of my dreams, Nicholas Branson. Did I make a hasty decision? Maybe I did...with Nick behaving erratically and bordering on the bizarre. Sadly, my perfect world with Nick has started to unravel with the realization that everything was not as rosy as I had imagined it to be. As the lines between dreams and reality blurred, I was left to navigate the labyrinth of deception and truth to ascertain if Nick, the billionaire CEO and the most eligible bachelor in Manhattan, and the one I thought was my one true love, is indeed the one that I can truly find happiness with.

A Sultry Betrayal

A sultry betrayal. An unwavering love.

My life is flawless. My kids are perfect. My husband, the very epitome of it.

A picture-perfect family.

I built this life for myself, and for us, with one goal in mind... perfection.

Until perfection blinds... It consumes and overshadows, begins to reveal the cracks, the imperfections, and all my faults. Because here's the truth—while we're all striving to become better versions of ourselves, we don't change at the same pace.

This is Gisele's story and her reflection on the life she's built, and the woman she is becoming to doubt.

Call it a midlife crisis or a late-at-life awakening, but read it with an open heart and hold your judgement.

Clause of Attraction

Two lawyers. One partnership. Zero self-control.

Ubiquitous workplace anxiety building up.

Innate attraction brewing over.

And the underlying intense desire all set to explode.

Alina and Reign are locked in a high stakes battle for the ultimate prize: a coveted spot as Partner at the prestigious law firm where they both work. With a career-shaping case on the line, their fierce rivalry collides with the scorching chemistry they've buried for far too long.

When an audacious client openly flirts with Alina, Reign feels the tug of desire. That's when their professional boundaries blur, spiraling into a game of passion, secrets, and ambition that neither can escape. As power-plays turn personal, the lines between desire and betrayal become dangerously thin.

Winning the partnership comes at a great cost, but losing each other in the process might cost them even more. In a winner-takes-all world where want trumps need and ambition beats emotion, they'll have to decide how far they're willing to go and what they're willing to risk. Lose everything or win it all.

Join the mailing list to be the first to preorder the next book in the series.

Website: https://www.deliadukebooks.com/

Instagram: https://www.instagram.com/deliadukebooks/

BookTok: https://www.tiktok.com/itsdeliaduke/

Facebook:https://www.facebook.com/deliadukebooks/

About the Author

A new and upcoming author, Delia writes contemporary romance with a deliciously stubborn alpha male, strong female, and plenty of steam and angst.
A travel enthusiast and a foodie at heart, she loves incorporating her life experiences into her stories and will never say no to girls' night out.
An analyst by day and a writer by night, if she is not working, you will find her traveling the world with her family or eating out with her friends.
To know more about Delia, please visit her website @ https://www.deliadukebooks.com/